E. M. Kkouua

# The Trials of Neptune

## Ships of Britannia

### Book 3

PublishNation
www.publishnation.co.uk

# By the same author

*Wrath of Olympus: Ships of Britannia, Book 1*

*Prey of the Huntress: Ships of Britannia, Book 2*

*Son of the Sea: a Ships of Britannia novella\**

*Dark Blessings, a Portus Polis story\**

*\*available through emkkoulla.com*

*For Stephen*

# Contents

# I

She'd done it. This huge new vessel was hers to command. Maia greedily extended her awareness, marvelling at the multitude of mechanisms and devices installed and waiting for her touch. True, it felt like she'd been given a new body that was several sizes too large for her – three masts instead of two and a multitude of cabins, decks and holds instead of the smaller ones the *Blossom* controlled, but she assumed she'd get used to it in time.

Flesh, blood and bone were but a memory now as she explored her vessel using her Ship's senses, overawed at the vastness of the space. It was unfamiliar, raw and rough around the edges, but eventually she would smooth out the channels and operate it with ease.

Or so she hoped.

After a few minutes, she became aware of two other presences on board. She turned her gaze to them, seeing them from different angles now that she was no longer dependent on just one viewpoint.

Pholus stood on her quarterdeck, hooves firmly planted despite there being no movement, as she was in dry dock. The Chief Naval Architect waited patiently for her to acknowledge him, brawny arms crossed over his chest, with only the slight swish of his tail an indication of his anticipation.

The other one was Raven.

She switched her gaze to face him directly, centring it so that it was coming from her Shipbody. He looked no different than before; still shrunken and wizened, his wispy hair drifting around his pink scalp and his opaque eyes staring into space. A little breeze moved through her rigging and Maia guessed that her mother was near. That could mean that her sister was too, though she couldn't detect any tell-tale silvery wisp floating in the air.

Away to the east, a dark storm cloud squatted on the horizon like an angry bruise; it seemed that her Aunt Cymopoleia wasn't far away either and Maia hoped that the Goddess' curiosity wouldn't entice her to come any closer. She made a mental note to arrange a sacrifice of appeasement in that direction as soon as possible.

She took some satisfaction in making them all wait a few moments longer. Her emergence would be on her terms.

An image surfaced abruptly: being wrapped in the earth's cool darkness as the Mother Tree claimed her body for eternity. She felt herself shudder before she could push it aside.

"Steady there. It's over with now, Maia. You're safe."

She focused on the Master Mage. She must have given some outward sign of disquiet.

"Is everything all right?" Pholus rumbled, his blunt features screwing up in concern.

Raven raised a hand.

"She's just settling in. It will take time, especially under the circumstances. Maia, is everything as it should be?"

She bit back a sharp retort. Was it? Shreds of memory still clung to her like burrs. Flashes of emotion mingled with faces; none of them real. Her husband, her child. Mere figments of her imagination and gone forever. The cold wind from the sea slashed them to pieces and whipped the tattered remnants away into oblivion. It was time to face her responsibilities and the reality of her metamorphosis. But why did her future have to include Raven? Or had she imagined his appearance in her trial too?

"I'm fine."

Her voice echoed around the vessel, coming from several different places at once. She'd have to remedy that.

Pholus smiled. "It's always a shock, you know. I'll help you as much as I can. I might not be a Ship, but I've a lot of experience."

Maia concentrated. This time, her voice came solely from the vicinity of her Shipbody.

"Thank you."

"You haven't formed properly yet, but that's understandable," Raven said. He sounded even hoarser than usual. "You might want to hold off on your final appearance until you're named."

Maia turned her attention to the living wood that now anchored her to her vessel. Raven was right. She looked like a twisted block of solid oak rising from the deck, the grain spiralling around a central core.

"You can appear as anything you like," Pholus told her. "It might be a good idea to practise when you've a moment. Don't worry about it now."

Various images shot through her, complete in every detail. It was true. She could even look like something from a nightmare, if she preferred. The memory of the hydra's writhing form made her shiver again and she felt the vessel twitch slightly.

"Put it from your mind!" Raven commanded. Pholus shot him a look and nodded.

"It's true, Maia. Remember, there's more at stake now. Your emotions directly affect your vessel, until you learn to keep them separate. Calm yourself."

Maia did as she was bid, forcing the fear down deep inside. She would have to choose a shape sooner or later and she hadn't decided yet what it would be. It would be easier when she was named, for sure. She remembered *Blossom* telling her about the *Elephant*. That designation was still up for grabs.

An involuntary snort burst from her and she knew that she was still shaky.

"Rest now," Raven ordered. "Blank your mind and allow yourself to drift. We'll speak soon."

Both he and Pholus turned and left. Maia noticed the squad of marines placed on guard around her perimeter and allowed herself to sink gratefully into a kind of stupor. It wasn't quite sleep, but it would do for now.

She didn't know what to think about Raven being the one to call her forth. Part of her was grateful; he was a known quantity at least, but the rest of her wanted to pick him up and dash him to pieces against her shiny new deck. She'd never dreamed that he would be assigned as her senior Ship's Mage. Would she be able to work with him at all now? The pain he had caused her was still too raw.

It didn't seem long before the centaur reappeared, his great hooves ringing as he clopped up the gangplank, to be greeted by the marines. Maia checked her internal chronometer and realised, to her surprise that several hours had passed. She greeted Pholus, noting with relief that Raven was absent.

"Hail to the new Ship!" he announced, cheerfully. "I'm afraid that this will be your designation until you're named, but it won't be for long. The King is eager to set you on your way."

"How long do I have?" Maia asked.

"Well, we need to get everything ready, so I'd give it a few days, but preparations are underway. Your initiation took longer than expected."

"I don't know how long it normally takes," she replied warily. She'd lost track of time in the forest and had no clue as to how long she'd been in her dream world. At the time, it had seemed like months. The memories were bright, but becoming more indistinct and they made her uneasy. She'd always been able to recall every detail of her life, however hard she'd tried to forget some of it.

Pholus shifted his bulk. "It normally takes a single day and night," he said.

"And?"

"You were gone for a week."

Maia heard his words in disbelief. A week? It had felt like mere hours. Everyone must have been worried sick. She didn't know what to say.

He clopped over to her and took up position by her side.

"It doesn't matter. You made it and that's what counts. You should feel more settled now."

Maia thought about it. It was true, she did, as if she had somehow expanded to fill all the empty spaces whilst she had dozed. It still wasn't as comfortable as being partnered with the *Blossom,* but she was beginning to feel part of the whole, instead of some hastily tacked on appendage.

"I do," she admitted.

"Excellent!" He flashed her a smile. "In that case, it's time to take you through some of the primary checks. That'll take your mind off things. You're a fully paid-up Ship now and it's time to earn your keep."

He was right. Her long life of service had just begun.

\*

4

Pholus knew more about her vessel than she did, Maia reflected. It was reassuring to have his patient guidance as he took her through basic operations. She was glad that she was in dry dock, where he could observe all her mechanisms, including her rudder as it responded to her commands.

"Have you thought any more about your final shape?" the centaur asked her, when they paused for a break. Being half-man, half-horse, he had to consume large quantities of food.

Maia regarded her wooden skin.

"I think I'll wait," she said and he nodded, chewing.

"Good idea, though you can change it as you will. Your name will depend on the King's wishes, of course. I expect he'll choose something that sounds grand and regal."

Of course. She was to be a Royal Ship. Tullia, her classmate from the Academy, might be called the *Regina* now, but she wasn't a Royal.

"It could be difficult to take a shape, if it's something figurative," she observed.

"True, but you need to have something ready," he warned. "You don't want to take too much time over it, not with everyone standing there watching."

It was good advice. Maia was tempted to choose something outrageous and not at all human. The image of the deadly hydra came to mind again. She'd had the chance to see one up close and it had been an impressive creature, though she hadn't appreciated that fact as it was trying to kill her at the time. As far as she knew, there wasn't a Ship of that name. Coming face-to-face with a wooden version would definitely strike fear into her enemies.

One thing was for sure: there was no way that she was going to be some sweet little Ship, smiling benevolently on everyone with a pretty little *tutela* in her hand.

She wanted claws and fangs.

Pholus was regarding her with a grave expression.

"I heard you had it rough," he said quietly, so that the few workmen still aboard wouldn't hear.

If she had been human, Maia would have sighed. Now, she just let the stillness of her Shipbody overtake her.

"Just a bit," she admitted.

"If you want to talk about it…?"

"I'd rather not."

His huge brown eyes gazed at her for a few moments longer, before he continued to pop compressed cubes of what looked like hay into his mouth. Did he ever eat human food, Maia wondered, or was it all stuff that horses ate?

He swallowed and grinned at her through his beard.

"I know what you're thinking. I do eat human food, as well as grass and such. I have two oesophagi, one for each stomach."

Maia couldn't help but be impressed.

"It sounds complicated."

He shrugged.

"It's normal for centaurs. It means I'll never starve while there's plenty of fodder. I might die of boredom, though. I do love apple pie and cream."

She laughed. "So do I!" then stopped, abruptly. "I did," she corrected herself.

He cast her a look of sympathy.

"It will get easier."

"That's what everyone says," Maia reflected miserably. When she'd been a child, she'd hoped that life would improve when she left the Foundling Home. When she'd been a servant, she'd looked forward to being freed from her indenture, and when she'd been a Ship-in-Training with no Potentia, she'd looked forward to a pension and the chance to make a new life somewhere on her own terms.

None of it had turned out as she'd hoped it would.

"Have you spoken to any other Ships yet?" he asked.

"Only the formalities," she replied. She hadn't felt like talking to anyone except her close friend Briseis, who was now the *Patience*. She'd even cut her mentor, *Blossom,* off short, saying that she had to do her initial checks. She doubted that it had fooled the old Ship, but she'd been wise enough not to push it. Her conversation with *Patience* had been a little longer, but even then she didn't feel that she could tell her everything. It was easier and less painful to hide behind protocol and regulations. There wouldn't be much chance to chat until she was named anyway, as some Ships were superstitious and preferred to wait until everything was official.

6

"You'll be getting all the gossip in no time," Pholus observed. He pointed a calloused thumb over his shoulder. "See the *Jasper* over there? Biggest mouth in the fleet and proud of it. Don't tell her anything you wouldn't want broadcast to every Ship in the Navy!"

Maia looked over at the smaller vessel in the next dock.

"Thanks for the warning. *Blossom* and Captain Plinius mentioned her as well."

She'd have to learn who to trust and who not to confide in. She'd already added the *Jasper* to a mental list of 'nots'. It couldn't be good if the Ship had that sort of reputation and it was important to make the right impression from the start.

"Yes, I'm afraid she's notorious," the centaur remarked. "Anyway, as you've probably noticed, the preparations for your naming and launch are coming along nicely."

It was true. The dockyards were beginning to assume a festive air, with banners, flags and bunting being hung from walls and lampposts. She noticed with interest that there were more Britannic Dragons flapping in the breeze than Imperial Eagles.

"Are there any other candidates yet?" she asked the Architect.

He pulled a face. "No, not yet. We were lucky to get you three at virtually the same time. The Board is already looking further afield. We live in hope that we can get to them before the Priests do."

A dwindling supply of girls with Potentia meant more competition and Maia had no doubt that some would run to a temple before allowing themselves to be drafted into a life at sea. She would probably have done the same, if Jupiter himself hadn't given her an ultimatum: become a Ship, or die. Well, she'd become a Ship, for all the good it would probably do her.

Pholus finished the last of his food and brushed off his hands.

"Now. Let's check your rigging."

Maia set to work.

*

The afternoon brought a pleasant surprise in the form of a heavily-laden cart trundling along the dockside, pulled by two mules. The driver was a large, burly fellow, but it was the man perched on the seat next to him who caught Maia's attention. His cowl was thrown back, blond hair shining in the sun and the strawberry mark on his face redder than ever against his pale skin.

"Ahoy the new Ship!"

"Robin!" she called out. "Come aboard!"

"I've brought you a present," he shouted back, his face alight with enthusiasm. Maia knew instantly what was under the tarpaulin in the back of the cart.

"I can't wait!"

The driver tied up the mules and several workers came forward to help unload the cart, with the young Mage hovering around them like an anxious parent on their child's first day of school.

"They're to go straight to the Mage workroom," he instructed them. "Carefully, please."

The men lifted down the boxes and chests with exaggerated caution. Nobody wanted to upset a Mage, especially when the latter was almost dancing with impatience. Robin oversaw the handling of each piece; only then did he follow the line of men across the gangplank and onto the vessel. He saluted Maia, regarding her unformed state with interest.

"Greetings! I come bearing gifts."

"Good job you're not Greek," she said, wryly.

"Indeed," he laughed, quite unabashed. There was hardly a trace left of his stammer now and she saw that he'd become a very confident young man. The silver badge of the Guild of Artificers winked on his robes. "Congratulations on your initiation."

"Thank you." Maia knew that he would have undergone his own trials and hoped they had been less traumatic than her own. "I haven't decided what form to take yet," she added.

"So I see," Robin said. "I didn't know if you'd look like yourself, or choose something different." He cast an eye over her Shipbody. "Interesting. I haven't seen a brand-new Ship before. It must feel strange."

"It's taking some getting used to," she admitted. "The default setting is the gracious and beautiful maiden."

Robin blew a raspberry. "Boring!"

She had to laugh. "Choose a monster," he urged her, enthusiastically.

"Heron would love me to look like a kraken."

"You could do several things at once and pick up people with your tentacles," he said, his eyes twinkling.

"That's a thought. So, talking of krakens, I heard you got your device approved."

"All sorted." She thought that he might burst with excitement. "It worked in controlled trials and then we tested it on an old inanimate loaded with bait. Worked like a charm!"

"Am I the first to get it?" she asked, curiously.

"No. We gave the first one to the *Emerald*, or the Navy would never have heard the last of it. I *think* it's helped her, but then again it could fuel her obsession."

Poor *Emerald*: her vessel had been destroyed by a kraken almost as soon as she was launched. Maia didn't begrudge her the first device. It might give her more peace of mind if she knew one of the creatures was in the vicinity and could take action to either fight or avoid it. Either that, or she would be constantly on edge waiting for the signal.

"They're being fitted on several Ships as we speak. Catching the one that took the bait has provided us with more tentacles, *ergo* more devices!"

He beamed at her. It was as if they'd never been parted.

"That's wonderful. Are you going to stay aboard for a while?"

His face fell.

"I can't unfortunately. I'm working on something major, so I have to get back to the Artificers' Guild. I swear I spend more time there than at the Collegium, but it's where I'm needed most."

The fact that he'd taken time to come and install his device himself meant a lot to her and she told him so.

"I wanted to see you again," he said. "After…you know…everything, I thought you might like to see a friendly face."

"You don't know how glad I am to see you," she said, meaning every word.

"Me too. I'm just relieved you're all right. I'm hoping that this is only the first of many new devices."

9

"Will you be able to manage on your own?" she asked.

"Raven's at the palace."

"Oh yes. I'll get on with it now. Raven understands it, but Magpie will be the one that takes a real interest. He has a mechanical bent, as well as several other specialisms. Being junior Mage means that he'll have more time to indulge himself in research than if he was alone, which suits him just fine."

She'd have two experienced Mages then. That would be a bonus.

"I'll meet you down there," she told him.

The kraken detector was just the latest of several innovations to be added to her already impressive armaments. New breech-loading guns, a coating for the sails that made them less likely to rip, and chemical storage units to ensure that her supplies would last longer and in a far more palatable state. Mages could use spells to maintain the food, but these devices would be something that wouldn't be magic dependent and thus available for anyone to use at any time. Pholus had explained that they would need topping up at intervals, but otherwise looked after themselves. The metal cabinets were heavier than the boxes, barrels and crates she had been expecting, but strengthening had been built into her decks and hull to compensate.

Maia flowed down to the Mage quarters, where Robin was busy fixing a familiar-looking piece of rubbery flesh into a nest of wires and crystals. The alarm bells sat in their crate, carefully packed in straw and waiting to be attached. The young Mage muttered over his equipment, sending the odd spark to shoot through the tangle and causing the small piece of tentacle to jerk and flex as if it were still alive. He reminded her of Heron, his old master and she wondered if he would grow to be as eccentric as time went on. Maia was glad to see that the device was nowhere near the size of the prototype; indeed the whole apparatus was contained in a frame about two feet square.

"You managed to make it smaller then," she remarked.

"Yes, we've made some big improvements."

He adjusted a crystal, tweaking it into place, then reached for a bell. "All I've got to do now is attach the bells and make sure that the sensory field is operating. You'll have to listen for the alarm: I'm afraid we haven't yet worked out how to integrate it with your senses."

"Why are there different bells?"

"To indicate strength. One chime is something small – or small as krakens go. If more go off that means something bigger's approaching."

His long fingers deftly fastened each bell to the frame as Maia watched, not wanting to interrupt him further.

Eventually, he stood back to examine his handiwork.

"There. That should do it. Of course, we can't do a proper test until you're at sea facing a kraken, but there are ways of fooling it into sounding off."

He levered open another crate. Instantly, a familiar pungent smell filled the air. If Maia had still been human, she would have wrinkled her nose, but Robin seemed unaffected.

"Fresh kraken tentacle – or as fresh as possible. Pickled or dried ones don't work. Ready?"

"Yes."

He lifted the slippery chunk of flesh from its bag of ice and walked over to the detector. Immediately, the bells began to quiver and one let out a low note of warning.

"Excellent! It's reacting."

"I'd ask how it works, but I think the explanation will be beyond me," Maia said.

"It has several components, mostly physical but some magical. The crystals react to the life force of anything large, sensing the emanations that all living things give off. They then translate this into energy, which powers the bells."

He gazed fondly at the contraption.

"You make it sound simple," she said.

He shrugged. "Everything's simple when you know how it works. We're learning more and more all the time. I have friends who are talking about using steam engines to power everything. They're already working on ways of producing heat without the need for conventional fuel. We're living in an age of marvels, Maia!"

"So I won't need my lovely new sails for much longer?"

She was teasing, but he considered her words carefully. "Who knows? Give it time. Maybe your next vessel will look totally different."

"I've got to get used to this one first."

"So you have." He pulled a watch from his pocket and flipped the lid. "Got to go, but I hope to see you again before too long. Tell Raven or Magpie to let me know when you're back in Londin, so I can pop over and say hello."

"I will."

He packed the smelly lump of tentacle away once more. "Don't worry, I'm taking this with me."

"Glad to hear it," she said. No wonder *Blossom* had complained. The larger piece Heron had inflicted on her would have been revolting if this was anything to go by. Robin was probably inured to the smell by now, but she wouldn't want it to linger and neither would her crew.

It wasn't long before he was waving cheerfully as the cart trundled away over the cobbles once more.

"Goodbye, Maia!"

It felt strange to hear her name again. She supposed that even her friends would call her by her new Ship name. How long would it be before hardly anyone remembered the person she had been?

\*

It was only after several days of hard work and practice runs that Maia felt anything like a real Ship. She watched the comings and goings on and around her, noting that the rate was steadily increasing as the day of her naming drew nearer. She'd had a slow start, but it would be more than made up for soon. Pholus was very attentive, but his time with her was nearing its end. He had other vessels to supervise, whether they would be inanimates and rigged for a large crew, or be allocated to existing Ships to transfer into, like so many hermit crabs finding new homes.

She was grateful for the time he'd given her and was thankful for his patience.

"I think you've grasped the basics," he remarked, one afternoon. The spring air was sweet, as a stiff south-easterly breeze was blowing most of the Londin smoke away inland.

"I should hope so. I'll have to put theory into practice soon enough," she observed. This was where a good memory helped.

"You learn quickly," he agreed, sniffing the air with every sign of enjoyment, his wide nostrils flaring.

"What happens now?"

"You'll be getting a visit. Senior admirals, for a start, and some of your new crew. The King's insisting on appointing your Captain himself."

There was an edge to his voice that alerted her.

"Who is he?"

He looked pensive. "There is a likely contender, but nothing's certain yet. The Naval Board will try to influence His Majesty's decision. This is a very prestigious appointment."

"Surely I'll get an experienced Commander?" she asked, puzzled.

"I hope so," Pholus said darkly, "but the King has favourites."

Maia's heart sank in a not dissimilar fashion to when it still beat in her breast. Surely she wouldn't have Admiral Albanus? She dismissed the thought in a second. He wouldn't want to leave Court and the King's ear, not even for her. It would probably be some other lackey. She thought of Silvius' grim face and groaned internally. She definitely didn't envy the *Regina* on that score, though the man was competent and respected. Some experience was probably the best she could hope for. The worst would be some fool who'd jeopardise the safety of her crew, and provoke trouble, if not mutiny.

Maia brought herself up sharply; only just installed and thinking about mutiny? She gave herself a mental kick. The sooner she was working, the better; if only to turn her mind from such grim musings.

"I hope I'll get some notice before they arrive," she said.

"I doubt it," Pholus said, "but keep one eye open. They might come by water, but I wouldn't bank on it. If they're portalled in you'll get no warning at all. Not that it matters. You just have to reply when spoken to and put up with them until they decide they've seen enough."

"I can do that. I've spent a lot of time in the background, trying not to be noticed," she answered.

"It will hold you in good stead, then. Remember, eyes and ears open, mouth mostly shut and you won't go wrong."

He was right, though Maia imagined that some of the chattier candidates would have found it harder to adjust to the new rules. Her thoughts strayed to Tullia again. That girl had always loved the sound of her own voice. No wonder the Ships talked as much as they could amongst themselves and joked that the two most important words in a Ship's vocabulary were 'aye' and 'sir'.

All she could do was to wait and see whom King Artorius chose.

Later, she glided through the vessel, choosing the privacy of a lieutenant's cabin to try out her ideas for her new form. It wasn't a bad size. She hadn't dared use her Captain's; besides which, there were still workmen around putting the finishing touches to the fittings and she didn't want to be observed.

It was larger than the cabins she'd occupied on *Blossom,* both her original one, invaded by the *Livia,* and the one Durus had relinquished for her afterwards, so she'd have some room to grow if necessary. How large could she be, anyway? Surely the wood imposed some sort of limit? The Shipbodies she'd seen had all been within reasonable parameters. It wouldn't make sense for her to be unable to fit inside her vessel. She decided to rein in her ambition and keep to roughly human size, though the thought of towering over her officers did have a certain appeal.

Maybe she wouldn't look entirely human at all. It might be better to be some sort of hybrid, like the *Leopard.* If so, which animal could she choose? She ran through various pictures in her head, unable to decide. Of course, if she was to be called *Lion,* or *Tiger,* the choice would be virtually made for her, but she had the feeling that it would be something that fitted in with the other Royals.

It was no good. Her brain refused to offer any viable possibilities. Eventually, she decided to just practise changing into something, so she knew that she could. For a few seconds, she toyed with the idea of contacting *Blossom* or *Patience* and asking for advice, but just as quickly decided to try it herself. It didn't matter if she made a mistake here.

Maia cleared her mind, concentrating on the great block of Britannic oak that housed her consciousness and watching from various angles to see the results. The sense of her old body sprang to mind and she allowed it to rise from her will and memory.

There. Her external eyes told her that the wood was softening, melting like wax in a flame and moulding itself into the desired result. Colour appeared from nowhere, forming on the surface of the Shipbody like a layer of paint. Slowly, the image rippled before becoming solid once more.

The face that swam into her vision was one she'd seen many times in the mirror of her dreams. An elegant, titled lady stood in the sunlight that was streaming in through the porthole. She was complete; the dress, the chestnut hair, the storm-grey eyes and the elaborate silk gown. A necklace of pearls, interposed with gems, glittered around her perfect neck. The Lady Gemma Valeria, in all her glory.

Maia saw the figure's mouth contort in a soundless scream of pain, then instantly clamped down on her emotion, forcing it back. This wouldn't do; it wouldn't do at all. At this rate, she'd rouse the whole dockyard! She savagely dismissed the form, watching with satisfaction as it slumped and collapsed under her will, the features dissolving into a misshapen lump of pale oak, all definition gone. Only then did she release her grip, sending her awareness up and out to the topmost spar of her mainmast, to perch like a resting seabird alongside the pennant that streamed in the breeze, its dragon symbol rippling as if alive.

Pain and grief slashed into her. She felt like howling, but how could she grieve for something that had been mere illusion?

It seemed to take forever, but finally Maia wrenched her mind back to the present, focusing on the life and activity around her and burying the emotions as deep as she could. The sense of the moving air helped to calm her as she centred herself on her vessel and its surroundings.

Below, men scurried like ants, erecting staging and tentage to cater for the crowds that would flock to her naming. It would be a big day for the locals. Many others would come from Londin too, to join in the celebrations as a brand new Royal Ship began her long journey and catch a glimpse of the young King with his fabled sword. There would be feasting and pageants, with her at the heart of it all, mute and bound throughout. For a split second, she almost wished that she'd taken Diana's offer. It would have been wonderful while it lasted, without pain or fear. Or, then again, she could have defied Jupiter and thrown herself upon the mercy of the Mother as Ceridwen had advised, and become a Priestess living in the seclusion of the Great Forest. She spent a few more minutes calming herself before a familiar voice broke into her mind.

<*Blossom* to the new Ship!>

The mental call took her by surprise and, for a few seconds, she groped for an answer.

<This is the new Ship.>

<Ah! Maia! How are...you're not all right, are you?>

Maia realised that her distress was leaking through the link and forcefully pulled herself together.

<Teething troubles, that's all. Nothing to worry about.>

Maybe if she told herself that often enough, she'd come to believe it.

<I was just wondering if you wanted a chat,> *Blossom* ventured.

Maia pulled herself together. She couldn't hide away forever, even if she wanted to.

<Yes, that would be nice,> she replied, trying to cover her confusion. <Pholus has finished with me for the day and it's not as if I have anything else to do at the moment.>

<Your main job is to familiarise yourself with your vessel,> the other Ship agreed. <How are you finding it?>

<Enormous.>

*Blossom* laughed. <Yes, it is, isn't it? I've no doubt that you'll lick everything into shape in no time. Have you had a visit from the high-ups yet?>

Maia scanned her surroundings automatically. Everything seemed to be in order.

<Not yet. I'm expecting them any time now. I'm getting named the day after tomorrow.>

<So I hear.> *Blossom*'s tone became avid and Maia sensed her excitement. <Have you decided on a form yet?>

<I've been practising.>

She decided not to mention her first attempt.

<Good. Most of us just decide to look like ourselves, but a lot prettier!>

*Blossom* thought that was funny. Tullia had certainly improved on her human looks, but did she really want to do that?

<I'll decide when I'm named,> she said. <I can always change my mind later, if I don't like it.>

<True.>

The conversation was awkward, on both their parts. Maia was still fond of her mentor, but Ceridwen had opened her eyes to the fact that the training Ship was just doing her job. After all, if she had been cold or unwelcoming, candidates would refuse to go through the process so it made sense for her to be motherly and kind. A niggling thought insisted that she was being unfair; *Blossom* and her crew had fought to protect her, but she still couldn't shake the suspicion that she had been manipulated from the start and that was throwing up a barrier between them that hadn't been there before.

<Promise you'll keep me updated on your new crew,> *Blossom* said.

<I will.>

It wasn't like the whole Fleet wouldn't know almost immediately, but she resolved not to start any gossip. Her gaze slid to where the smaller *Jasper* rested in an adjacent dock. Her refit was almost finished and she would soon be back on duty. Maia hadn't been hailed yet, but she felt that it was only a matter of time before her sister Ship's curiosity got the better of her.

She was relieved when *Blossom* broke the contact. So much for not being human; her emotions and thoughts were all over the place.

Suddenly, a flurry of activity from the marines caught her attention. A small group of men exited the main offices and were heading purposefully in her direction. Immediately suspicious, Maia magnified her vision and focused on the leader of the group.

He was hooded and cloaked, but something about his walk set off alarm bells. The others were definitely escorting him, so he was a person of importance. One of them was Admiral Albanus, his uniform distinctive even at this distance. Flanking the central figure was another, also in uniform, but this time belonging to the army. She noticed the resemblance to Pendragon immediately. This had to be his son, Prince Marcus. The other man, bringing up the rear, was dressed as a Captain.

She tried to make out the latter's features, but Albanus was in the way and she couldn't get the angle right. Oh well, he'd be here soon enough and then she could get a good look at him. Perhaps he was going to be her Captain? It was better that they meet sooner rather than later.

She concentrated on the lead figure instead, catching glimpses of him beneath his hood. Now, why would he be concealing himself?

The marines snapped to attention as the men passed them and she made out more details of her mystery visitor. He was young for sure and he was wearing a sword. She could see the end sticking out behind him, lifting the cloak.

If she'd had a mouth, she would have gasped. It had to be the King.

Abruptly, Maia realised that her Shipbody was still in its embryonic state down in the cabin. That wouldn't do. She quickly shot her awareness back into the oak and retrieved it, fountaining up from the deck just in time to catch the party striding up the gangplank. For a second, she bridled, wondering whether to challenge them for daring to set foot on her vessel without her permission, then memory and training kicked in. The Sovereign was the only person who could. As she remembered, a senior marine bellowed out.

"His Royal Majesty, Artorius the Tenth, King of the Britons! His Royal Highness the Prince Marcus! The Honourable Admiral Lucius Albanus Dio!"

Even as he announced her illustrious guests, she sounded her Ship's bell in acknowledgement and wondered who the fourth member of the group was. She could see him more clearly now, so she tore her eyes from the King and focused on the Captain's face.

Recognition flooded through her. For one heart stopping moment, she thought the dead had come alive again. The same fair hair, the shape of the eyes and nose, even the way he moved screamed to her that she'd seen him before. Panic flooded in, even as they approached where she stood fixed in horror. For once, she was glad that her wooden anonymity could give nothing away. The sight of this man did something that even the Revenant had failed to do – reduce her to a horrified wreck. Why did he look like her father? Who was he? She could sense his feet on her deck, so surely he was mortal and not some accompanying wraith?

The King threw back his hood and turned, gesturing to the vessel, his face alight with pride and enthusiasm. He had the same dark eyes as all his family, with black hair cut short in the Roman style. A slim gold fillet rested on his head, proclaiming his status to the world.

"Marvellous, isn't she!"

"Indeed, your Majesty," Albanus said, smoothly. "A true and potent sign of Britannia's superiority in all things maritime."

Prince Marcus was staring at her Shipbody, his forehead creased.

"What's that?" he demanded.

Maia felt all eyes turn to her.

"Ah, our Ship has not yet taken her form," Albanus told him. "No doubt she's waiting to be named and will adjust accordingly. This often happens," he told the King.

Artorius looked unimpressed. "Why doesn't she look like a woman? This isn't what we expected!"

"She can look like anything, your Majesty. It's sometimes a difficult decision to make."

The King looked her up and down. Maia forced herself to remain perfectly still.

"Can she speak?"

"Yes, Your Majesty. Perhaps you would care to ask her something?"

The young man smirked at his cousin, then walked slowly around Maia's mute form. "It looks like an old tree's been uprooted and jammed down on to the deck. I've never seen one like this." He raised his voice and addressed Maia.

"Ship? Can you hear me?"

Prince Marcus rolled his eyes. "She's not deaf, Sire."

Maia found her voice.

"Greetings, Your Majesty."

Artorius took a step back. "So, there's someone in there after all!" He walked up to her Shipbody, examining it carefully. "It looks like ordinary wood to me. Perhaps we ought to call for a carpenter to turn her into something more presentable."

Maia realised that the King had started his celebrations early. What she had taken for a swagger, was more of a drunken lurch and his eyes were slightly glazed. She didn't think that the others caught the flash of annoyance on the Admiral's face. Why hadn't Pendragon come with him? He might have moderated the young man's behaviour.

"A chair, maybe, or a table. Isn't that what oak is usually turned into?" He grinned at his own joke. Maia felt the nearest marines bristle and, for a second, she had the urge to turn into something that would wipe the smirk off his face.

"I'm sure that she is only thinking of a more pleasing form, Sire," Albanus interjected.

"She'd better be," the King snorted, "otherwise everyone will think she's just another Imperial. One more worm-eaten branch parroting instructions!" He burst out laughing at his own wit, then threw an arm around the Captain.

"Sorry, old friend, we wanted you to have a pretty maid to look at! You'll have to state your requirements." He leered at his friend. "What do you fancy? A beautiful redhead?"

"I love them all, Sire!" the Captain announced and they both burst out laughing. After her initial shock, Maia could see the differences. This wasn't her father come back to life, but surely they had to be related.

"Of course. You weren't introduced," Artorius said, raising his eyebrows in mock chagrin. "Purposefully, we hasten to add. We wanted to surprise my new Ship. Ship, this is Tiberius Valerius Severianus Leo, your new Captain!"

If she'd had a jaw to drop, it would have done so. The last surviving Valerius, save herself. Why had no-one told her that he was a Captain? Something told her that he hadn't been one for very long. Thoughts piled into her head like a barrage of grenadoes, exploding on impact.

This man had what should rightfully have been hers; the house, the land, the money and the family name. He'd probably had a life of ease, while she did laundry and emptied slops. Nor was he an experienced commander. Albanus' stony face gave nothing away while Marcus looked on with barely restrained boredom.

The King must know he was her cousin. He probably thought it was a great jest.

"Ma'am," Valerius stepped forward and saluted. She responded automatically, part of her Shipbody folding out and across before she had realised it. Artorius gasped.

"So, she can move after all! Turn into something else: we command it!"

This time, Albanus stepped forward as if he was about to intercede, but Artorius waved him back.

"Did you hear me, Ship? We gave you an order! Obey your king!"

Rage pulsed through Maia. Her Shipbody was the one thing that she had control over, the sole bit of independence left in her regulated, command-ridden life. She had no choice as to the rest, but nobody, not even her Captain, told a Ship how they would appear. Ever.

She reared up, the dense wood flying apart into a roiling mass of jagged shards that spiralled up to her lowermost spars. At the same time, a blast of air swept across the deck, echoed by a loud crack of thunder above them. Her family was rallying to her side.

"Gods protect us!"

The king staggered back, automatically reaching for his sword, alarm and incomprehension writ large on his face. Before he could unsheathe the weapon, Valerius raced to shield him with his body. The King landed flat on his back on the deck, staring at the dark funnel cloud above their heads and the whirlwind before them. Albanus was the only one who moved forward, arms upraised, to pacify her.

"Steady now, steady now, Ship. All is well; nobody will harm you. The King meant no offence. Calm yourself."

He continued, speaking slowly and quietly as Valerius and the Prince picked up the King and moved off to a safe distance. The Admiral kept one eye on her and the other on the sky as he soothed her and, gradually, Maia felt herself shrinking back into the wood.

"That's it. Control yourself. Concentrate."

21

She wanted to order the arrogant, spoiled young man off her deck, but knew she couldn't. A white-faced Artorius was being propped up by his cousin, both of them casting fearful glances at her position. Valerius hovered between her and the King, as if uncertain what to do. Overhead, the storm cloud began to disperse, though the air still had the thick, greasy feel of undischarged energy. Gradually, the tension abated and silence fell over the deck.

Now that it was over, Maia watched the men warily, rage still bubbling inside her. The marines hadn't moved, she noticed. Interesting.

Artorius looked as if he was going to be sick, while Marcus and Valerius glanced at the Admiral for guidance.

"As you can see, your Majesty, the Ship is still coming into her power. I'm sure she didn't realise her own strength. Imagine what she'll be able to do to our enemies!"

To give him his due, the King rallied somewhat. Colour began to return to his cheeks.

"We have to admit it was impressive." He swallowed. "Perhaps we should leave the rest of the formalities until later."

"An excellent idea, Sire. I have arranged for refreshments –,"

"No. We shall return to the palace." His glare said it all. He'd been shocked and humiliated and Maia knew he wouldn't forget this meeting in a hurry.

"I'm sure that's for the best, Sire."

Maia wondered if she'd doomed her chances of him actually launching her in person. The look he cast in her direction as he left was angry and awed in equal measure.

"We hear that you nearly didn't pass your trial," he snapped. "We truly hope you're worth all the faith people have in you!"

He swept from her vessel, pulling the rest behind him like an irresistible force. Albanus pursed his lips and followed. His eyes slid to hers as his lips moved silently.

"It'll be fine. Leave it to me."

She watched them return to the main offices, on their way back to the capital. Artorius obviously hadn't fancied a trip by land or sea; he'd be back home in no time. The ominous sense of heaviness in the air lifted as her aunt's Potentia retreated back to the horizon, the wind fell back to a gentle breeze and the late afternoon sun shone once more. A couple of gulls wheeled above her, but she was too miserable to take much notice.

All she'd had to do was be a stump of wood and she hadn't even managed that. Still, what could they do about it? Maybe she should have stuck to her previous form; however much it had pained her, she knew that it would have found favour. Instead, she'd lost her temper and made a mess of everything when she should have made a good impression. Still, Albanus hadn't seemed too bothered. Maybe he'd enjoyed seeing his Sovereign so terrified? But this didn't change the main facts of the situation. The King was an ass and her new Captain was wet behind the ears and probably useless too. They could all go to Hades as far as she was concerned.

She fixed her eyes on the continuing preparations and settled into a determined sulk.

# II

Raven had chosen geography for the third lesson of the day. His sole pupil was at her desk writing notes, as he expounded on the major rivers of Gaul and how they promoted the economy of the Empire as a whole. Her Royal Highness, the Princess Julia, sister of the King, pretended to be absorbed in the details but he could tell that her thoughts were elsewhere.

Her lady-in-waiting, elderly Priscilla, was already beginning to doze over her needlework. It wouldn't take much to tip her over into a deep and refreshing sleep.

The Princess was getting restless. They'd covered politics and history already and doubtless she'd decided that enough was enough. There were far more important things to learn and little time left to study them. Finally, he took pity on her. A whispered word and Priscilla's head sank on to her ample bosoms. Julia sighed with relief.

"I think Your Highness has grasped the importance of the river Rhodanus to trade?"

"I certainly have," the girl replied. "I wish you wouldn't keep me in suspense, Master Mage."

Raven knew that her large, dark eyes were fixed on him in reproach. Julia looked like a younger, female version of her uncle, with the dark hair and thin face of the line, finished off with a determined expression. She was certainly nothing like the simpering princesses in the storybooks.

"Patience is a virtue."

She scowled.

"Time waits for no man."

"Slow and steady wins the race."

"*Carpe diem.*"

He grinned at her. "You're right, we should begin. I don't know how long we've got."

She twisted her face in disgust. "Before I'm sold off to old Parisius, you mean. I'd rather pass on that, thank you. I can't see the point, anyway. He's impotent. You know that a God cursed him."

The Mage frowned at her in reproof. "Baseless gossip."

"Oh yes? Two wives and no children. Not even by-blows. There's something wrong there. Plus he's, what? Sixty two? It's the triumph of hope over experience."

"Then you won't be married to him for long."

Julia stood, stretching her back. "I still think it's a waste."

"Politics. Or would you rather be sent to the North?"

He ignored her scowl.

"I'd *rather* stay here and complete my studies."

"I know. Count yourself lucky that you weren't married off years ago. You're getting to be old for an unmarried princess.'" Raven glanced over at the gently snoring Priscilla. "I think we should see how your ability is progressing. Have you been trying things out?"

"When I can," Julia admitted. "It's getting harder to find excuses to send people away. I sometimes make a break for it into the gardens, but it's too risky. I resorted to practising in the lavatory, but they even try to follow me in there!"

He sympathised.

"I understand. Now. Let's start with something small."

He extended his senses, checking that they were unobserved. All clear.

"Begin."

Julia concentrated, staring at her notebook. It shifted, as if knocked by a careless hand, then rose into the air, turning gently. A smile of triumph shot across her face as she held it with her mind.

Raven nodded in approval. She was improving. If she had to be used as marriage fodder, then at least she'd be *trained* marriage fodder.

"Excellent. Now, let's try that fire spell…"

His speechstone sent a pulse of heat through his arm.

<Yes, what is it?> he replied irritably.

<Admiral Pendragon sends his compliments and asks that you check on the new Ship.>

Favonius' tone was even drier than usual.

<Why?>

<There was an incident during the King's visit.>

Raven bit back a curse.

<I'm on my way.>

Blast it! What had happened now? He became aware that Julia was standing, arm upraised and waiting for him to give her the word that would produce magelight on her open palm.

"My apologies, Your Highness, but I'm called away on urgent business. This will have to wait."

"It must be urgent indeed." He felt her examining him. "I know you'll return as soon as you're able."

"Believe me, I shall. In the meantime, do what you can and I'll leave you to wake Lady Priscilla. Gently, mind. I don't want her seeing dancing rats again."

Julia stifled a grin.

"Of course."

He gave her a stern look, which he knew wouldn't fool her at all, bowed politely and left for Durobrivis. He would use the portal in the Palace – it would be quicker.

What had Maia got herself into now?

*

Julia watched him leave, bubbling with frustration. She was so close! Every day her skills and Potentia were growing and she'd been so looking forward to calling up light. Lowering the notebook had been more difficult and left her feeling tired, but nothing like it had the day before. It was definitely getting easier.

What could be so important to call Raven away now, of all days? He was the only one she'd trusted enough to tell when strange things started to happen around her. He'd taken charge immediately and she'd been training with him, in secret, for over a year. So far, their clandestine lessons hadn't been discovered and he'd warned her to say nothing. It had taken all the willpower at her command to clamp down on her Potentia, especially lately with all this talk of marriage.

She glanced over at Priscilla. The woman was high-ranking, but had little in the way of stimulating conversation. What little brain she had was solely devoted to making sure that Julia didn't do or say anything she wasn't supposed to, and that included being alone for any longer than it took Priscilla to attend to the essentials. Julia was tempted to leave her in the arms of Morpheus for a little longer.

She wondered whether to try the light spell on her own, then abandoned the idea. It wouldn't do for it to get out of control. Perhaps a simple illusion? A plate of oranges stood on a small table. She took one and held it, feeling its weight and the texture of its dimpled skin against her fingers.

As her concentration grew, the peel rippled as if obscured by a heat haze and the skin smoothed out, becoming green. It still felt like an orange, but her eyes were telling her that she was holding an apple. She adjusted the colour, adding a blush of red. There. Now it looked like a real apple. She added darker flecks and a stalk, keeping the image in her mind.

There were footsteps outside. She dropped the illusion and whispered the counterspell to wake Priscilla as the door swung open. The footman bowed.

"Your Royal Highness, the Lady Drusilla."

Priscilla snorted as she awoke and the footman looked around, startled.

Drusilla swept in, expensive silks wafting perfume.

"This is a surprise, my Lady!" Julia said, pleased for once. They were old friends and both Senator Rufus and his wife had been very kind to her after her father's death and her mother's re-marriage.

"Highness." Drusilla curtsied. "His Majesty asked me to help you to prepare your trousseau, so here I am."

Julia stared at her, the mask slipping, despite all she could do to hide it.

"Oh, my dear, you knew this day would come," Drusilla said, taking her to a couch, then belatedly noticing the other occupant of the room. "Lady Priscilla! How lovely to see you."

Priscilla blinked, momentarily bewildered by her rapid awakening.

"My goodness. I must have nodded off."

"The Master Mage was just called away," Julia said, hastily. "Let's have some refreshments."

She looked at the women's eager faces, feeling a wave of hopelessness sweep over her. There was little chance of escape now.

*

The dockyard was nearly ready for the momentous day. Everything had been cleaned, swept and decorated with garlands of flowers. Maia had become accustomed to the constant stream of workers respectfully asking for admittance as they tramped aboard, bearing tools and fittings to finish her cabins, or boxes, barrels and crates to fill her holds. It took such a lot to supply a Ship. Throughout it all, she remained fixed in position, only speaking when it was absolutely necessary. She caught the occasional glances thrown in her direction, but mostly the hands were too busy to do more than give her a cursory salute as they went about their business. It was less than a day before she would be named, whether by the King or not. She was brooding over the chances of him being indisposed, when a familiar voice hailed her from the quayside.

"Raven to the new Ship, requesting permission to come aboard!"

Naturally, he would be the one they sent to talk to her.

"Permission granted."

She kept her tone neutral, watching as he walked up the gangplank, his staff tapping on the planks. He only carried it to reassure others; Maia had seen him without it often enough and knew that the old Mage had his own ways of seeing the world. Once aboard, he made a bee-line for his cabin. His servant, Polydorus, had preceded him, so most of his master's belongings were neatly in place. Maia watched nervously as they exchanged greetings. The accommodation seemed to meet with the old man's approval. Raven dismissed Polydorus before starting to arrange various multi-coloured jars and bottles on purposely designed shelves. She was just beginning to think that he wasn't here for her at all, when he spoke.

"Maia, would you come to my cabin, please?"

His voice was light, but she knew she was in trouble. Reluctantly, she withdrew her Shipbody down into the deck and

28

flowed along through the structure, to emerge on a bulkhead like a supporting beam. He cocked his head as she entered, then turned to face her.

"You haven't chosen a form yet."

If she'd had teeth, she would have ground them.

"It's within my rights to appear as I please," she told him, unable to keep the edge out of her voice.

"It is indeed," he said, calmly. "A fact that our Sovereign failed to understand, or so I hear."

When she didn't reply, he sighed.

"Maia, you must control your temper. Detachment is the key, or have you forgotten your training already?"

"He was drunk!"

Raven raised an eyebrow. "And you've never come across drunks before, have you? Didn't you use to work in a tavern, or was that some other girl?"

His words hit Maia like a dash of cold water. He was right. Why had she reacted so badly? She'd dealt with enough befuddled men before – what had been different this time? Did she still believe that she was a great lady, unused to insults?

Raven sank down into an old leather chair that looked as though it had given several decades of loyal service. The arms were worn and the seat sagged but he seemed comfortable enough.

"It was that damned trial, wasn't it?" he asked her. "I know that you resent me for pulling you out of it, but it was either that or lose you forever."

All Maia's despair rose at once.

"It wasn't just that. You don't know what happened afterwards."

He was instantly alert.

"Tell me."

"The Huntress interfered. I ended up in a forest, somewhere in the Fae lands. Then she turned up and gave me a choice. I could stay in the dream world and have everything I'd ever wanted, if I abandoned the trial."

Raven grew very still.

"And when you refused?"

29

"She set a hydra on me. I fought it off, but it wasn't really me. I was used by Nemesis, called by the *Livia* in revenge and I'm sure it was sanctioned by the Thunderer himself. I burned the Goddess too, marking her arm, and she ran off. Lesser Fae found me and guided me back to the Priestesses."

Raven put his head in his hands.

"You see?" Maia continued. "I was being manipulated all along – we all were. This was some play of the Gods. The final act started when my mother rejected the Huntress and chose my father instead!"

"Or possibly long before then," Raven answered. "They don't measure time as we do. Nemesis, you say?"

"Yes. And surely she wouldn't act without permission. We know that the Thunderer's been involved all along."

Raven raised his head and stared blankly into space. "This is beyond all of us. I have the horrible feeling that another chain of events has been set in motion. There have been murmurings of a failed power play on Olympus. I know that some of the younger deities have become restless and chafe at the restrictions their elders put on them. It's possible…"

He trailed off.

"And here we are, caught in the middle of it all," Maia said.

He nodded. "I sincerely hope that it's run its course and we'll be allowed to get on with things in our own way. Has there been any other evidence of Potentia on your part?"

Maia shifted uneasily. "I…well…I sort of exploded when the King ordered me to change form. There was a funnel cloud too, but I think that was my aunt. She was hovering about."

"Ah. That explains a lot. A funnel cloud, eh? I take it that it didn't touch down?"

"No."

It was good job too, Maia thought. It could have been nasty, especially if Artorius had been snatched up and deposited in the sea, although then the joke would have definitely been on him.

"Still, it's frightened the King enough that I've been sent here to have a chat."

"Nemesis called me '*child of the air*' and told the Huntress that she had underestimated my power."

"Did she? It's very possible that something has been unlocked, but I wouldn't try to use it, unless you really have to. You have no training and you could wreck yourself."

It was a sobering thought. She shied away from it and changed the subject.

"Oh and I met my new Captain, too. One Tiberius Valerius Severianus Leo; the cousin who inherited everything. I think the King chose him deliberately."

"What? Gods of Britannia, is the man insane? He's only a first lieutenant!"

"Not any more, apparently."

"Jove's beard! Pendragon will be furious. There's no way that he's ready to command a Ship of this size!"

He fell silent, but Maia knew that he was talking to somebody higher up. Probably hoping that she was mistaken. She waited until he broke the connection.

"Well, it seems that you're right. My source has confirmed it."

"And Admiral Pendragon?"

"His hands are tied. This is a Royal appointment and you can be sure that Albanus will have been whispering in the King's ear. He probably thinks it's funny, as you're related. The youngster hasn't got a lick of sense."

*Wonderful*, she thought. *All I need.* "When will the rest of my crew arrive?" she asked.

"Most will be here tomorrow, for the naming, though you'll have to wait for Magpie, your other Mage. He's returning from the New Continent and has been delayed by storms. Anyway, it's not as if you're going very far initially. There'll be sea trials first and the formal offering to the Gods before you can even think about being sent on a mission."

Maia heard him with relief. She would need lots of practice before she became really comfortable in this new vessel.

"I'm worried about operating it efficiently," she admitted.

"Understandably," he replied. "You're still training. Nobody expects you to get everything right at once. This is where you need an experienced Captain."

"Doesn't look like I'm going to have one."

"No," he admitted ruefully.

31

Why had she thought that it would be easy when she was installed? Here she was, a Ship at last, and things still weren't right.

"I don't think the King will name me now."

Raven barked a short laugh.

"Of course he will! To back out now would be unthinkable. I just hope he stays off the drink long enough to get through the ceremony. It's not as if he has to do much, just parade around and give the dedication." He looked disgusted. "The place will be full of hangers-on."

"I'll choose my form when he names me," Maia said.

"You'll have to think quickly, then. Look, why don't you do the usual and turn into a beautiful maiden? Then everyone will be happy."

Maia felt a sullen lump of stubbornness settle in her Shipbody.

"Don't want to."

"Now you're being awkward."

"So? If I want to be awkward, I'll be awkward. I don't have to look like anything I don't want to."

"I never took you for a sulker," he remarked.

"That's because I didn't know how I've been used and manipulated from day one!" she flared. "Part of me wishes I'd taken *her* offer. At least I'd be happy!"

"Happiness doesn't last."

"This would have. She promised me everything!"

To her astonishment, he sagged in his chair.

"I'm sorry about that, believe me," he whispered. His hands gripped the arms and Maia saw that he'd lost the tip of his little finger. The wound still looked raw.

"What happened to your hand?"

He smiled at her sadly.

"It was a necessary sacrifice. I had to destroy your necklace too as part of the spell to get through to you. There was no other way, believe me. I know how much you treasured it."

So, her cherished gift from her friend was no more. For a second she wished she'd kept it with her human body, even if she would never have seen it again, but common sense took over. Had she really wanted to remain in her deadly fantasy?

"I understand," she said, though a tiny spark of resentment towards him still smouldered.

He sighed. "The Mother demands a price, but it was worth it. You're a Ship and I'm your Mage. This is what we've both been working towards for so many years. Swallow your pain and pride. Accept what is, not what might have been in some nebulous dream. It wasn't real. This is. Now, can you work with me, or do I request a transfer to another Ship?"

"Do I have a choice?"

His clouded eyes lowered.

"I will bow to your wishes."

Maia was surprised. Was he really willing to leave her?

"So you'd leave me in the hands of that...that..." She groped for a word.

"Inexperienced young Captain? I'd rather not."

"What will you do if he tries something stupid? Turn him into a toad?"

He grinned at her suddenly. "I'll tell you one thing. He'll be wetting his breeches at the thought of having me as your Mage."

"Will he?" she asked.

"Oh yes. I've a fearsome reputation, you know."

He seemed quite happy at the thought. She stared at his wrinkled face and wondered just how old he was. Perhaps she would be better with somebody younger. He might not last her first voyage and, if he became unwell, where would that leave her?

"Of course, I won't be your only Mage," he remarked. "Leo will have both of us to contend with; that is, if the Navy decides to let him run things solo. I wouldn't. They might keep him as Post Captain and put in an executive Commander, thus not going against the King's wishes, but adding safeguards."

"We'd both be in training," Maia said, with disgust. Damn these politics!

"Yes, you would," he admitted. "It's time to undergo the Trials of Neptune and deal with whatever his realm can throw at you."

"More trials?" she asked in alarm. He smiled.

"It's just what they call it in the Navy. Sometimes life at sea feels like one big trial."

She thought quickly, weighing her advantages. Raven was experienced and, if her Captain feared him, he'd be less likely to get them both in a mess.

"All right," she said, grudgingly. "Besides, you've moved your stuff in already."

"Thank you. Polydorus will be extremely relieved that he won't have to pack everything up again."

Maia liked the Master Mage's servant, a quiet Greek who always seemed to be around when his master needed him. She wouldn't have wanted to put him to any trouble.

"Well, I suppose that's that," she said.

Raven inclined his head. "I'll get on with settling in then. If you want to know anything, especially about tomorrow, let me know."

"I will, but *Blossom* and *Patience* have explained what I'm to do."

"Excellent."

She left him to his unpacking and returned to the deck. Activity had really ramped up now. Her officers' belongings were being ferried aboard as she watched; there would be no chance to use the lieutenant's cabin again. Idly, she wished that Durus could have followed her from the *Blossom*. He would have made an excellent second-in-command and his steadiness would have offset any recklessness that the King's favourite might show. She still couldn't think of Leo as her cousin and hoped that he didn't know about their blood relationship.

Maia spent the next couple of hours giving permission to all and sundry to come aboard, including several marines and ordinary seamen, who greeted her respectfully before moving below to stow their gear and begin their duties.

Then it was time for her to meet the rest of her senior officers. They came aboard, mounting the ladder with ease and lining up at attention before her. The tallest of the three seemed familiar, until she realised that he looked like his father. This had to be Lucius Albanus Sabrinus, her second-in-command. The others would be second lieutenants. She remembered their names. Claudius Atticus Amphicles and Marcus Faustus Drustan. The first was a slight man, with short brown hair, who gave her a smart, if stiff salute. She wondered whether his new uniform was causing him any discomfort, but he would wear it in soon enough. The other was a dark, curly-haired youth whose expression showed how excited he was to be aboard.

Neither was the older officer she had hoped for. It seemed that familial connections stood for more than experience these days. It wouldn't have mattered so much if she'd had a few thousand nautical miles under her keel, but Maia felt as green as they looked. Naturally, Albanus Sabrinus took the lead, introducing his fellows. She hadn't missed the momentary look of surprise on their faces as they'd spotted her; they must have been expecting a sweet and pretty maiden too. All three were looking very smart in their expensive new clothes, but their servants would have their work cut out to keep them looking that way. Behind them, the aforementioned men were helping to lug various chests, bags and cases aboard to be taken to their cabins. Her officers were lucky. Their cabins were positively luxurious compared to the ones she and Durus had on the *Blossom*. Fewer bodies aboard meant more room for her crew – another reason why sailors preferred to work on Ships.

Everything had to be ready for the big day.

She wasn't looking forward to it. She'd been focused on being a Ship for so long, but now she was, it didn't seem that great. Perhaps she'd feel better when she was at sea.

<*Jasper* to the new Ship!>

Maia was jolted out of her less-than-pleasant reverie by a cheerful voice over the Ship link.

<How are you? Are you ready for your big day? It's so exciting!>

Maia glanced over to where the smaller Ship was in her dock, spotting a small figure waving madly from the deck. So this was the infamous *Jasper*. She waved back. The other Ship's red hair shone in the sun, contrasting well with her elegant green gown. Golden jewellery adorned her neck, ears and fingers, set with her named stone. She certainly conformed to the 'pretty maiden' ideal.

<Hello, *Jasper*,> she replied.

<Ooh, they're really going to town on you, aren't they?> her sister Ship prattled on. <It's going to be a real party!>

She sounded as though she was about to burst at the seams with every remark and Maia suppressed a groan.

<I suppose so.>

<Oh, don't be nervous!> *Jasper* trilled. <I don't suppose you've any idea about your name? I didn't, you know, but the two before me were *Amethyst* and *Peridot*, so I had a feeling I'd be a gemstone. I suppose it's different, with you being Royal. I like your banners. You look lovely!>

Maia began to reply, but the *Jasper* continued, undeterred.

<Who was that visiting you the other day? I couldn't see clearly.>

*Well, thank the Gods for small mercies.*

<Oh, just the usual dignitaries.>

*Jasper*'s mental voice dropped lower.

<There's a rumour going around that you're getting a handsome new Captain.>

What was she to say? <I'm not sure,> she hedged.

<Oh come on! Everyone will know soon enough. You're getting Leo, aren't you, you lucky girl?> The Ship sighed dramatically.

Maia felt backed into a corner.

<Nothing's formalised,> she insisted.

*Jasper* gave a knowing snigger.

<It makes sense. He's the King's bosom companion, from when they were young. They're almost like brothers. Do you know how he got to be called Leo?>

<Wasn't he born with it?>

<Oh no! It's because he's fearless. When he was a midshipman, aboard *Garnet*, they were facing off against a bunch of pirates and he just charged the lot of them screaming his head off. He was fourteen years old and mad as a sack of snakes. Captain Plotinus said he roared like a lion and the name stuck. He's one for the ladies too. I hear that his last Ship, the *Centaur*, is quite fond of him. I'm sure she'll tell you more if you ask her.>

The *Centaur,* eh? It was useful information, but Maia would have to be discreet.

<It's his first command, then?>

<Yes. Oh, you'll have such fun! Better than getting some crabby old sea-dog. I bet there'll be great parties! Who's your Mage?>

<Raven.>

There was a startled squeak

<No! Raven? Blood and sand! I thought he'd retired!> *Jasper* was clearly shocked. <Isn't he really old? He must be over a century, surely? He was ancient when I started and he hasn't changed as far as I can see.>

<How long have you been a Ship?> Maia asked.

<It'll be fifty-five years next month. This is my second vessel, but I needed a spruce-up so here I am. At least I get to see your naming first-hand,> she added, brightly. <Who trained you up?>

<*Blossom.*>

<Ooh, me too!> the little Ship squealed. <I just love her! I don't talk to her as much as I should really, but with this refit I've been having some downtime for a few weeks. I'm only just properly awake.>

So, it could have been worse.

<I'm sure she'd love to hear from you,> Maia offered.

<And now I know you too! You'll still speak to me when you're named, won't you, not like those other hoity-toity firsts?>

<I will,> Maia promised, hoping that it wouldn't be too often. Still, she needed to learn the ropes and possibly the things that the more staid and proper Ships wouldn't tell her. She was beginning to see that not everything about a Ship had been covered in her training.

<Wonderful! Well, then, bye for now!>

*Jasper's* voice faded as she ended the Sending, leaving Maia feeling mentally quite exhausted. No wonder there were times set aside for non-essential Ship-to-Ship talk, as clearly for some it would be too easy to do nothing else.

Something the other Ship said caught in her mind. So, Raven had been old for at least fifty-five years? Something didn't add up. Would she get this reaction every time her Mage was mentioned? If he came with baggage, it was best that she knew now, rather than to appear ignorant, especially as Ships were supposed to have essential information about their crew, to be used when the occasion warranted.

37

She decided to ask him now before they both got too caught up in events and the opportunity passed. A quick check found Polydorus busy elsewhere, so she knew that they wouldn't be disturbed. Maia was careful to keep an eye on what was happening all around her vessel as well as focusing on her Mage.

"Raven?" Her voice echoed in his cabin.

"Yes, Maia?"

"May we talk? There's something I feel I need to know."

"Of course. Come on in."

Maia gathered her resolve and moved to his quarters once more. He'd made progress – a few empty chests were piled in a corner waiting to be moved to the hold and the room looked more occupied. Raven was sitting at his desk, head tilted attentively as she emerged.

"How can I help you?" he asked.

Maia thought for a second. Demanding to know how old he was straight off would just be rude.

"I was talking to another Ship," she began.

"Good, you need to make connections," he said approvingly. Maia ploughed on.

"She was surprised that you're my Mage. She thought you'd retired."

Raven's expression didn't change, but she sensed him catch his breath.

"Technically I never retired, though it's true that I haven't been a Ship's Mage for many years. I've been working behind the scenes, so to speak, teaching and staying mostly within the Collegium. I'd believed that the fact I was in Portus when you were brought in was sheer coincidence, but I'm beginning to doubt that now."

"Because of my heritage?"

"Yes. I firmly believe the Gods were at work."

Maia didn't have to ask him to elaborate.

"The Ship I was talking to said that you hadn't changed in over fifty years."

Raven fell silent, then his eyes closed and he sighed. For an instant an expression of pain crossed his wrinkled features.

"I knew someone would say something sooner or later. I've just lived longer than most. A magical accident. I take it that it wasn't *Blossom* who pointed it out. Would your informant be the *Jasper*, by any chance?"

"I couldn't possibly say," Maia prevaricated. She didn't want to get the little Ship into trouble.

"Humph!" the old Mage grunted. He was starting to sound more like himself. "That Ship is one of the biggest gossips in the fleet and now she's nearly refitted, she's back on the circuit with a vengeance. Little madam! Did she say anything else?"

"She said that Leo is known for being, well, a bit reckless." She could hardly say 'as mad as a sack of snakes.'

"Reckless, eh? Well, he may be, but all we can do is pray that he'll take guidance. Not all Captains are as experienced as Plinius. Has the *Centaur* contacted you yet?"

"No. Will she be able to tell me about him?"

The Mage pursed his lips. "She may give you a few pointers – all officers have their own foibles and preferences and she may miss him. Some Ships sulk when their favourites leave."

Maia could believe it. "As long as he doesn't wreck us within the month. He must have some competence to get me."

"Let's hope so." Raven didn't sound as if he believed it. "A lot will depend on your First Lieutenant as well. I hear that Sabrinus is a steady and reliable young officer."

"Well, we'll find out in a few hours. He'd better respect me."

"I told you, I scare people," Raven said, deadpan. She shot him a look of reproach.

"You don't scare me," she pointed out.

"Glad to hear it."

A sudden memory of the strong, handsome young man he had been briefly, so long ago, caught at her heart. No-one else would remember him that way now, save her. It was obvious that he'd neatly side-stepped the personal question. Maybe it was too painful to talk about? Anyway, it didn't seem that he'd drop dead of old age any minute, which was a relief.

*

It was a long night. Maia felt that she'd spent it only half awake, as if this was her final chance to rest before her long career began. She was aware of her surroundings at all times, but

39

she found that her mind wandered back to places she had known, conjuring the sounds and smells of her past life, everything from the smoky, ale-laden air of The Anchor, back to the cold mustiness of the dormitory at the Foundling Home and the comfort of her room at the Academy. She drifted between them, caught on a current of memory until, at last, daylight began washing over the dockyard, bringing out the colours in the flags and banners and lighting up the sky.

Activity soon resumed, with an army of workmen appearing to put the finishing touches to stages, altars and seating. She watched as two of them unrolled a great length of carpet for the King and his entourage to walk on, whilst others erected barriers to keep the crowds contained. Most of the population of Durobrivis and the surrounding area would turn up to enjoy the show and take advantage of any free food and drink. Loud hails rang out in the chilly morning and the atmosphere began to be charged with a subtle air of anticipation and excitement.

Maia felt impatient for everything to begin so she could get it over with.

It was going to be a very busy day.

# III

Julia stared moodily out of the carriage window. The browns and greens of the spring countryside were punctuated by toiling figures going about their daily tasks and she wondered what their lives were like. Their faces were a blur as she passed by, merging into one single image of wide eyes and open mouths as they watched the cavalcade. To the front, the Royal cavalry escort trotted ahead, barking orders to clear the road, their elaborate parade helmets glinting in the mild sunshine. Beside her, two heads were bent over a tray of dice.

"Venus! I win again!"

The King shot his cousin a look of pure disgust.

"It seems that your luck is better than mine, Marcus."

The prince shrugged, trying not to smirk.

"Can I help it if the Gods favour me?"

Artorius gathered up the ivory and gold dice once more.

"A few more throws, I think."

She watched as her brother rolled them in his hands, blowing on them before releasing them in an exaggerated gesture. They hit the tray and bounced before settling. It wasn't a good result. Artorius swore.

"Dog! *Merda!*"

Julia cast him a look of sympathy.

"I'd give up if I were you."

He frowned in her direction.

"Surely Fortuna must smile on a king!"

Marcus chuckled. "You'll have to offer her something nice, then she might be more inclined to favour you. As it is, I think this pot is mine. Pay up!"

Artorius scowled and reached into his purse. He'd already lost more money in an hour than most of his subjects would earn in a year.

"All right, but I want the chance to win it back later."

Marcus raised his eyebrows.

"Of course, Sire. If you wait a while, perhaps all will be different."

"It better had be." The king pouted and flung down several gold coins. "There!"

He glared as his cousin scooped up the winnings, then flung himself back in his seat, arms crossed in a sulk. Julia watched him, trying not to feel the usual mixture of hope and despair; hope that her brother would grow up before too long and despair that he never would.

"How much longer will it take?" he said, crossly. "We've been on the road for hours! We should have used a portal."

"It's not far to Durobrivis," Marcus assured him. That was true enough. There were more people by the road now. Many were craning their necks to get even a brief glimpse of the King and most were waving. Julia composed her features into the royal smile and waved back.

"Your subjects are happy to see you," Marcus said. Artorius pulled a face.

"I wish I hadn't bothered. All this way just to name a Ship!"

"Well, you would announce that she was going to be a Royal," Julia pointed out. She loved her little brother, but sometimes she just wanted to smack his bottom and send him to bed early.

"It seemed a good idea at the time," he replied. He gestured languidly out of the window, acknowledging the cheers.

"Have you decided what to call her yet?" Marcus asked him.

Artorius chewed his lower lip.

"Oh, I can think of plenty of names for her. The Admirals want me to name her *Fortitude,* or *Valour.* Something boring, anyway."

"How about *Holy Terror?*" Marcus remarked, snidely. "She certainly put the wind up us."

The king scowled.

"Or maybe *Fury?*"

Julia had heard about what had happened. It had been her brother's fault for behaving like an idiot. No wonder the Ship had lost her temper. Unfortunately, Artorius wasn't interested in his sister's opinion, just her compliance. She was here to be seen, not to comment, like a good Roman woman should, though it was getting harder to bite her lip and stay silent.

"I had a dream last night," Artorius said. "I think a God might have sent it."

Julia was instantly alert. Her brother wasn't the sort to have meaningful dreams, or see omens in every little thing, so this was something new.

"What sort of dream?" she asked.

The king took a deep breath. "I was in a tiny boat, on the open sea. There weren't any oars or anything and I couldn't see land. It was calm at first, then it got rougher and rougher and I had to hold on to the sides, for fear of being tipped out. Then a storm sprang up – thunder and lightning and everything. I looked up to see a giant wave crashing down on me."

The memory clearly wasn't a pleasant one. Marcus whistled.

"What happened then?"

"I woke up."

Artorius lowered his eyes and fiddled with the hilt of his sword, as he did when he was nervous. He rarely let Excalibur out of his sight these days.

"You must have eaten something that disagreed with you," Marcus said, briskly. "It doesn't sound like anything serious."

His cousin looked up hopefully.

"Do you think so?"

"Oh yes! It's nothing. You were probably just thinking about the sea and Ships because of today. Isn't that right, Julia?"

"I expect so," Julia replied, trying to ignore the tiny trickle of alarm that was creeping up the back of her neck. "You should have summoned a dream interpreter, but if it worries you ask Aquila about it. Thunder and lightning are usually Jupiter's signs, so he'll know if the God is giving you a message, or if it's just an ordinary nightmare."

Artorius' face cleared. "Good idea. He'll be able to tell."

"Really, cousin," Marcus drawled, shooting a look of annoyance at Julia. "If Jove wanted you to know something, surely he'd tell Aquila and Aquila would pass it on. You are the King, after all."

"I suppose so."

43

"Don't worry about it! Now, are you going to tell us what you've decided to call this Ship?"

Artorius regarded them both.

"No."

"You haven't decided, have you?"

"I have!"

Julia doubted that he had. She only hoped that it wouldn't be something silly or frivolous. Her uncle's patience was already wearing thin and she wished that the Lord High Admiral wasn't away on manoeuvres to the west on the *Augusta*. He was the only one who could talk any sense into his nephew these days. Even Senator Rufus was finding it difficult to corral the headstrong young man and as for Albanus, the man was a snake.

She sighed inwardly. She'd have more to worry about soon enough, as she was packed off to Gaul to marry an impotent old man. A worm of revulsion squirmed inside her, followed by a spark of hope. Perhaps he'd die of old age before she arrived. Failing that, she'd been secretly practising the sleep spell Raven had taught her.

The whole thing didn't bear thinking about. She'd had to plead with her brother to be allowed to attend this naming – anything to get out of the palace and away from interminable dress fittings. Most of the court were following on in their own carriages, ready to be all smiles and compliments in the hope of getting into her brother's good graces. Also, to tell the truth, she was curious to see this new Ship. They'd passed off what happened as a joke, but she'd seen the fleeting look of fear on her brother's face.

There had been plenty of rumours about this candidate, whispers that she was of high birth and either favoured by the Gods, or cursed by them. After Echidna had attacked Senator Rufus' villa, people had muttered about Diana's involvement, though nobody could say where the gossip had started. She was sure of one thing: Raven knew more than he let on, though he'd refused to answer her questions. Perhaps she could talk to the Ship directly? Curiosity gnawed at her. Here was someone else who had been shackled to a life that probably wasn't of her own choosing, though the Navy made a great thing of their candidates being volunteers. Her musings were shattered as her brother decided to change the subject before Marcus could press him further.

"The negotiations with Parisius are finished," he announced. "You'll be leaving for Gaul in a couple of months."

Gods protect her; it wouldn't be long then.

"Good news, cousin," Marcus told her. "Just think of it. Queen of Gaul!"

She regarded him stonily.

"Wonderful."

"And when he croaks, you can come back."

Artorius smirked. "You never know; there might be a miracle. The next King of Gaul could be my nephew. Sister, I hope you've been praying to Juno to bless you with a son."

"Of course," she lied, adopting a pleasant expression. He smiled back at her, mollified.

She wasn't going to admit that she'd been praying that Diana would intervene on her behalf and spare her. She didn't want to be any man's wife.

"Come on, Sire." Marcus picked up the dice and the king's face brightened. "Why don't we have a few more games? Time for you to win some money back."

Outside, the noise of the onlookers had increased until it was one continuous roar like waves on a beach. The faces blurred into a mass of colour, moving and heaving like the restless sea.

Julia began to wave, her face composed but her mind elsewhere.

\*

Maia scanned the dockyards, quietly amazed at the transformation from working space to a scene of festivity and celebration. The barriers were already packed with thousands of people in their best clothes, all out to enjoy themselves and make the most of the occasion. It wasn't only the nearby towns that had emptied, but seemingly most of the south-east. The wealthy had come in their carriages, parked in ranks nearby, whilst lesser folk had taken public coaches, or even walked. The anticipation was building ahead of the King's arrival, the atmosphere becoming more charged as the minutes ticked by.

A light breeze sprang from the south as the hours passed, setting her bright flags and pennants rippling and fluttering, though the official ones were still furled until she was formally named.

&lt;*Jasper* to the new Ship!&gt;

Maia suppressed a twinge of annoyance and answered through the link.

&lt;Hello, *Jasper*.&gt;

&lt;You must be so excited! It's such a great occasion! I'm glad I'm still here so I can see it too!&gt;

The smaller Ship was beside herself, twittering on before Maia could answer.

&lt;The King will be here soon. You're all over the newssheets, you know!&gt;

Maia had been expecting that. Pamphlets were being eagerly hawked in the streets, more to publicise the might of the King and his Navy than to reveal anything about her. There were comments describing her as 'a maiden of impeccable reputation and noble blood, willing to offer her life in service for Empire, King and Country,' together with a printed illustration of a generic fair maid standing on a vessel. It was the same one they always used; she'd seen it several times before.

The *Jasper* giggled with excitement. &lt;Is Leo aboard yet?&gt;

&lt;Yes. He arrived first thing this morning to oversee everything,&gt; she replied.

&lt;And you've got young Albanus Sabrinus as your First Lieutenant as well. His father must be so proud!&gt;

Maia made a non-committal sound. It wasn't fair to be prejudiced against the young officer simply because of his father, but it all smacked heavily of nepotism. She only hoped that he would rise to the challenge of his new position. So much for having an experienced set of officers.

Fortunately, the other Ship wasn't in contact long and broke off after wishing her luck.

&lt;I'll be able to use your name later!&gt; she declared happily.

Maia was relieved that the other Ships were waiting until after the ceremony to greet her properly – *Jasper* was the exception and seemingly didn't give a fig that she was breaking protocol. Maia suspected that her Captain wasn't yet aboard to chide her, or possibly he wasn't bothered. Perhaps he liked his Ship's saucy attitude and cheerful disposition.

There was to be another exception, however.

<*Blossom* to the new Ship!>

Maia linked to her old mentor, watching as several actors took to a nearby stage to the delight of the crowds.

<Hello *Blossom*. Are you watching all this?>

<I am indeed,> the Ship replied. <The *Jasper*'s busy relaying it – noisily, I might add, and providing a running commentary to boot. Are you ready?>

<As I'll ever be.>

<You know what to do, then. I understand that you're only part formed?>

Maia's shape had become more of a rough-hewn carving of a female than anything more lifelike and she intended that it stay that way until the last minute. It was a small act of rebellion, but one nonetheless.

<I might change it when I'm named,> she said, grudgingly. She could sense *Blossom*'s concern through the link. The other Ship was dismayed at the change in her after her initiation, but Maia wasn't inclined to explain.

<Yes, of course. Is everything ready? I hear that you've got young Albanus aboard?>

<No surprise there,> Maia snorted. <Is he any good?>

<I've heard he's a fine young man,> *Blossom* told her.

<It's just a pity that my new Captain is wet behind the ears, and his previous Ship wasn't much help,> Maia grumbled. <Why couldn't I have been assigned an experienced Captain?>

<It is what it is,> the older Ship acknowledged. <The other Ships will be able to advise you on that.>

Maia was intrigued.

<What do you mean?>

<Oh, nothing,> *Blossom* said, innocently. <You know that the *Persistence* is always up for a good chat. She's a wise old girl, that one. Your sisters stand ready to help you in any way they can, remember.>

*Persistence*, eh? There was one who wasn't afraid to speak her mind. It would soon be time to learn the finer points of dealing with a Captain and she'd need some pointers.

<I'll catch up with her soon,> Maia promised, wondering what advice she'd receive.

<Or the *Leopard*. She doesn't suffer fools either.>

This was getting interesting. Maia was about to ask more, when a flurry of movement below decks caught her attention. Her officers were on the move.

<Something's happening.>

*Blossom* was silent for a moment, as if checking.

<It's the Royal party,> she confirmed after a moment. <I've had a heads up. Now, remember. Don't frighten the Very Important People, whatever you do!>

Maia's heart sank. So, the word had leaked out.

<I won't, if they behave,> she said, stubbornly. *Blossom* sighed.

<Maybe one day you'll tell me what happened to you, girl?>

Maia doubted it, but then again, she had nothing but time to decide otherwise.

<Let's just say that I learned a lot.>

*Blossom* radiated nothing but care for her, but Maia refused to allow herself to respond. Ceridwen, the High Priestess of the Mother, had sown too many seeds of doubt for her to let her guard down that easily.

<Well, then. We can talk when it's all over,> *Blossom* Sent. <Try to enjoy the experience. It's a singular event, after all.>

Maia thanked her and broke the link. For a second, she was tempted to raise her friend, the *Patience*, but decided against it. She needed to be on full alert: it seemed that proceedings were about to kick off and she'd need her wits about her.

She ran through the checklist in her head. The protocol for naming Ships hadn't changed for centuries, though, as she was to be Royal, this one would be a little more elaborate than if she were to be in a lesser vessel. The fact that the King was attending added another layer of ritual and lengthened the proceedings. Maia was glad that she wouldn't end up with aching feet, though a sudden pang hit her, like a ghostly memory from the girl she had been; she'd have enjoyed being part of the crowd, watching the performances and waiting to cheer for the King. There would be free food and drink, too, courtesy of the Treasury. People were already crowding around the stalls and specially rigged fountains, jostling to grab what they could.

Others were watching a brawny fellow dressed as Jason, slaying a cunningly wrought dragon that was guarding a very showy Golden Fleece, to the delight of the audience who urged him on with cheers and shouts of approval. They were obviously impressed with the amount of fake gore that spurted from the creature in the form of ribbons, as it writhed and bellowed. Jason grabbed handfuls of the red silk, throwing them to the crowd who snatched them up as good luck tokens, before he seized the fleece and held it aloft in triumph.

Maia looked away. The dragon's writhing reminded her unpleasantly of the hydra in its death throes, even though this monster was only made of painted cloth and board. Her gaze roamed over the throng searching for something else, only to see the most popular tableau there. A large sign proclaimed *'The Goddess of the Lake presents Excalibur to Artorius Magnus!'* Unlike the play, this performance was largely static; the actors were trained to hold position for several minutes at a time before performing one or two short scenes, usually silently. The curtain would then fall and, after a short break, the whole thing would start again.

People were surrounding the raised circular stage, waiting for the next showing. Many were eating and drinking, their faces alight with anticipation and enjoyment. As Maia observed them, chatting with friends and swinging tiny children on to their shoulders for a better view, a strange sense of detachment overcame her. She was now a creature apart – metamorphosed into a symbol of Britannia's superior sea power and, as far as these people were concerned, near immortal. Their concerns were hers no longer and the barrier erected between them was one that could never be breached. Maia, or whatever she would become, would be sailing the sea when they were all mouldering into dust.

She stood on the deck, surrounded by thousands and felt the loneliness eat at her. In that moment, if she'd had the chance to turn back time she would have told Jupiter to do his worst and his judgement be damned.

The sound of a trumpet broke into her ugly reverie. The show was starting. Faces turned to watch the fabric being lowered, to fall in neat folds around the base of the stage.

The setting was beautiful. It was constructed to look like a pool of still, deep water, glittering like silver in the light. To one side, there was a boat in which the actor playing Artorius was standing, looking about him as if wondering what he was doing there. He was dressed in elaborate mail covered by a surcoat bearing the Britannic dragon of his house and he looked every inch a monarch. After a few moments, the water began to ripple and a figure rose to face him, until she appeared to float on the surface. The 'Goddess' was clad in white, her long dark hair falling to her waist and bound with silver filigree. Her eyelids and lips were painted gold and her face was stern, as if to impress upon the young king the seriousness of the gift.

The sword itself, a copy of the real Excalibur, lay across her open palms. They both stood like statues for nearly a minute, then the Lady moved, proffering the sword. 'Artorius' knelt to take it from her, bowing his head in acknowledgement of her power. As he took it, the 'Goddess' smiled and slowly sank beneath the water which closed over her head with barely a ripple. The crowd gasped as she vanished and 'Artorius' stood, examining the sword as if he couldn't believe his luck, before raising it over his head.

"For Britannia!"

The answering roar drowned out all other sounds. The blade flashed in the sunlight and the actor smiled. He was very handsome and Maia felt a stab of memory. She thrust it ruthlessly aside, thinking instead that probably the original Artorius wasn't half as impressive. The lake would likely have been choppy and it had probably been raining.

'Artorius' froze in his heroic pose as the curtain rose and the audience clapped wildly, before making their way to another entertainment, others pushing past them to take their places for the next show. Maia wondered how the actress playing the Goddess had managed to stay dry, then dismissed the thought. It probably wasn't really water, or, if it was, they must have hired a Mage to provide the special effects.

It was just the distraction she'd needed and Maia wrenched her thoughts to more practical matters.

She reviewed the arrangements for her launch. It would be a so-called 'float-out'. The dry dock gates would be opened to admit the water that would lift her and allow her to sail straight out. It was the gentlest and safest way and would cause the fewest problems for those on board. It allowed her more control, although she wouldn't be going far, only to anchorage in the harbour. She'd then get the rest of her crew complement before being readied for trials. Maia turned her gaze to the interior of her vessel.

Raven was in his cabin being fussed over by Polydorus, who was insisting he change into his ceremonial robe. Valerius was in his cabin, likewise preparing himself. She didn't linger there; he'd be in command and she would have to interact with him soon enough. Elsewhere, the Ship's altar was being readied for the sacrifice of a bull to Neptune, which would be performed by the Sea God's High Priest, a grizzled old fellow with long, flowing grey hair and piercing blue eyes. He'd given her a sharp look when they were introduced, though he hadn't been unfriendly. He must have heard some of the gossip about her, but he'd said nothing to make her suspicious. His full attention was currently being given to burning incense and muttering preliminary prayers to get the God's attention. The chanting made the air thicker, as if Divine power was already funnelling her way and it made her a little uneasy.

A momentary flash above her resolved itself into a fine ripple of silver, like a wisp of low cloud.

<Sister? Is that you?> she Sent. The answer came immediately as a whisper in her head.

<I am here. What is happening?>

Maia reminded herself that Pearl was unfamiliar with many human customs.

<I'm being named and launched.>

<Because you're a Ship now.>

<Yes. Despite everything a certain Goddess did to stop me.>

<The Huntress is being punished,> Pearl informed her, her tone satisfied. <She went against her father's wishes and angered the Mother, so she must pay.>

Maia could only agree with her sister's sentiments. She hoped that the Goddess was having a thoroughly rotten time of it, too.

<Good. Do you know that she set a hydra on me?>

Pearl hissed in anger. <No, I didn't. I was told that she desecrated the ritual and that Nemesis was summoned as the instrument of her punishment.>

Maia remembered the words in her mouth, put there by a higher power, and tried not to shudder.

<I know that the Livia had something to do with it as well. All along, I thought our father's murderer wanted to be revenged on me, but she used me instead.>

<As well as bequeathing you her gifts,> Pearl observed.

<Yes, but I don't know how to use them. I've no control!>

Pearl's laugh was like a sudden blast of air.

<You'll learn, my sister. You will have time and the ancient one is a good teacher.>

<Do you mean Raven?>

<Him too.>

Maia frowned to herself. How many ancient ones were there? Surely no mortal had lived longer than her Mage?

<I don't know any other,> she objected.

<You will.>

Maia felt her sister's presence wrap itself around her oaken Shipbody.

<I don't want to do this,> she whispered. <My vessel's too big and I'm afraid I'll fail.>

<You won't. It will be all right, you'll see. Plus, we can be together for a long time, you and I.>

Maia was curious.

<Are you immortal, Pearl?>

She sensed amusement. <Nothing and nobody lasts forever, my sister. We all change in the end. Don't be afraid now, not after all you've been through. Look! There's the Swift One!>

<Mercury? Where?> Maia followed her sister's direction and saw a familiar curly head of hair disappearing into the crowd. So, the God was present? She hoped he was enjoying himself in his latest disguise and uttered a quiet prayer in his direction. She was rewarded by the glimpse of a smile and a sense of reassurance. It was nice to know that she had friends. She wondered which other

Gods were watching, maybe even mingling with the crowd, unnoticed.

<Is Mother here?> she asked, feeling a little ashamed for her previous condemnation of Aura and her actions.

Pearl's tone brightened. <She is! Can't you feel her presence?> It was true that the breeze had sprung up, swirling through her rigging and making the flags flutter and snap.

<I'm glad she's here,> Maia admitted. <I hope she can forgive me for my unkindness.>

Even if her motherhood had all been a dream, the glimpse she'd had of it had given her a new understanding.

<Of course!> Pearl said, happily. <She will always love us both equally. She's so proud of you!>

Maia had to ask the question.

<Has she seen my new Captain?>

<Yes. It pains her to see how much like our father he is, but she hopes that he'll do a good job.>

<So do I,> Maia said, glumly. <He hasn't much experience.>

<Then you'll just have to train him up, won't you? What about the rest of the crew?>

Maia had already met some of them. The biggest surprise had been when she had been hailed by a familiar face and realised that Danuco had been appointed as her Priest. It seemed that the King of Olympus was still keeping an eye on her.

"I already met my Priest on the *Blossom*,> she said. <I think he's one of Jupiter's.>

<Mother thinks so, too,> Pearl confirmed. <She still has friends in high places, so she'd know.>

<The others seem competent,> Maia admitted. Raven was familiar with Hawthorn, her new Adept and she suspected that the Master Mage had pulled a few strings to get him assigned to her, which meant that he had to be good. Magpie, her ancillary Mage, was still delayed, but would be arriving before too long.

That left Osric, her Captain of Marines, a big blond fellow with a huge moustache, who struck her as being extremely capable and respected by his men; Corax, the purser, who kept an eye on the stores and finances, and old Musca, the Master Gunner, who'd fixed her with a cheerful eye and given her a toothless smile, before disappearing off to check on his beloved cannons.

She'd get to know the rest of her crew as she went along – in fact, it would be one of her first duties. She'd already made a note of the new recruits and would make sure that they got extra attention until they learned the ropes.

Talking to her sister had lifted her mood and she remembered Campion's words, months ago on the *Blossom*, when she was healing.

*"Too much time moping about doesn't do anybody any good. The busier you are, the better you'll feel."*

He was right. She'd have to keep busy.

<*Our aunt's here too,*> Pearl said suddenly.

<What's she doing?> Maia asked her in alarm. <You do know that she can be trouble?>

<*Oh yes,*> Pearl said cheerfully. <*She likes causing chaos. Don't worry, Mother and I will keep an eye on her. As long as mortals show her proper respect, she's usually happy. That is, if she understands what's happening.*>

Maia wondered if her aunt was going senile. It would explain a lot.

<I really don't need her to make a scene,> she said urgently.

<*I know. I'll go and see what she's up to. I think she's just curious and keen to see that you're treated properly.*>

<Good idea. Tell her that I appreciate her good wishes and will make sure she gets her due.>

<*I will!*> Pearl called. Her voice was already receding. <*I'll be near!*>

One brief swirl, and the Tempestas was gone.

Maia had barely a minute to ponder her sister's words before her new Captain-to-be emerged on deck, closely followed by, Osric, Hawthorn and Raven. The latter two were deep in conversation. She tuned in immediately.

"…good idea to appease the Lady of Storms as well," the Master Mage was saying quietly. "I've already had a word with Danuco. It wouldn't do for her to kick off in the middle of the ceremony."

The Adept grimaced. "We wouldn't want that. I take it he was in agreement?"

"Thankfully. An offering will be made after the bull. That should appease her. Right, they're nearly here. I must speak to the Ship."

Raven left the main party and walked over to her.

<Are you ready?> he Sent, privately.

<I hope so,> she retorted. <It's a bit late if I'm not and it wouldn't make any difference anyway.>

Aloud, he said "The royal party is nearly here, ma'am. Is there anything you need to ask?"

Maia glanced over at the altar and the great gold cup that would be filled with the finest wine and used to consecrate her vessel.

"I think everything's in hand. I understand the procedure."

There would be a lot of speeches, magically amplified and relayed to the crowd, then the King would drink from the cup before pouring libations to the Gods. Once she was afloat, the cup would be cast into the sea as her first offering to Neptune. Next, her Captain would receive his earring and they would be linked then. After that, Artorius would pronounce her name. Maia's first duties would be to form the letters at her bow and stern, even as she unfurled the great flag proclaiming her to be a Royal Ship of His Majesty's Britannic Navy. She would then be expected to mould her Shipbody into an appropriate form, whilst guiding her vessel out of the dock. She tried not to balk at the thought. It was hardly something she could practise beforehand.

"I'm sure that the other Ships are on stand-by to advise you, should you think it necessary," Raven told her.

"I'll manage," she said, shortly. "It's ridiculous that I can't be told my name beforehand."

He shrugged. "Ancient custom. It's supposed to be bad luck until the Gods have been petitioned."

The sacrifices and ceremonies would be happening simultaneously, but the animals would be dispatched before she moved.

"I hope the bull goes peacefully," she remarked. "It wouldn't do to have it charging about the deck."

Her Mage grinned. "Why, do you think that Neptune might object?"

"Dear Gods, I hope not. He's always been fair, even when he had bad news for me."

She knew that the Sea God had tried to warn her about the perils of her initiation, even if he couldn't go into details.

"He supports his brother," Raven agreed. Far out to sea, a brief flash of lightning caught her attention.

"Cymopoleia's around."

"Ha! We all know that."

Danuco walked past them, carrying a cage containing a pair of doves.

"Looks like they've found her a sacrifice," Maia said. "Doves."

He snorted. "That should do it."

Just then a roar went up, as the onlookers caught sight of the royal party. Maia focused on the quayside. Several carriages had drawn up and she could make out the figure of the King alighting from the most splendid. His gold circlet flashed in the spring sunshine, then he was surrounded by his guards. She wondered if he was apprehensive about meeting her again. Artorius stopped to talk to the portly figure of Aquila, also here for the ceremony, though Neptune's High Priest would be officiating on this occasion. They seemed to be having a hurried conversation, but they had turned away so she couldn't quite make out what they were saying. It was only at the end that she could read the Priest's lips as he murmured to the King.

"I'll arrange for a propitiation. It will please the God."

Nearby, she saw Albanus looking self-satisfied, and once more found herself wishing that it was Pendragon who was here instead.

She decided that they were talking about the sacrifice and turned her attention to the King's other companion. This was clearly the Prince, also looking resplendent in his military uniform though everyone knew that he'd done little to earn it. The other occupant was far more interesting and, for once, not another male.

"Is that the Princess?" Maia asked Raven.

"Yes. She wanted to come and meet you," he replied. "I think you'll like her."

Maia glanced at him and waited for the ceremonies to begin. There were official greetings and presentations, whilst the crowds cheered and waved flags. The free food and drink was going down well. Stallholders were doing a great trade in model Ships, wooden Excaliburs for the children and printed pamphlets

Gradually, the royal party made its way over to the gangplank, accompanied by much bowing and scraping by officials. Pholus was waiting at the bottom to greet the King and they exchanged a few words. Maia noticed that the Princess was looking about her with great interest. She was dark-haired, like her brother and uncle and was wearing a naval-style coat over her gown. A fancy bicorn topped the whole ensemble, complete with silk cockade in the latest fashion.

Pleasantries over, the King strode up the gangplank, his retinue pulled along behind him like a comet's tail. Maia was pleased to see the imposing figure of Senator Rufus, accompanied by his wife, Drusilla Camilla, and she hoped that she'd have time to speak to them at some point. Even though she knew that what had happened at Saturnalia wasn't her fault, she couldn't help the sudden flood of guilt. If she hadn't been there, Echidna wouldn't have entered the villa and caused such devastation. Still, she was alive, so she had something to be thankful for, though the terrible fate of the monster's victims still hung like lead weights on her conscience.

Osric called his marines to attention with a rattle of muskets as they prepared to be inspected. The officers were lined up ready and Artorius greeted his friend joyously.

"Leo! Well, here we are at last!"

"Sire." The young officer snapped off a salute. "Welcome aboard."

"Glad to be here," the King said. Any trepidation he might be feeling was well hidden, though he didn't look at Maia directly. "I take it that all is ready?"

"We await your order, Sire."

Artorius nodded, then signalled to the Priests, who began the sacrifices. The bull went quietly, much to everyone's relief, and the blood sluiced away down channels into the dock. The carcass would be butchered and its bones and fat burned, as was customary, to feed the Gods. The meat would then be salted and added to her stores. Everyone stood respectfully to attention as the beast was ceremonially opened and its entrails inspected.

"The omens are favourable!" Neptune's Priest announced. Maia heard the exhalations as everyone breathed out at once. Anything else would have been a disaster. "We have an additional sacrifice," he continued. "Lady of Storms, O mighty Cymopoleia, we beseech your favour!"

The doves were beheaded and their blood sprinkled on the fire. A rumble of thunder answered the sacrifice, but Cymopoleia seemed content to keep her distance. This time, it was Aquila who bent over the corpses, probing the soft guts, before raising his eyes to the heavens.

"The Lady accepts the sacrifice!"

"Glad that's done," Raven said, under his breath. "Can you see any birds?"

Maia scanned the skies. "Only the usual gulls."

He nodded. "Right. No omens then. Be prepared. You're onstage any second now."

She glared at him, but he was right. This whole thing was as showy as any stage play, except there would be no taking off this costume after the performance was over. If she'd still had a human heart it would have been beating furiously, but instead all she felt was a strange sense of dislocation, as if she was watching from the side lines and not really part of the action at all.

The High Priest of Neptune washed his hands in a silver basin and dried them on a linen cloth before lifting the great golden cup from its place. It had caught a fair amount of the bull's blood as it had spurted from the animal's throat, thus sanctifying it as a ritual object. Now it was the King's turn to finish the ceremonies.

Artorius stepped forward to face the Priest. He inclined his head, acknowledging the power of the Gods, and took the cup. This was it. Maia forced herself to concentrate. The King walked over to her and was handed a sprig of mistletoe, the sacred plant of Britannia. His dark eyes regarded her thoughtfully as he dipped it into the cup and sprinkled the blood over her Shipbody.

The wood drank in the scarlet drops thirstily. Maia felt a shock run through her as the binding took hold and the ancient compact was sealed.

"In the sight of the Gods and of the people of Britannia, I name this Ship…"

He paused, prolonging the tension. Maia felt that every second was an eternity, the moment stretched out as if she were trapped in amber. She could feel the connection to every part of her vessel, the link to the other Ships, the thread that connected her to Raven. From being an observer, she was now at the centre of everything. All times seemed to converge for one eternal moment as the person she was about to become stepped up, ready to take form.

"His Majesty's Ship…*Tempest!*"

A chain reaction ran through her Shipbody, as if she were a mechanism fired up and whirring into motion. Gilded lettering formed on her bow and across her stern as she put forth her will to unfurl the great ensign of the Britannic Royal Navy. Instantly, a stiff breeze sprang up, catching the fabric and making the great red dragon ripple and writhe as if alive. Around it Pearl danced, her airy form weaving around the colours and shining silver in the light, mother and daughter rejoicing together.

The King, accompanied by the Priests, processed to the four points of the compass and offered the blood and libations of wine to the Gods. A deafening wall of sound erupted as his subjects celebrated the birth of their new Royal Ship.

Maia Abella was gone from the world of mortals. There was no time for her to mourn, as the other Ships flooded the link with congratulations and messages of welcome for their new sister. She responded as best she could, all the while tracking the dozens of minor operations necessary for her first short trip out into the harbour.

The King finished the ceremony with a triumphant smile and a gracious wave. The cup was placed reverently on the altar, ready to be given to the sea on her maiden voyage as the first of many offerings. Next, it was her Captain's turn. The old High Priest summoned him, marking him on the forehead with the blood of sacrifice to consecrate him and help forge the link with the Gods. The red smear stood out sharply against his tanned skin. A few words were spoken, then she felt the link snap into place as the earring connected.

There was a moment of confusion as he adjusted and she remembered what it had been like for the anxious girl on the deck of the *Blossom*. She reached out automatically, as if to steady him, feeling his presence and the sudden closeness as if he were pressed against her instead of feet away. Leo blinked rapidly, then his voice echoed in her mind.

<Captain to *Tempest*!>

She answered him immediately.

<*Tempest* acknowledges, Captain.>

A delighted grin flashed across his face.

"*Tempest* acknowledges! The link is strong!" he declared. Everyone burst into applause and the mood relaxed a little. Now there was just the small matter of exiting the dock.

*Tempest* saw Pholus give the signal and all eyes turned to the huge gates as they began to move. The water trickled in, slowly at first, then becoming a torrent as the sea sought to reclaim its own.

Raven's voice sounded in her head.

<Are you going to change your form?>

She was startled. In all the commotion, she'd forgotten to do anything about her outward appearance. *Tempest*, eh? Her aunt would be delighted. But what should she look like? A quick check showed that everyone's attention was diverted. The King was with Leo and her officers, accepting refreshments and plaudits, whilst the rest were watching as the water foamed higher up the side of the dock. She could sense it as a tickling sensation against her hull, and knew that it would soon be able to support her great weight. Blast it! She'd have to act quickly. She could sense Raven's impatience through their link and blocked him off, cudgelling her mind for inspiration.

Suddenly, Diana's face flashed before her. Cold, haughty and superior at first, then convulsed with rage and, finally, fear. It gave her an idea. She might not be a Goddess, but she'd been born of one. She could never disclose this, but she'd make sure that she was respected as someone to be reckoned with. A slow smile crossed her face as she seized hold of the sacred oak and *willed* it to change.

\*

60

There was so much to look at that Julia didn't know what to focus on first. She would have loved to mingle with the crowds and enjoy the plays and tableaux, freed of her responsibility, but that wasn't an option for a princess. She acknowledged the cheers and followed her brother as he made his way towards the dock. As she'd suggested, he stopped for a while to speak to Aquila. Whatever the Priest said seemed to reassure him, for he looked more relaxed as they ended their conversation. Presumably his fears about the dream had been allayed. A bridge led onto the deck of the vessel and Julia followed her brother and cousin aboard, straining her eyes to catch the first glimpse of the Ship.

It was most disappointing. She didn't look like much at all, just a crude block of oak that someone had stuck in the middle of the open space, as if a woodcarver had started then couldn't be bothered to finish. It wasn't what she'd expected at all. Her attention was caught by the inevitable introductions, so she locked her expression into a gracious smile.

"Delighted to be here on this happy occasion," she murmured. "It's all looking splendid."

She continued down the line, greeting Senator Rufus and his wife warmly, until reaching the towering bulk of the Chief Naval Architect. He was wearing a naval sash and a hat that was as fine as hers, though his cockade was a matching blue. His hooves were firmly planted on the deck and his tail swished idly, betraying his nervousness. An equerry murmured in her ear.

"Your Highness, may I present Master Pholus?"

The centaur bowed low.

"You should be very proud," she told him. "She's magnificent."

He smiled. "I am, Your Highness, but I'll feel better when we're out of the dock."

Julia grinned back. "I'm not surprised." A sudden thought struck her. "Could you tell me why the Ship isn't..." she groped for a word.

"Looking like anything much?" he supplied. "She's probably waiting for her name, so she can choose something appropriate."

So that was it. "Thank you. It's all very interesting. I'm looking forward to meeting her."

Pholus bowed again and she was guided on to her allotted place. Ahead of her, her brother was talking to Albanus, who stood with a smug look on his face as if he were personally responsible for everything. Again, she wished that her uncle had been here, then his second-in-command would have been relegated to a supporting role instead of being the most senior admiral present. Albanus glanced over at her and Julia smiled politely, secretly gritting her teeth and wishing him at the bottom of the sea. She couldn't explain why her hackles rose at the sight of him, but she trusted her gut. If only her brother didn't hang on every word the man said!

Raven was standing a short distance away, near the inanimate-looking Shipbody. Julia weighed up the situation and took the chance to sidle over to him.

"Hello, Raven."

He inclined his head, his opaque eyes looking through her, as usual. She had the sneaking suspicion that he'd known she'd been there all along. He might be blind, but there was nothing wrong with his hearing.

"Princess."

"Master Mage. How's it all going?"

"We'll know more after the sacrifices."

Julia's eyes slid towards the Ship, but he forestalled her in the uncanny way he had, as if he knew what she was thinking.

"I'll introduce you later. She's a lot on her mind at the moment and it wouldn't be appropriate now anyway. You wouldn't know what to call her, for a start."

"That's true," she acknowledged, "but don't forget!"

"I won't. Give her a chance to get us safely into the harbour and settle down a bit. Now, I'd get into position if I were you. It looks like Decentius is about to start the sacrifice."

"Oh. Yes."

Julia looked across at Neptune's High Priest who was standing and looking expectant. A commotion behind her heralded the arrival of the bull, pure white and garlanded for the sacrifice. She quickly returned to her place and watched as the animal was brought forth and offered up with the appropriate prayers. It didn't struggle but went meekly to its death, which was a great relief. The High Priest opened it up and poked about, looking for signs. Julia prayed that the animal was healthy, with no signs of diseased organs. The sweet incense didn't quite mask the stench of blood and she was glad that they were out in the open where the breeze would carry it away.

It was always tense just after a sacrifice and she realised that she, along with everybody else, was holding their breath and waiting for the verdict.

"The omens are favourable!" Decentius nodded benevolently and Julia exhaled with relief. It would have been awful if Neptune hadn't approved, even though they'd given him no reason not to. She watched in surprise as a pair of doves followed the bull to the slaughter. The Lady of Storms? That was interesting. Away on the horizon, an ominous cloudbank caught her eye. She hoped it didn't mean that rain was heading their way. A low rumble of thunder made her twitch.

"The Lady accepts the sacrifice!"

Good, Julia thought. If she hadn't there would have been trouble. She could see that others were puzzled too and there were mutterings in the crowd. There had been some terrible storms of late, so it must just have been a precaution to curry the Goddess' favour. She certainly seemed to be hanging around more than usual and vessels had been lost, especially in the Great Bay of Gaul. Cymopoleia was an unpredictable and capricious Goddess and it paid to get on her good side, if indeed she had one.

The blood sacrifices were concluded and it was time for her brother to play his part. He accepted the sacred gold cup, ready for the libations and the sealing of the pact between Britannia, represented by her King, and the Sea God. At last they'd know what he'd decided to call her.

Again, she prayed that it would be appropriate and not something more befitting one of his hounds.

His choice caught people by surprise.

"That's interesting," she heard Albanus mutter. Eyes were drawn to the horizon once more and the chatter resumed, to be drowned out by the cheering and applause from the assembled multitudes on the dockside who'd been avidly following the action. Julia thought that *Tempest* was a good name; better than *Valour* or *Fortitude*, anyway. It just irked her that there was seemingly more to the story than she knew, and she resolved to winkle out as much of it from Raven as she could later. He was bound to know about it – he always did.

There were oohs and gasps as the great ensign was drawn forth, flying bravely in the breeze. Something was moving around it, partnering it in a stately dance and causing her Mage sense to tingle. There was Potentia in the air, rippling over her skin and giving her the shivers. It had to be some sort of God or spirit.

She watched as her brother processed around the vessel and Valerius received the magical earring but, to her disappointment, the *Tempest* remained unresponsive, even when her Captain confirmed that the Ship was operational. If she was going to change form at all she was taking her sweet time about it and Julia wasn't the only one casting curious glances at the Shipbody.

Just as she was wondering what would happen next, Pholus gave a signal and the dock gates began to open. They would soon be away from land and anchoring in the harbour. Trumpets rang out as churning water began to surround the vessel. Now that the official ceremonies were concluded, people relaxed and split off into groups to mingle, as servants slipped among them with delicacies and refreshments. Julia took a glass of wine absently and sipped it, her eyes fixed on the Shipbody. She couldn't have explained it, but she knew that there was going to be a change now that everyone's attention was diverted.

Her instincts were right. Slowly, the Shipbody began to ripple and twist, features rising to the surface as if something within was pushing its way out of the living wood. Julia could only stare in fascination as the *Tempest* took shape, growing in size until she was fully as tall as Pholus. Colour flowed over her surface, dark grey, black and silver, looking more like metal than a once living substance, refining and sharpening by the second. One arm stretched out to the fore, a mass of swirling cloud coalescing over the open palm, complete with tiny lightning bolt. The other grew a dagger, its blade long and sharp. At last, the *Tempest* was complete.

Her torso was clad in a back and breastplate, her skirt a rippling sheet of armour. Hair the deep hue of storm clouds streamed behind her as if wind-blown and black eyes set in a silver mask surveyed the scene before her, unyielding and implacable. She was magnificent and not a little terrifying.

"Jove's beard!" a voice exclaimed behind her. Just then she felt the vessel sway slightly as it lifted clear of its supports. The tremor caused laughter and not a few spilled drinks, but Julia could only gaze at the Ship, transfixed. As if sensing her scrutiny, the *Tempest* slowly turned her head and their eyes met. Julia screwed up her courage and made her way over to the Ship, feeling dwarfed and a little awkward.

"Hello," she said. "I'm Julia."

The Ship regarded her solemnly, then dipped her head.

"Your Highness."

"Julia, please. Raven promised to introduce us, but I decided not to wait. I hope you don't mind?"

Unexpectedly, *Tempest* smiled, silver lips stretching over even teeth. Her voice was low and pleasant.

"Not at all. I'm glad. Raven's told me about you."

"Congratulations on your installation and naming."

"Thank you. It's not been easy, but here I am. I suppose this is it now for the next several hundred years."

Julia could only nod. "I suppose it is." A sudden urge caused her to add, "They're marrying me off, you know."

The Ship's face twisted in sympathy. "I've heard. I can't say I envy you."

"Did you really have a choice?" Julia found herself asking, before stammering, "Oh Gods! I'm sorry. Sometimes I just say things I shouldn't."

"It's all right," *Tempest* reassured her. She seemed to think for a moment. "A choice? Not really."

Julia's eyes widened. Just as she opened her mouth to ask the Ship what she meant, a familiar voice cut in.

"Ah, Your Highness. I see that you've already become acquainted with our newest asset!"

She turned, only to almost bump into a smiling Albanus.

*Asset? What a revolting term.* "Admiral. Yes, I was congratulating the *Tempest* on her naming and launch. I'm delighted that everything has gone according to plan."

"Naturally," he replied, with a bow. "I'm sure that she appreciates your good wishes, don't you, *Tempest*?"

65

"Yes, sir," the Ship answered. "The Princess is most kind."

In a sudden flash of insight, Julia knew that the *Tempest* couldn't stand the man either. There was some history here between Albanus and whomever she'd been before. It was something else to ask Raven about. An equerry appeared.

"Your Highness, Admiral. The King requests your presence."

"We shall attend him directly," Albanus told him and the man hurried off. "Princess?"

He offered Julia his arm and she took it. To do otherwise would have been an insult, even though he made her flesh crawl.

"I hope that we shall have further opportunities to meet," she said to the Ship.

"As do I, ma'am," *Tempest* replied, her black eyes steady. A look of mutual understanding passed between them and Julia had the certain knowledge that they would see each other again before too long. Until then, she would just have to bide her time and wait to see what developed.

One thing was clear. Both she and *Tempest* were caught in events beyond their control. And the Gods help the pair of them.

# IV

*Tempest* watched impassively as her illustrious passengers were rowed back to land and their waiting carriages, thankful that it was all over.

Her choice of form had clearly startled some. Perhaps it had been the dagger? Whatever it was, she had spoken to a few people, including Rufus and Drusilla, but she could see the unease in their eyes at her martial appearance.

<You've made quite an impression.> Raven's voice slid into her mind. She couldn't tell if he approved or not from his neutral tone. <Most Ships aren't so scary-looking from the off.>

<Really?> she replied, sarcasm creeping in. <I wonder why?>

<You weren't joking about the sweet and pretty bit, were you? You look like one of Rufus' automata.>

<There's not much difference is there? Captains order, Ships obey, right?>

He was silent for a moment and she could feel his exasperation through the link. She was just about to add another pithy comment, when Valerius' command broke in.

<*Tempest*, status?>

She glanced over to where he stood, in front and a few feet to the right. He looked confident enough, but she could feel his uncertainty.

<All's well, Captain.>

She felt the burst of excitement as she responded, as if he were a child with a brand-new birthday toy, and part of her quailed.

<Excellent. The remainder of the crew should be boarding shortly. Inform me when you sight them.>

<Aye, sir.>

He ended the Sending though she could still feel his presence at the back of her mind, a closeness that wasn't physical but was nonetheless strangely intimate. It was different to what she experienced aboard *Blossom* with Captain Plinius. There, she'd had the Ship as a buffer; here there was nothing between herself and Valerius. It didn't make her uneasy exactly, but it was something she'd have to get used to. Maia supposed that after a few years it would become more comfortable, even necessary, like a background noise that is only noticed when it stops. She concentrated instead on checking over her vessel for any signs of strain or stiffness, running her awareness through the mechanisms for the umpteenth time, whilst keeping an eye on the land. She was expecting a few more crew, including Magpie, who was classed as a junior Mage, though anyone would be junior to Raven. The ancient was currently in his quarters, consulting over something with Hawthorn. The younger man, sandy haired with a short, neat beard and piercing green eyes, was examining something with interest. It appeared to be a dried root, then she realised that it was ginger.

"I mix this up with peppermint and a little something of my own devising," Raven was saying. Hawthorn put down the root and sniffed a small, uncorked bottle.

"It's similar to what I make too, but without the other ingredient. Magic?"

"A tiny amount of will," the Master Mage admitted. "Mostly to improve the spirits. There's nothing worse than sharing a vessel with groaning men."

Hawthorn grunted in agreement. "We have a few new hands and some of them will welcome this. I take it you keep Admiral Pendragon well supplied?"

He smiled mischievously.

Raven shared the joke. "I do. His Highness is fortunate that nobody dares to remind him of the time he was seasick before he'd left Portus harbour."

"Except you, I take it?"

"I think I'm the only one who remembers."

"That's probably another reason he doesn't spend too much time on land."

"And a lesser one, I fear." Raven frowned. "I hope he'll return to oversee his nephew sometime soon. It isn't doing the youngster any good to be constantly surrounded by lackeys and yes-men."

"You said it. Meanwhile, here we are with our new Captain."

Raven rolled his eyes, whilst Hawthorn's face told Maia everything she needed to know on that score. It seemed that she and Raven weren't the only ones to be less than impressed. She left them to their discussion and focused on her surroundings.

It had been a long day and the sun was setting away over the land, slipping into the dark line of the horizon. The nights were shorter than they had been, but she had to remind herself that it was still only the month of Martius, though warmer times were ahead. Maia thought longingly of the spring flowers she would never see again, unless somebody brought some on board just for her. They were hardly part of standard naval supplies.

Her time in the forest seemed aeons ago. She banished the memory and lit her lamps with a thought, watching as the warm glow spread across the vessel and reflected in the inky water. To tell the truth, now that all the excitement was over she wasn't sure what to do, except keep her unceasing watch over the lives that had been entrusted to her care. No wonder Ships passed their quiet time chattering amongst themselves like magpies in a tree.

Answering lights flickered on across the harbour. The lapping of the sea on her hull was soothing as she rocked gently. The tide would be turning before long, pulled back to the land by the swollen moon whose implacable face stared down silently, a mute witness to her transformation.

<*Augusta* to the new Ship.>

Maia acknowledged the Sending immediately.

<*Tempest* here, *Augusta*.>

There was a pause and she could feel the old Flagship's confusion.

<*Tempest?*>

<Aye, ma'am,> she supplied quickly. <I've just been named.>

A moment more, then the *Augusta* seemed to realise what had happened.

<Good. My Admiral tells me that the King named you himself.>

<He did, ma'am.>

<My Admiral wishes to speak to you. Relaying now.>

The Ship's voice faded, to be replaced with Pendragon's. She could picture him, sitting at his desk in his quarters, his dark eyes earnest.

<*Tempest*. I offer you my congratulations! I regret that I couldn't be there in person.>

<Thank you, Your Highness. You were greatly missed,> she added, daringly.

<So I've heard, but the country's security comes first.>

Fortunately, he only seemed amused at her presumption. <I dare say I'll be back before too long. I also heard that the Lady of Storms was hovering. She must be pleased by your name.>

Of course, he had been told who and what she was. Or had been. She wasn't sure if her half-Divine status even counted now that she was bound, but he might be counting on her connections. Wind and weather were of paramount importance to a sailor.

<I couldn't say, sir.>

<Perhaps it's just as well. You wouldn't want her following you about. She's been busy enough lately, though all the storms to the west can't be laid at her door. They're common enough this time of year, though tailing off now.>

<Glad to hear it, sir.>

She felt his attention shift. <Well, as I said, congratulations. Don't forget to ask Raven anything, or Send to the other Ships for advice when needed.>

<Understood, sir. Thank you.>

She felt his approval. <Carry on, *Tempest*. My compliments to Captain Valerius. End Sending.>

The Flagship broke the link, leaving Maia thinking hard. Pendragon couldn't be happy with Leo's appointment either.

Did anybody, save the King, have any trust in her new commander? Was he truly experienced enough? Oh well, she'd find out sooner rather than later, but if he expected her to follow incompetent orders he was in for a shock.

\*

The rest of her crew complement straggled in over the next couple of days, together with further supplies that were stowed neatly in her holds under the watchful eye of Corax, the purser. The pernickety old sailor mumbled and tutted over his lists of goods and glared at anyone he thought wasn't moving fast enough.

70

Maia was glad to see that most of the ordinary seamen and gunners knew what they were doing. She didn't need as many men as an inanimate vessel, being able to do many of the operations herself, but she still had a fair number of men who worked on deck and maintained and fired her many cannons and guns. It left room for more marines, so that she could move a small army at a moment's notice, faster and more safely than any other Empire or Alliance Ships could hope to do, plus her communications were far more reliable. She was already getting regular updates from the rest of the Fleet. Apart from the western storms, things were generally quiet and most Ships were undertaking routine duties.

One huge fellow climbing up the rope ladder from the boat sparked her interest. She trained her gaze on him, feeling the joy of recognition as he swung himself aboard, followed by several more men.

"Permission to come aboard, ma'am!" one of the others said. The big man smiled shyly in her direction.

"Big Ajax!" she cried. It was he, the quiet giant who had been her friend on the *Blossom*, and had been so concerned for her when she was burned. He shuffled his feet then stared at the deck, as usual.

"You come right here," she told him, as his companions slapped him on the back. One of them was old Hyacinthus.

"I can see the pair of you," she called to them. It was a lovely surprise, but she wondered how they'd got transferred from the *Blossom*. To her relief, there was no sign of Scribo or his foul-mouthed pet.

The group made its way over to her, saluting as protocol required.

"I'm glad you're here," she told them, returning the greeting. The other men hurried off to stow their belongings, whilst Big Ajax stood like a rock and Hyacinthus grinned under his bushy sideburns.

"*Blossom* sends her compliments, ma'am. She thought we might come in handy, seeing as you're new an' all."

"It's very kind of her," Maia laughed. They all knew that it wasn't up to Ships who moved where, though their suggestions were usually heeded. "I think I'll need all the help I can get."

It was only as they stood before her that she realised that she was fully as tall as Big Ajax. She'd always had to crane her neck to look up at him before. His mild brown eyes met hers as he pulled a small object from a pocket, wrapped in a handkerchief.

It was the little dog he'd carved for her, so many months before. She didn't know what to say, or indeed where she could put it. Technically, Ships had no possessions; the Navy didn't approve of anything that could hold memories and cause distress as the donors were lost to time, but she knew that most Ships had a few cherished items squirrelled away.

She thanked him, taking the carving in her gauntleted hands and admiring the craftsmanship. The little creature's floppy ears and laughing expression reminded her that she had been loved for who she was, not just for what she was fated to become. She stroked it gently. But what could she do with it? She darted a quick look around; it would be awful if it was spotted and taken from her. Maia came to a decision and split her Shipbody just above the breastplate, forming a little hollow where she could tuck it away, unseen.

She immediately felt better for having something of her own again, resting just above where her heart once lay.

"You do right, ma'am," Hyacinthus told her, tapping the side of his nose with one finger. "We won't tell will we, lad?"

Big Ajax shook his head solemnly.

"I'll treasure it always," she told him.

"An' if there's anything else you'd like, you've only to ask," the old sailor continued. "Just say the word an' me an' any of the lads'll sort it out for you."

"I'll let you know," she promised. "What do you think of the new me?"

"Very impressive, ma'am. This'll put the wind up them savages, you see if it don't."

So, he thought she'd scare the Northmen? Good, and not only them if she had anything to do with it.

"Go and settle in," she said. "I take it you know where you're going?"

"Oh aye. We're on the same gun crew with a couple of old Shipmates. You'll soon get to know them all as well."

"I certainly will."

They saluted and she responded, watching as they made their way below decks. They were soon followed by a steady stream of crewmen. The oldest had to be sixty at least, whilst the youngest were still children. If they had sponsors, they would be servants or midshipmen if they were training to be officers, learning from the older men, but if they were from poorer backgrounds they'd be assigned to the gun crews as powder monkeys and general factotums. She'd keep an eye on them, as she would be expected to be their surrogate mother for the time they were aboard her.

Maia observed them as they scampered about. Some looked confident enough, though there were a couple she'd need to talk to. This was a time when scary and intimidating wasn't the best look but she wasn't going to change her mind now. They'd get used to things after a few days and soon, they'd all be one happy family.

Or so she hoped.

\*

Milo was staring gloomily into his second mug of beer and wondering whether to just go back to his room, when the stranger sat down opposite him. The Agent glanced up warily as the man threw back his hood and waved to the barmaid.

"Ah, Cara, my dear! Wine for me and whatever my friend is drinking."

"You have me at a disadvantage, sir," Milo said flatly.

Cara hurried to serve them. Milo stared at his new acquaintance, whilst surreptitiously checking that his pistol was at the ready.

"Hello, Master Velox. I didn't see you come in." Cara was all smiles and Velox winked at her.

"See?" the man grinned across the table. "I'm a respectable merchant and well–known hereabouts."

There was something about the man's manner, if not his appearance, that niggled at Milo, as if he should know him though he'd have sworn they'd never met before.

Milo was only just back from Kernow, by sea this time, and was thoroughly fed up. The weather had been foul, the food worse and the only bright spot was that The Anchor had had a room available for him. The building might be mostly new but the atmosphere was still welcoming.

Velox looked surprised. "Why, don't you recognise me, Milo? And after we did a spot of grave robbing together as well."

Milo felt his stomach drop. He'd have sworn that this wasn't Celer, the Priest who had helped him disinter and burn Captain Valerius' body several months ago, but then again….The Gods could change their forms at will and he'd thought that there was something familiar about him.

"Oh, don't worry," Velox reassured him. The man, or whatever he was, took a long swig of his drink. "That's better. I needed that." He gestured to Milo's mug. "What do you think?"

Milo cautiously took a sip of the free beer, never taking his eyes from the stranger's, and nearly choked. Instead of beer, it was the best wine he'd ever tasted.

"I know you shouldn't mix your drinks, but you'll be all right," Velox said airily. "Now, I just wanted a word with you. Thanks for the sheep, by the way. As you've gathered, I've been keeping my eye on you lately."

Gods of Olympus! He was talking to Mercury. He knew there'd been something funny about the Priest at the temple when he offered the ram.

"May I ask why?"

"Why not? I feel that we're friends already and having a convivial evening together is what friends do."

Milo felt that he was standing on very thin ice. Velox seemed unperturbed.

"I suppose so," he said, slowly.

"You're thinking of heading back to Londin, right?"

"Yes."

"Good. Now listen. You're going to be assigned to protect the Princess."

"I am?" Milo was surprised. He was more the skulking in corners type and being given royal duties was out of his league. That was usually Caniculus' bag.

"Yes. Do you still have that old sword you found in Kernow?"

Sword? Milo frowned, before remembering.

"Erm, yes. It's still in my pack. It's not much good for anything," he added.

Mercury nodded. "I just wanted to check."

Milo stared at him blankly. It was getting hard to focus on the man and his vision was going blurry at the edges.

"Don't worry about it," the God continued. "Drink up and then I think it's time for you to sleep. Nice meeting you again."

It was easier to do as he was told. The wine filled him with a sense of warmth and well-being. Milo yawned.

"Think I'll head off to bed." His voice sounded strange and far away, even as he said the words. His companion smiled.

"Off you go."

Milo stood and made his way to his room, barely managing to undress before his head hit the pillow and he fell into a deep sleep.

By the morning, he'd forgotten all about his unexpected encounter.

*

"*Tempest*, weigh anchor!"

The Ship obeyed, turning the capstans to raise her chains and free herself from the sea bed. This was it. She was about to make her maiden voyage.

Her officers stood on the quarterdeck, the fresh wind giving their cheeks a ruddy glow even as it snapped at her pennants and ensign.

"You have your course," her Captain continued. "Make sail when ready."

"Aye, sir." Maia turned automatically to her training as she ran through the procedures. She was to set sail to the east, around the Isle of the Dead and then head west through the Britannic Ocean. Her first destination was Portus. Part of her was glad that she would be returning to familiar haunts. After that, she would retrace the journey she had made several times aboard the *Blossom*. The first part would be the trickiest, making her way around the point and avoiding the treacherous sands that lay off the coast. Still, she had memorised their location and knew what to expect.

She could sense Leo's excitement, tinged with a little nervousness as he surveyed his new kingdom. Over to one side, Amphicles was taking some midshipmen through navigation exercises, whilst the rest of her crew were about their duties. She knew that most were on stand-by to assist her and to ensure that all the mechanisms were working smoothly. They shouldn't have to climb up to the yards to free tangled lines, but it wasn't unheard for there to be initial snags. All these sailors could run a vessel on manual if required.

She released her sails, feeling them drop and catch the wind. Gradually, she began to move, her hull parting the water and picking up speed.

"So far, so good, sir," Sabrinus reported, scanning her masts and rigging. Leo nodded.

"I'm glad. It's a damned nuisance when there's stiffness."

Across the harbour, several guns fired to salute the Navy's latest Ship.

"Return the salute."

Maia felt a shiver run through her as one of her main guns answered, its deep roar echoing over the water. Her crew cheered and waved their caps, whilst below the men manning the gun hauled the mass of wood and iron back to swab it out. She would have the chance to run her drills later, using cannonballs this time. The blank cartridge had been impressive enough, but the sensation had been strange. She couldn't imagine what it would feel like when she was firing broadsides. It was yet another thing that *Blossom* had shielded her from, though the smaller vessel couldn't compete with hers in power.

<I take it nothing's exploded.>

The Master Mage's dry voice startled her.

<No. As my First Lieutenant has just observed, so far so good.>

<Everything working?>

She considered for a moment.

<Seems to be. It's a different kettle of fish to the *Blossom*, I can tell you.>

She sensed his amusement. <It certainly is. At least Leo is taking it easy for now. There'll be no speed records broken on this trip.>

Maia eyed her Captain. <He's very quiet. Plinius and *Blossom* are always talking, but he's hardly said a word to me.>

She adjusted her vision to peer into the Mage quarters. No portion of her vessel was off-limits to a Ship and her crew accepted their lack of privacy. Raven was decanting a liquid into bottles, his touch sure.

<He's probably nervous. I know I would be.>

Maia wasn't sure. She didn't know Leo well enough yet. <Maybe,> she Sent, doubt in her tone, <but I have the feeling it's something else.>

"Hmm," Raven said aloud. "Why not just ask him? You might be together for a long time and there's nothing worse than unease between a Ship and her Captain."

"I'll think about it," she said, her voice loud in the cabin.

"Ouch!"

"Sorry."

"Well, that's one thing to adjust, or we'll all be deaf by the time we reach Portus."

She obliged him. "Is that better?"

"Much."

"What are you making?"

"Magic Drops."

Her chuckle burst out before she could stop it.

"Seriously?"

He smiled. "Yes. I find that adding the word 'magic' to anything instantly makes people feel better, even before they've taken the stuff in some cases. Oldest trick in the book."

"What do they do?"

"They'll help with sea-sickness. I'll let Hawthorn do the actual administering, though, as I suspect that most of the crew would rather give me a wide berth. He has his own remedy, but I like to keep my hand in. They cure hangovers, too."

"Always good to know," she replied, watching as he inserted corks. "I think there'll soon be a big demand."

"Oh yes, especially for the new lads who'll be taken unawares. After we get to Portus, they'll all be begging for them again, but not for sea-sickness this time!"

Maia knew that all too well, from her days in The Anchor. It seemed to be the norm that sailors would go ashore, find

77

convivial company and get roaring drunk, in that order. Then when they'd finished, the whole cycle would begin again until they either ran out of money, or ran out of shore leave. It had certainly kept Casca, Cara and herself busy enough and the tavern in profit. She imagined that it would have been rebuilt by now, after the *Livia* had destroyed most of it. She'd find out soon enough.

"It'll be strange to see Portus again," she said, wistfully.

"And from a new perspective," he observed. "Everyone will be pleased to see you. I imagine there'll be dignitaries."

She groaned. "Yes, lots of important people traipsing aboard to be wined and dined. Well, Valerius should be used to that after being at Court with Artorius."

"That's true. The King kept him away from his last Ship longer than he should have. He was always finding an excuse to have him nearby."

"Oh yes. That would be the *Centaur*, under Captain Rhys." Maia had spoken briefly to the Ship. She had a sound reputation, as did her Captain. "She liked him, so that's one thing in his favour."

"Ah, you've spoken to her, then. Good. You're too used to keeping things to yourself; it's understandable, but Ships tend to be more open between themselves. Our Captain's quite impetuous, or so the rumour goes. Very close to Artorius as well."

"I don't give two figs about that," Maia told him. "I only want to know if he's up to being my Captain."

Raven sucked his teeth. "He'll have to be. Have you spoken to the *Persistence* yet?"

Maia was puzzled. "*Blossom* told me to have a chat. Why her?"

"Oh, no particular reason." She didn't believe him for one second.

"What have you and *Blossom* been cooking up together?"

"What makes you think that?"

Maia wasn't getting anywhere.

"Has anyone told you how annoying you are?"

"Lately, or generally?" The old Mage was enjoying himself.

"I see that Ship baiting is your new hobby."

He laughed at that. "No, it's an old one. You ask the *Justicia*."

Maia remembered that *Blossom* hadn't got on with that Ship either, from when they were candidates together.

"You mean the one *Blossom* threw a vase at? The 'total cow'?"

This time Raven's shoulders shook uncontrollably. "Oh, you don't miss a trick, Maia. The other Ships will have to be wary of you!" He took a minute to calm down. "How is your memory, by the way?"

Maia sighed. "As it was, except I can't remember much about the last part of my initiation. It's all gone fuzzy. I can picture bits and pieces, but they're all jumbled up."

Raven was suddenly serious. "That's good, believe me. It was a fantasy and you don't need it any more. It's best to put it behind you."

"Will I ever dream again?"

He nodded. "Of course. You'd go mad if you didn't, but they will be daydream images, swift and fleeting. Much of your humanity is in the keeping of the Mother, and you must trust her to look after you, as she does all her daughters."

"But what will be left of me?"

"As much as you want there to be. Remember who you were, but accept who you are now."

Acceptance, patience, obedience. That was what was expected of her. Well, she'd see about that and bide her time.

"Good advice," she replied. Raven lifted his head, as if suspecting that she wasn't entirely sincere, but wisely decided not to push his luck. She turned her attention away from him, monitoring her vessel as the coastline slipped past them, until she felt that she was fixed and it was the land that was moving, drifting away to the west like a shadow, further and further out of her reach.

\*

Maia soon had another chance to test her mechanisms when she was ordered to drop anchor out at sea, several hours into her voyage. There were a couple of hours of daylight still remaining and the sky to the west was clear, allowing the weak evening sun to gild her masts and spars. It was time for the formal offering to Neptune.

Valerius' communications had an edge to them that told her he was nervous. Maia opened the link to the *Patience*, who was off the coast of Gaul and more than happy to chat. She was once again ferrying diplomats, this time to discuss the Princess Julia's dowry with her prospective bridegroom, the aged Parisius.

<*Tempest*! It's good to hear from you. Are you under way?>

<I am. Danuco's getting ready to call upon the God. My Captain's nervous about it. Is there something I should know?>

Her friend's laughter echoed down the link. <He will be! It's an important moment.>

<But it's only a sacrifice and throwing the gold overboard,>she objected. <Why is he getting his breeches in a twist over it?>

<He's worried that the God will actually appear,> *Patience* explained. <It's rare, but if he's in the area he sometimes manifests personally.>

<But isn't that a good thing?>

<Well, it *can* be,> said the other Ship, <but nobody wants to attract that kind of attention, you know?>

Maia did know. She wished she could tell her friend that it was too late in her case. She had spoken directly to three Gods, though only Mercury had been really approachable. Pearl, as a lesser entity, didn't really count and anyway she was family. Sometimes it was hard to keep everything to herself. Maybe she was about to add Neptune to her list?

<Let's hope he's not around,> she agreed. <Oh, it's starting.>

Indeed it was. The whole company was formed up, officers to the fore, facing her altar where Danuco was sacrificing a goat.

<How's it looking?> *Patience* asked, anxiously.

<I'll show you.> Maia activated her relays and let the other Ship see through her eyes. They watched together as the Priest carefully parted the flesh and inspected the animal's organs.

<What do you think?>Maia asked her.

*Patience* sent a mental shrug. <They seem all right to me.>

Sure enough, Danuco's voice rang out confidently.

"The God accepts the sacrifice. There are no blemishes or signs of disease!"

He signalled to several burly crewmen, who had been chosen to carry the chests of gold from below and cast it into the sea. As she was a Royal Ship it was a king's ransom; no wise monarch would stint the Sea God or deprive him of his dues.

<What do you think they do with it all?> she asked *Patience*.

<The Mer-people? I think they adorn themselves and their underwater palaces. They must have tons of the stuff.>

<Perhaps they eat it?>

*Patience* snorted down the link. <Who knows? We just keep throwing it overboard and they keep accepting it. Look! There goes the cup!>

The heavy vessel, still stained with the blood of sacrifice, went over the side first and disappeared from sight immediately. As it did so Maia felt it give off a tone, as if a great bell had been rung in the deep to catch the God's attention. Some of the crew shifted their feet; she knew that they'd felt the vibration running up through her hull. If something was going to happen, this would be the time. The rest of the treasure soon followed, falling into the deep in a golden cascade of coins and objects. The sailors' eyes followed it as it disappeared, probably thinking what they could do with that much wealth, but they were idle fancies. Not even the smallest coin would be taken, for fear of offending the Sea God.

"Hail, O mighty Neptune!" Danuco intoned, arms raised. "We offer these riches on behalf of His Majesty's Britannic Royal Navy, and beseech you to permit us free passage over your realm!"

The crew cheered. Some stepped forward to offer tokens of their own, muttering their own pleas and prayers as they did so. Few sailors would pass up the opportunity to piggy-back on the major ceremony.

The water remained undisturbed. Everyone scanned the waves eagerly, as if expecting the God to come fountaining from the depths like an excited porpoise, but as the minutes stretched on and nothing happened, the air of anticipation faded. Maia almost felt disappointed.

<Well! That was an anti-climax.>

<He didn't turn up for me, either,> *Patience* consoled her. <He must be busy elsewhere, or watching from Olympus. Maybe he's throwing a party?>

They both laughed. Leo had a brief word with his officers, then dismissed the company. An air of normality returned to the vessel.

<How are you finding your new Captain?>

<He doesn't say much to me, to be honest. All I do is give reports and say 'aye, sir.'>

*Patience* was shocked. <Really? What about the daily briefings?>

<What about them?>

<Doesn't he ask for your opinion?>

<About what? I know we're going to Portus and if there's a problem I'll let him know. Apart from that, he's letting me get on with it.>

Maia could tell that her friend was taken aback.

<What about the social side? There are usually some sorts of entertainments in the evening.>

<Give him a chance. I've only just got going.>

<Didn't you have some sort of party in the harbour?>

Maia didn't know what to think. <No. He just dined with the officers, then retired to his cabin. All very boring. I mostly talk to the crew.>

<What does your Mage think of him?>

<Raven? I'm not sure, apart from the fact Leo's only been given this commission because he's the King's favourite. Heaven knows how many capable officers were passed over in his favour.>

<It's not ideal,> *Patience* admitted, <but give him a chance, won't you?>

<Do I have a choice?>

<You always have a choice, though admittedly, they might not be good ones. Look at it this way, you can all train him up.>

<I need to train myself first!>

<Then you'll train together.>

Trust her friend to find the silver lining in every situation.

<I suppose so. If I don't end up wrecked first.>

<Hush! That's no way to talk!> *Patience* reproved her. <Stop feeling sorry for yourself and make the first move. Show an interest in him and he might open up. Perhaps he's lonely. A Captain doesn't always have somebody else he can confide in.

That's why it's important for you to get to know each other well.>

<Besides which, he's my cousin,> Maia blurted out without thinking. There was a stunned silence. She sought to cover it up, adding lightly, <Didn't you know? My father was a Valerius.>

<I'd heard a rumour,> *Patience* replied cautiously. <There was all that business with the *Livia*'s Revenant in Portus.>

<She was after me. She thought she was my mother, but she was quite mad. She killed my father, her Captain, and I had to be hidden away.>

Maia had had enough of concealing her identity. If she couldn't tell her best friend, who could she tell? The rest she would have to keep to herself.

*Patience* hid her shock as best she could. <Your poor thing! All that time and you never knew. What happened to your mother?>

<Gone.>

It wasn't the whole truth, but it would have to do.

<How dreadful!>

<I know you won't tell anyone.>

<Yes, of course!> They were almost whispering, even though nobody else could hear. <I'll keep the secret. I take it the Navy knows?>

<Oh yes. They know all right and so does the King. I think he chose Leo deliberately. He probably thinks it's a good joke.>

*Patience* sighed. <Let's pray that the Gods grant him wisdom.>

<Too right, and the sooner the better. How are your diplomats?>

They were both happy to change the subject.

<Taking advantage of my stores, when they're not being sick or arguing. Most just want to get where they're going as quickly as possible. I think it shouldn't be too long before they come to some sort of agreement about the Princess. Parisius wants it sorting as soon as possible.>

<It's not like time's on his side,> Maia agreed. <I don't think the Princess is looking forward to it. I met her at my naming.>

<What was she like?>

Maia brought up the picture of Julia in her mind's eye. Slim and intense, the King's sister had seemed far too intelligent to be sent away to market like a prize heifer.

<Too good for him.>

<Oh dear. It's at times like this that I'm glad I'm a Ship. Imagine having to marry someone you'd never met.>

<And old enough to be your grandfather.> She made a disgusted noise.

<*Tempest*. Report to me in my day room.> Her Captain's voice interrupted their chat.

<Got to go. Leo wants to talk to me,> she explained quickly.

<You know where I am and I'm always here if you need anything.>

They signed off and Maia sank down into the deck, gliding smoothly through the wooden planks until she re-formed on a bulkhead in the Great Cabin.

It looked very different to the first time she'd seen it. Now, instead of empty space, it was filled with the paraphernalia of command; a large table, strewn with charts and papers where the Captain would conduct and discuss the business of the day, and his work desk, placed to get the maximum light from the great windows that stretched across her stern. He was just finishing what appeared to be a letter, signing it with a flourish and sprinkling it with sand to dry the ink. Maia watched him as he shook off the grains, folded the paper and sealed it.

"There, that's done," he remarked, as if to himself, before turning in his chair and fixing his gaze on her unmoving Shipbody. "A letter to the King," he explained. "His Majesty insists that I write to him once a day, even though he won't get them until I can send them from Portus."

This close, she was struck again by how young he was, only four years older than the King and, at twenty-three, the least experienced Royal Captain. The initial shock she'd felt on seeing him had mostly gone, though sometimes the way he held his head, or the way the light shadowed his face, reminded her very much of the brief dream she'd had of her father. She had no doubt now that it had been sent by a God, though she couldn't say which one. Maybe it had been her mother, Aura, trying to communicate through a secret channel? His eyes weren't blue but hazel shading to green, and for that she was thankful.

Leo cleared his throat.

"I feel that we haven't really had the chance to talk at any length," he began and Maia had the immediate suspicion that Raven had had a word with him. He paused, looking at her expectantly.

"It has been rather busy," she replied.

"Exactly! Everything's new for both of us, but I don't want you to think that I'm neglecting you."

Maia kept her face composed. "Of course not, sir."

"We'll have lots of time to get used to each other."

"Indeed."

He might have a reputation as a charmer, but he was floundering here.

"I got on well with my last Ship, the *Centaur*, you know."

Maia kept her expression neutral. She'd sheathed her dagger at her side, as it wasn't practical in everyday situations, but her miniature storm still hung about her left hand, moving slowly. She had the sudden urge to hurl the little lightning bolt at him to make him get to the point. To her surprise, he flung up his arms in a gesture of defeat.

"I'm sorry, *Tempest*! The King told me who you are. I couldn't believe it. We had no idea that Vero had any offspring and it came as a bit of a shock. Then to hear that you'd been a servant, and nearly murdered as well, compounded the horror."

He rose and walked over to her, gazing up into her silver mask. "Please believe that I never asked or expected to be given this honour. I know I haven't got half the experience of some of the other candidates, and I was as shocked as everyone else. Artorius – His Majesty – thinks he's doing me a great favour, and indeed he is, but I'm going to need help."

His eyes widened as he appealed to her and Maia felt her wooden heart melt a little. Everything he said had the ring of truth and he hadn't attempted to hide the awkwardness of his situation. He'd been awarded her inheritance and he knew it.

"You should have been a great lady, living a life of comfort and respect. I understand that. I don't know exactly how you ended up here, but your sacrifice is appreciated, I assure you."

Hmm. Now that sounded more rehearsed.

"It's better than scrubbing floors," she said. His face fell. "I worked in a tavern, too."

From his slight twitch, she knew that he'd jumped to the same conclusion everyone else did, but she didn't care. "Now the Gods have decreed that I should be a Ship. That's the way it goes and you can be sure I'll do my best to be a good one. Would I have wanted an experienced commander? I'd be lying if I said I didn't, but you're my Captain and we have to make the best of it."

There, she'd said her piece. Leo nodded.

"Thank you for your honesty. I don't know if I can ever make up for what happened to you, but I promise I'll do my very best. Agreed?" He held out his hand and she reached out, feeling his warm fingers in hers.

"Agreed."

His face broadened into a smile. "And we can both ask Raven what to do when we're stumped."

That did it. His smile was infectious and she found herself responding.

"We won't have to. He'll tell us, whether we want him to or not!"

Leo laughed and Maia felt the tension she'd carried inside her gently ease. He might be young, but at least he wasn't arrogant enough to think he knew everything. There had been genuine feeling in his words.

"I know Ships aren't really supposed to have possessions as such," he told her, "but I would like to give you this."

A present? Maia was intrigued. He went back to his desk, slid open a small drawer and brought out a little hinged case, covered in red leather.

"I found this when I was going through my father's things, after his death. Your father and mine were cousins and Vero had no siblings, so this must have come though the family to him."

Maia took the case and opened it. Nestled inside was a miniature picture, painted in delicate colours on what looked like ivory. The subject was a young man, dressed in a naval uniform, with fair hair and familiar blue eyes. A small, involuntary noise escaped her before she could stop it.

"It was his mother's. She had it commissioned when he became Second Lieutenant on the *Leopard*. He served with Admiral Pendragon, you know. I thought you might like to have it."

She could no longer shed tears, despite her welling emotion. "Thank you." Maia gently touched the portrait, once more regretting that she had never had the chance to meet her father.

"He was a fine Captain," Leo said, softly. "I'll keep it open on my desk so you can look at him whenever you want. Unless you'd prefer to take it yourself?"

She shook her head. "I think it's fitting that he's on your desk. You've followed in his footsteps, except I hope you have more luck than he did."

He regarded her levelly. "You know how he died, then?"

"Yes." She couldn't tell him that her parents' actions had almost cost her her life too.

"Tragic." He stared past her for a moment. "Still, I pray to the Gods that he's at peace."

"As do I," she echoed. "We must forge a new path for ourselves now."

The two remaining members of the Valerius family faced each other in the light, both understanding that they were now bound, not only to their duty, but also to each other for as long as their partnership should last.

*

Milo was in the Portus Morgue consulting with Scabious, when the muffled boom of guns penetrated the thick walls. Jackdaw, who'd turned up for a chat with his friend, raised his eyebrows and swallowed a mouthful of meat roll, despite Milo's amazement that he could even think of eating in this place.

"The *Tempest*'s just arrived then," the Mage remarked. "I hear she's quite a sight."

"She is," Milo answered, remembering his first glimpse of the vessel in the Durobrivis dockyards.

"I'd heard they'd built her big."

"Bloody enormous and bristling with guns," Milo confirmed.

Scabious was more interested in the corpse on the slab.

"You can go and ogle her later. For now, I can safely say that this gentleman was murdered by suffocation. See the broken capillaries in the sclera?"

Jackdaw brushed crumbs off his robe and trotted over to take a look.

"Oh yes. They must have rearranged the body. He was found in his bed. Quite peaceful, by all accounts."

"I knew I smelt a rat," Milo said, satisfied that his initial suspicions had been confirmed. "His family thought he'd died in his sleep."

"Well, I suppose he awoke briefly," Scabious said, "Presumably when someone put the pillow over his head. Any idea who could have done it?"

Milo blew out a breath. "He was named as a go-between for smuggling. I believe his shop was being used as a meeting and storage point."

"He must have outlived his usefulness, or threatened to go to the authorities," Jackdaw said. Milo could only agree. It was a setback to his investigations.

"Probably wanted to turn King's Evidence, but they got to him first."

Damn it! He'd been so close. The man would have squealed like a stuck pig if he'd thought he could escape the arena.

"Have you questioned the household?" Scabious asked, wiping his hands on a cloth.

"Yes. We haven't anything on the wife and daughter, but one of the household slaves is missing. We've put out the word and hope to apprehend him."

Milo doubted they'd find the fellow, but stranger things had happened.

"If he was the guilty party, I imagine that the gang will have made sure he'll be following his master down to Hades." Jackdaw grinned. "Perhaps they'll end up in the same queue for the boat."

"Would you pay the ferryman his fare?" Milo asked. "I'd happily leave him wandering forever on the shore if he'd killed me. Charon doesn't work *pro bono*."

"Too right." Jackdaw shuddered. He regarded the supine corpse. "This chap will have the coin; his wife will see to that. Are you going to release the body?"

Scabious sniffed. "That's up to the Prefect, but I don't see any reason to keep him. He's hardly going to sit up and accuse his murderer, even if you do find him."

"Maybe his wife did it for the insurance money?" the Mage teased. Scabious' eyebrows rose and he shot his friend a reproachful look.

"Come on, you know women generally use poison."

"Of course!" Jackdaw was unrepentant.

Milo rolled his eyes as the pair of them sparred cheerfully. "You two are better than a comedy duo."

"Nah. You and Caniculus have got those parts sewn up."

Milo punched the young Mage playfully on his arm.

"Ow!"

"If you've *quite* finished, gentlemen," Scabious said, in mock reproof, "I'd like to go and get some lunch."

"Good idea!" Jackdaw brightened.

"You've just eaten!"

"That was just a snack. Come on, let's go and have a gander at this new Ship and then we can go and get hot meat pies. Milo?"

"I wouldn't say no to a pie."

They exited the morgue by the back door, avoiding both Placidianus' office and the front desk, where Sergeant Grumio would be casting a disapproving eye over the antics of Portus' finest, to emerge on to a side alley. The buildings afforded a narrow view of the harbour, the sparkle of the sun on the water an inviting contrast to the gloom of the narrow passage. There was already a crowd gathered to stand and watch as the *Tempest*, pennants and ensign flying bravely, dropped anchor. Milo fancied that he could hear the rattle of the chains from here, though it was so noisy that he could have been mistaken. The Ship was certainly looking spectacular in the sunshine, bright and gleaming with new paint. He spared a thought for the Ship herself. Did she find it strange to return to her old home like this, or would it bring back unpleasant memories? He had no way of knowing.

The three men stood and watched for a while, until their empty stomachs and the lure of hot pies drew them away.

*

Portus looked much as she remembered it; smoke rising from thousands of fires and factories, warehouses and civic buildings looming over everything. Maia had always assumed that she'd been born there; it was certainly all she'd known for the first sixteen years of her life.

Her crew were happy, as Leo had granted shore leave. He and Sabrinus, who was a pleasant and efficient young man, if a little serious, were going ashore to be treated to a civic reception. The word had got out that Maia had been a Portus girl, so the locals were seeking to capitalise on it. At the rate things were going, there wouldn't be another new Ship for a while and re-installation wasn't quite the same thing. It seemed several ages since she'd seen the *Diadem* processing down to this very harbour to take up her new vessel.

After the land celebrations, Leo had invited all the Portus dignitaries to a reception on board. Her cook, Pertinax, was already terrorising his juniors in the galley as he aimed to produce a feast worthy of the newest Royal. He was generally a mild-mannered man unless food was concerned, when he would roar like a lion and brandish a cleaver as if it were Excalibur. Some of the boys were awed by his fearsome appearance, aided by the livid scar that twisted his lip into a snarl, but they soon learned to sneak down and listen to his stories while he fed them titbits.

Maia didn't mind hosting the reception, but the highlight of her stay would be seeing Matrona and Branwen again. They were coming aboard beforehand for a private visit and to see how she was settling in. She hadn't seen either of them for months and couldn't wait to show off her new vessel. Meanwhile, the other Ships in the harbour were sending congratulations. When one of them was the *Persistence*, she seized the opportunity to find out why everyone was telling her to talk to this particular Ship. For once, she wasn't grumbling.

<How's it goin', girlie?>

<Everyone keeps saying '*so far, so good*'.>

<Hah! That's better than yer think. There're usually some issues on yer first trip out. No fouled lines or fires in the galley, then?>

<Not yet, thank the Gods.>

<Well, be prepared for the unexpected,> the *Persistence* said wisely. <Don't try to struggle on if yer think somethin's wrong. It's not up to yer to sort everythin' out on yer own. What about yer crew? I 'ear there are some old mates aboard.>

Maia thought of Big Ajax and Hyacinthus, among others. <Just a few. I'm getting to know them all better.>

<Good.> The other Ship approved. <But let's get down to brass tacks. What about yer officers? Yer Captain's as green as grass, fer all he did well on the *Centaur*. Think 'e'll shape up?>

Maia knew that her hesitation spoke volumes over the link. <I don't know him well enough yet,> she said cautiously. The *Persistence* snorted.

<Yer've not had *the talk*, 'ave yer?>

Talk? That was what *Blossom* and the others must have been meaning.

<No.>

<Right, then.> She felt the *Persistence* mentally roll up her sleeves. <This is how it is. *Captains order, Ships obey*, right? Well, don't think they 'ave it all their own way. There's plenty of Ships been saddled with useless officers. Yer just 'ave to make sure that yer not caught at it.>

<I don't know what you mean?>

<Yer make sure they're removed. Put out of the picture, so to speak.>

Maia was shocked at the knowing glee in the Ship's voice. <You don't kill them?>

<Jove's beard, no! Yer just make sure that they are, 'ow shall I put it, *inconvenienced*.> She pronounced the word carefully. <One Ship I know unlatched a port 'ole in an 'eavy swell and 'is cabin was swamped. Said it was a faulty catch. Another made sure 'e was always trippin' over somethin'. As long as yer crew can't be faulted, it's quietly accepted and the man's transferred. Of course, if he's really bad yer could put things in 'is bed. Find out what scares 'em an' go fer it. Snakes, spiders, beetles. One

was got like that with frogs. Hated 'em, 'e did. Screamed the place down!>

<Who did that?> Maia asked, trying not to laugh.

<No names. Though I will say that she ain't too far away from yer right now.> *Persistence*'s snigger confirmed Maia's suspicions. <Yer crew will always 'elp, 'cos if they're annoying yer, they'll not be popular with anyone else either an' everyone aboard will want 'em gone.>

Maia didn't dare ask if any Ship had done anything worse – not with her family history.

<So it's just little things really?>

<Aye,>Persistence answered, thoughtfully. <Don't go too far an' cause lastin' damage, or yer'll be in trouble. The Navy doesn't mess about.>

An image of a blazing blue eye in the charred remains of a Shipbody rose from the depths like a warning.

<I see yer know somethin' of that,> the old Ship said, her tone subdued. <They 'ad no choice there.>

<She was mad.> Maia didn't want to say the *Livia*'s name. The Ship's Revenant might be finally gone, but her unquiet shade still lurked in the shadows, haunting her still.

<It's true then? Valerius was yer father?> *Persistence* genuinely wanted to know. The news must have leaked, though she knew that it wouldn't have come from the *Patience*. She might as well admit it if it was all over the Fleet.

<Yes, though I never knew him. He died before I was born.>

Sympathy flooded down the link. <The Gods are cruel sometimes an' the Fates can be worse. But,> she added quickly, <it's all right now. Yer with us an' we look after our own. We might gossip an' bitch, but an insult to one is an insult to all. Remember that!>

Maia felt a little battered. <Yes. Thank you.>

<What do they say? Uncomfortable truths. Yer'll 'ear more of 'em before long, mark me words.>

<I've already heard quite a few,> Maia admitted. <There are lots of things they don't tell you at the Academy.>

Persistence agreed vehemently. <Yer right there! Still, it's a grand life if yer don't weaken. Eh, looks like visitors. Remember

ter keep an eye on yer surroundin's at all times, even when yer thinkin' of somethin' else. I'll let yer get on with it.>

She broke the link, leaving Maia with a lot to think about, but she took the Ship's advice and concentrated on keeping her observation channels open. It wouldn't do to be lapsing all the time and she'd nearly missed the boat heading her way. In it, she could see two female figures and her mood abruptly lifted. At last she'd get to see Matrona and Branwen once more. If she lived to be a thousand, she'd never forget the love and care they'd given her when she was injured. It had gone beyond the call of duty, despite what Ceridwen had said before her initiation. Maybe the Priestess had been testing her in another way, by sowing doubts in her resolve? She hadn't thought of that. She had to stop being so eager to believe what she was told by others and, instead make up her mind about people, based on her own judgement. She was a big Ship now.

She alerted Drustan, who'd remained aboard to supervise the preparations for the reception, and the young officer hastened to welcome their guests. Maia took up her position on the quarterdeck and waited for them to be helped aboard.

Matrona was wearing a heavy cloak over her uniform, complete with the unflattering cap that Gallus the stylist had compared to a washerwoman's. Branwen brought up the rear, her ginger hair escaping from similar headgear. Maia realised that she was glad that she'd never have to wear one of the blasted things ever again. Seeing the familiar faces brought back so many memories that she had to force herself to bundle them aside and concentrate on the present. Perhaps, in time, the images and emotions from her human life would stop ambushing her at the most inopportune moments.

"*Tempest*, permission to come aboard?" Matrona's clear voice followed the customary protocol.

"Permission granted!" Maia replied, smiling.

The two women reached the deck and shook out their cloaks, smoothing down the material. Then Matrona looked up and her eyes widened.

"Matrona, Branwen, it's lovely to see you," Maia said, taking the initiative. "Welcome aboard! May I present my lieutenant, Marcus Julianus Drustan?"

The young officer stepped forward and they exchanged greetings.

"It's been a while, Drustan," Matrona said. "It doesn't seem a minute since you were running around at the Academy."

He smiled at her warmly, "No, I suppose it doesn't. Funny how the years pass so quickly. It's good to see you again, ma'am. Won't you come below, out of this wind?"

Matrona agreed with alacrity. "Certainly. It's definitely chillier out here on the water, isn't it, Branwen?"

"Oh yes, Matrona." The maid's eyes flicked nervously to Maia and she realised that it was happening again; the constant reminder of the gulf between who she'd been and who she was now. Did they think that she'd changed all that much? Perhaps she had.

It was much warmer in the State Cabin, reserved for visiting dignitaries and royal passengers. Much of the food was already laid out under covers and the whole area was looking splendid with its gilded mouldings and painted panelling. They'd only have a short time to catch up, before the rest of the boats arrived in a triumphant flotilla.

A servant took their cloaks and the women settled themselves on padded chairs, whilst another served drinks.

"Please excuse me, ladies," Drustan said, "but I have duties elsewhere."

"Of course," Matrona smiled. "I'm sure we'll be able to chat again before we leave."

"I hope so, ma'am."

He bowed and left, just as Maia rose from the deck, re-forming alongside the table, as if she were in the next-but-one seat. She didn't really want to hang off the wall like a decoration and she thought this might be more appropriate.

"Well, I must say that I'm relieved to see you, Maia, or *Tempest* as we should call you now," Matrona began.

"Me too," Branwen added quickly.

Maia decided to cut to the chase.

"You must have been so worried," she said.

Matrona nodded. "We were. You took longer than any other candidate I've ever known. I understand that there were…*difficulties*."

94

"Yes," Maia replied bluntly. "It was horrible and I nearly died. *She* decided to interfere."

Nobody dared mentioned the Goddess' name.

"So I understand," Matrona said, a flash of anger crossing her face. At that moment, the resemblance to Ceridwen was even more pronounced. "I hope she got what she deserved."

"It was certainly painful for her," Maia replied, unable to stop the feeling of satisfaction. "I hope she's decided to leave me alone now."

"You're protected by powerful Gods now and out of her reach," Matrona confirmed, "though it won't stop her being curious."

"Doubtless she'll find someone else to torment. I had the feeling that she enjoyed it."

"Who knows? The main thing is that you survived and you're installed on your amazing new vessel. I can't believe how big it is!"

"I couldn't either," Maia admitted. "To tell the truth, it's taking a lot of getting used to."

"It will, after the *Blossom*," Matrona agreed.

Maia had to ask the question. "Have you found any more candidates?"

Matrona's face fell.

"No. There were rumours of Potentia among the Gaels and Caledonians, but it came to nothing. They have their own Gods there and don't want poaching. I hate to say it, but we're going to have to outbid the temples and try to bribe parents and guardians."

Everyone loved the idea of Ships, but many parents didn't want to lose their daughters so permanently. If they entered a temple, at least they could stay in contact and maybe have descendants.

"It's easier if there are no relatives," Maia said, with the bitterness of experience.

"True. So, where are you bound after this?"

"Oh, just a cruise west along the coast and back again, while I check that everything's working. I've been warned that there might be snags."

"There will be snags," Matrona confirmed, "and not all of them will be mechanical. Your new crew have to get used to everything as well."

That was true. Two marines had already nearly come to blows over an old quarrel and received a warning from Osric. Apparently it had been going on and off for years, but they'd both been told that they'd better cease hostilities whilst they were on board. Maia didn't bet on it lasting until the next shore leave; they were itching to fight and settle the matter once and for all. If it got any worse, she'd set up a makeshift arena herself and everyone could place bets.

"I should have the time now to get properly settled down," she said. "At least we're not at war."

"No, thank goodness. Portus is full of Northerners, you know. They have some beautiful silks and jewellery for sale. All the local merchants are complaining."

"The competition might bring prices down," Maia observed, thinking how she would have loved to go shopping. As it was, apart from buying presents, there was no need to any more. Some Ships did bring goods aboard and there were always small boats that flocked to sell sailors their wares in port. It might be worth taking a look then. Technically, Ships were paid, though they never saw any of the money. She'd have to put a chitty in to Corax, who'd sort it out for her.

This time, she'd remembered to keep watch. A string of boats, some of which were her own, was braving the choppiness of the harbour. Out to sea, she spotted dark clouds massing to the south-west; she had the feeling that a storm was on its way. Perhaps the reception would have to be cut short? If it got any worse, the Magic Drops would be in demand. She extended her awareness to her boats, speeding them through the water so that they would arrive first; the rest would have to rely on the brawn of their rowers. Leo was striking a heroic pose at the bow of the lead one, looking like a figurehead himself and clearly enjoying the trip. She hoped that he wouldn't fall in. She relayed the information to her companions.

"Time for a quick freshen up before they get here, I think," Matrona said. Branwen had been very quiet, but smiled at Maia as she rose.

"I haven't forgotten how kind you were to me," Maia said, abruptly. "If there's ever anything I can do for either of you, you must let me know at once."

"Thank you, my dear," Matrona answered. "I'm just glad you succeeded."

"We were very worried," Branwen said.

"No more rose petal baths for me, though," Maia said, trying to lighten the moment, making her former maid smile.

"Oh, you were so dirty!" she burst out and they all laughed.

"Dirty and ragged, that was me. Good job you took me in hand, Branwen."

"I miss looking after you," the woman said with a sigh. "I'm taking care of some of the little boys at the moment, young limbs of Pan that they are. I seem to remember that Drustan was a lively one."

Maia grinned. "Oh, you must tell me all about it!"

"Now, now," Matrona said, in mock reproof. "Give the poor man a chance. Of course, if he misbehaves just let us know and we'll give you something to cut him down to size."

"I don't suppose you remember Leo?" Maia asked, innocently.

"Sorry, can't tell on Captains! Now, which way to somewhere we can freshen up?"

# V

Julia was enduring yet another round of tiresome gown fittings, when an announcement heralded the arrival of Raven.

"Master Mage! Aren't you supposed to be on the *Tempest*?"

"Your Highness." He bowed in her direction. The dressmaker, her mouth full of pins, cast her patron an anxious glance.

"Leave us!" Julia commanded, relieved at the chance for a break. The woman scuttled off, and Julia stepped off the low plinth she'd been forced to stand on for what seemed like hours. Her back ached and all she wanted to do was to get out of the heavy fabric and into something more comfortable.

"Give me a minute," she told the Master Mage, disappearing behind a screen and undressing herself for once. The loose robe she chose would do for now, as she was under no illusion that this would be a long respite.

"So, what brings you to the palace?"

"I wanted to see how you were."

"Oh," she said, knowingly. "You want to make sure that I haven't set anything on fire or caused a major structural collapse." She emerged in time to catch his grin.

"That too. I hear that negotiations are nearly finished."

Julia shuddered. "Seems like it. I hear that my future bridegroom is very keen and praising my beauty at every opportunity. I could be a hunch-backed, warty old hag and he'd say exactly the same thing."

"Naturally."

Julia blew a raspberry. "I don't suppose you know a spell to put him off?"

"No. Face it, you should have been married years ago."

"Gods save me!" She threw herself on to a couch. "Stop hovering and sit down. Would you like a drink?"

"What is there?"

"Wine."

"You've persuaded me."

Julia poured them both a glass. "I've been practising," she told him with pride. "I can lift a couch now and I only singed the curtains a little. I blamed it on a stray candle."

Raven looked thoughtful, pressing his lips together. "I can't leave you like this," he said, "barely trained and a danger to yourself and others."

Julia sipped at the ruby liquid. "It seems that you won't have a choice as the dowry is settled. I'm to be gift-wrapped and parcelled off very soon."

Raven grimaced. "I know, but not yet. I've had an idea."

Hope rose at his words. If there was any way of delaying the inevitable she'd agree to it, whatever it was.

"Go on."

"You need to prepare for your wedding by making a pilgrimage to the temple of Juno Rigana in Portus. I've just portalled in from there."

Portus? What was he planning?

"And that will help me how?"

"Have faith, Princess! You'll be going to make offerings and be ritually purified. That will take at least a month."

A month! Still, it wasn't a tempting prospect spending hours each day having to undergo endless boring ceremonies whilst listening to a bunch of twittering women singing the praises of the Goddess. She didn't really want to be prepared for marriage at all.

"You won't be there, of course," he continued, grinning mischievously.

Her jaw dropped. "I won't?" she managed, when she'd remembered how her mouth worked.

"No. The *Tempest* needs an apprentice Mage and I think you'll fit the bill splendidly. A little diversionary magic about your person will make sure nobody questions you. I'll have to tell the Ship, but I can't see that that will be a problem and Hawthorn's an old friend of mine, as is Magpie, the other Mage. Claudia Modesta, the High Priestess in Portus, will keep quiet if I ask her to."

Julia could only stare at his wrinkled features.

"You'd risk that for me?"

He snorted. "I've had more excitement recently than I have for a very long time and I find I've been missing it. Time for some more. So, Your Highness, what shall we call you? Do you have a favourite bird?"

Julia's eyes slid to the small shrine in her room. "I do, actually."

She thought it would be an excellent choice. All she had to do now was to persuade her brother to let her go.

*

Julia had to wait two days, fretting over the delay, until the King returned from his hunting lodge to the north of Londin. She knew that he'd rather stay there, but there was government business to conclude and they couldn't do it without him. No doubt he'd be off again as soon as he could get away, so she would have to act swiftly. She decided to ask him over lunch, as he was more likely to be amenable whilst eating.

"Sister! Come and let me tell you of my success!"

Thank the Gods he was in a good mood, laughing as he reclined on the couch. Julia joined him, nodding at her cousin who was already helping himself to some choice dishes.

"The Huntress favoured you, Sire?"

Artorius waved his goblet, his face already flushed. A slave rushed forward to fill it.

"She did indeed. I shot a fine stag yesterday. Its head will look wonderful mounted on the wall, won't it Marcus?"

"It will look very fine," the Prince replied. "You're an excellent marksman."

Artorius was pleased. "I am, aren't I? Marcus saw it first, but he wasn't quick enough."

"Alas, my gun misfired."

Julia kept her face composed, but suspected that it was a very timely failure. Artorius would have sulked for days if anyone else had killed the animal.

"I intend to serve it at the Ambassadors' Banquet," the King said, "after it's hung for a while, naturally."

He cast his eyes over the plates and selected a quail. "Mm, delicious. I like the sauce."

Julia joined them, picking at the food as they ate and waiting for the right moment. Fortunately, her brother pre-empted her.

"Everything's sorted," he told her. "Parisius has agreed to our suggestions about the dowry, though it's not like that old skinflint needs the money. He's as rich as Croesus, despite the paltry tribute he gives the Emperor."

"He pleads poverty, but we all know it's a ruse," Marcus agreed. "Get him to shower you with jewels, cousin, then when he dies you can keep them and make a run for it."

Artorius laughed so hard he started to cough. A slave was at his side immediately, but he gestured the man away.

"What a wit you have, dear cousin!"

"I speak the truth," Marcus said, languidly. "Surely he can't be much longer for this world. Having a young wife might be the end of him."

Julia gave the Prince a polite smile, but seethed inwardly.

"Talking of my marriage, dear brother," she began, "I would like to pray for a fruitful outcome."

"Wouldn't we all," Artorius interrupted. "I'll order sacrifices throughout the land."

"It would be better if I were to appeal to the Goddess directly, say at her temple in Portus. A few days of ritual could make all the difference."

She gazed at her plate modestly.

"Portus? Well, it's not far from Dubris."

"I could sail straight from Portus, if the weather was favourable," she pointed out, sending up a silent prayer.

"It's a good idea, Sire," Marcus chimed in, unexpectedly taking her side. "Think of the stakes. We want *your* nephew on the throne of Gaul, not one of Parisius', and the Goddess can achieve things impossible to mortal man. Do you think Julia has a chance otherwise? We need Divine aid."

Artorius chewed thoughtfully on another quail.

"I agree. I'll get Aquila to arrange it with what's-her-name, the High Priestess. Then you can go directly from Portus. Uncle can sort out a Ship to take you."

"Why not use the *Augusta*?" Marcus offered. "I believe she'll be back from the west by then, unless the Fae decide to invade again."

The King shuddered theatrically, "Don't even jest about that, cousin! But it would be fitting that the Flagship take her. Yes. Have a word with the Admiralty and tell them it's what I want, though we can't wait for too long."

"Thank you, dear brother," Julia said, outwardly demure, but bubbling with relief inside. With any luck, Parisius would be heading for the underworld before she got half-way to Gaul, and in the meantime she had a sea voyage and a lot of training to prepare for.

It was only as she returned to her suite that she remembered her presentiment aboard the *Tempest*. It seemed it had come true, after all.

*

The speechstone activated just as Milo was waking. The afternoon sun slanted through the windows of his small room at The Anchor, filling the air with dancing motes of gold. He groaned and rubbed his eyes.

<Blue here.>

It had been a long night on the waterfront, keeping watch for suspicious activity. His last lead had ended up dead, forcing him to grasp at any clues he could find. It seemed that most people had been either bribed, or intimidated into silence.

<Agent Blue,> came the familiar voice of the Controller. <You have a new assignment. You are to report to HMS *Tempest* immediately. Inform Master Mage Raven the instant you arrive. He's expecting you.>

<Acknowledged.>

He hoped for more information, but the link ended. He heaved himself out of bed and rang for some hot water, wondering what the old man was up to now. Milo was tempted to contact him directly, but he'd find out what was happening soon enough. His small window didn't face the harbour, but he could still picture the new vessel, admiring its trim lines and impressive firepower. What was more surprising to him was that the girl had managed to survive long enough to be installed. He wouldn't have given a worn copper coin for her chances, especially after learning who was against her. Raven had clearly had more faith in her than he.

As he scraped at his bristles, he wondered how she'd managed it. Perhaps he'd find that out too, when he was aboard?

Sure enough, he'd just finished stuffing his clothes into his bag when the speechstone flared into life once more. He knew who was at the other end even before he answered.

<Hello, Raven.>

There was a second's pause and he knew that the Mage was disgruntled.

<You're not following protocol. Suppose it wasn't me?>

Milo had a moment of satisfaction.

<I knew it was. What are you hatching now, you old troublemaker?>

He felt the chuckle down the link. <Never you mind. Just be glad that I'm saving you from yet another long boring night of skulking in alleyways.>

<At least I have a comfortable bed that doesn't move. You honestly want me to trade it for a hammock?>

<There's nobody else I can trust with this.> The Master Mage's voice was suddenly serious and Milo was instantly wary.

<So, it's not routine?>

<If you mean smugglers and separatists, definitely not. Get here as soon as you can. They're ferrying crew back and forth. You're already vouched for so you shouldn't have any trouble.>

Raven was being his usual cryptic self, Milo thought in exasperation. What didn't he want to tell him over the link? <Are you going to tell me what's going on?>

<When you arrive. Get a move on. End Sending>

Milo was left hanging for the second time that morning. He stared at himself in the shaving mirror, adjusted his coat collar and headed down to the bar. He'd grab some food before he left, at the very least. Best to start his day with a full stomach.

"Master Milo." The landlord greeted him as he walked past. The Agent had been a regular at the tavern for many years and Casca valued his regulars, especially when they always settled up on time.

Milo leaned on the bar. "What've you got on the menu today, Casca?"

"Pie. Beef or pork."

"Beef, please."

"Veg and gravy?"

Milo considered his options. He really had to hurry.

"I'll take it to go. Oh, and I'm settling up."

Casca was used to Milo's abrupt arrivals and departures. "Right you are."

He disappeared to get the paperwork sorted and Milo cast an eye over the other customers. Most were sailors on shore leave, but there were a couple of businessmen talking animatedly in a corner.

"You off again then, Master Milo?" Cara breezed past with a tray of empties and took up position behind the bar.

"I am. Duty calls, alas." He gave her a smile and she batted her eyelashes at him.

"Have you seen the new Ship?" he asked her, just to make conversation. Cara's smile faltered for a second, before she regained her composure.

"Oh yes. She's very impressive!"

Her enthusiasm sounded forced and Milo was instantly alerted. He'd struck some sort of nerve there. Of course, Maia Abella had come from Portus, hadn't she?

"Did you know her?" he asked. Cara's eyes flickered and she leaned closer.

"She used to work here. Nearly got us all killed."

The Revenant. Several pieces clicked together in Milo's mind. He'd suspected there was a link, but hadn't been sure.

"I heard what happened. It must have been terrifying."

"I had to tell it where she was," Cara told him, her eyes filling with tears. "It would have ended me. It wasn't my fault!"

Milo pitied her. The woman had clearly been carrying the guilt for months. Maybe she even thought he was spying on her? People got strange notions sometimes.

"Of course wasn't your fault," he insisted. "You did what was necessary to save yourself and others. Put it from your mind. It's all over now, anyway. Nothing's going to be coming for you. The thing's gone, believe me."

Cara exhaled. "I hope she doesn't blame me."

"The Ship?"

"Yes."

"I doubt she knows, and even if she did, you weren't unkind to her, were you?"

"Oh no!"

He patted her work-roughened hand. "It's fine. I bet she's happy that you're unharmed and she's installed now, so it all worked out, didn't it?" Cara's face cleared. "There, that's better." Casca bustled back with a bagged-up pie and his receipt. Cara shot Milo a look of gratitude as he tucked a coin into her apron with a wink.

"There you go," the landlord said. "Have a safe trip and hopefully we'll see you again before too long."

"Thanks, Casca."

He paid, then grabbed the pie in one hand and his bag in the other before heading out on to the crowded quayside. He didn't know why sometimes people felt the need to tell him their worries, but he was glad that he'd been able to help Cara rid herself of her guilt. He had to admit to himself that, under the circumstances, he would probably have done the same.

\*

*Tempest* rode at anchor in the calm harbour, enjoying the milder weather now that Aprilius had arrived. The reception had been and gone, much to her relief. It had mostly consisted of a long round of introductions and speeches, with Portus worthies enjoying themselves at the Navy's expense. Now that the formalities were over, she would soon be free to continue on her way. All of her crewmen had been signed on, straggling aboard to stow their belongings and adjust to their new situation, whilst waiting for their new mates to return from their jollies on shore.

Maia was grateful that her memory seemed to have returned to normal. Ships generally had superior computational and retrieval abilities, essential to the work they did, but her attribute was a bonus. It was the one thing she could truly call her own.

She tried not to think of the unexpected gifts bestowed on her by the *Livia*, even though they had saved her life. They had no relevance now. Unleashing fire wasn't something any Ship would want to do and surely that one time it had been triggered by Nemesis' intervention. There hadn't been any sign of it since.

This voyage was as much for her to become accustomed to her new life as it was for the men who served aboard her. Her vessel was now fully crewed and she would be expected to know everybody's name and details, from her Captain down to the lowliest powder monkey. That was a lot of sailors, even though she didn't need as many as an inanimate; there were still warrant sea officers, interior warrant officers, petty officers, idlers, seamen and that wasn't counting her complement of marines, led by a captain and his own officers.

Naturally, there were some who'd work more closely with her than the majority, who would mostly see her at a distance, but she had to be ready and able to assist any who asked for her help at any time of the day and night. She was their guide, their compass and their protection against the perils of the sea and so it would remain, barring destruction of her vessel or her own dissolution. Maia pushed away thoughts of what she would become after the passage of several centuries.

She scanned her vessel, noting who was still aboard and running through the shore lists, so as to be ready when the men returned. It wasn't unknown for some to go missing, either by design or accident, and she had to be prepared to spot any discrepancies immediately. The younger members of her crew were kept aboard for their own safety, especially if they had no family to meet them in port.

Some of the latter comprised the half dozen eager faces clustered in the galley to listen to one of her cook's stories. Pertinax had a reputation for telling tales and this time he had a rapt audience of Ship's boys, all hanging on his every word whilst making the most of the dinner he'd provided. Light duties in port meant they had more time for leisure; that would change when they were back out at sea and their days would be filled with schooling and duties. These weren't the superior class of midshipmen, but boys from the gun crew whose task it was to fetch powder during drills and battle. Their teachers would be the senior members of their little group, but today they had some time off and had come to pester her cook. He was already in full flow.

"Tentacles as big around as a horse's belly, there were. Dozens of 'em, writhing like a pot o' mad snakes up the sides of the vessel an' a-grabbin' anythin' they could!"

One boy, eyes like saucers, paused in the act of shovelling in a mouthful of stew.

"Did it eat 'em?"

"Aye, Sprout. It dragged 'em under, towards its great beak. Then it smashed their vessel into matchsticks!" He crushed an imaginary vessel between his fingers. "Bodies everywhere. We steered clear. Some of the lads were for tryin' to rescue them as still lived, so the Cap'n checked with our Priest first. 'E said we could have a go as the Gods had spared 'em, but there were only 'alf-a-dozen and one of 'em died anyway."

The boys looked suitably impressed.

"An' that's why yer don't insult the Gods of the Sea by usin' dolphins fer target practice, lads. Turned out that them we saved 'ad objected, but their officers were drunk. Wouldn't 'ave 'appened on a Navy Ship. That's why yer stop yer mates from doin' summat stupid. Got it?"

Heads bobbed frantically.

"Will we see krakens?" Sprout was full of questions. He was from the Foundling Home too, Maia remembered. Her flawless memory supplied a name. He'd come a few years after her. Vinicius, that was it, assigned his place in the alphabet as she had been. Sprout suited him better, with his round head and brown tufty hair that wouldn't lie flat, no matter what he did to it. The nickname seemed to have stuck.

"Let's 'ope not, eh? Anyway, this vessel's a big 'un, so it 'ud 'ave a job to get us. Besides, the Ship 'll spot anythin' that big, mark me words!" He ruffled Sprout's hair and the boy grinned back.

Satisfied that they were fed and cared for, Maia checked on the rest of the crew. The midshipmen hadn't been excused lessons and were being shown how to take readings to determine position, all dutifully logging their findings and taking it in turns to use the instruments.

"Mr Drustan, sir. Doesn't the Ship do all this for us?" one asked, clearly annoyed at having to do something he thought unnecessary. His bearing and crisp tones told her that he was upper-class and used to having things done for him. He'd be a younger son of some lord or other, she thought wryly, making a note of his attitude.

"Indeed she does, Mr Egnatius," the lieutenant replied, "but you can't always count on being assigned to a Ship and it would be a poor show if you ended up unable to perform the simplest of calculations, wouldn't it?"

Some of his fellows quietly smirked behind his back. Lordly Egnatius hadn't made many friends, for all his rank. Maia would have a word with Drustan later; she didn't want any trouble this early on and a few words could prevent any brewing up later.

Corax was checking his beloved stores so, after a quick word to confirm that all was well, she left him to it.

The only Mage currently aboard was Magpie. He'd arrived at first light, ferried across from the *Intrepid* who had finally made it to port. Maia already knew that she'd faced storms off Gaul as she'd spent the past hour telling everyone who'd listen all about it.

<Not seen waves that high for a bit,> she announced. <We had to have the shield up for longer than I liked.>

<I see you're getting a new Mage,> the *Swallow* said. She was a fourth-rate and seemed nice enough. Maia had had a little conversation with her and knew that she would shortly be heading into the Oceanus Germanicus on patrol.

<Yes. My loss is *Tempest*'s gain,> *Intrepid* replied. <I'm to be assigned Kittiwake. He's young, but keen.>

<Sounds like he's suited to a Ship, with a name like that.>

<I hope so. Not many seabirds around these days.>

<Not many of anythin',> *Persistence*'s raspy voice cut in. <There aren't any candidates, either.>

A ripple of unease ran through the link.

<We've had three lately, so I'm sure more will be found,> *Intrepid* offered hopefully.

<I 'ope yer right. We 'ad to wait long enough to get them.>

Interesting. Maia hadn't realised how worried her sister Ships were about the lack of suitable girls. *Blossom* had always seemed pragmatic about it. No wonder Jupiter had decided that she should go to the Navy; the gratitude and worship he'd receive would more than make up for the bending of his decree and, if there had been trouble on Olympus, as Mercury had hinted, the King of the Gods would want every ounce of Potentia that worship could afford. It was all wheels within wheels and she'd been but a tiny cog in the machinery of events.

<How did you find Magpie? Anything I should know?> she Sent to *Intrepid.*

<Very competent,> Intrepid answered promptly. <Is it true that you have Raven?>

<Yes.>

<Well, you'll be well protected. I've heard they've worked together before, so you shouldn't have any clashes.>

<That's good.> Privately, Maia thought that if anyone tried it on with Raven, they'd soon be put in their place.

There was some more inconsequential chat, but Maia's attention was soon diverted by a hail from the shore.

<Ahoy, *Tempest!* I'm on my way back. Raven and Sabrinus are here too, so we'll share a boat.>

Her Captain sounded cheerful, as well he might be after a couple of days being wined and dined in Portus. She could tell that Leo was enjoying his new status as Captain of a Royal Ship. Obediently, she linked to her boat and prepared it to bring her officers across the short stretch of water to where she lay at anchor. A few minutes later, she reeled it in, feeling the added weight of its passengers. It wouldn't be long before she would receive her orders and make her way westwards. She had to admit that she was looking forward it. Being in Portus had brought back some unpleasant memories.

"Captain on board!" she announced.

The crew stood to attention as Leo made his way up and onto the deck, followed by Sabrinus and the robed figure of the Master Mage. Just after him came a smaller young man in the lighter-coloured robes of an apprentice. She'd seen Robin wearing them aboard *Blossom*, but he'd since graduated to full Mage, so this was somebody new. Maia scanned him carefully, wondering that she hadn't been told about him.

Her Captain and his second made their way down to the day cabin, but Raven approached her Shipbody, the youngster in tow.

"*Tempest*, may I present Little Owl, my new apprentice?"

"Greetings, Little Owl." Now that he was up close, she could see that he had black hair and a smooth, thin face. In truth, the lad didn't look old enough to be at this stage of his training, but he might be small for his age. He looked her straight in the eye, seemingly unworried by her martial appearance.

"Greetings, *Tempest*. I'm honoured to be aboard. Please call me Owl, as there aren't any others to confuse the issue."

Maia felt the shock ripple through her. She knew without any doubt exactly who Raven's new apprentice was. What plot was this?

<What in the name of all the Gods are you doing, Raven?>

<Hah! I knew there was no fooling you. Give me a minute and I'll explain.>

<You better had!>

"Owl is here to complete his training," Raven said aloud. "I want him somewhere he'll be safe. I don't want him to get into trouble."

<Trouble? That's what you've brought me!> she snapped at him, whilst outwardly she remained calm.

"The Master Mage will show you to your quarters presently," she said sweetly, resisting the temptation to add, 'Princess'. What was the old man playing at? Was Julia in danger? "We must talk, Raven."

She gave him one of her best meaningful looks, which was wasted on him, but he inclined his head at her tone.

"Of course, ma'am."

She supervised the return of several more boatloads of bleary-eyed sailors before bearding him in his cabin. Magpie was on deck showing Owl around and Polydorus was absent, so she had him all to herself. She emerged from the bulkhead and crossed her arms, watching as he ran his fingers along a shelf. She could see that the jars were labelled with raised markings. He moved so confidently that sometimes she forgot he was blind.

"Well?"

He broke off his task and muttered a word. She felt the silence spring up around them as he hid their conversation from others. Raven forestalled her next question.

"It's best if we talk normally, then anyone will assume it's government business. If we just stand here it will look strange."

110

"There's nobody here but us."

"Good, but it pays to be cautious. Yes, Owl's the Princess and yes, she's still going to be married, but she's also got a large amount of Potentia. If I don't train her, she'll be a danger to herself and others."

Maia found it hard to believe. "Doesn't anyone else know?"

"No. It came upon her suddenly about a year ago. She was a late bloomer."

"But why all the subterfuge? Couldn't you train her at the palace?"

He sighed. "I *have* been training her at the palace. That's why I've been away so much, but now you need me too so the best thing was to bring her here. Hawthorn and Magpie know, but nobody else does. I can't risk the news leaking out."

Maia was shocked. "But where do people think she is?"

"At Juno's temple in Portus. Claudia Modesta, the High Priestess there, is in on it and is covering for us. We'll go along the coast and back, then she'll be smuggled back into the temple and leave to board the *Augusta* with due pomp, on her way to Gaul. The Gods know that I wish she didn't have to, but there it is."

"And you thought I wouldn't realise? A change of hair and clothes and suddenly nobody will notice?"

"Actually, no," he said, wryly. "Most people don't have your powers of memory and observation. They expect to see a boy, so that's what they see."

"But surely Leo will know her?"

"Yes. So I cast a glamour on her. To him and everybody else, she appears as a fair-haired and slightly spotty youth."

"I didn't see that."

"No. I wonder why?" He tilted his head. "Maybe it's your heritage allowing you to see what's really there."

"Maybe."

"I'll have to test that," he said. He gestured and abruptly his shape rippled as if obscured by smoke, resolving back into himself. "What do you see now?"

"You."

"Not a strapping young man?"

"No."

He grimaced. "You definitely have a gift. It might come in useful one day. We'll have to work on it. Have you ever seen supernormal beings, apart from Gods?"

Where should she start? "A few."

"Fae?" Maia remembered the helpful little sprites she had met in the forest.

"Yes. Minor Fae helped me during my trial."

He lifted his chin. "Ah. Not many can see the wee folk, or the spirits of the land."

"One was busy stuffing himself with my picnic, so I could hardly miss him."

Raven smiled. "But that's just it. Ordinary mortals would have." He closed his eyes and Maia knew that he was remembering the naiad he had spoken to, so long ago.

"We're not ordinary."

"No. And neither is Julia. I think that all the Potentia of her forebears has surfaced in her. Oh, why couldn't she have been born male?"

Maia felt a stab of outrage on the Princess' behalf. "Because Potentia isn't the exclusive right of over-privileged men!"

He held out his hands in appeasement. "You're right, but it would have been easier. She'd be King and her younger brother would be off messing about to his heart's content, with nobody worse off. As it is, he's an idiot and she's to be bartered away like a parcel of fish." He ran his hand over his face. "I'm too old for this."

"I'll help where I can," she told him. It would be nice to have female company, if only for a short time.

He smiled at her, his face stretching into a mass of wrinkles. "Thank you."

"But don't forget – you have to spend time with me too!"

He arched a brow. "Why, ma'am, are you jealous?"

They laughed together at the thought.

*

Milo sat in the boat with the other sailors and watched the *Tempest*'s flanks grow in size as they drew nearer. She truly was

112

big, dwarfing many of the other Ships that were anchored nearby or drawn up against the harbour walls for loading and unloading.

His companions talked quietly among themselves, or stared ahead, lost in thoughts of their own as they returned to work. A couple dozed, still clearly the worse for drink and probably lamenting the fact that for now the fun was over. The seaman to his left caught his eye. His enormous sideburns and bulbous nose reminded Milo of Silenus, the cheerful old companion of the God Bacchus, though this man didn't carry as much extra weight.

"Haven't I seen you at The Anchor?" the older man said. Milo smiled.

"You have. I stay there sometimes, when I'm in port."

"You'll know Casca then?"

"I do. Damn good beer, eh?" The man's face split into a smile, showing the stumps of teeth.

"Aye, yer right there!" He held out a hand. "Hyacinthus is the name, and this is Teg."

"Milo." He didn't see the need to adopt a pseudonym, as it was common enough.

"We got given our names 'cos of our great beauty, didn't we?" Hyacinthus jabbed his mate, who fixed Milo with a bleary eye. The Agent suppressed a laugh. Teg had to be a nickname, as no-one could call him 'the beautiful one' without sniggering.

"That's right," Teg said, amiably enough. "We're on the guns."

"I serve the Mages," Milo said, further information having been finally Sent by a distracted Raven.

Teg pulled a face. He was one of those men who'd be able to swallow his own nose, much to the amusement of all. "Can you do magic, then?"

"Me? I'm only a servant," Milo hastened to say. He stopped himself from elaborating on his previous naval experience. If they thought he was beneath them, it would be better.

"Ah. I guess it has its own perils, eh?" Teg said.

"If yer don't look lively, they'll make yer 'op to it!" Hyacinthus said, with glee. Milo stared at him blankly.

"'*op to it!* When they turn yer into a toad!" the old sailor announced, delighted at his own wit and looking around to see if anyone else had got the joke. Milo smiled ruefully.

"I've 'eard things about that Raven," Hyacinthus continued. "Yer don't mess with 'im."

"Absolutely not."

"'E once turned a boatload of pirates into fish!"

That was a new one. "Really?"

"Oh aye. Best keep on 'is good side."

"I'll certainly try to."

Hyacinthus subsided, satisfied that he'd said his piece. Teg leaned over, his rubbery face screwed up in puzzlement.

"What sort o' fish?"

"Dunno, Teg. Why don't yer ask 'im yerself? I'll be ready ter throw ye overboard when yer floppin' about on deck."

They were still bickering over the question when they reached the *Tempest* and began the scramble up her flanks. The sailors shot up like so many monkeys. Milo followed, looking around and hoping to spot the Ship herself, but the vessel was so large, she could have been anywhere.

He gave his name to the lieutenant on duty, who checked his list and pointed the way to the Mage quarters, aft and near to the Captain's own. As Milo made his way there, he marvelled at the space available on this new vessel; he was more used to being crammed in cheek by jowl and having no room to move. Maybe he'd even have a little bed for himself, instead of having to sling a hammock from the beams.

He found the door and knocked, sliding it back as a voice bid him enter.

"Milo, reporting for duty, sir."

The Mage looked up and fixed him with a pair of piercing eyes. This had to be Magpie. His tight black curls were already showing signs of silver, though his brown skin was unlined. Milo guessed that the man had to be in his forties and wondered if he found his new position galling as, with his experience, the Mage was well able to have a Ship of his own.

"Ah, Master Milo. Welcome aboard. Raven has told me of you."

"Only good things, I hope?"

Magpie grinned. "Of course! You'll be mostly attending to me and Raven's new apprentice, Owl."

Milo's eyebrows rose.

"He didn't mention that he'd taken on an apprentice."

"Oh yes. He'll want a word with you about that. I'm aware of your calling, though I'm the only one Raven has confided in, so to everyone else you're a servant."

"I understand."

"It'll be the usual stuff."

"No problem. I've done a lot worse." Milo had had many jobs in his time. One thing that could be said for the life of an Agent was that it was rarely boring for long.

"Excellent! There's a cubby hole for you behind that curtain."

Milo followed his eyes to a space containing a little bed and a chest, where he could put the few possessions he'd brought with him. Compared to most berths it was luxurious.

"Raven wants to see you before you start work," Magpie continued. Milo could already tell that the Mage's mind was on other things and wondered what his specialism was. Knowing Raven, he'd probably picked someone with a bent for devices. There weren't too many clues in Magpie's cabin, but he might see more in the main area.

Milo poked his head into the cubbyhole and dropped his bag on the bed.

"I take it he's in the workroom?"

"He is."

"Then I'll go now, sir." He inclined his head as any humble servant would and caught the flash of a grin from Magpie. Good – the man had a sense of humour.

The main working area was at the end of the corridor and took up the whole width of the stern, taking advantage of the light afforded by the large windows and directly below the Captain's quarters. He went in to find Raven standing next to a table, showing a lad in apprentice robes a cunningly constructed maze of tubing and bottles.

"This should distil the root sufficiently for our purposes."

The boy turned as Milo entered. He had a pimply face and round features, topped with a shock of fair hair. Milo was about to greet him, when the stone around his neck gave off a shrill warning.

Fae magic! The dagger was out and his hand was on the apprentice before the youth could let out even a squeak. Milo's arm snaked around his neck as he jerked the boy's head back, dagger at his throat…

…and the *Tempest* erupted from the floor.

"Stop!" she bellowed, her silver mask inches from his face. "There's no danger!"

Milo felt a stasis spell snap around him. The Ship's black eyes met his own and he felt a shiver run through him. She looked like an angry Goddess, with her flying hair and armoured body, as if Nemesis herself had appeared to seek vengeance.

"Oh, Gods! I forgot you had the stone!" Raven slapped himself on the forehead in frustration. "Milo, it's all right. He's under a spell, but I put it there. You'll find out why in just a minute."

*Tempest* regarded the Agent, her face immobile.

"Back off, *Tempest*. Milo, stand down. This is all my fault."

The Ship glanced at her Mage, then retreated. Raven gestured and the spell encasing Milo vanished with a tiny pop, allowing him to release the boy, who scuttled over to his master, eyes starting from his head. The stone's warning grew louder and Milo winced. Only then did he realise that he was still holding his dagger and slowly tucked it away again, his eyes never leaving Raven's.

"A little misunderstanding," Raven said. A gesture from him silenced the alarm, leaving Milo's ears ringing in sympathy. He felt a muting spell rise to replace the binding. "Your Highness, may I present Agent Milo, who's charged with your security whilst you are aboard *Tempest*."

Milo's mouth dropped. *Your Highness*? He squinted at the boy, calling up his meagre skill in *revelare* magic and caught a brief glimpse of female features. He swallowed and dropped to one knee.

"Your Royal Highness," he said, hoarsely. Suddenly, everything he'd heard about Julia from Raven made perfect sense. Still, she'd been the last thing he was expecting.

The Princess smiled, causing Milo to have double vision again.

"Don't worry, Agent. I blame Raven for this." She cast a cool eye on her mentor, who stared ahead innocently. "But what is this stone you mentioned?"

*Tempest* remained to one side. Milo could tell nothing from her expression, but he knew she wasn't pleased.

"It's a singing stone that alerts the wearer to Fae glamours. I gave it to him as a protection, but the magic was too alike and it caused a false alarm."

Too alike? Milo filed that fact away for further reference. There had long been questions about where Mages received their Potentia, though most assumed it was from the Gods.

"I apologise," Raven said, a little grumpily. He was embarrassed, and with good cause. "I had hoped to see you first," he added, though Milo decided he was just trying to save face.

"Oh well, no harm done," Julia said, rubbing her neck. "I think that was an excellent demonstration of your skills, Master Milo. I've never seen anyone move that fast. Please rise."

He did so and stood, slightly awkwardly.

"If I'm not needed here," *Tempest* said, pointedly, "I've a vessel to run."

"Of course. Thank you, *Tempest*."

The Ship nodded respectfully to Julia and sank into the floor, which rippled briefly in her wake. Milo resisted the urge to let forth a juicy oath. This wasn't the way he'd have wanted to meet royalty. If Caniculus ever heard of it, he'd be sunk.

"Well, Milo," Raven began. "I'd better brief you on your mission, hadn't I?"

\*

The other Ships' good wishes echoed in Maia's head as she weighed anchor, set sail on the evening tide and headed off into the west to rendezvous with the Flagship.

"We're to escort the *Augusta* back to Portus," Leo told her as they stood together on the quarterdeck. "Then we'll join with the royal convoy to take the Princess to her new husband. Artorius wants a show of strength and power that will be reported all over the Empire."

"It's an important occasion," she agreed, watching dolphins leap playfully under her bow.

"It is." His face darkened for a moment. "We all hate to lose her, but she knows her duty."

Maia sighed to herself. Duty, obedience and all the rest. She couldn't imagine what it must feel like to be free, unless that meant starving on the streets, a fate she once feared lay in store for her. It pleased her that Julia would have some time without her responsibilities. The Princess was wisely keeping out of Leo's way; easy to do on such a large vessel. Plus, as a very junior Mage, she wouldn't always be invited to dine with the Captain. It had all so nearly ended in tragedy. The Agent, Milo, had been like a striking cobra.

Ahead, the sun's chariot was sinking into the waves, staining sky and sea with red and gold. It was going to be a good day tomorrow, with the wind in her sails and the open water before her. Below decks, the dog watch were readying themselves to take over for the night, led by Amphicles, though her watch was constant and unceasing. She liked to talk to her men as they worked by night, keeping up their spirits against the darkness. It was a time to check on the others too, as they rested after the labours of the day. Sometimes the boys would be missing their families, or want a story and she would be there for them, too. It was all part of a Ship's life and *Blossom* had taught her well. The resentment she'd felt after her initiation had faded to acceptance and the knowledge that the Ship had genuinely cared for her, despite what Ceridwen had said. There had to have been a reason for the woman's cynicism, but that was her problem, not Maia's.

As the watch changed and the officers departed below to dine, she decided to broach the subject with *Blossom*. Not having any candidates to train, her mentor was putting a crew of cadets through their paces instead.

<*Tempest* to *Blossom*!>

<*Tempest*! Good to hear from you!> The older Ship's voice was full of warmth and, Maia thought, a little relief.

They chatted for a while about the usual subjects of interest to Ships, which mostly consisted of the weather, new postings, and all the latest gossip.

<It's a pity you're not in Portus,> Maia reflected.

<I know! I'm just off Dubris. Guess who's anchored nearby?>

It couldn't be the *Patience*, as she'd returned to Gaul. <Not the *Regina*?>

<How did you know?> *Blossom* said cheerfully. <And I don't have to tell you that you've put her nose severely out of joint.>

Maia was puzzled. <Me? Why?>

<Because everyone's talking about you! The new Royal this and the new Royal that. She's having to grit her teeth and bear it.>

<So everyone's talking about me?> She hadn't heard that side of it.

<Oh yes. How big you are, plus the fact you've got Leo as Captain and Raven as Mage.>

<I'm glad that one of them knows what he's doing,> Maia muttered darkly.

*Blossom* laughed. <I trained you well! I think Leo will settle in soon enough. It won't be long before you turn around and he's an admiral, believe me. You just get used to them and they're gone.> She sighed. <It doesn't seem a minute since a certain young prince came aboard as a midshipman cadet, and look at him now. Enjoy the time you have together.>

Maia knew she would learn to take the long view. She decided to ask *Blossom* about Ceridwen directly. It would clear the air between them, if nothing else.

<I must ask you something,> she began. <When I was in the forest, some things were said that made me question a lot of things.>

She felt *Blossom*'s puzzlement.

<What things?>

<Oh, that the Navy just wanted Ships at any cost and you only cared about me because it was your job to.> The link went silent and Maia quailed inside. <Perhaps it's all part of the trial?> she suggested. Sowing doubts would weed out all but the most committed, but her friend *Patience* hadn't said anything. Then again, if she thought it was part of the Mysteries, she wouldn't have.

<I've not heard of anything like that,> *Blossom* said slowly, <and it certainly wasn't done in my day. Of course, back then Ceridwen wasn't High Priestess. Have you mentioned this to Raven?>

<No,> she admitted.

<I'd say something to him and see what he makes of it.> The Ship sounded grave. <She didn't actively try to stop you, did she?>

<No.> Maia was definite about that. <She gave me good advice, but I got the feeling that she didn't think I'd succeed.>

<It's not up to her. But…I do wonder….>

<What?>

<I told you about the girl who failed, didn't I?>

<Yes. You said that she had to be virtually dragged off to initiation and that was the last you saw of her.>

<Yes, naturally you remember,> *Blossom* replied. <But I didn't tell you that she was Ceridwen's daughter, did I?>

That would explain a lot, but if Ceridwen was somehow trying to stop new Ships being created, she hadn't been successful, as the three of them had all come through the trials, though in her case it had been a close thing.

<Perhaps she thinks it's her duty to make sure we're fully committed,> she told *Blossom*.

<Maybe.> Maia could tell that she wasn't convinced. <But I'd still tell Raven. He'll know what to do.>

Maia promised she would and left the conversation feeling more confused than ever. Had she been wrong to bring it up at all? Maybe all she'd done was to open up a Pandora's Box? All in all, she wished she'd left the subject alone.

She sighed to herself, then, mind fixed firmly on her duty, she sailed her vessel westwards into the gathering dark.

# VI

As promised, the dawn brought fine weather. Leo breakfasted well, then called his officers to the day room for the morning briefing. Everyone filed in and Maia took up position on her accustomed place on the wall, nodding greetings as the men appeared. They made a respectful space for Raven, who made his way unerringly to her Captain's right hand and stood, hands tucked inside his robes, his frail figure a strange contrast to the strapping officers clustered around him.

<Morning. How is the Princess doing?> she Sent.

<She started feeling sick,> Raven replied. <I've dosed her up with Magic Drops and she's having a lie–in.>

<The privileges of rank?> She sensed his amusement, though he gave no outward sign.

<Not at all. I didn't want her puking up as I was eating.>

She chortled silently. Julia must take after her uncle, as he was rumoured to be a poor sailor until he got his sea–legs.

Just then, Leo started speaking.

"As you all know, our orders are to meet up with the *Augusta* and escort her back to Portus. It's been a smooth trip so far, thank the Gods, but I want to know the second anything seems off. *Tempest*, report please."

"Only minor adjustments needed so far, Captain," she said. "Nothing a little grease hasn't solved. I've been over the main structure with Master Vestinus."

"All seems sound, sir," her carpenter agreed. "The lads at Durobrivis have done a bang-up job."

"Excellent. I hope to make a good report to the Admiral. *Tempest*, time of the rendezvous?"

"At our current speed we should sight her at eleven hundred hours and thirty-four minutes, sir."

Maia had already fixed the *Augusta*'s current position at fifty-five nautical miles off Bolerium, the Place of Storms which most people just called Land's End for obvious reasons. She was headed west-south-west; thus they would meet about halfway between Kernow and the Isles of Sillina.

"That gives us about two and a half hours then, gentlemen. We must be prepared to greet the Flagship and fire a salute. Admiral Pendragon will perform a full inspection and I want everything gleaming. Is that understood?"

"Aye, Captain," all replied.

"He and his senior officers will be coming aboard to dine. This is our chance to impress. Any questions?"

There weren't, so Leo dismissed them and settled down with Sabrinus to the business of the day. Maia reported on the weather and relayed routine communications back and forth to the Admiralty, whilst Osric drilled his men on deck and Musca checked the cannons. She knew that it was vital to make a good impression and was pleased to see that things were going smoothly. She could sense her Captain's excitement and nervousness, but didn't think he had anything to worry about.

She scanned the skies for any hint of bad weather, but everything was clear. In fact the breeze was being particularly helpful, blowing steadily from the east to help her on her way. Maia looked carefully to see if there were any tell-tale flashes of silver, but couldn't see anything. She hadn't seen Pearl since she was named and hoped that the Tempestas would appear before too long so they could catch up. She had the feeling that Aura was about, but knew that the only way the Goddess could communicate was by sending a fair wind, which after all was the best thing any Ship could ask for. She would ask Danuco to provide a sacrifice as soon as they were on their way back as thanks, but Maia reminded herself not to always count on her mother's attentions. Natural powers also held sway and Aura couldn't spend all her time and attention watching just one Ship. Still, she offered up a quiet prayer and fancied that the breeze blew just that little bit harder in response.

<*Tempest*. Please contact the *Augusta* and confirm rendezvous position,> her Captain ordered. She suppressed a smile. He was very polite.

She acknowledged and complied, opening the link and Sending the message.

<*Tempest* to *Augusta*.>

There was a long pause before the reply came – much longer than she was used to, even in her limited experience.

<This is *Augusta*.> The Ship sounded weary, like an aged dame who was already fading into her memories of the past. <Who is this?>

<This is *Tempest*, ma'am. I'm to confirm the point of rendezvous.>

Silence stretched over the link and Maia knew immediately that something was wrong.

<Ma'am? *Augusta*?>

"Captain, something's wrong with the *Augusta*," she said. Leo looked up in alarm as the *Augusta* finally spoke.

<All Ships! The enemy is sighted! Keep formation and prepare to fire on Admiral Titus' command!>

Cold dread shot through Maia, as she realised that the Flagship was reacting to something that was not of this time and place. The *Augusta* had broadcast widely and other Ships began to react in bewilderment and alarm. Another, male voice broke into the link.

<All Ships, this is Pendragon. Disregard the last message. The *Augusta* is failing. I repeat, the *Augusta* is failing. *Tempest*, proceed here with all speed. We're having to bind her.>

His voice was calm, but he was unable to hide his distress.

"By the Gods! Full sail!" Leo snapped aloud as confusion continued to pour from the stricken Flagship.

<I'm too far out!> That was the *Diadem*, rapidly echoed by several others, including the *Victoria*, the *Empress* and several other smaller Ships, all of whom were too far away to do anything to help. The link was filled with oaths and frantic communications, until the *Victoria* cut through them all.

<Be quiet, all of you! *Tempest*, you're the nearest. Keep trying to talk to her and keep her going. She can't fail so far from land.>

<She isn't answering!>

<Try anyway. Do what you can to reach her. Thank the Gods that the Admiral is aboard and can keep us informed. Use your Mages too – they have speechstones.>

The older Ship knew what she was talking about.

<Raven!> Maia Sent frantically.

<I've heard. I'm contacting Cormorant now.>

<*Victoria* says to try and talk to her!>

<Do it.>

Maia reached out through the link. <*Augusta*! Respond!>

All she got was a burst of confusion. Maia stretched out, willing the connection with all her power, and...

...*she was in the midst of battle.* The sea around her was filled with shattered debris and bodies that stained the ocean with murky clouds of blood. The remaining enemy Longships were ahead, their animal spirits howling and shrieking to urge on their crews. The *Britannia* had been rammed and was listing. Her Mages had accounted for at least two of their attackers who were slowly sinking, but it would be all the Ship could do to keep afloat. Spells hurtled between vessels as conjured blasts sought to disable the enemy.

<*Augusta*! I'm not much help to you like this!> the *Britannia* Sent.

<Concentrate on yourself and get out if you can,> she ordered. <Prepare to disengage and let me in!>

She was confident that her rowers were strong enough to get her vessel between the battle and her stricken sister, but it wouldn't be much use if she was hit by a stray spell. Titus was shouting to her Mage.

"Raven! Prepare to drop the shield!" Titus' face was strained, but she felt his determination through the strong bond they shared and loved him all the more for it.

"Aye, sir!" Raven called back. He was already punching holes in the shimmering barrier to shoot fireballs that slammed into the wooden hulls, holing them below the water line. Despite his appearance, he was the strongest of their Mages and had already single-handedly destroyed over half-a-dozen of the spirit-bound Longships. Over to her dexter side, the *Dragon* was accounting for another of the barbarians, despite half her oars being sheared away. Her Mage seemed to be down, but a steady stream of arrows poured from her flanks to find their mark.

Her own rowers, aided by the power she provided, were pulling strongly to get her vessel to intercept the enemy, as the *Fortuna*, the *Sceptre* and the *Fortitude* moved to assist. The

Northmen's line had already been smashed, leaving them weakened and vulnerable.

<I can't attack!> the *Dragon* Sent. <I haven't enough power!>

<I have!> came the answer, as the *Lioness* charged through the water, her great ram parting the waves. Directly ahead of her was a Longship with a spirit in the form of a great stag. The *Lioness* roared in defiance, as she smashed into the enemy's prow, to be answered by a grunting bark of agony from the stag as his vessel was mangled beneath him. It began taking on water immediately, forcing some of his defenders overboard to cling to whatever wreckage they could find. The enemy Ship, seeing that he had lost his chance, detached and swam away as fast as he could. The stag would have to take his chances and try to get to one of his fellows, just as the *Honour* and several other smaller vessels, too damaged to stay afloat, had done already.

The *Lioness* began to back out, her crew cheering as the abandoned vessel heeled over and was rapidly swallowed by the ocean, leaving the field clear for her sister. Titus ordered her to drop her shields so that her crew could pour Greek fire on the last of the Northmen's Ships. The crew went up like torches, burning bodies falling like meteors into the sea as the deck was consumed. The wolf at the prow howled and raged, so close that she could see his slavering jaws and rolling eyes, but he knew his time was up. Another spirit was forced to abandon his vessel and crew to their fate.

<We've got 'em!> Titus was jubilant and his weary men echoed his sentiments. The Britannic Ships were mopping up the stragglers as the last of the seaworthy Longships were limping away, as fast as their spirits could sail them. He turned to her Shipbody and gazed into her eyes, a grin on his sweat-stained face, and she returned his smile, stretching out her arms to him as he stepped towards her.

And pitched forward into her arms. She stared in frozen horror at the arrow in his back. Across the water, a last defiant Northman yelled in triumph and waved a bow. A second later he was felled in his turn, but it was too late for her Admiral.

<*Martia...*>

Titus raised his head and his brown eyes met hers before the life within flickered out, only blankness remaining…

…and Maia was snapped back, still reeling from the *Augusta*'s agony.

Her training kicked in. Emotion forced aside, she ran a lightning check through her systems. She had been gone for exactly two seconds.

<*Tempest*! Can you get through to her?> Leo demanded.

<I think she's going.> Maia could now see the *Augusta* on the far horizon. At this speed it wouldn't be long before she reached her. The Flagship was drifting, her sails limp. Maia half–expected to see floating bodies and blood on the waters, but all was calm.

<They're lowering the anchors manually,> Raven reported.

Maia tried once more to raise the stricken Ship.

<*Augusta*?>

There was a breathless pause, then the *Augusta* gave a great cry.

<My Admiral!>

There was a burst of joy then, abruptly, emptiness. All sense of the Flagship's presence was snuffed out. Maia recoiled as the other Ships wailed their loss, feeling as if she were standing on tiptoe at the edge of a great void. The *Augusta* was gone.

The shockwave rippled through the fleet. Wherever they were in the Empire, every Ship had felt the passing of one of their own and not only that, but the oldest and wisest of them. Their grief flew across oceans, from the southern seas to the distant shores of the New Continent back to the Mediterranean and the heart of Empire.

Raven moved first, making a beeline for Leo.

"We have to recover her quickly. Only the Gods know who else is about and we can't risk unfriendly powers making the most of an opportunity."

"They wouldn't dare, surely?" Leo asked him, his face showing the shock they were all feeling.

"Who knows? There are pirates and worse. We don't need a fleet of Longships to come and offer their 'help'. The longer we can keep this under wraps, the better."

Sure enough, Maia felt the Admiralty link open.

<New orders, Captain.> She relayed the message.

<*Tempest*. Proceed to the remains of the *Augusta* and report on the situation. Follow Admiral Pendragon's orders. Keep us informed. Albanus, Admiralty.>

She Sent an acknowledgement and stood with her Captain as she grew closer to the now inanimate vessel. She felt Leo's shock and pain, together with Raven's sadness, which was mirrored by her crew, many of whom stood with tears running down their cheeks. The death of a Ship was a terrible thing and many of her hands had served aboard the *Augusta* in years past.

"Cormorant reports that Admiral Pendragon is bearing up well," Raven said quietly.

Leo nodded. "He must be devastated. He loved her more than his wife."

"So he did."

*But she didn't love him half as much as she loved Admiral Titus,* Maia thought. His death, so long ago, had broken her heart. No wonder she'd always seemed a little distant. A girl who had once been called Martia had died that day too, even though she must have known that there wouldn't be a happy ending for either of them. It had been her doom to live for centuries without him. Maia hoped that wherever they were now they were together, perhaps running happily through the Elysian Fields in an eternal summer, never to be parted again.

It was too much. She turned away from them, struggling to find her composure.

<Are you all right?> Both Raven and Leo were concerned, though it had been Raven who spoke.

"I felt what she felt, at the end," she said. "She was reliving the Battle of the Oceanus Germanicus and the death of Admiral Titus. She loved him."

Leo looked startled, but Raven nodded. "I know. She never really recovered from his loss."

They were almost at the vessel now and the many questions that Maia had for her Mage would have to wait. Leo took a deep breath.

"*Tempest*, shorten sail and heave-to. I'm going aboard to see what the Admiral has to say. Sabrinus, take command."

"Aye, sir."

127

The young lieutenant took up position next to Maia, his telescope trained on the other vessel. He reminded her of his father, but she'd seen none of the slyness and cunning she associated with the Admiral. Her second-in-command was an earnest and diligent officer and he was rapidly earning her respect.

"I think it best that I accompany you," Raven told Leo. His Captain thought for a second, then nodded.

"Very well. I think the Admiral will welcome your support."

Maia lowered a boat and the men climbed down, relying on her motive power to travel across to the inanimate. She could see the deck clearly now. Pendragon wasn't in sight, but the vessel was a hive of activity as her crew began to rig her for manual. Everything the Ship had done automatically would now be the responsibility of her crew, from navigation to steering and making sail. The *Augusta*'s absence felt huge, not only because of her status, but because her guiding presence had always been there. The thought that she was gone was almost too much to bear.

<All Ships!>

It was the *Victoria*. She was now the oldest of them and the *Augusta*'s responsibilities had passed to her.

<We have suffered a grievous loss, but we continue. I have seen more Ships pass than any of you, but still the Fleet survives. We have our new sisters, *Patience*, *Regina* and *Tempest*, who will carry our traditions into the future and take us from strength to strength. Hold your heads high! This is *Victoria*! Gods save Britannia! Gods save the King!>

The Ships answered, one by one, oldest to youngest until at last it was Maia's turn.

<This is *Tempest*. Gods save Britannia! Gods save the King!>

The Ships fell silent, each turning to their own Captains and crews for comfort in the days ahead.

Had the *Augusta* still thought of herself by her human name, or had Martia faded over the years? Maia thought she was the last person in the world to know the answer to that question.

*

128

The remainder of the day was spent securing the *Augusta*'s vessel and preparing to tow her back to port at the mouth of the River Fal, in Kernow. There, it would be stripped of its guns and devices before being decommissioned.

<What will happen to the hulk?> Maia asked *Blossom*, who was on hand to offer comfort to the younger Ships.

<I think it will be taken out and sunk,> the older Ship replied, sadness dripping through the link like falling tears. <Would you want to reuse anything that had been hers? She was due a new vessel anyway and had been for a couple of years. I think the Navy saw this coming and put it off. If you ask me, they waited too long. She would have gone soon anyway, but the pressure on the Admirals to keep her active was too great.>

Maia could only agree. She remembered wondering if the Ship was failing in her wits when *Augusta* referred to Pendragon as Titus.

<It was so sad!> the *Cameo* said. <We all heard her cry out for Pendragon at the end. The poor man!>

Maia didn't contradict her, though she had the feeling that Pendragon knew that it wasn't his face that the dying Ship saw at the last. As much as he'd loved her, he could never have taken the place of Titus.

A message from Leo confirmed what she'd thought. <Some of my crew are going to man the vessel,> she said.

There were murmurs of sympathy from the others.

<This is hard on your first trip out,> *Blossom* said.

<I wonder who'll carry the Princess now?> the *Regina* cut in, with typical bluntness. <I'll ask my father if I can do it. I'm heading towards Portus right now, so that would make sense.>

Some things never changed. Maia didn't feel like arguing with the self-absorbed creature and resisted biting back, focusing instead on the preparations aboard the inanimate. She'd already had to relay the dismal scene to her sisters.

<She should 'ave been allowed ter slip away in port,> *Persistence* muttered. <It's a bloody disgrace!>

<Well, she's gone and we must all offer prayers,> *Blossom* said practically. <Also, please keep *Tempest* in your thoughts, as she's having to deal with everything on the spot.>

She was indeed. Another order came through. To ease progress, she was being ordered to come alongside the vessel and tie on, to expedite movement of men and resources. Obediently, she unfurled a little sail and nudged up to the inanimate, feeling a little like she was nestling up to a cold, dead thing. Glancing over to where the *Augusta*'s Shipbody had stood, she saw that it had transformed back into the ancient branch that had housed her *anima* for over five hundred years. All Potentia was gone; it was nothing more than a crumbling piece of old wood.

Sabrinus came back aboard and he, Drustan and Amphicles began allotting men to help with the inanimate, aided by the *Augusta*'s officers. Both crews were subdued, faces grim as they worked quietly without the usual banter.

<We're to make sail as soon as possible,> her Captain informed her. <You shouldn't have any trouble and the weather's set fair for the next couple of days.>

<Are you coming back aboard?> she inquired, already missing his presence.

<Yes. There's not much I can do here. The Admiral's refusing to leave just yet. I think he needs time to grieve.>

<I'll manage just fine,> she reassured him. <I'm sure that the wind will be in our favour.> She felt his curiosity at the remark, but he didn't press her.

<Make preparations. I'll be back in a few minutes, then we can take up position.>

<Aye, sir.>

She opened a link to Raven.

<Oh hello, Maia.> he sounded bone tired. <I'm with Pendragon now.>

<How is he?> She hated to think of him in pain.

<I told him that he needs to get very, very drunk, but he's refusing. Says he needs to see her vessel home.>

<It might be easier if he came aboard me,> she offered. <It can't be good for him there without her.>

She heard his exasperated grunt down the link. <There's no chance at the moment, though he might change his mind tomorrow. Don't bet on it, though.>

<Are you coming back with Leo?>

<Yes. Cormorant and Shearwater are more than capable of doing what's necessary.>

<What will happen to her Shipbody?>

<It will be taken back to the forest.>

Come to think of it, she'd seen some fallen branches around the grove of the Mother. The thought that they marked the graves of Ships was disconcerting, as was the realisation that it would be her eventual resting place too. Still, everything returned to the earth at some point. She tried not to think of the body of Martia, only now beginning its final dissolution in the ground, or of her own, buried there in the silence.

"Captain on deck!"

The shout brought her to attention and dispelled the morbid thoughts that had sidled into her mind. Leo strode on board and began to confer with Osric and Sabrinus, Raven following on. The old Mage made his way across the deck, stopping to talk to some of the hands and exchange messages of sympathy. When he finally made it to where Maia was standing, he somehow produced his staff from under his robes, though she'd have sworn it wouldn't have fitted there, and leaned on it with a sigh.

"That's that. Pendragon should be asleep now."

Really? I wouldn't have thought he would be willing to go to bed?"

"He wasn't. I drugged him," Raven said absently, his clouded eyes seemingly scanning the horizon.

He was probably the only Mage who would be able to get away with that.

"We need to talk," she told him, firmly.

"Oh yes, about Owl."

"No," she contradicted him. "Not about Owl. About what I saw and felt as the *Augusta* was dying."

Raven went very still – whitening knuckles as he clutched at his staff the only outward sign of his discomposure.

"You were there, as you are now. Five hundred years and you haven't changed a bit."

She was shocked to see moisture well up in his eyes as he drew in a sharp breath.

"Not here. Meet me in my cabin when you're able. For now, I think you need to be ready to take the vessel in tow."

He left her then, stumbling blindly away to his cabin, as if the weight of centuries had caught up with him at last.

*

There was a lot of manoeuvring and not a few oaths from all concerned, but by the end of the following morning, the shell of what had been the Navy's proud Flagship was secured and fastened to the *Tempest* with the thickest rope available. Maia was just waiting for the order to make sail, knowing that she would have to wait for the crew on the other vessel to climb the rigging and release the sails manually, after hauling up the heavy sea anchors. Until then, all she could do was hang around and twiddle her thumbs.

"Nearly ready," Leo reported. He frowned. "I wish we could get the Admiral over here. I think it would do him good to talk to a Ship."

"He'll have to leave at some point," Sabrinus said. "Sir, have you ever seen a Ship pass before?"

Leo shook his head. "No. The last one was a fourth–rate, the *Prosperity,* about three years ago, I believe. She'd just come into Noviomagus and her crew were granted shore leave. One minute she was there, the next, she was gone, but her Captain had seen it coming, so they had some warning." He cast a thoughtful gaze over the water. "I can't believe they didn't know she was failing."

Sabrinus raised his eyebrows. "It's hard to admit it, I suppose. They must have thought she had a few more years left in her."

Maia doubted that. If she'd picked up that something was wrong after a few brief conversations, surely her Admiral must have been alerted sooner. It was probably political, though surely it would have made more sense to retire the old Ship and let her go gently before Maia was named? Then the loss of her passing would have been eased by the celebrations around a new Ship. She knew the Navy was stretched, but a line had to be drawn somewhere. She was alerted as the Admiral's link opened. Unlike Captains, Admirals could Send to any Ship, which was coming in useful at the moment. He sounded his usual brisk self so the sleep must have done him good, involuntary or otherwise.

<Pendragon to *Tempest*. We are about to weigh anchor.>

<Acknowledged, Your Highness.>

As he broke off, there was a violent noise belowdecks, as many bells rang at once and a simultaneous pressure beneath her hull, as if something vast was rising from the depths.

"Kraken!" she shouted as the message was flashed across to the empty vessel.

"All hands! Battle stations!" Leo ordered.

Osric bellowed at his marines, who rushed to form up along her rail on both her dexter and sinistra sides, to load their muskets as quickly as they could in the hope that massed firepower would deter the creature. The sailors who weren't manning the guns grabbed axes to chop at anything that wormed its way over the side. Even Pertinax and his team snatched up knives and cleavers.

"No! Stop!"

Danuco forced his way through to the Captain. "It isn't a kraken!"

The chiming had become more insistent. The Priest turned to the nearest crewmen "Fetch the best and largest animal we have and all the gold. Now!"

Maia extended her undersea sensors as far as she could to the deep currents swirling beneath her hull. She couldn't make out what was down there, but something was approaching, rising upwards rapidly. Something big.

There was a similar commotion on the deck of the *Augusta* as a figure forced its way to the rail and leaned over the side before shouting and gesticulating to the crew. She could see it was their Priest and was momentarily puzzled. What could he see that she couldn't? Maia felt the enormous shape below emit a pulse of energy as it turned its attention to her. Suddenly she felt like a tiny piece of driftwood on the surface of a vast and bottomless ocean and had a familiar sense of being examined by a mind too large for her to comprehend.

"The God comes!" Danuco shouted, before heading amidships to where the altar stood. Frightened faces turned to follow his progress and the noise redoubled as the crew alerted their fellows.

"It's Neptune," Maia said quickly. "I've felt this kind of presence before."

She checked below, to see Magpie disconnecting the bells. The clamour shut off abruptly, then the younger Mage hurried to join his fellow Mages on deck. Julia was standing behind Raven, looking apprehensive but determined. She'd stayed in the Mage quarters at Raven's insistence, but clearly wanted to see what was going on, and the Ship didn't blame her. The Agent was hovering at her elbow, his gaze flickering back and forth as he assessed the danger.

Maia whispered in his ear. "If I tell you to, get her below."

To his credit, Milo didn't flinch, though his eyes slid sideways to where she was standing on deck. He nodded once, then returned to his monitoring.

"Yes, bring it here!" Batacarus and Caphisus, two brawny gunners, had left their posts at Danuco's insistence and were leading one of her sheep over to the altar. It was true that Neptune preferred bulls or horses, but this would have to do. As it was a short voyage, she didn't have much in the way of livestock.

"Is it really Neptune, then?" Teg muttered to Hyacinthus.

"Seems so."

"Some bloody lovely cruise this is."

"Just ask fer yer money back," his friend quipped. "It's all fun, ain't it *Tempest?*"

"Have you seen the God before?" she asked them.

Teg nodded but it was Hyacinthus who answered.

"I 'ave. Listen, lads, don't look at him directly. Keep yer 'eads down and admire the Mer- ladies instead."

He jiggled his hands at chest height, suggestively.

Teg and some others within hearing distance shot him worried glances, not even appeased by the thought of pretty naiads.

"Good advice," Maia told them, while fielding a dozen queries from other crewmen. She tried to control her fear as the presence grew closer. Neptune was taking his time, she noted and had given them some warning, which she took as a good sign. The other Priest was organising a similar sacrifice, performing his duties with an admirable calmness that spoke of a long familiarity with the task. She wished she had half his confidence.

Danuco began the rite of appeasement immediately, slitting the sheep's throat and spilling its blood on the sacrificial altar.

The crew stood by respectfully, many clutching talismans as the air grew thicker and charged with power. Maia could feel it thrumming through her hull, a deep note below the range of human hearing, like the song of a great sea creature amplified and carried through the water.

The low tone was soon joined by others, audible this time as calls, clicks and haunting songs. The Mer-people were praising their ruler as they travelled in his entourage. It sounded as though there were a lot of them.

She checked on her officers. Raven, as usual, appeared calm, but she knew he was concentrating on something else. Probably reporting back, as Leo hadn't ordered her to do so. The steady chant of prayers hovered over both vessels and the sickly-sweet smell of expensive incense drifted over the water. Leo's face was set and her junior officers looked excited and terrified at the same time.

To her sinistra side the sea began to boil, great green bubbles rising and bursting to create massive ripples that rocked her hull. *Tempest* clung tight to her anchors, feeling them digging into the sea bed to brace and steady her as each man found something to hang on to. The churning water was suddenly broken by heads, then bodies rising up, scales flashing iridescent colours like oily rainbows in the sunlight. Some were carrying spears or tridents and all wore necklets and bracelets of gold. A low murmur of awe ran through the men as the Lords and Ladies of the Sea drew nearer. But this was nothing compared to their ruler.

Three gleaming points of light burst upwards, lengthening to become the points of a mighty trident rising higher and higher, followed by what seemed to be a huge pile of blue kelp that resolved itself into a mane of hair. The God's face followed, dripping and bearded, the size of a carriage. Maia caught a glimpse of piercing eyes beneath shaggy bows before she quickly dropped her gaze.

All around her the men were kneeling save Danuco who stood with arms upraised in supplication. She bowed her head in respect, feeling Neptune's eyes sweep over her vessel with intense curiosity and glad that her Shipbody gave her strength. Her Priest stepped forward, arms bloody and eyes averted.

Behind him, smoke rose in lazy billows from the remains of the sheep.

"O Great Lord of the Seas," he intoned, "We humbly beseech you to show us your favour as we travel over your domain. To this end we offer you tribute and ask that you bless this new Ship, the *Tempest*, granting her safe passage by your divine will. All of Britannia sends you worship and respect, as shown by this sacrifice offered by Artorius the Tenth, King of the Britons and your most humble petitioner."

For the space of three long heartbeats all was still, then Neptune spoke,

"Greetings to you, *Tempest*." His voice was the sound of the waves' thunder on the beach and the song of the Mer-folk, low and musical, but not overpowering. She felt the vibrations of it through her whole vessel and remembered that he was also Poseidon, capable of toppling cities as well as drowning them. And he was speaking to her. She lifted her eyes to the God.

"Hail Neptune, King of the Ocean. I, His Majesty's Ship *Tempest*, salute you on behalf of the people of Britannia."

His penetrating eyes regarded her with interest. Though the sensation wasn't as terrifying as her encounter with his brother, Jupiter, she still sensed the weight of his presence, as if the mind behind his words was vaster than she could know. He bent towards her, excluding the crew and her waiting officers, his voice sounding directly in her head.

<So, you have come into your own at last. My brother's decree is fulfilled.> His enormous mouth stretched into what she realised was a smile. <Your mother Aura submits to her punishment, but you should know that she is proud of you.>

His golden eyes looked up, watching something in the sky and suddenly she knew that Pearl was near. His next words confirmed it.

<Ah, I see you, sprite of the air. You keep a watchful eye on your sister then. Good!>

<*Greetings, mighty one!*> came the whispered reply.

To her relief, the God resumed speaking.

"You have my favour, *Tempest*."

The old Maia would have gulped and shivered, but HMS *Tempest* gathered her courage and looked him full in the face.

"I thank you, mighty Neptune. I and mine are yours to command. I also know my duty to the Gods, Empire, King and Country."

A deep rumble of approval answered her words, making the sea ripple outwards. A giant hand lifted from the water as he took a firmer grip on his trident.

"Your king was not mean with his gifts, but I have another reason for coming here. I see that the *Augusta* has departed. My condolences. She was a fine Ship and we had dealings many times. But such is the way of things. You will have to find another to teach you. The *Victoria* perhaps?"

"As you say, O great one," she replied. The *Victoria* still had more than four hundred years of service behind her and a great wealth of experience. She would take over as the new Flagship.

"I had got used to the *Augusta*," he said, softly. "As a mark of my respect for her memory you will have safe passage back to port – but you should move swiftly. One last thing I would say to you. As you have already seen to your cost, not all peril comes from the sea, or from the hands of the Gods. You must be vigilant in the days ahead, but especially now. Danger comes in many guises, some of it from the most unexpected sources."

His tone was serious and all bowed their heads.

"We thank you, O mighty Neptune!" Danuco called up to him.

Neptune's eyes took in the kneeling men, before alighting on Raven. "Still going then, Raven?"

"Oh yes, Lord. I'm still here," the Master Mage replied, resignation in his voice.

"Some things, it seems, never change," the God remarked. "And here is my Priest. Greetings, Lentulus. I suggest you put in for a transfer to another Ship as soon as possible, if you can find any that are able to stand your gloomy disposition."

Maia focused in on the *Augusta*'s Priest, whose beaming face was filled with adoration as he beheld his God. "Indeed, O Divine One. I need a new berth now."

Neptune smiled at his own joke and nodded his massive head. Then, pleasantries over, he turned. For a second the great scaled arc of his body was revealed as he dived back into the depths. Sheets of water poured from golden flukes that flashed and shimmered brightly before vanishing beneath the surface. His court gazed upwards with curious eyes before disappearing in his wake, leaving the swell of the waves undisturbed once more. The sense of heaviness slowly lifted as normality returned and Maia felt everyone relax. The dolphins called to each other before heading off to feed, though she knew they wouldn't go far.

"Well, that was unexpected," Leo said, adding privately to his Ship, <he favours you, it seems. Did he say something else to you?>

Maia thought quickly. <He remembered my family.> It wasn't a lie.

<Ah, yes. Of course. He tends to talk to Ships rather than men anyway.>

"It's good to know that the God is watching over us as we sail home," Sabrinus said. From the looks on her crew's faces they wholeheartedly agreed with him.

"Speaking of which, *Tempest*, please inform the Admiral that we await his command," Leo ordered.

"Aye, sir." <Your Highness, all is ready.>

<Proceed.>

She relayed his reply and unfurled her sails at Leo's word. The great expanse of cloth billowed as they caught the wind. There was some initial resistance as she took up the burden of the other vessel, but the late *Augusta*'s crew knew their business, and soon one live Ship and another that would never live again were making good speed towards the mainland and safe harbour.

"It won't take long at this rate," Sabrinus observed.

"No," Leo agreed. "We should be there tonight. Time for some food, I think." Sabrinus saluted as his Captain went below, then took up his post on the quarterdeck where he had a good view of both vessels.

"I don't know if we need the tow lines," he said, and Maia had to agree. "They're doing a good job of sailing her and she's no slouch." A pained expression flitted across his usually stoic features. "It, I mean. Still, better to be safe than sorry, I suppose."

"Aye, sir," she said. Her crew were slowly returning to their usual routine, helped by liberal amounts of food from the galley for those coming off watch. Maia knew that she should check in with the other Ships, but had no inclination to do so. She didn't

138

feel prepared for the endless round of questions, wanting nothing more than to have some time to digest all that was happening to her. So much for a quiet maiden voyage!

She looked hopefully into the skies for any signs that her sister was near, before catching sight of a silvery swirl around her mainmast. It was time to catch up with Pearl.

\*

Back in the Mage quarters, Julia was full of questions.

"Is that the first time you've seen Neptune?" she asked Magpie. Raven had gone into his cabin. She thought that the old man probably needed a rest after all the excitement.

"Yes. He doesn't appear as often as he used to," he replied, "though it was unusual circumstances."

"My poor uncle. What will he do now?" A thought struck her. "Maybe he'll return to the Admiralty and supplant Albanus at Court!"

Magpie cast her a look of annoyance, raising a bubble of silence around her almost as soon as the words left her mouth. Her face fell.

"You must be more discreet, Your Highness!" he told her sternly. "Anyone could overhear you and then all this will have been for nothing."

Julia felt herself flush. "Yes, I'm sorry. I'm just worried about him. He did his best for us when we growing up, but my brother could do with his guidance. What do you think the God was warning us about?"

The Mage shrugged. "I don't know. Wiser heads will have to ponder that one. Maybe we're due a natural disaster, or another war? He was quick to absolve Olympus of blame, whatever it was."

She chewed her lip. "*Tempest* will let people know, won't she?"

"Yes, and I should imagine that the Admiral will be reporting back as we speak. We don't have to rely solely on our Ship when he's around."

Julia looked towards the closed cabin door. "Do you think Raven's all right?"

He sighed. "I think he's had a shock. He served with the *Augusta* for years, just like your uncle, though I think it was before he became an Admiral. This has been a trying time for all who loved her. Ships usually fail in port, not out on the open sea."

"It's a terrible shame. What will happen now?"

Magpie started putting out equipment on a table, selecting vials and retorts. "We'll get to port and then there'll be a memorial for the *Augusta*. I should imagine that every sailor both at sea and on land will get very drunk. So that's why, ma'am, the lesson for this afternoon is going to be how to create Magic Drops."

Julia nodded and went to get the ingredients. She had hoped it would be something more interesting, but she could hardly refuse after feeling the benefits of the potion. Magpie gestured and they were audible once more. It was time to concentrate on the magic required whilst remembering to keep a guard on her tongue. If nothing else, that lesson would benefit her in the future. Wherever she ended up.

\*

The Sea God was as good as his word. Maia sailed into the harbour without further incident, accompanied by pods of dolphins and wheeling clouds of birds whose cries filled the sky as if in mourning for the loss of the Flagship. The two forts, one on either side of the river mouth, both saluted as she approached, towing the sad relic and she could see people already lined up on the quayside to pay their respects.

"Prepare to lower the boats," Leo commanded. She would drop the lines and use her boats to manoeuvre the hulk further up the river, which was deep enough for even the largest vessels. There it would lie until it was stripped and the Navy would decide what to do with it. The operation was carried out quickly; the remaining crew aboard the vessel would see the remains to their final resting place.

<What will happen to it?> Maia asked her Captain.

<They'll reuse the guns, naturally and any other devices that weren't too personal, but the rest will be disposed of,> Leo Sent. <She was due a new vessel anyway.>

<Even if it were a new vessel, nobody would want it,> she replied. <It would be like possessing a corpse.>

<That's true, I suppose.> Maia's attention snapped to a boat being rowed across to her. Admiral Pendragon had left at last.

<The Admiral's on his way here.>

Leo put the telescope to his eye and pressed his lips firmly together. She got the impression that he wasn't pleased.

<He'll be giving us new orders. It wouldn't surprise me if he supplants Latinius on the *Victoria* and demotes him to Flag Captain. It's a given that she'll become the new Flagship. There are a few more years in her yet.>

<Is it always the oldest Ship who's the Flagship?> Maia asked him.

<The oldest Royal, yes. The *Victoria*'s vessel is fairly new, so she's impressive enough. Why, do you fancy the position?>

She threw him a look of annoyance. <Hardly!>

It didn't bode well that she'd had such a crisis on her first trip out and she didn't want to get the reputation as an unlucky Ship. The *Emerald* had had to sail without incident for years until sailors stopped being leery of her. Leo caught her mood.

<Don't worry. This could have happened to anyone. There have been no problems so far and the God appeared to you himself, so that's a mark in our favour.>

She was grateful that he'd said 'our' not 'your', acknowledging that their careers were bound together. It had been a strain on him, too.

<Here he is. Have everyone form up.>

Maia relayed his order and watched her crew rush into position ready to welcome the Admiral, just as Pendragon came through her link.

<*Tempest*, you have new orders. I am to assume command. Leo will be Flag Captain.> A second later, he added, <I think it will do both of you some good.>

She didn't know whether to feel relieved or dismayed for Leo. She'd been quietly complaining that her Captain had little experience, so she could hardly wish things otherwise. Maybe it was only temporary? He'd surely prefer the *Victoria*. Still, a small part of her was quietly exulting that she would be linked to a man she both admired and respected.

141

<Aye, my Lord.>

<I'll tell him myself shortly.>

Pendragon was piped aboard with all ceremony and the usual salutes were exchanged. Maia noticed that Raven had come on deck to greet the Admiral, with Magpie close behind. Her crew watched, all faces solemn and aware of the Navy's great loss.

"Men," Pendragon began, turning to the assembled hands. "I would like to thank you personally for the assistance you have provided at this difficult time. I know that it isn't what you were expecting on your new Ship's first voyage, but you have all acted commendably. The *Augusta* was a great lady who will be remembered for her untiring service to Empire, King and Country and I pray that the Gods are welcoming her into Elysium. Gods save Britannia! Gods save the King!"

The crew answered with a great shout that echoed across the harbour, as the remains of the *Augusta* slowly glided up the river and disappeared into the hazy distance.

# VII

Maia's reverie was broken by a call through the Ship link.

<*Patience* to *Tempest*!>

It was a relief to hear her friend's voice.

<Hello, *Patience*.>

<I've just heard what happened – with the God I mean.>

Was it her imagination, or was there a tiny bit of reproof in the Ship's tone?

<Oh, yes. It was unexpected.>

<I'll say! Still, she was the Flagship.> *Patience* hesitated, before asking, <Are you all right?>

Maia took a deep mental breath. <Of course. Why wouldn't I be?>

<Because it's your first voyage and you're having to deal with a death, not to mention a change of command. It would be surprising if you weren't affected. We all are, you know.>

She was right. Maia had been so wrapped up in her own feelings that she hadn't given a thought to the other Ships, all of whom had known the *Augusta* a lot longer than she had.

<I'm sorry,> she said, feeling a pang of guilt. <I haven't really had a moment to think about how it's been for everybody.>

<We were all worried about you.>

<I suppose I'm still getting used to everything,> Maia said. She racked her brain for something to say. <It's strange how they don't say 'died'. We 'fail'.>

<Yes, we do,> Patience said, sadly. >Maybe it's easier for people to think that way about us.>

<I don't want to be thought of as a thing!> Maia said, fiercely. <Why do we have to be *things*?>

<We aren't.>

<Really? Tell that to the *Augusta*, or any of us!>

<She is mourned. >

Maia's frustration spilled out before she could help herself.

<Yes, as a mighty Ship! I bet you don't even know her name! Does anybody?>

Her friend was silent. <It's the way of things,> she said after a time.

<Well, it shouldn't be. She was a woman called Martia and that's how I'm going to remember her!>

She felt the shock through the link. <How do you know?>

Damn it! How could she explain? Maia thought hastily.

<She told me. At the end, when her mind was wandering. She referred to herself by her name.> It wasn't really a lie, though the Gods knew how many times she'd had to bend the truth already.

<Oh, you poor girl. It must have been horrible, trying to communicate with her when she was like that. Nobody else could get through.>

<I didn't realise,> she replied, her anger vanishing as quickly as it had come. <How is everyone else?> She was sure now that *Patience* had been nominated to contact her.

<Oh, shocked, though many knew that she wouldn't last much longer. It's just that she's always been there. I think that *Victoria* is feeling the weight of responsibility already. She's fretting that she's going to lose Latinius.>

<Tell her not to worry. Pendragon's staying with me.> The words left her head before she could stop them.

<I know, but he'll transfer soon, won't he?>

<Don't bet on it.> Maia couldn't have said how she knew; she just did.

<Your Captain won't be pleased, surely?>

<Leo doesn't get a say in the matter. He's not experienced enough, anyway. I'd rather have the Admiral in charge.>

<As long as you're happy with that,> her friend said cautiously.

<Oh, I don't get a say either! I do feel a little sorry for Leo, but I think it's worked out well under the circumstances.>

She felt *Patience*'s mental sigh. <I think you're right. Look, don't brood over things. I know you, Maia Abella! You'll worry away at things until you get yourself in a tizzy. That's why Ships talk all the time. We have to.>

<So you do remember my name, Briseis Apollonia!>

<I don't remember you being this stubborn!> Her usually placid friend sounded almost exasperated.

144

<I have my moments,> Maia admitted. <At least I wasn't a madam. Talking of madams, how is the *Regina*?>

<Still hoping to convey the Princess to Gaul and boring everyone to death moaning about it.>

<Typical. I bet she's still mad that she isn't a Royal.>

<Now who's being catty?> *Patience* pointed out. <That's more like it!>

They both laughed. <Gossip and more gossip,> Maia agreed. We'd better exchange some, I suppose, or we wouldn't be Ships!>

They chatted for a while, and by the time *Patience* signed off Maia realised that her dark mood had passed and she felt much better.

*

Leo appeared to take the Admiral's order well, but Maia could tell that he was secretly disappointed. He'd enjoyed his brief taste of absolute command and now he was to be supplanted by the older man.

"I'll move cabins immediately, sir." As the ranking officer, Pendragon would naturally be at the heart of the action. The Admiral nodded.

"I know that it must be galling, but I think that it will benefit you in the long run. Of course, it won't be forever."

"You'll be moving to the *Victoria*, then, sir?"

Maia sensed a reluctance in the Admiral. "I've not decided yet. Believe me, I'll let you know when I do."

"Of course, Highness."

"Admiral, please," Pendragon said, his mouth relaxing into a rueful smile. "I get my bellyful of titles when at Court. Now, I need a full report on your progress so far. This Ship still needs to prove herself."

"At once, Admiral." Leo signalled to the servants for refreshments, as the two men sat down at the table and began to confer.

"*Tempest*, please inform the crew of the changes," Pendragon ordered.

"Aye, Admiral."

The Ship's voice echoed through the vessel and the men exchanged knowing looks. Her Shipbody was still on the quarterdeck, though her eyes were all over her vessel, monitoring the men's reactions.

"That was quick," Sabrinus muttered to her. "It's probably only until he can get on board the *Victoria*, eh?"

"Possibly," she whispered back.

The young officer looked surprised. "He won't be staying, surely?"

"I think he might."

Sabrinus raised an eyebrow. "We'll have to wait and see. The Admiral doesn't always do what's expected of him." She was glad that he didn't seem bothered. "I suppose I'm to have Drustan's cabin, then?"

She checked. "Looks like it. Everyone's going to have to shuffle."

Drustan joined them as he was speaking. "Ma'am, sir. I'd just got used to that cabin." His tone was rueful.

Sabrinus smiled. It made him look younger. "The fortunes of life at sea. Look at it this way. We have the opportunity to serve under a great officer, and how many can say that?"

"Indeed, sir. Are we to head back to Portus?"

"I've not heard anything yet. *Tempest*?"

"They're discussing it now," she said. She had one ear on the conversation, but was mainly wondering what the Admiral would say if he found out that a certain apprentice Mage wasn't all that he seemed. Raven would have a lot of explaining to do. And, talking of explanations, she hadn't forgotten that he owed her a whole raft full of them.

<*Tempest.*> Leo's voice came over their link. The Admiral could and would talk to her, but everyday operations would still be handled by her Captain. <We're to remain here for the night, then we're to head down to Gaul before returning to Portus. The Admiral wants to do more sea trials.>

*And he'd rather sail away from land right now* was the unspoken message.

<Aye sir. Are you all right?> She felt his snort down the link.

<I'm not going to fall over and beat my fists on the deck, if that's what you mean.>

146

She had to laugh at the image. <I'm glad to hear it!>

<I might sulk for a bit, though.> He paused. <There. Did you feel me sulking?>

<It was a good sulk.>

<Thank you. Finished now. There'll be a feast on board tonight. The Admiral's paying for a bull at the local temple, so there'll be beef for all and plenty of drink. No shore leave. They've all had enough and we want to be setting sail tomorrow with the tide.>

<The crew will appreciate it.>

<Just warn them not to overdo it. A hangover is no excuse for slacking and I'll make an example of anyone who's stupid enough to drink themselves insensible.>

<Acknowledged.>

<That includes me.> His face broke into a grin.

Maia was starting to appreciate his humour. <As if you would.>

He assumed a look of innocence that made her laugh.

Leo ended the conversation and she returned to watching the bustle aboard the vessel as everyone changed cabins and got themselves sorted. The men who'd been sent to sail the hulk would be back soon to join their mates and there would be songs and stories aplenty below decks tonight, honouring the *Augusta* and the Navy.

Later would be as good a time as any to get some answers and find out just what Raven was going to do now.

*

Below decks, Milo watched and waited. What had been planned as a quiet training cruise had turned out to be something much more interesting and, quite frankly, problematic. Events were threatening to overtake them and he wasted no time in pointing this out to Raven.

The old Mage had mostly kept to his cabin, but long acquaintance told Milo how upset he was that the *Augusta* had failed. The Agent used the excuse of taking in some clean laundry to try and have a word. He knocked quietly on the cabin door and waited for permission to enter.

"Come in." That was Polydorus. The faithful servant was at his master's side, as vigilant as any well-trained guard. The man's dark eyes fixed on Milo with an implicit challenge.

"I need to talk to him."

The Greek's gaze flicked to the curtained alcove where Raven slept.

"He's resting."

Milo bit back a sharp retort and raised his eyebrows. "I wouldn't disturb him if it wasn't important."

There was a rustling, then the old Mage's voice sounded from behind the heavy fabric.

"I can hear the pair of you. Milo, give me a minute. Polydorus, please could you pour us something to drink, then ensure we're not disturbed?"

"Yes, master," Polydorus answered. Milo could see that he was worried. He must have served Raven for nearly thirty years now; the man was well into his forties and going grey. Raven had freed him years before and offered to provide him with money to make a life of his own, but Polydorus had refused to countenance the idea. Milo couldn't fathom the man's reasoning, but he applauded his devotion. The servant gave Milo a meaningful look, as if to say 'don't overtax him', before fetching a decanter and two glasses from a wall cupboard and pouring the wine. Then he slipped noiselessly away, closing the door firmly behind himself with a click.

There was more rustling and the curtain drew back. Raven swung his legs to the floor and ran a hand over his face.

"I was just resting."

"Aren't you feeling well?" Milo had never known the old man to be ill, not even with a cold. He seemed to tread a constant path, never deviating or weakening despite his great age.

"I'll be all right," he grumbled. "I've already had to order Polydorus not to fuss. Sometimes I just need a little time with my own thoughts."

He moved unerringly across the room and sat down in his favourite chair. Milo took a stool and handed him a glass. Raven took it from him, raising it in a toast.

"To the memory of the *Augusta*, one of the finest Ships the Navy has ever produced!"

Milo echoed him and they drank in silence. Now that he could see the Mage, he thought that he looked more shrunken than usual, as if he had aged in the last day. Then the moment passed and Raven seemed his usual self.

"You want to know what we're going to do," the Master Mage said. Milo felt the air grow flat as the spell of silence surrounded them.

"It would help." Milo admitted. "I think the Princess has had enough excitement for one trip. It's all I can do to keep her in the workroom and she's starting to chafe at the restrictions. How is her training coming along?"

"Very well. She picks things up quickly and I've noticed that her power is growing. There's a large store of Potentia there, which is worrying. It's as if everything has been pent up for years. I've not seen anything like that for a long time."

"She's got more than she bargained for," Milo observed. "First the *Augusta*, then Neptune turning up in person. I never thought I'd see that! Now her uncle's aboard as well, so that's another person to avoid."

"I can't see that he'll want to meet a young Mage," Raven said, "but you're right. It's going to be tricky. Claudia's keeping me informed as to the wedding plans, but if the King suddenly decides she's to go, we'll have to move quickly and portal her back to the temple." His face creased with worry. "I don't want to send her anywhere as she is, but what can I do? Parisius will want her sooner rather than later and there's only so long we can delay the inevitable."

"We're heading south, not east. Word is that the Admiral wants to run more trials."

Raven swore quietly. "It would be better to stop messing about and go back to Portus, but I know I can't persuade Cei to do so without a very good reason."

"Any bad weather due?" Milo asked hopefully.

Raven considered this. "There's nothing forecast."

Milo stared at him glumly. "Look. We can't do anything at the moment. If the situation changes, we'll decide what to do then. Was there a date set for her departure?"

"No, fortunately. That gives us more time. I'll see if I can find out how long the Admiral intends this voyage to be. With any luck it won't last for more than a few days, then we can get back to Portus without anyone being the wiser."

Milo could only agree and left Raven to finish the wine. As he returned to his menial duties, nodding to acquaintances as he went, he reflected that the situation wasn't ideal, but what choice did they have?

*

That night Maia watched as her crew celebrated the life of the Navy's Flagship by eating, drinking and telling stories. In the officers' quarters they dined well, seated around the great table with Pendragon presiding as they swapped tales of long voyages, strange creatures and people they had known. The younger men listened with rapt attention as the old sailors reminisced about times gone by and the events that were now part of history.

It was less decorous below decks. The crew sang songs, danced and told tall stories, many of them bawdy, some horrific and others heart-rending. Past comrades were toasted, old enmities resurrected and battles re-fought. It was like being back at The Anchor, Maia thought, except she wouldn't have to clean up after them and watch out for wandering hands. She was pleased when they toasted her and her good fortune. Everyone had seemingly decided that she was favoured by Neptune and thus a lucky Ship.

After a time, she left them to it and prowled the vessel, gliding from deck to deck like a restless ghost unable to settle. To her satisfaction, all seemed in order and the sailors on watch were keeping sober, though by the looks on their faces they weren't happy about it. She'd have to see that they were relieved before they missed out on all the fun.

The lights on shore twinkled in the clear night air and she watched them for a time, unable to lift herself out of her dark thoughts. She felt more alone than ever, before remembering that she had unfinished business.

<Raven? Can we talk?>

She switched her view to his cabin and saw the Agent just leaving. The man was quiet, unobtrusive and diligent in his duties. If she hadn't known that he was a government operative, she would never have guessed it from his bearing and manner. She wondered whether he remembered the little skivvy he'd sometimes slipped a coin to, back in another life.

<Ah, *Tempest*. Yes.>

She reformed in Raven's cabin, rippling up out of the floor to stand like a temple statue. The old Mage was huddled in his chair, a glass of wine in one claw-like hand.

"I can guess why you're here," he said, without preamble. "You want explanations, don't you?"

"Yes." She couldn't deny it.

"That ability of yours is proving interesting, to say the least. How many heads have you got into so far?" He sounded guarded, as well he might. She thought about it.

"Only three. *Blossom*'s, yours and the *Augusta*'s."

"Only three, eh?" he said, drily.

"That's three more than I wanted to!" she snapped. Did he think she was doing it on purpose?

He raised a hand to pacify her. "Calm yourself. I intended no criticism. If anything, it's my fault for not having helped you before now. It could be a useful ability, if controlled."

"Controlled?"

"Oh yes, though it would be more useful to an Agent. Don't tell Milo, he'll be jealous."

Maia thought of the pain she'd experienced and shuddered. "I wouldn't wish this on anyone. I seem to pick up on the worst parts of somebody's life."

"I only had a hangover," Raven smiled.

She pulled a face. "Well that must be the worst thing that ever happened to you, then."

His smile faded. "Oh no. I can assure you that it wasn't, which leads me to what you picked out of the *Augusta*'s memories. Tell me, what exactly did you see?"

Maia told him about the battle. "I lived it all," she ended. "As if it were happening to me. I *was* her. I felt what she felt..." She trailed off.

"And you saw me, fighting from her deck. Four hundred and sixty-eight years ago."

She didn't answer, watching his face intently. He grimaced. "I could tell you that you were mistaken, but it would be a lie."

Maia realised that she *had* been hoping that she was wrong. How could he still be here, after all this time? A thought struck her. Hadn't he mentioned a magical accident? There were stories of people entering portals and ending up where they weren't supposed to. "Did you go back through time by mistake?"

Raven closed his eyes. "No, it wasn't that. Look, Maia – and yes, I will still call you Maia – I've been blessed by the fact that you've accepted me as you find me, and not had your opinion coloured by rumours and garbled versions of the truth. I can see that it's time to be honest with you, before you hear a load of rubbish from somewhere else." He put his glass down on a side table and clasped his hands in his lap.

Apprehension flooded her, but she caught it automatically before it spread to her vessel. What could he be hiding? She didn't trust herself to speak and though she had no pulse to quicken, her Shipbody suddenly creaked as if under strain. Raven's eyes flew open.

"It's all right! I haven't deceived you in any way – I am what you see before you. An ancient, crippled Mage."

He raised his arms in emphasis, then let them fall back to rest on the worn leather.

"I'm going to tell you something of my history. There are only a couple of people alive who know anything about it. The truth is strange, if not as colourful as some would have it. Sometimes I feel that I've become a creature of myth, the object of legends and fantastical tales and not a flesh and blood man at all."

"I've noticed that people respect you," Maia said.

"Respect, fear, take your pick. I annoy quite a few as well," he said, with a trace of his usual dry humour. "Bullfinch, for one. He'd rather I was safely tucked away out of sight somewhere or, failing that, six feet underground. He feels that I have outlived my usefulness."

"I didn't like him one bit," Maia said, loyally, recalling the haughty Prime Mage.

"Personally I wouldn't trust him as far as I could kick him. Some people confuse disagreement with hostility and lash out, even at those who would be their friends. Politicians!"

He spat the word in disgust. "I think I stayed in the Collegium just to spite him. Anyway, back to my history. I think it best that you hear it now and I think that I'm finally ready to tell it. If of course you want to hear the whole sorry tale."

"I do," she said quietly. He nodded slowly, readying himself.

"I was born far away from here, in the land of the people the Romans called the Deceangli, among the mountains to the west. Apart from mining, sheep and rain there isn't much industry there and most people just bypass the area on the main roads. Central government doesn't bother with the place much, so long as the taxes are paid and goods delivered. The old ways still linger, including the speaking of the old tribal tongue. I didn't know any Latin at all until I was seven. It was even more remote when I was born on a small farm on the side of the mountain, in an old stone house. My parents scratched a living from a flock of sheep and whatever vegetables we could grow. I had another name then, though I've not heard it for many, many years.

"My siblings and I spent our time learning to look after the flock and that was pretty much what was expected of me. I was going to follow in my father's footsteps and my sisters would join my mother and the other women of the village in spinning the fleece ready to be woven into cloth in the winter months, when no farming could be done. That was how things had been since time immemorial, you understand.

"There was a spring above the house where we got our water. My parents made the usual offerings to appease the local naiad and the water was always sweet and fresh. It was one of my jobs to fetch it daily, as soon as I was strong enough to carry the buckets and I soon got used to trudging up and down the track. Then one day, when I was seven, I saw a woman sitting by the spring.

"She was very pretty, with big green eyes and I remember being fascinated by the blue hair that tumbled all down her back like a waterfall. I'd never known anyone could have that colour hair. All our family had black hair, like most of the people I'd met until then. She smiled at me and asked if I was Cadog's son, so she clearly knew my family. I was quite happy to chat away, as little boys will do when they find a willing ear, until my Mam called up to me. I said goodbye and trotted back down.

153

"Where have you been?" she asked me.

"I was talking to the pretty lady," I told her. Of course she wanted to know who on earth I was talking about, as we knew everyone in the district, so I explained. "She was sitting by the spring and her hair was blue."

"My Mam didn't know what to make of that, but I thought nothing of it. She gave me some job or other, but I overheard her whispering to my Da later and looking in my direction. I often saw the lady after that; my parents were pleased and gave me little presents to give to her – flowers, a bit of bread or milk, things like that. It was only later that I came to understand that she was the resident naiad whom few could see, and only then if she wanted them to."

"Like the little Fae?" Maia asked with interest.

"That's right," he agreed. "Well, a few months later a Priest visited the local village for the harvest celebration. As it was a market day as well, we all went along. My little brother had been born a couple of years before and I remember wanting him to be grown up so that he could play with me and share my chores. There had been another before him, but he hadn't lived. So, off we set down the mountain with sheep to sell, as well as some cloth in heavy packs. Anyway, Da must have spoken to the Priest because I was taken to him and he asked me questions about the lady. Had I seen anyone else? I told him about the figures on the mountain and how there were people in the trees. I accepted it all as perfectly normal. Why shouldn't people have leaves for hair, or stride about the hills like moving stones? I was impressed that such an important man as the Priest should want to talk to me about it, but I remember wanting to get back to the fair to watch the jugglers.

"After that, my Da went off with him somewhere and we enjoyed ourselves at the market, thinking no more of it, but, a few weeks later, the Priest came back. I was going to go to school to learn to be a Priest, like him. My parents were overjoyed – it was an honour for them to have produced a child who had some Potentia and who could help them in the years to come. Their social standing increased overnight, not to mention the bounty that the Temple would pay them for reporting my gift. As for the farm, they would be able to afford to buy a slave or two as well as more sheep and, all being well, my little brother would inherit after my Da passed. I thought I'd only be gone a short while, so I said my goodbyes and happily trotted off to the Priestly College, all the way to Deva.

"I couldn't believe that there were so many people in the world after the silence of the mountains. The only civilisation I'd seen before that was the village and some there still lived in roundhouses. Deva was like a small version of Londin and I swear my mouth stayed open for two whole weeks."

He paused to take a sip from his glass and Maia took the opportunity to speak.

"I saw a woman with bark for skin and leaves for hair. She came out of the trees and called me sister."

He raised an eyebrow. "During your initiation?"

"Yes. I was very shaken at the time as I'd just fought *her*."

"It seems we're both favoured."

"If that's what you call it. But you're not a Priest. What happened?"

"No. I was only there for a few weeks before some older novices decided they'd have some fun with the little farm boy from the back of beyond. There were three of them, big, stupid and cruel as all these types are. They terrorised the younger boys in rotation, where the masters couldn't see. This day it was my turn. They cornered me behind a tree where I was playing jackstones with another boy and started taunting and pushing me around. Suddenly, stones started flying from a nearby wall and smashed into them. I remember that there was a lot of blood and screaming. I just stood there yelling my head off until a Priest ran up and cracked me one."

He rubbed his wrinkled cheek. "I can still feel the slap he gave me. Pulled me out of it, he did. Well, after that little performance they decided that I was better off becoming a Mage, so away I went again, this time all the way to the Collegium in Londin. Barely eight years old, with hardly a word of Latin and only an old Priest to guide me. It was a bloody long walk and I was terrified and excited all at once. I'd enjoyed the power, see?"

Maia could understand how he'd felt.

"My teachers said I was a quick learner and I soon picked up the Londinium way of speaking and became fluent in Latin. So that was that for the next fourteen years. I, too left my past behind.

"I was a holy terror growing up. You wouldn't believe it now, but I was a handsome lad, hair as black as a raven's wing and eyes that changed from blue, to grey, to green, depending on the light. I soaked up everything like a sponge – there wasn't any task I couldn't accomplish, any aspect of spellcraft I couldn't master with ease in half the time it took my fellows. I was a cocky, arrogant young idiot who thought he could do anything without consequence because he had a silver tongue and a whole load of Potentia to use as he pleased."

A note of bitterness crept into his voice.

"How wrong I was. There's a saying; 'there are reckless Mages and old Mages, but no reckless old Mages.' Just like that young fool in Portus, burnt to a crisp because he thought he could do anything and didn't have the sense to run. Well, that was me, except I lived. Like this."

He gestured to his ruined face and withered body, then fell silent.

Maia could only wait, feeling helpless. She hadn't wanted to hurt him.

"You don't have to –" she began, but he interrupted her forcefully.

"I must finish my tale, as it contains the part you really need to know if you're to understand why everyone treats me as they do. I warn you – it's not…pleasant."

"I've seen unpleasant things," Maia said. "Blandina was killed in front of me, remember? Not to mention the poisoned necklace."

That was two corpses, for a start. She tried not to recall Xenia's bulging eyes and bloody face.

He nodded. "Yes. I suppose you've seen your fair share of horrors."

And that was before her initiation. Raven took a breath.

"You saw how I was, before. I was doing well, completing several assignments successfully and winning praise from my superiors. Everyone tipped me to rise through the ranks and have a bright future, until one day I was sent on an urgent mission.

"The country was in trouble. A blight had descended on the land, killing crops at first, then animals and after that people started to die of disease and starvation. The Collegium was in a panic trying to determine where it had come from, but neither the Mages, Priests nor Adepts could find the cause. Bodies were lying in the streets unburied and those that were collected ended up on huge pyres to try and contain infection. Every Temple was full of desperate petitioners and civil authority was in danger of breaking down. They had troops and Mages guarding the grain stores to stop looting. We all thought the world was ending, such was the despair, until at last word came through from the Gods.

"There was a curse upon the land. A magical attack. Whence it had come, whether from within Britannia or elsewhere, no-one was sure. Now I suspect that the threat came from a summoning or working gone horribly wrong, but who knows? Perhaps not even the Gods, as they were slow enough to respond. The contagion certainly had a magical feel about it because of the way it destroyed indiscriminately.

"Eventually, they told us that the remedy was to locate a powerful stone that had fallen to earth from the heavens, long ago. This stone contained a substance that would somehow repel the curse and keep it at bay, acting as a protection to the nation. Furthermore it was located in the very mountains where I'd been born. The Gods wanted us mortals to deal with it – a 'test of worthiness' the High Priest called it. I couldn't see why the immortals didn't deal with it themselves, but you know that we can't fathom their reasoning most of the time. They do what they do and that's it. The Collegium was ordered to find this stone and, to that end, they called me in as a native of the region. They didn't have anyone else who could speak to the locals, though to tell the truth I couldn't remember much of the dialect. I was hoping it would come back to me when I got there. I was immensely flattered that they would choose me for such an important assignment and I fear that my head swelled even more as a result."

"Were you glad to be able to see your homeland again?"

Raven bowed his head. "No, I wasn't looking forward to that part. I'd never been back and I'd convinced myself there was no point in sending a message, as my parents and most of the people we knew were illiterate. We had a rich oral tradition, but unless you were going to be a Priest it wasn't then thought necessary to be able to read and write. I supposed they could have found someone to read a letter to them, but I'd come to be ashamed of my humble origins and glossed over them at every opportunity. What a wretch I was! But orders were orders and there wasn't anyone else, so back I went, with three other more senior Mages to seek the cave under the great mountain of Yr Wyddfa, and get the stone.

"Time was pressing, so we used portals until we arrived in Deva. The rest of the way would be completed on horseback, as it would be quicker than a carriage. I hadn't spoken my birth tongue in many years, though strangely I still dreamed in it occasionally. I was a bit rusty at first and got some funny looks as I asked the way, but eventually we reached the slopes of the mountain. Some of the landmarks seemed familiar and I realised that we weren't too far from my parents' farm.

"A local shepherd was hired to be our guide; he knew the location of the cave and took us straight there, though he didn't seem too happy about it, as apparently it had an evil reputation and his sheep would never shelter there, even in the worst weather. I was in high spirits, confident that we'd grab the stone without any trouble, activate its defensive power and be back in no time to a heroes' welcome.

"My companions had more misgivings, especially Nightjar, an older man with a permanently dour expression who didn't approve of my youthful optimism. Skylark and Curlew were only about ten years older than me, but as twins their abilities complimented each other's, so they usually worked together. They had the annoying habit of saying half a sentence each, like they only had one brain between them, so I called them Skycur. It annoyed them no end. I had a mouth on me in those days that often got me into trouble. Anyway, it was thought that three Mages and several men-at-arms would be more than a match for whatever might be down there.

"The cave mouth was a good size and we went in without any difficulty, though the shepherd refused. He tried to warn us, saying he had a bad feeling about it, but we brushed his concern aside. He was a young man made older by a life of hard, outdoor work and we were clever, sophisticated and powerful Mages from Londinium, so of course we knew better."

It was clearly getting harder for him to speak, but he took another drink and carried on almost mechanically, though Maia could see the effort it was costing him.

"The cave was dark and dank, with the noise of dripping water echoing all about us. We scrambled over the rocky floor, conjuring light so that we could see where we were going with the soldiers following on behind. They were handpicked by the King himself. Their Captain was a man called Balba, a big scarred fellow with a lot of battle experience. I don't think he thought much of us, except possibly Nightjar, but he had the sense to keep quiet about it. He certainly didn't lack for courage and insisted on going first into the darkness, sword drawn."

Maia pictured them in her mind, clambering into the depths of the cave, the only sounds the clinking of armour, footsteps scuffling on stone and the endless dripping water.

"We must have been over two hours groping our way into the bowels of the earth, when our eyes began to register a soft glow in the distance that had nothing to do with daylight. We knew then the object of our search was near and we picked up our pace.

"Balba called two of his men to the fore with Nightjar, who was checking for magic with a device he carried. He said it would measure the stone's emanations and he'd been using it as a sort of compass to get us through the cave system. It would have been very easy to get lost down there. I was never sure where he'd obtained it, or even if he'd invented it himself and I never got the chance to ask him later, alas!"

Gradually, the world seemed to fade away, shrinking inward to the whispery sound of Raven's voice. She listened, aware of a mounting sense of horror and dread that was not her own, before feeling it crash over her through the strange link they shared, like a tidal wave from the past that engulfed her, dragging her down until she saw…

…*the stone*. It was resting on a sort of rocky altar at the back of the large cavern. To the left of him another opening gaped like a dark maw, but all was still, though he strained his ears to hear any movement. Even the soft patter of drops had ceased in this place.

It didn't look very impressive, just a half-melted looking lump of blackened rock, possibly some form of iron, less than a foot or so long and half as wide again. His first thought was that it looked like a piece of old slag discarded from a foundry, instead of a highly magical object.

Nightjar stepped forward, motioning the soldiers back. He lifted his eyes from his device, evaluating the stone carefully.

"I'll get it," he said, pulling a leather pouch from a bag slung over his shoulder.

A blurred shape erupted from the depths of the cave. Something huge shot by, so close that he could feel the rush of its movement. Before anyone had time to react, the creature grabbed Nightjar and bit down on his head with a sickening crunch.

It was roughly man-shaped and pale like the belly of a frog, its clammy skin stretched tightly over ropy tendons and muscle. It whirled to face them, still clutching Nightjar's body, while lipless jaws chewed and wide nostrils flared below empty pits where its eyes should have been.

A yell burst out to his left and Balba charged, sword darting forwards to stab and slash. His men followed, their own battle cries rebounding from the rocky walls as they leapt to support their Captain. The creature bellowed in answer, dropping the luckless Mage's corpse and reaching for its assailants with lightning speed. Razor claws ripped into flesh and three men fell eviscerated, the sharp stink of spilled entrails filling the air.

He couldn't believe how fast it was. It spun and leapt over its assailants to block the exit, a rapid clicking noise rattling from its open jaws. He loosed fireballs at it, as did the twins but it dodged them all, somehow sensing the approaching spells.

"Shields!" Curlew screamed. The brothers raised their strongest defences, trying to keep the creature off for as long as possible, their entwined voices ringing out whilst the remaining soldiers slashed and dodged frantically.

He felt that time had fractured. His mind was slowing, everything taking on a strange sticky quality as if he was merely an observer watching something that was happening very far away. A hand grabbed his shoulder and yanked him round out of the stasis. Balba's craggy face thrust into his own, wide-eyed and spattered with blood.

"Get the stone!" A shove punctuated the order.

Bile rose in his throat, but he stumbled over to Nightjar's mangled remains and tugged the leather pouch from his dead fingers. Behind him, the clicking bounced from the cave walls and he could feel the air vibrate as the creature hurled itself repeatedly at the Mages' shield.

The stone was very heavy for its size. They'd all been warned not to touch it, so he opened the pouch, jamming it over the rock and scooping it up before fumbling to secure the ties. He risked a glance over his shoulder. Curlew and Skylark were on their knees, arms raised and struggling to maintain the defences which flashed with purple light each time the creature attacked. Another man was down, splayed bonelessly on the cavern floor, leaving Balba and the remaining soldier to harry their foe as best they could, but it was obvious that it wouldn't be long before the creature's frenzied attack would force them to give way.

He was moving to throw his Potentia into the shield when, with a last explosion of light, it finally cracked and failed. The soldiers rushed forward but the creature was faster, leaping with taloned feet outstretched to clutch the two Mages and they all went down in a writhing mass of limbs. He desperately loosed arrow spells, praying that they would not hit his comrades. The creature ignored them, though a sickly yellow ichor dripped from several wounds. A limp body was thrown aside. Balba. Hoarse screaming and pools of blood, black in the dimming magelight told their own story. Panic rising, he concentrated on the light – if that failed, he knew he was dead.

He edged around the creature. Despite his shock and horror, he knew he had to get the stone out, or all this would have been for nothing. Abruptly the screaming stopped, leaving the thing crouched, panting and clicking, its long fingers pawing the corpses at its feet as if reassuring itself that the battle was over.

He flattened himself against the cave wall, heart pounding and sweating despite the chill. The only sound he could hear was wet snuffling as the thing bent its head to the pile of bodies as if preparing to feed. Whilst it was occupied, he seized his chance and fled, simultaneously hurling the spell he had hastily prepared not at the creature, but at the roof of the cavern.

The crack as it smashed into the stone was immediately followed by a thunderous roar as tons of rock broke loose, collapsing on to the creature as it raised its head in alarm. He kept running through the choking dust, coughing and clutching the precious pouch as the rumbling and shaking faded behind him, his head empty of everything save the light spell and the need to get away.

Then there was only running and tripping over rocks, banging his knees and shins when he slipped and fell, once coming to in total darkness with sticky moisture trickling down the side of his face. It was a nightmare of endless tunnels, mud and water mixing with his own blood from cuts and scrapes that he barely felt any more, all spells forgotten in the disorientation and shock. He prayed incoherently to every God he could recall in wordless appeals that never left his lips.

Even in his dazed state, he became convinced that he could hear a dragging, scraping sound behind him. At first he dismissed it as a trick of his overwrought senses, but it persisted, growing louder. Something was following him.

He stopped and hid himself as best he could, kneeling behind a thick pillar of rock that grew from the cave floor like a giant fang.

Slowly, the noises got nearer and, in the dim magelight, he could see that it was the creature. It was using its talons to claw at the rock, dragging itself along on its belly like a hideous snake. Its lower body was crushed, the once powerful legs trailing uselessly as it heaved itself along to leave a viscous, foul-smelling trail of ichor. Its head swung from side to side, nostrils snuffling at the air; even blind and maimed it continued to track him.

Horror pinned him in place. His breath froze and he could only stare, hypnotised like a rabbit before the creature's slowly weaving face. Abruptly it stopped, its nostrils flaring and empty eye sockets fixed on his hiding place. The eerie clicking noise started up again, but stronger now, reminding him of a rusty wind-up toy. It changed direction, moving steadily towards him, jaws agape.

Exhausted, he leaned against the pillar, summoning up the last of his strength and racking his brains for any advantage. What did he know about it? One thing was clear, it could sense magic, but there was one last chance now that it was wounded. He had to work two spells at once. A muttered phrase sent a fiery ball of light zipping around his hiding place to plunge into the creature's chest, while he concentrated on pushing another through the base of the stone pillar. The rock groaned, toppling even as the creature gurgled and choked, flailing on the ground as the wound in its chest began to sizzle and stink. A cloud of foul smoke, like something burning and rotten, billowed up, making him gag. The stone pillar swayed, toppled and finally fell, smashing down to pin the thing in place. The creature emitted a last bellowing scream of anger, frustration and pain.

He watched as its struggles grew weaker, until, after an age, it twitched one last time and lay still. Gales of harsh laughter echoed off the tunnel walls around him and at first he didn't realise that it was his own.

He staggered painfully round what was left of the pillar, to stare at the dead abomination. Surely the eyeless horror was nothing natural of this earth?

A small voice in his head warned him to leave it, to get out and let it rot in the dark, but a flare of greed and curiosity urged him closer. Many potions called for unusual ingredients and this monster had been largely immune to magic. Perhaps there was something of value here that he could use? The claws alone looked as though they might be worth the trouble and would prove that he had bested the thing. There was no way he could drag it all out of the mountain even if he'd wanted to, but he might be able to salvage a part of it.

He was groping for his knife to make the first cut in the clammy flesh, when the thing's head reared up. It spat out a stream of ichor, drenching him before slumping back down to shrivel and dissolve, until nothing remained save a bubbling, glutinous mass spreading like vomit where it had lain.

He fell to his knees, clawing at his face as his skin began to burn…

….and a jolt of Potentia hit Maia like a slap, forcing her back to the present.

Only a handful of seconds had passed, despite the hours she had seemed to spend in the cave with him, being him. Raven was bent almost double, arms gripping the sides of his chair and breathing heavily. His glass lay shattered on the floor, the remnants of its contents trickling to stain the deck red. She was just about to call for help when he raised his head, eyes wide.

"No, don't. I'll be all right."

She doubted very much that reliving the worst moments of his life left him feeling all right, but didn't argue. Her Shipbody had protected her from any physical effects she might have felt, though, as with the *Augusta*, the ghost of his fear and agony still echoed in her mind. Raven muttered something else that she didn't quite catch, some ancient oath, then he straightened and leaned back.

A few minutes later, he spoke at last.

"You shouldn't have seen... that."

Maia didn't know what to say. Was she forever doomed to seize on the worst parts of someone's life and experience their pain? If so, it was a talent she would willingly forgo.

"What was that thing?"

"We never knew, though some suspected that it was attracted by the power of the stone. It certainly didn't want us to take it. Nothing like it has been seen since and I hope that it was the only one of its kind."

She hoped so too. The creature had been too strong and its resistance to magic was worrying.

"What happened next?" she asked, hesitantly.

"Somehow I managed to crawl out of there. I hadn't dropped the stone, thank the Gods, though they couldn't prise the pouch out of my hand for hours afterwards. The shepherd had waited by the entrance and would have helped me out, but I screamed at him not to come close. I could tell that the creature's ichor was eating into me and transforming me into something else. I was already losing my vision and my hair had turned white. I think I'd tried to wash the poison off in a pool of water on the way out, which might have saved my life, but to be honest I'm not sure.

"The shepherd got me down off the mountain by making me hang on to his crook for support. He took me to his parents' house, which wasn't far away. It was only then that I knew him

164

to be my brother, Alawn, whom I hadn't seen since he was a tiny child. In our arrogance we hadn't asked him his name, you see. I thanked the Gods that neither my Mam nor my Da recognised me – I was half-mad and too exhausted to speak anyway. I don't remember much for a long time after that, but I was told later that over the next week I went totally blind and my body shrivelled to what you see before you now, though it hasn't got any worse since then. I seem to be stuck in this form. Even the Adepts can do nothing and magic is worse than useless. I think that the creature lived by different physical laws to ours and so its final curse can't be altered, though my ability to do magic remains unaffected.

"I got my wish in one respect. The King pronounced me to be a Hero of Britannia. The stone was melted down and the metal forged into the Luck of the Land. It's heavily guarded somewhere on the island, still doing its job. Needless to say, the Great Blight vanished soon after it was installed."

Maia was struck dumb with horror. So this was his secret, the reason for the looks, the whispers, the fear and respect. Over five hundred years of life.

"I can't die," he whispered. "What is left to me but to serve my country and the people in it? I tried to kill myself, you know. Even poison doesn't work. Wounds that are usually fatal heal up. The Gods are silent on the matter – I don't think they know what to do either. I gave up trying after a while. It was all my fault anyway, caused by my stupidity, arrogance and greed."

Maia, still shocked, found her voice, "You couldn't have helped them. It all happened so fast. If you hadn't hung back it would have killed you too and any others that followed. You got the stone out and that's what matters."

"I can still hear the screams," he muttered.

"You saved the whole country," she insisted. "That was your mission and you succeeded. I learned about the Great Blight as a child – we all do and how brave men stopped it by finding the Luck. Surely you've punished yourself enough."

"I've certainly paid," he said softly. "I've become an object of fear, curiosity and pity. That's why I value the few friends I make, until I have to bury them as well. Immortality as far as I can see it just means attending a lot of funerals. I asked that my

165

family be told that I'd died a hero; I sent them money, saying that it was compensation from the Collegium. They never knew that I was the gibbering Mage they tended."

A tear rolled down his ravaged cheek and he raised his hand to touch it. Maia's eyes were drawn to the stump of his finger. Yet another sacrifice he had made.

"They're all dust now and distant descendants hold the farm. Look at me, I didn't think I had any tears left. Forgive me, Maia, please, I never meant to burden you with this." His voice broke. "I'm a stupid, selfish old fool!"

The bitterness and grief burst through as the weight of his years pressed down on him, bowing his shoulders as if he were Atlas, condemned to an eternity of suffering. Maia went to his side immediately, taking his unresisting body in her wooden arms. She cursed her lack of flesh as he clung to her, his shrivelled head on her breast as if he were shipwrecked on a great ocean and she his only chance of salvation. All her resentment towards him melted away like morning mist. Why had she believed that she was the only one who'd suffered?

"You're *my* Mage now," she told him. "Whatever comes, we'll face it together. All curses can be broken."

He raised his head and smiled, sadly.

"Well, there's always hope. The thought of spending an eternity in this body holds little appeal."

She patted his shoulder. "It seems that we're both in it for the long haul. Nothing lasts forever. I promise you, if there's a cure, I'll do my best to find it. Even if we have to travel to the ends of the earth."

"Now that's a thought," he replied ruefully. "Who knows what lies beyond the horizon?"

Maia stayed with Raven all that long night, watching as Polydorus wrapped him in blankets when he refused to leave his chair and holding his hand, whilst around them the noise of commemoration lasted into the early hours. He dozed fitfully, once waking with a start, but her presence reassured him and, finally, he slept for a short time.

When Raven woke, just before dawn, they talked for a while.

"I wish this would stop," she whispered at last. "I don't want to get inside people's heads but I can't control it."

"It only seems to happen when you have a mental connection with someone."

"Yes," she said, feeling wretched. "I don't want this power, believe me."

"Oh, I believe you. I can stop it happening to me now, at any rate, though it took a lot of Potentia to break the link. You've been given this ability for a reason, I'm sure, even if we don't currently know what it is."

"It was the *Livia*," she told him, shuddering at the memory.

"Yes. The Thunderer said as much. Look, we'll make some experiments when you're more settled in your Ship work. It didn't happen with Captain Plinius, did it?"

"No," Maia admitted, "it only seems to happen when someone's thinking about their past and going over it in their mind. At least, that's what it seems like."

"Good. I really don't want to have to explain this to the Admiral and Leo. Are your functions affected?"

Maia had already checked. "Not that I've noticed. It only lasts for a few seconds. My lamps stayed on and I have a continuous surveillance record."

"Well, that's a blessing. I am truly sorry that you saw what you did. I would have spared you the full horror of it all – a few words would have sufficed. Do you know, when the *Livia* attacked I truly hoped my time had come at last." He gave a great sigh. "I didn't think that even I would survive being burnt to a crisp by supernormal fire. I was resigned to my fate, maybe even ready to welcome it, until a certain young lady threw herself to the fore."

A wry grin stretched his death's head skull.

"Then the Revenant was gone, along with my chance. The Gods have not finished with me yet it seems."

"I don't think they've finished with either of us," she told him.

*

The next day brought new orders. She was to leave Britannia behind and turn southwards towards the coast of Gaul, for 'a quick trip down the coast' as Leo put it.

"I've never been abroad," Maia said.

167

He laughed. "It's not far, but at least you'll glimpse another land, even if it's just northern Gaul. More cliffs and beaches at first, then it flattens out. We won't be stopping."

"It'll give me more time to get used to everything."

"So it will. A couple of days, that's all, then it's back to Portus. I think that the King wants to send his sister off in style."

She frowned. "I thought the *Regina* was going to take her? That's what she's telling everyone."

Leo sniffed. "Well, she's going to be disappointed. The King's ordered the *Victoria* to Portus with all speed. I think he'll want his newest Ship there too, just to make a point. Tell you what, we might let *Regina* the diva tag along behind, eh?"

He gave her a wicked grin and she couldn't help but return it. It seemed that her sister Ship was already getting a reputation. Leo and she had fallen into an easy relationship after the initial friction and Maia appreciated his kindness. He'd put the miniature of her father on his desk as promised, too. She would have to tell Pearl about it when she was by next. Her sister rarely had time to chat and Maia wondered just what it was that kept the Tempestas so busy. Maybe they regulated air currents, or something?

She had a quick peek into the Mage quarters. Raven was busy teaching the Princess spellcasting, which seemed mostly to involve concentration and visualisation. A nebulous shape appeared between them, forming out of the air. She thought it looked like a rose.

"That's it," Raven instructed. "Now, imagine the colour, the texture and the smell."

Julia set her jaw and, slowly, the flower appeared. A delicate scent filled the cabin as it bloomed, hanging in mid-air. Maia was impressed.

"Excellent. Now, take it."

Julia put out a hand and slowly closed her fingers around the stem. Her eyes snapped open and she cried in pain.

"Ow! Bloody thorns!"

The rose fell to the floor and dissipated into smoke.

The Princess sucked her finger and glared at Raven accusingly. "You could have warned me!"

Raven stood, immobile. "I never mentioned thorns."

Julia's eyes widened. "I made it too real."

"There was nothing real about it," the Master Mage admonished her. "Illusion is illusion and don't you forget it."

"But it pricked me."

"Just so. It wasn't real, but it still had an effect on our world because it was an extension of your will, and *that* has magical substance. The object will be part of the world for as long as you can maintain your concentration. Now. Try again."

Maia watched for a while longer, knowing better than to interrupt them. Did she resent the time that he was spending with Julia? It was silly; the girl would be taken to Gaul, forced into marriage and that would be that, whereas it was possible that, as the *Tempest*, she would spend several centuries with Raven. She didn't know why, but the thought was oddly comforting, as if there was something more, hovering in obscurity at the back of her brain. Something she'd forgotten.

\*

The Admiral was very thorough. The *Tempest* and her crew were drilled mercilessly, day and night, until all was working to his satisfaction. Nobody grumbled. All were aware that their lives and the lives of their Shipmates might depend on their swift actions, not to mention the fate of their country should hostilities break out once more. Maia often caught him staring out to the west, a troubled look on his face as if he was trying to peer into the far distance.

It was the end of yet another battle drill, this time early morning before the change of watch. Maia made her report to her officers who had assembled in the day room. She was aware of Leo's quiet apprehension, but the Admiral seemed satisfied.

"Send Musca my compliments," he said.

"He was a good choice, my Lord," Leo agreed. "The man knows his business and there's healthy competition among the gun crews."

Pendragon smiled thinly. "They all want to be the best and I demand nothing less. We'll give them a short break, then we'll go again."

<He's pushing them,> Leo Sent to her.

169

<It's his prerogative,> she replied, <and we'll thank him for it. Wouldn't you have done the same?>
<I would.>
Part of her wondered whether he'd have been so exacting. It wasn't as if she could accuse him of cutting corners, but there was a certain air about him that worried her, as if he was easily bored with the routine and mundane. She suspected that he would come into his own in more trying circumstances, but action needed a solid underpinning and that was what the Admiral was making sure of.
<You're not getting bored, are you?> She saw him twitch.
<Not at all.>
*Liar.* She suppressed the thought, maintaining a dignified silence. His hazel eyes flicked to where she had formed on the bulkhead, then to the Admiral again as talk turned to the weather and nautical miles covered. Maia relayed the information mechanically.

A yell caught her attention, below decks. One of the new hands had been too slow and incautious as a gun was dragged backwards for cleaning, and the heavy wheels had caught his foot. He was lying in a heap on the deck, whilst Musca stood above him letting rip with a series of choice curses.

"Master Gunner, report."

The red-faced man glared at the unfortunate hand.

"This idiot didn't move fast enough, ma'am. He was told 'n' all. We've got to get our speed up 'n' this is what I've been given to work with!"

The youth cringed, clutching at his foot.

"Get him to Hawthorn if you would, Master Musca," she told him, groaning inwardly. Crushed fingers and toes were a hazard of life at sea, but this lad would have to sharpen up quickly if he was to survive and not be seen as a liability to his mates.

"Accident with number twelve cannon, Admiral," she reported to Pendragon. "One of the new hands."

"Just as things were going so well," Pendragon said in annoyance. "Is it serious?"

"Crushed foot."

In the Adept's quarters Hawthorn was seeing to the casualty. "You're lucky not to have smashed it completely," the Adept told the man sternly. "New, are you?"

"Yessir," the crewman sniffed. He didn't look more than sixteen, his freckled face streaked with tears.

"Well, jump back quicker next time or you won't get a chance to learn anything and I'll have to practise my amputation skills." The lad's eyes widened, but Hawthorn only snorted.

"It's only bruised, but this ointment will help it to heal quicker. I don't think you'll be allowed to stay off it for more than a day or two, but rest it when you can. Off you go now!"

"It's nothing serious, sir," Maia relayed.

"Good," her Admiral said crisply. "Pain is the best teacher."

The boy hobbled off, wiping his face on his sleeve and no doubt wishing he'd never signed up. Musca would have to keep an eye on this one. She checked her records for his name and found it.

"Hello Cunomoltus," she said, making him stop dead and look around him in confusion.

"It's *Tempest*," she said, wondering if he really was so green that he didn't realise that she was the only female on the vessel, or at least, the only obvious one.

Cunomoltus tried to salute to all points of the compass at once.

"I'm sorry ma'am," he whimpered, probably expecting another bout of censure. "They call me Monkey."

"You've been unlucky, Monkey," she told him gently, "but you really must be more careful."

He nodded vigorously, gulping an affirmative, then winced as he put too much weight on his injured ankle.

"Go and lie down," she ordered. "Try to sleep for a while. I bet you didn't have much rest last night, did you?"

If the boy had been tired, that could explain his clumsiness. He looked green about the gills too. Come to think of it, she thought that he'd been one of the ones who had spent most of the night bidding an unpleasant farewell to their dinner.

"No ma'am. I was sick," he said miserably. She couldn't help but feel sorry for him. Hopefully he'd toughen up soon.

"I'll get you something for that," she consoled him, intending to have a word with Musca. Somebody should have pointed him in Hawthorn's direction before now. She watched as he limped away, stammering his gratitude and hoped that he knew that he had at least one friend on board. It was only then that she had the horrible thought that it had been her job to have taken more care of him.

It seemed that Monkey wasn't the only one who had much to learn.

<Raven, some of the crew need your Magic Drops.>

She felt his acknowledgement and switched her attention to the officers. It was time she stopped merely watching others and starting acting like a Ship.

# VIII

"Ship ahoy!"

Maia's call alerted Leo immediately, both inside his head and through his ears.

"Who is it?"

"Inanimate. I can't make out the name at this distance, but there's something wrong. It's anchored, but there's no sign of life."

Leo pulled out his telescope and raised it to his eye, his junior officers following suit. Sabrinus was down in the day room giving the four new midshipmen, known as middies, their morning lessons, so his lieutenants, Amphicles and Drustan were standing with their Captain. All three strained their eyes to make out the mystery vessel.

It was a smallish, two-masted craft with sails neatly furled, probably a merchantman plying the coast carrying wine and oil up from the Mediterranean. The coastline loomed behind it, consisting of a stony beach sloping upward to high cliffs. The vessel was moored just off shore, rocking gently at anchor as the waves rolled past.

"Can anyone see any crew?" he asked her. Maia focused on the empty deck, a sense of unease forming. They were off the coast of Gaul, miles from the nearest fishing communities and harbour. Why would the traders have abandoned their vessel to the tides without leaving at least a skeleton crew on board?

"I can't see anyone aboard," Maia replied, increasing her magnification to maximum.

"Approach slowly," Leo ordered. She obligingly slackened her speed and adjusted course to take her towards the smaller vessel, scanning all the while.

As they sailed nearer, more details began to emerge. Magpie and Raven joined Leo as they assessed the situation, whilst Maia could see the Princess standing behind them. Her uncle was in his cabin, so she'd taken the chance to get some fresh air.

"It could be plague," Magpie offered. "Maybe the crew have all been struck down, or the survivors went ashore for help."

"They would have left some warning for other shipping," Leo said. "I can't see any plague signal."

Maia checked again, just to be sure, but the red and black flag hadn't been raised. She alerted Pendragon, who was busy below conducting Admiralty business in private through his personal link.

<Have you hailed them yet?> he asked.

<Not yet, my Lord,>

<Be cautious,> he ordered. She could tell that he suspected something but didn't want to commit himself yet.

"*Tempest*, hail them," Leo said, his attention still fixed on the anchored vessel. Other crew members had paused to watch with interest.

"Somethin's not right," Hyacinthus muttered to Teg, who screwed up his rubbery face in agreement.

"Merchant vessel, this is HMS *Tempest*. Respond."

Her augmented voice echoed over the waves, but there was no answer or movement. She scanned for any signs of violence, but could find nothing amiss, save for one thing.

"Their boat's gone," she reported. Leo raised an eyebrow.

"So they abandoned it? It's not pirates – they would have grabbed what they could and left the area as soon as possible, scuttling the vessel to cover their tracks." Her Captain was clearly thinking out loud. "I'll send a small party over to check. Ready a boat please, *Tempest*. Mr Amphicles, take Captain Osric and six marines."

"Aye sir!" The young lieutenant saluted smartly and made his way amidships where the marines had gathered, weapons at the ready.

Maia watched as Amphicles relayed Leo's order to Osric. The huge, blond man showed no emotion as he received his orders until his Captain had finished, when a wolfish grin appeared beneath his bushy moustache. The small dark Briton looked like a child next to him.

"Leave it to us, sir." She could see that he was relishing the thought of action after days of repetitive trials and drills.

Six more men were promptly chosen. Maia lowered her number one boat and they all clambered down into it, weapons at the ready. She felt the small craft respond to her will as she propelled it briskly across to the silent vessel.

Just before it reached the merchantman, she halted it at a gesture from Leo.

"Report!" she called.

Amphicles raised his megaphone. "It's the *Bonaventura!*"

She had seen that there was a name in faded paint, but couldn't make it out from her angle. Now she knew the vessel's name she could quickly check the lists in her Ship's record.

"It's out of Vada Volaterrana in the north of Italia. Just a regular trading vessel," she informed her Captain. "It works the coastal routes up to Londinium carrying olive oil. It should have a crew of fifteen."

"Tell them to proceed with caution."

"Aye sir."

Amphicles acknowledged the command with a wave as she pushed the boat into position and the men, led by Osric, scrambled up the sides and on to the *Bonaventura*'s deck. They took their time, climbing cautiously before checking the upper deck. Amphicles signalled a negative before disappearing below, followed by Osric. They weren't gone long.

"No-one's aboard!" Amphicles bellowed. For a small man he had a good set of lungs on him. "We can see the boat on the beach! Everything's been left! No sign of attack!"

"I don't like this," Raven muttered, head tilted as if listening to the wind.

"Bring us alongside," Leo told Maia. "It seems safe enough for now. I just can't imagine what would cause a merchant crew to abandon both cargo and vessel."

"*I can!*" Pendragon strode on to the deck, grim-faced. "Belay that order. *Tempest*, initiate siren protocol!"

She heard the sudden intake of breath from her crew as they rushed to obey her loud alert. The Admiral had been monitoring events from his cabin and had wasted no time in acting. His mouth was set in a thin line as he scanned the vessel and the shore beyond. At her hail, the boarding party had virtually fallen into

175

her boat and were already readying the waxen plugs that were carried at all times as standard naval issue.

"There haven't been any reports of danger in this area, Admiral," Leo said.

"If there had been, they would have been acted on," Pendragon replied. "These creatures are rare now, but infestations can appear without warning. All it takes is a brood female to escape a bombardment and start up a new colony. We can't afford to take any risks."

Maia quickly reviewed what she had been taught about the hazards at sea. There were a number of deadly creatures, including various sea monsters like krakens and serpents that would attack Ships if they felt like it, but sirens were something else. Their song enticed mariners ashore, where they could be torn to pieces and eaten at leisure, sirens being exclusively carnivorous. They roosted on rocky cliffs, just like the ones that they faced now, though the beach would be an advantage to them as their prey could get to land under their own power.

"I can't hear anything," Drustan ventured.

"Good. If they were singing you'd already be halfway to shore. They must have dined well not to have reacted to our presence immediately," Pendragon replied shortly. "Make sure that all crew have their earplugs at the ready. We may not get another chance."

Maia focused all her senses on the distant shore line. As a Ship, she was immune to the sirens' song and any warning she could give might mean the difference between life and death.

"There could be some survivors," Raven pointed out. "It's unlikely that a handful of them could have eaten the whole crew at once. Some might yet be saved."

Pendragon pressed his lips together, clearly weighing up the risks.

"They rely on surprise to attract prey and are usually small in number," he said at last. "A well-armed party should be able to deal with them, especially with magical support. My preference would be to blast them from here, but we may cause more deaths. Call for volunteers – and make sure that they know what they're going into. They'll need strong stomachs."

"I'll take command," Leo offered. Maia realised that he was annoyed that he hadn't seen the danger sooner and he was eager to prove himself. Pendragon shot him a sharp look, then nodded curtly.

"Very well, but I'm not risking the Ship. We'll stand by to offer firepower if needed. If you find the filthy things, eradicate them without mercy, no matter what they *appear* to be." Leo nodded.

"I understand, my Lord."

Maia drew her boat back to her as quickly as she could and waited for the report.

"Everything was just left, sir," Amphicles reported, pale under his tan. He had already inserted one earplug, she noticed. "They took the boat and went ashore, leaving all their cargo and personal possessions."

"Are there caves in the cliffs?" Pendragon had clearly made up his mind.

"Yes sir, quite a few."

The Admiral's gaze unfocused and she knew that he was making a direct report to shore.

"It's agreed," he said abruptly, "We're to remove any threat. Make ready."

As per the protocols, all crew inserted their wax earplugs and Raven and Magpie readied a sound barrier around the Ship that would deaden some of the noise if and when it came. Maia continued to scan the shoreline for any sign of movement, but still nothing stirred save the wind. She checked to see if her sister was about, but somehow she knew that the Tempestas was far away. It was too much to expect her to stay near all the time, but she would have come in very handy in their current situation. All communication from now on would have to be done mentally or with hand signals, as no ear could remain unblocked. Deafness was their primary defence now.

<We'll look pretty silly if the crew have just decided to go ashore for food or water,> she Sent to Raven.

<I pray that it's so> he Sent back. <Rather that than the probability that they've gone to a horrible death.>

She was ashamed immediately, but felt his reassurance as he added, <I know what you mean. Let's hope we find a boat load

of drunken sailors flat out after a happy party on the beach, eh? Then we can all feel silly together.>

<Be careful!> she Sent to Leo, wishing that she could detach herself and follow him. The shore was full of dangers that she couldn't protect him from and she hated to feel helpless.

He smiled up at her from the boat and patted the hilt of his sword. She was relieved to see that he was also carrying two pistols on his belt.

<Don't worry. I'm surrounded by armed men who won't hesitate to strike. Send Owl below to stay with the youngsters. He'll be of more use there.>

She did as she was bid, watching the apprentice's back disappear below decks.

Unlike some threats, sirens could be dispatched with powder and steel as easily as a human, as long as their attackers remained deaf to their irresistible song. As she sent her boats away, she saw that some men were wrapping cloths around their heads as an added protection and to keep their earplugs in place. It would be fatal if they were jolted loose in a battle with the deadly creatures.

A flicker of movement ashore caught her eye. A large sea bird? Something with wings anyway. She quickly relayed her observation to the others, watching carefully to see if it appeared again. There – a brief flicker as something darted across the cliff face. She couldn't quite make out what it was but surely it was too large to be a gannet or other bird. Come to think of it, she'd seen nothing in the sky for quite some time. It was frustrating to be too far away to see clearly.

<No sea birds,> Pendragon's voice sounded in her head, steely and commanding, much like his speaking voice. <They'll have caught and eaten them, too. Sirens devour anything they can get their claws into.>

She felt his disgust, tinged with fear and knew that he spoke from experience.

<Have you come across them before, my Lord?>

<Yes. On my first voyage. We lost half the crew.>

She heard the pain that he was unable to hide and knew that he would try to save as many men as he could. If there was no-one left alive he wouldn't hesitate to order a devastating bombardment.

<Ready the guns,> he ordered.

She signalled to Musca and his gunners obeyed, loading and priming ready to fire when required. She could feel Leo's anticipation and eagerness as the boats approached the shore, as well as his apprehension. Few sailors had met sirens before and lived to tell the tale. At least the rocks were obvious enough and the sirens, if they were there at all, weren't bothered about wrecking the vessels. Perhaps they hoped that leaving them would lure in other victims?

<I can see half a dozen figures,> Leo Sent. She could feel him looking through his telescope. <They're women.>

<Naked and beautiful?> Pendragon interrupted.

<Yes,> Leo confirmed. <They're waving at us and smiling.> His tone held fascination mingled with horror.

<I can hear singing!> Maia Sent immediately, as the first sweet notes flew towards her over the water.

"Good job we're already deaf!" she heard Musca tell his men. Most of the gunners were skilled at reading lips, as when the guns were sounding off the noise was incredible and hearing loss came with the job. Still, all of them had taken the mandatory precautions.

"Eh?" Teg shouted, which got a laugh. Maia was reassured. They were fine at least. She checked below decks. Julia was standing guard over the midshipmen, who were huddled together with their hands over their ears and their eyes as big as saucers. Hawthorn and Rowan, his assistant, were preparing the Adept quarters for casualties.

A movement at her side heralded the arrival of Danuco. The Priest's features were creased with worry as he gazed shoreward and she caught his eye. He smiled at her weakly and she saw that his lips were moving. Behind him, smoke was already ascending from the Ship's altar.

The siren song had grown louder now, as if the creatures had realised what was happening and more were joining in the hellish choir. She analysed it, noting the interwoven harmonies that were designed to overpower the human will and compel them to follow the sound to its source. It wasn't a tune as such, just a

179

series of overlapping chords that flowed from high to low tones in a repeating pattern over and over, like birdsong magnified and augmented with magic. It had no effect on her, but she watched her crew closely just in case there was someone who was more susceptible or foolish enough not to have secured their waxen plugs properly.

Some men had rammed their hats or caps down but still showed a certain glassiness about the eyes that she didn't like. Pendragon's face was set like concrete, all his attention fixed on the boats that were finally approaching the beach.

<They're all singing now,> Leo reported back.

<Fire as soon as you're close enough,> Pendragon ordered tersely.

<We're going in,> he replied.

<Be aware that they may attack from the air.> He turned his attention to his Ship.

<Report.>

< All guns ready,> she assured him, trying to project a confidence she didn't feel.

<Heave-to,> Pendragon ordered. She did as directed, until they could all make out several figures on the beach. They appeared to be beautiful women, with long, flowing hair, all smiling and waving suggestively at the boats. She could see how the unwary would think that they had suddenly found a paradise filled with willing partners, even more tempting after long weeks at sea. The sirens truly had a perfect hunting technique. Leo had timed it so that both boats beached simultaneously and she approved of his strategy. With any luck her crew would get most of them with the first volley and she knew that they carried explosive grenadoes as well. Hand–to–hand combat would be a last resort.

She felt Leo tense, then, as the boats' keels scraped up on to the shingle he stood, drew his sword and signalled.

The marines were already loaded. They leaped from the boats with military precision, lining up two deep on the shore. The creatures approached, arms outstretched, lips open wide in song. The first rank knelt, the rear one closed up behind and, with a sudden crack of exploding gunpowder, they fired. The noise of the volley echoed from the cliffs and a great cloud of smoke arose, obscuring her vision, followed by further explosions as lit grenadoes were hurled into the crowd of sirens.

The song ended abruptly, replaced by inhuman screeching. Several scaled creatures lay dead on the shingle whilst black feathered wings thrashed as the wounded tried to escape, only to be finished off with swords and pistols. She heard her crew cheer.

"That's taught 'em!" Drustan muttered.

Pendragon nodded and went to remove his earplugs. At that instant, Maia saw the danger they were in.

Sirens were pouring out of gaping holes in the cliff. Their cries filled the air as they dived, hurtling down at their attackers. She screamed a warning down her link and grabbed the Admiral's arm.

Maia could see them clearly now. All pretence of beauty was gone as claws grabbed and fanged beaks snapped. Leo shot one out of the air with his pistol before pulling out a second. Before he could cock it, great talons snatched him off the ground and he cried out with pain as he was lifted into the air. A firebolt streaked like a comet and hit the creature in the chest, forcing it to drop him. He fell heavily to the shingle and she feared for broken bones before another siren swooped down, only to be met with a pistol ball. It fell like a stone, writhing weakly on the ground before switching back to its female form and holding up a hand imploringly, crying like a human woman. Osric strode up and impaled it with his cutlass.

<Leo, can you get up?> she Sent urgently.

<Sprained my ankle,> he replied, gasping with pain, but he managed to get upright with Osric's help and hobble back to a boat. His coat was stained where the creature's talons had pierced his flesh.

<There are too many of them,> Pendragon ordered. <Captain! Retreat so we can fire!>

The men stumbled back to the boats. It wasn't only sirens' bodies that littered the beach now. Maia could see that several of her crew were already on their way to the realm of Hades, their prone bodies being fought over by the ravenous monsters. Raven and Magpie stood on her deck, pouring a steady stream of spells into the rest of the screaming creatures as they harried the survivors. A well-aimed fireball crisped three at once and she felt a flash of pride at her Mages' abilities.

As they fell into her boats, two marines weren't quick enough, snatched from the side as they ran, to be plucked up and dismembered in mid-air as she watched. The others turned their attention away from the fleeing sailors and began to head in her direction. And still they came, swooping from their cave nests like winged nightmares. There had to be more than fifty of them.

<They're clear. Target the cliffs and fire!> Pendragon's voice echoed through her head. Musca received her signal with grim satisfaction and almost at once her guns blazed forth, sending their iron shot into the cliff face and smashing into the wheeling sirens. Showers of rock and earth erupted from the cave mouths as her gunners found their range and began to methodically demolish the nest site. Maia extended her Potentia through the wood to speed her boats back to her vessel, noting the bloodied limbs and faces where talons had taken their toll. Hawthorn and Rowan would be kept busy for a while.

<Maintain fire!>

Pendragon was implacable in his desire to see every one of the sirens dead. Some had turned back to their nests, perhaps hoping to rescue young, but others were heading in her direction, wings beating frantically as they sought an advantage. Raven spoke a word and a lance of flame arrowed into the air, slicing into feathers and flesh. Sirens fell like burning cinders. Men rushed to load her deck guns, firing canister shot at the swooping enemy as they came into range. Those that fell into the sea were picked off with deadly aim as her cannons blasted away, pounding the cliffs into rubble.

Thick, sulphurous smoke poured from the gun decks, reducing visibility, though she thought that the attack was lessening.

<Cease fire!>

The great booms and heavy vibrations stopped. Slowly, the fog of battle cleared, to reveal her boats and a sea awash with corpses. A few creatures still flew above, but well-aimed shots put paid to them. If any had survived, they were nowhere to be seen.

The men were brought aboard in a silence all the stranger after the cacophony. Eight men had been lost to the creatures.

"We were lucky," Pendragon said, his face bleak. "I've never heard of so many. They usually live in small groups, not more than a dozen. I don't know how this has gone unnoticed for so long." His tone boded ill for someone.

"We don't know how long the *Bonaventura* has been here," Raven pointed out. "Perhaps the glut of food led to rapid breeding. These creatures haven't been studied as much as some other perils."

"And I'm not going to start now," Pendragon said firmly. "I will want answers though, especially from the Hispanic and Gallic authorities. Someone must have noticed that vessels were going missing."

Maia resigned herself to relaying a large amount of official correspondence in the near future. Meanwhile, sacrifices were being made on behalf of the lost sailors, both her own and the unfortunate crew of the *Bonaventura*, who were presumed to have been devoured. Pendragon ordered Drustan to assemble a scratch crew and sail it back to the nearest harbour. From how it was sitting in the water, the hold was probably still full of goods. The crew hadn't stood a chance. Maia wondered what she could have done if she had been taken unawares; she could have responded, but there would have been a great loss of life. Men would jump overboard and swim to get to sirens, abandoning all reason, although many sailors couldn't swim and would drown in the process. These sirens had shown more intelligence than most of their kind in persuading the men to use the boat – another reason to ensure that none was left to spread their plague.

Leo had been lucky. She'd been sure that he'd broken his ankle, but he insisted that the most badly injured of his crew were treated first. His servant, Cato, was quite distressed but insisted on staying with his master, watching as his damaged shoulders and swollen ankle were bound and treated with salves. Hawthorn muttered a healing prayer as he fastened a small silver amulet on to the bandages. Next to him, Rowan was also working flat out, sewing up a nasty gash that had sliced open a marine's cheek. He had been fortunate that it had just missed his eye, but he would be left with a scar. The apprentice had deft fingers and chatted as he worked.

"You'll be able to impress the ladies with your battle honour," he told his patient.

The marine fixed him with a jaundiced eye. "No thanks," he grunted. "I knew there was a reason I distrust beautiful women. I'll stick to my own kind."

Rowan rolled his eyes at him then slathered on some pungent ointment and a dressing.

"Just try not to smile or laugh while it's healing."

The marine, Marcellus, sighed. Maia knew that his mates would promptly dredge up the funniest jokes they could think of to try to get him to crack. It was cruel, but there was no accounting for their warped sense of humour and if she told them off they'd try it on even more.

"Go and rest," the Adept said and Marcellus grunted his thanks before marching off stoically. Rowan washed his hands in astringent vinegar before turning to the next man.

The marines would mourn the loss of their own, packing and moving sea chests to be returned to next-of-kin and holding their own ceremonies, which mostly comprised telling stories about the dead and both thanking and cursing the Fates.

Musca had resumed his bombardment as soon as both boats were secured, until there wasn't much left of the caves. They'd been hollowed out to provide a refuge for the sirens, but now they were scarred and gouged by cannon shot. There was no sign of life and she hadn't spotted any escapees from the carnage. Torn and bloodied bodies, both human and siren lay scattered and broken along the shoreline, tinging the waves with red.

"I'll take a party ashore myself, to check," Pendragon told Leo. "We can't leave even one of the creatures alive. Round up all uninjured marines and a few crewmen too. *Tempest*, if you see anything in the air that could be a siren, fire on it immediately."

"Yes, Admiral."

"Good. Well done."

She was puzzled. "I'm sorry, sir. What do you mean?"

He raised his eyebrows. "You remained calm. Many a young Ship would have panicked. You didn't."

She felt a warm glow at the praise and respect in his tone, as she knew that it wasn't awarded lightly. She smiled back at him and resumed her scan of the shore, in case there were any signs that not all of the fallen creatures were as dead as they should be.

It had been bloody, dirty work, but sirens were just one of the many perils at sea that she would be expected to deal with. But why had there been so many of them? She settled down to watch, alert for further orders and only too aware that the Admiral would not rest until he was absolutely sure that every last one of the predators was destroyed.

Then, and only then, would the dead be avenged.

*

Leo had insisted on remaining on duty despite the pain of his wounds, until sheer fatigue had forced him to rest. Raven regarded that as simple foolishness, as Sabrinus was capable enough of commanding until the Admiral's return. Pendragon had been adamant on surveying the nest site himself and was even now on the beach supervising the cremation of the remains. The ancient Mage suspected that it was more a case of exorcising demons that had long haunted him, and laying at least some ghosts to rest.

Men and sirens had been separated into two piles, though with the humans it had been more of a question of assembling body parts. The freshest unknowns were presumed to have been from the doomed crew of the *Bonaventura*, whilst others were from other unfortunate and as yet unnamed vessels, salvaged from what was left of the sirens' nests and mostly consisting of gnawed bones. These last were laid reverently on pyres made from driftwood. Danuco was overseeing their final rites, placing coins in gaping mouths and empty skulls before making the offerings they would need to see them safely across the Styx, or to wherever they believed their souls would travel. The sirens' scaly corpses were piled up as far away as possible and burnt without ceremony, save a few muttered curses. Without their glamour they were revealed as winged lizard-like creatures, ugly in death and stinking of blood. The men had handled them with distaste, reluctant to even touch them.

"I asked Sergeant Osric to get me some bits," Maia heard Raven announce to his apprentice.

"Which parts do you think will be most useful?" Julia asked, with interest.

"Oh, feathers, talons. Scales. Maybe teeth. I've a couple of friends who'll put them to good use and the rest can be used in potions."

Maia, listening in, thought that Robin would be delighted. He was never happier than when he had a new project on the go. Doubtless he'd be straight on to his former master, Heron, to work out the best way to incorporate the parts into a new device. She didn't know what Osric would make of the request, though she didn't think it would give him any trouble.

She remembered *Blossom*'s reaction to the smelly kraken tentacle Heron had used on his first detector and hoped that the siren bits wouldn't be that bad. Even as the Mages talked, she kept most of her attention on shore, in case of any further threats.

<*Tempest*, have all Ships been alerted?>

<Aye, sir,> she answered. The Admiral sounded weary, though you wouldn't know it from his bearing and manner. She had come to respect him more and more as she spent time under his command. Though she didn't like to admit it, Leo's inexperience could have resulted in disaster.

<We'll be returning shortly. Sergeant Osric has been collecting trophies, it seems.>

<They're for the Collegium, sir.> That got his attention.

<Our young Mages are full of ideas. I approve. Anything to save lives from this scourge. We'll be returning shortly,> he added. <How is the Captain?>

Furious with himself for not seeing the danger, she thought privately. < Resting in his cabin. Sabrinus has taken charge.>

<Good. Make sure he stays there. I know he blames himself, but this was one time when experience counted. There hasn't been a siren attack for several years.>

<Thank the Gods that you were aboard, Admiral.>

<Indeed,> he replied softly.

Maia gazed east at the two roiling columns of smoke, one hallowed and one unclean. Fire was taking them all, though this stretch of shore would be avoided for many years to come. Other

186

Ships would pass and remember the carnage, whilst merchantmen would hurry by as fast as they could, eyes averted, remembering the horrific fate of their fellows. At least now no other vessels would fall prey to these implacable hunters.

"Your first battle at sea, *Tempest*," Sabrinus said. He'd moved up quietly to stand beside her Shipbody and survey the deck. His face was imperturbable as usual, but his eyes were shadowed. She knew he'd seen action against the Northmen before now.

"It isn't easy watching crewmen die," she said quietly.

"No. Whether it be at the hands of men or monsters, the outcome is the same. All we can do is honour the fallen by continuing to do our duty as best we can."

She turned her head to look him full in the face. "Indeed, Lieutenant. What will happen to the *Bonaventura*?"

Even though the vessel was an inanimate, it didn't mean that she didn't owe the sturdy little merchantman a debt, if only for the sake of the men who had put their faith in it.

"We'll take it back to Portus, where it can be collected and sailed on to Londin. It's part of a fleet, so the company will want it up and running again as soon as possible. The cargo seems intact and saleable."

They'd have to clear it first, she thought with a shudder. The new crew wouldn't want to see reminders of their doomed predecessors. She could only hope that the company would return all effects to the families of the deceased, but sentiment wouldn't be allowed to get in the way of profit and there would be sailors glad of the work.

"Who will take charge, do you think?"

Sabrinus rubbed his square chin thoughtfully. "Drustan would make a good job of it and we can spare enough experienced men to operate it. He's still a bit green if you ask me, but he's learning fast."

The young lieutenant had just been promoted from midshipman and hung on the older officers' every word. His father was a wealthy freedman in Londin who had been happy to sponsor his younger son's career in the Navy. So far, according to his son, he hadn't been disappointed with his offspring's progress.

"Yes, he performed well in the crisis," she agreed. "No-one can say that the guns haven't been thoroughly tested as well."

Sabrinus nodded. "Definitely," he agreed, surveying the ravaged coast. "Let's hope we got them all."

She could only nod.

\*

The beach was a mess, strewn with piles of boulders and churned earth from the *Tempest*'s bombardment. Milo could make out the figures picking their way through, collecting and sorting the bodies. The first greasy smoke was already starting to billow from the pile of sirens, cleansing fire consuming the shattered wings and scaly flesh. The Agent was glad the wind was off the sea and blowing the stench away inland. He'd wanted to volunteer for the unsavoury task, but his duty of care to the Princess came first. She'd left the youngsters below and was leaning on the rail next to him, her borrowed face pale and her eyes fixed on the land.

"My poor uncle," she whispered to him, once she was sure nobody was in sight. "He hates the creatures. Senator Rufus told me what happened to him, though he's never spoken of it."

"It was a hard thing to witness when so young," Milo muttered back, his eyes returning to the deck. "Thank the Gods he was aboard, or we'd have all been taken unawares. Even the Ship couldn't have stopped all her men from jumping overboard."

"Does it only affect men?" she asked. "Or are females immune? I had to plug my ears with the others."

He shook his head. "It's everyone. You'd see something different, that's all. Ships are unaffected, because they're no longer flesh and blood."

"Does anyone know what they sound like?" She turned curious eyes to him. He grunted.

"Well, I don't, that's for sure. Apparently Ulysses reported 'sweet singing that overpowers the senses', but you'll have to ask *Tempest*. She'll probably have a more scientific assessment."

Julia turned back to watching the activity on the beach.

"He must have been a brave man."

188

"Who? Ulysses?"

"Yes, though I prefer to call him Odysseus. Fancy risking his life just to hear their song! Do you think it haunted him, afterwards?"

"If it did," he replied, "It served him right. He was far too careless of his crews. Didn't they keep getting eaten?"

"He was cursed by the Gods," she pointed out.

"Yes, but he survived. His men didn't."

She chewed her lip. "That probably haunted him too." She shivered.

"Are you cold?"

Julia grimaced. "I just feel…" she broke off. "It's like something bad's going to happen, but I don't know what or when."

He straightened up. "A presentiment?"

She shivered. "I don't know."

"It's probably all the excitement." Privately, he thought it was something to watch. The Princess had the makings of a powerful Mage and they didn't have feelings like this without good reason. He'd have to report it to Raven. Just then, he caught sight of the Admiral and Captain emerging on to the quarterdeck. Even though they were amidships, he couldn't risk a meeting.

"I think we should go down," he said, taking her by the elbow and jerking his head in the direction of the officers. She caught on immediately and led the way back below, Milo following behind like a good attendant.

"Could you fetch some food please, Milo?" Julia asked and the Agent nodded, heading off to the galley. Julia watched him go. She'd had no midday meal with all the action and it was growing dark already. The men would work through the night if necessary, so that their fallen comrades were laid to rest with the proper rites. Nobody wanted angry shades to linger.

Back in the workroom, Raven was standing at a bench pounding herbs in a mortar. Magpie had gone ashore with the men for protection and defence, in case any sirens had survived the purge. The ancient Mage lifted his head as she entered.

"Ah, there you are. What's happening?"

"They're collecting bodies," Julia said. She crossed over to him and sniffed. "More Magic Drops?"

"Always useful," Raven replied, "and our good Ship neglected to tell her newer crew to come and be treated."

"She's had her hands full," Julia said, feeling that she had to defend the only other female on board. "It's her first voyage and look what's happened."

"You think I'm being too hard on her."

"Well, a bit," Julia said, idly conjuring a tiny light that drifted through her fingers like a gossamer thread. "She's learning too. We all make mistakes."

"Indeed, but she hasn't that luxury. Still, she won't forget again."

His apprentice cast him a look of annoyance and walked over to stare at the kraken warning device. The little crystals winked in the light as if reminding her that they could spring to action at any moment.

"Do you think we could devise something like this for sirens?" she asked.

Raven paused. "Possibly. Something that will react to the singing before the human ear, as by then it's too late. That's one of the reasons I've asked for samples."

Movement on the bulkhead heralded the arrival of the Ship, pushing out from the wood as an amorphous mass before her Shipbody took its usual form.

"Hello, *Tempest*," Julia said.

"Hello Owl, Raven. And Master Milo too, I see."

The latter had just entered, carrying a covered tray. Julia's stomach rumbled in anticipation. She really was very hungry all of a sudden. Milo set the tray down carefully.

"Would you like me to fetch some for you, Raven?"

The Mage waved a dismissive hand. "I've eaten, thank you. Polydorus watches me like a hawk and fusses like an old grandmother. Heaven forbid that I should skip a meal on his watch."

Julia rolled her eyes at Milo. "He can hardly force me to eat if I don't want to."

The Master Mage sniffed. "You need your victuals. I never had any trouble persuading Maia to eat, did I?"

Maia? Who was she? Julia looked at him in puzzlement, until the Ship answered.

"When you've not had much in your life, food is a luxury."

"Especially cake." He grinned at her, his wrinkles deepening. The Ship laughed and Julia realised that it was a private joke between them. So, the *Tempest* hadn't had a privileged upbringing? Interesting.

"I miss cake," *Tempest* said wistfully. "Now I understand why *Blossom* is always going on about cheese."

"It must be strange for you," Julia said. The Ship nodded.

"I just wanted to see how you're all doing," she explained. "The Navy's ordered us to try and find some explanation as to why the sirens had reached plague proportions. This coast is remote but on the shipping lanes, so somebody should have reported the infestation before now."

"And then we'll be heading back to Portus?" Julia sighed.

"Looks like it." Tempest cast her a look of sympathy.

Raven tipped the ground herbs into a pot and set it to simmer. "There. Another batch started. *Tempest*, have you checked for wrecks?"

"Not yet."

Raven gestured in Milo's direction. "He thinks the sirens sank their previous victims' vessels."

Julia jumped. She'd forgotten that Milo was there. The man had a way of fading into the background unnoticed.

"If I'm right," Milo said evenly, "they've learned a new trick. That's worrying."

"It was presumed that the recent storms took the smaller merchantmen," Raven said. "We are just to the north of the Great Bay after all and it's notorious for destroying vessels. *Tempest*, can you sense the sea bottom?"

"Some of it," the Ship admitted.

"Then I'd make a start, if I were you," the Agent told her. "It can't do any harm. New wreckage should be more intact."

"Good idea," Raven nodded. "Do it, but tell the Admiral it was your idea. Milo won't mind, will you Milo?"

The Agent smiled and Julia was hit by a feeling of familiarity. Had she seen him somewhere before coming aboard? She decided that he must have been assigned to the palace at some point. She'd probably come across him and forgotten.

"Not at all. We Agents rarely get credit for anything anyway, and you'll be doing all the work."

"It's very gracious of you, Master Milo," *Tempest* said, a smile on the silver mask that was her face. What had she gone through to form such a strange Shipbody? Julia had the feeling that whatever life she'd had before, the girl was better off as she was now. "I'm scanning," the Ship added, "though I'll have to move. Why didn't they sink the *Bonaventura*?"

"Time," Milo answered promptly. "They probably wanted to eat first."

"Ugh," Julia said. "It doesn't bear thinking about. I'm glad they're dead."

"It's their nature," Raven pointed out. "Numbers were low in the past, but more boats means more opportunities. At least there don't seem to be any on the New Continent."

"And now there are less of them here," *Tempest* said, with grim satisfaction. She surveyed the three of them. "I'll go and speak to the Admiral."

"Keep me informed," Raven told her.

"I will."

Her Shipbody shrank and melted back into the panelling, as if sinking back into deep water with barely a ripple to mark her passing. Julia took the opportunity to eat, whilst Raven deftly strained his herbs and filled his alembic with the remaining liquid, to distil it.

"After you've eaten, there will be a test on Trismegistus' Primary Laws of Magic. You should have had time to learn them all by now," he said.

Julia swallowed. She'd spent the last two days memorising the rules and hoped it would be enough to satisfy her teacher's very exacting standards. Milo, standing at the side, gave her a knowing grin, as if he knew exactly what was to come. Then again, she thought, perhaps he did. Whatever, it was better than what awaited her in a few short days.

She applied herself to her chicken pie with a growing sense of despair.

\*

192

Maia found four vessels, all lying in pieces on the sea bed.

"That explains their numbers," Pendragon told his officers. "Sirens are like rats. Their numbers increase when they find a regular source of food."

"One of them had a bright idea to sink the vessels, whilst leaving the latest as bait," Leo said, his face showing his disgust.

"We can only hope that a new brood mother didn't leave the nest and take her plan with her," Pendragon said, his tone ominous. "This could be an increasing problem. I've recommended more patrols in areas where we know vessels have been lost – with the necessary precautions, of course."

The others clearly agreed with him.

"Mr Drustan reports that the *Bonaventura* is made ready, sir," Sabrinus said. "He'll follow on behind us in his own time."

"A first command," Pendragon said. "I'm only sorry that it isn't under more favourable circumstances." There were murmurs of agreement. "In the meantime, we're to return to Portus for a happier occasion, Gods willing. We're to escort the Princess as she leaves for Gaul aboard the *Victoria*."

The atmosphere in the cabin lifted a little. Maia listened in, knowing that a certain new Ship would be spitting feathers that she wasn't to be the main attraction.

"*Tempest*, weigh anchor and make sail. I want to arrive as soon as possible."

"Aye, sir."

Maia doubted that the atmosphere in the Mage quarters would be as positive.

*

<Sirens! You really don't do things by halves, do you girl?>

*Blossom* sounded horrified and dismayed in equal measure as Maia relayed the events of the past day.

<Nasty creatures,> old *Persistence* offered. <Not run across 'em meself, but I know some who 'ave. All lost crew. Yer were very lucky.>

Maia's thoughts turned to her lost marines. <There shouldn't have been so many of them,> she explained. < Even the Admiral was surprised.>

<Do they know why?> That was the *Leopard*, on patrol in the Mediterranean where there had been reports of pirates lately. She sounded relieved that her route hadn't taken her further north.

<Probably because they were feeding well,> Maia replied with a shudder. <But no-one knows for sure.>

<As long as the foul creatures are all dead,> *Persistence* interjected.

<We think we got them all. I didn't spot any escaping and I blasted their nests to bits. The Admiral insisted that I was thorough.>

<Aye, 'e would be. They got most of 'is first crew when 'e was a young 'un, an' 'e's 'ated 'em ever since. Pox rot 'em all to 'Ades!>

The other Ships echoed the *Persistence*'s sentiment. Maia could tell that they weren't the only ones who were listening into the group as well, alerted by her general warning. Sirens appearing near busy shipping lanes wasn't normal. They preferred more out of the way places where a few sailors could go missing without causing too much alarm and they could hunt and feast in peace.

<Good job he was on board,> *Blossom* said. <How's Leo? I heard he was injured.>

<He's recovering. He wanted to lead the attack himself and the Admiral let him, but that was before we knew about how many sirens there were. He got clawed and hurt his ankle when they tried to drag him away. The Admiral's ordered him to rest.>

<Bet he loves that,> *Blossom* said, wryly. <Give him our best wishes for his recovery, won't you?>

<I will,> Maia promised. She could tell that the old training Ship had a soft spot for her Captain.

<Has anyone got any more cheerful news?> the *Cameo* asked. She was an easy–going fourth–rate who was off the south coast patrolling for smugglers who tried to dodge the import taxes levied on goods from the New Continent and the rest of the world. Walrus ivory, silk, amber and furs were lucrative luxuries and some traders tried to maximise profits by slipping into quiet creeks under cover of darkness. The smaller Ship was obviously unsettled by what she'd heard.

<We could certainly do with some of that,> *Blossom* seconded her.

<I've got a new Mage!> *Persistence* announced, to a few cheers. She'd been moaning about Plover for quite a while.

<Did you end up chucking him in the drink then?> *Leopard* inquired to general laughter.

<Didn't 'ave ter. 'E got a little too fond of the bottle and couldn't be woken during that storm I 'ad last month. The Old Man finally gave 'im 'is marchin' orders, thank the Gods. I've got one called Wagtail now an' 'e seems all right.>

<But can he put up with you?> *Cameo* teased. <The grumpiest Ship in the Fleet!>

<Don't know what yer mean,> *Persistence* shot back. <I'm a little ray of sunshine, I am!>

The conversation dissolved into sniggers.

<Well, I'd better get back to heading for Portus,> Maia said regretfully. It was always good to catch up on the latest news, even if she seemed to be the only one making it recently. Although she could talk to any Ship, in practice it was usually the ones that were nearest or she was familiar with already. Her bonds would strengthen as she gained in experience and years of service.

<Try and stay out of trouble!> *Blossom* told her.

<It likes me too much,> Maia groaned. She signed off and sped towards the rising sun with the wind in her sails, leaving the darkness behind her.

195

# IX

By the time the *Tempest* entered Portus harbour, Julia was feeling sick with mingled nerves, rage and frustration. Duty was at war with desire and she felt trapped in the middle of both, locked on a course that promised nothing but disaster. She told Raven as much.

"You always have a choice," he told her. His shrivelled face gave away nothing.

"What do you mean?"

"You're powerful. You could just say no and leave."

She stared at him in dismay. "And do what?"

He spread his hands. "Whatever you want."

"I would be denying my birth, letting everyone down and be the cause of a major diplomatic incident."

"Even so."

She glared at him. "How is that a choice? I can't do it!"

"Then you've made a choice, haven't you?"

Julia resisted the urge to throw something at him "I'm going for some air," she snapped and stamped out of the workroom, heading for the deck. A flicker in her peripheral vision told her that her ever-present shadow was near at hand. As usual, Milo took his responsibilities very seriously. She ignored him and climbed up the ladder to emerge into the freshness of the morning. A few hands nodded respectfully at her and she nodded back. As a Mage, even an apprentice, she was treated as a superior officer. She found she didn't miss the bowing and scraping that was her usual greeting.

The mouth of the harbour was now in sight, with the city clustered around it. The official buildings towered over the rest, the Polis Offices and major temples being the largest though she couldn't see the one dedicated to Juno from here. It was hidden behind that of her spouse, Jupiter and, as far as most people knew, was where she'd been spending the past couple of weeks. She leaned against the rail, turning her face into the west wind and closing her eyes, thankful that she'd had a little freedom before the chains of duty shackled her once more.

"Hello, Owl." It was the Ship, rising from the deck like a wave.

"*Tempest.*"

The two women stood in silence for a time, watching the land loom closer.

"Do you go up to the quayside?" Julia asked her.

"No. I'm too large. I anchor in the harbour and people use my boats," the Ship said.

Julia nodded. "I can't say I'm happy to see the place."

*Tempest* cast her a look of sympathy. "I grew up there, you know."

"In Portus?"

"Yes. In the Foundling Home. Then I was a servant, until my mistress tried to kill me. I never would have thought I'd end up like this. The most I ever hoped for was the freedom to run my own business and make my way in the world."

A difficult upbringing indeed. The Ship's earlier comment made more sense now. It also made her feel a little ashamed.

"And here I am, moaning about my lot," Julia said guiltily.

"Oh, I don't think you have it easy either," *Tempest* said. "I just meant, who knows what the Fates have in store for us? One minute our path seems set, the next everything's changed."

Julia smiled. "Are you trying to cheer me up? Everyone says that Parisius is on his last legs."

"Let's hope so," the Ship replied. "How are your studies going?"

"Apparently I know enough now to be less of a danger to myself and others. It will have to do, as I'm never going to be admitted to the Collegium, am I?"

"Probably not. Still, you'll know enough to deal with stubborn Gauls."

Julia thought of the sleep and illusion spells she'd already mastered. "Hopefully so. I've a plan."

"Always a good idea," *Tempest* said. "I'm glad I could help, even a little bit."

"I'm glad too. Thank you."

The activity on board suddenly increased and Julia glanced at her uncle's commanding figure, high on the quarterdeck and surrounded by his officers. He was definitely looking in their direction.

"We're here," the Ship said abruptly. "I'm ordered to drop anchor." A second later, the creaking of rope and noise of sails being furled, together with the rattling of chains told everyone the same thing.

"I'll have to go and get ready," Julia said. *Tempest* offered her a hand and she took it, feeling the strange, unyielding texture of the Ship's fingers. What had happened to her original, human body? Julia doubted that she'd ever find out. She smiled and went below, Milo following at her heels like a faithful hound.

Raven was nowhere to be seen, but Magpie was waiting for her.

"Time to go," he said. His face was sympathetic, but she guessed that he would rather be rid of her. It had been a terrible risk, after all. Milo went into her tiny cabin and she could see that he'd made a start on her packing, not that she had much to take. She could hardly wear Mage robes once she got to the Temple of Juno.

"I won't forget your kindness to me," she told Magpie.

He inclined his head. "It's always good to be owed favours, especially by a queen."

She smiled ruefully. "I'm not a queen yet."

"True." He made a sign to avert evil. "I didn't mean to misspeak, or tempt the Fates. I wish you nothing but good fortune."

"And I you. Where's Raven?"

"With Pendragon, but he should return shortly to take you to the temple, though if anyone asks, you're going to the Portus Collegium building to complete your training."

She sighed. "If only!"

He nodded, as Milo reappeared. "All's ready, sir."

The bag of belongings was pitifully small, but at that moment she'd have willingly traded it for her entire dowry. *Tempest*'s voice echoed in the workroom.

"Apprentice Owl, the boat is ready to take you ashore."

"Thank you, ma'am," Julia replied. Magpie bowed as she left and she felt the weight of duty settle on her shoulders like a heavy load she'd managed to forget for a time.

On deck, the sailors offered their best wishes. To her horror, the Admiral was among them. She blinked as he approached her, smiling.

"I hear you've made excellent progress in your studies, young man," he remarked, fixing he with his dark eyes. She swallowed, suddenly convinced that the game was up. Surely he would recognise her? "I hope you choose to remain with the Navy. We need good Mages."

Julia felt her knees wobble. "Indeed, Your Highness," she managed to whisper, before Raven was suddenly at her elbow.

Pendragon nodded indulgently before returning to his post, his duty done. For the Lord High Admiral and a Prince of the Blood to talk to a lowly apprentice showed how much he cared for all his men and she loved him for it. Fortunately, it would also explain her awkwardness, as Owl would be expected to be overwhelmed at the honour done to him. Still, Julia was glad when she had made it down to the water and was handed into the rocking boat to seat herself between Raven and Milo. The wooden flank of the *Tempest* rose above them like a wall, then receded as the boat made its way across the harbour towards the waiting city. On board, a silver-grey figure lifted a hand in farewell.

Julia turned her face to the city and offered up silent prayers to Diana and Minerva that they would grant her more time.

*

Maia raised a hand in salute as the boat sped away, feeling sorry for the slight figure in the stern, wedged between the men like a prisoner being transferred to an uncertain fate. She understood all too well the feelings of helplessness the Princess had to be experiencing, torn between her obligations and her duty, but there was nothing for it. Julia was better–armed than most to deal with whatever life threw at her, plus her Potentia would always give her the edge. It was interesting that it didn't seem to have surfaced in the rest of the Royals, who all seemed quite ordinary apart from their exalted status. Presumably the original Artorius must have had something to commend him to the Gods of Britannia?

She was still pondering this half an hour later when she saw Pendragon, who was writing in his cabin, straighten up and slam his pen down on his desk in an uncharacteristic show of frustration.

"If it's not one thing, it's another," he muttered to himself. "Don't we sacrifice enough? What more do they want from us?"

He must have received a message directly from the Admiralty. After a short time, he spoke aloud, presumably for her benefit.

"Understood, Favonius. I will take the Princess aboard *Tempest* and use the *Regina* as escort. Convey my sympathies to Captain Latinius and keep me informed as to casualties."

Captain Latinius? He was commander of the *Victoria*. Had something happened to the new Flagship?

The Admiral closed his eyes and sat back in his chair before addressing her. "*Tempest*, the *Victoria* is anchored off Noviomagus. She has sickness aboard and has been placed in quarantine. Please would you contact her? I want to know what it is and how many are affected."

Maia heard him with alarm. Contagion aboard a vessel was extremely serious. She promptly opened a channel and the *Victoria* responded immediately.

<I didn't want to broadcast it until I knew for certain. My Adept says it's the sweating sickness,> the older Ship said, resignation in her voice. <I've three dead this morning and fifteen others likely to die by nightfall. You know how fast it takes hold. They're fumigating my vessel now and offering sacrifices to Apollo.>

The God of Light was also the Sender of Plagues, using his golden bow and arrows to rain pestilence upon the heads of vulnerable mortals.

<I'm so sorry. I hope it abates soon,> Maia Sent, simultaneously relaying the information to the Admiral.

<I won't be carrying the Princess now,> *Victoria* added. <I've heard that you've got the honours.>

<Apparently so. The Admiral doesn't want to move if he can help it.> As soon as the thought was out of her head, Maia realised that she'd been less than tactful.

<Oh don't worry.> the *Victoria* said tolerantly. <I'm happy with Latinius for the present, though he'll probably have to bow to the inevitable before too long.>

It was only right and proper that the Admiral should spend time aboard the Flagship, whatever Captain Latinius thought. Maybe the latter would be promoted as compensation?

<I hope you don't lose too many men,> Maia told her.

<It happens,> the *Victoria* said. <It's my bad luck to be struck down now, whether by the God or not. It looks like you'll be carrying another Royal, *Tempest*.>

<We'll offer prayers for you,> Maia assured her, before the other broke the contact. Pendragon, too was resigned to the change in plan.

"I'll order the preparations. The Princess can use the state cabin; her attendants will bring everything she needs and the dowry will fit in your capacious holds, will it not?>

<It will, sir.>

<Good. Inform Corax and the Captain. I'll be holding a briefing at...> he checked his timepiece, <...fourteen hundred hours.>

<Aye, sir.>

Leo was sitting in a chair, an unopened book in his lap and one foot propped up on a stool, when she appeared through the wall and told him the situation in person. He groaned.

"Damn it! It's just one thing after another. No, it's not your fault," he added quickly as she opened her mouth. "It's just one of those things. It might have nothing to do with the Gods. Sickness can arise anywhere and vessels are very prone, you know that. Too many men in close quarters."

Maia shut her mouth again and regarded him steadily. He rolled his eyes. "As you can see, I'm following Adept's orders. No exerting myself."

"You must be feeling better," she told him. "You're starting to complain."

"Who, me? It's bad enough damaging my ankle without having puncture wounds as well, though they're healing nicely.

As for my foot, I should be able to get about in a day or two. Hawthorn says there's no ligament damage, just bruising."

"Still," she objected, "you've had a battering."

He stretched. "I'm more likely to die of boredom. So, Julia's coming aboard, eh? Poor girl. We'll have to cheer her up as she goes to her doom."

"You know her from the palace," Maia stated.

"Oh yes. We're of an age, though I didn't see as much of her as of the King, naturally." He looked thoughtful for a moment. "It's taken long enough for them to find her a husband. Pity it's a broken-down old man, eh?"

"Everyone's saying he won't last much longer."

"Who knows?" He struggled to sit up, grimacing at the discomfort.

"And what do you think you're doing?" she asked him.

He looked down his nose at her. "My job."

"Your lieutenants and Corax can do that. Do I have to call for Hawthorn?"

He scowled at her. "I don't need a nursemaid."

"No, you *need* to rest," she emphasised, "or you'll never heal!" Maia folded her arms and scowled back. Leo groaned and sank back into his chair.

"Very well, but not for much longer. I want to know everything that's happening."

"Understood, sir." She shot him another stern glance before leaving him to his fretting, calling for Hawthorn as she went. She wouldn't put it past Leo to get up anyway and try to hobble around and the Adept would have something to say about that.

So, Julia would be returning much sooner than either of them could have anticipated, and in far different circumstances. Maia opened the link and began to inform her friends of the new developments.

\*

Julia and Raven made their way into Portus without incident, ducking down a narrow alleyway to reach the rear door of the Temple of Juno. The Master Mage had cast a spell of

202

concealment that would divert eyes away from the pair of them and she took the opportunity to commit it to memory.

"A final lesson," he whispered to her as they trotted along a back corridor to where Claudia Modesta was waiting. The High Priestess ushered them into her rooms and shut the door behind them.

"Lady Claudia," Julia said. "I would like to thank you for your assistance in this matter."

The older woman bowed her head. "It was the least I could do, Your Highness, Raven."

"Lady Claudia. We must prepare the Princess with all speed."

Claudia surveyed Julia and raised her eyebrows. "Time to drop the illusion, I think."

Raven gestured and her borrowed shape fell to tatters, revealing her true face.

"I'll have to change," Julia said ruefully.

"I have everything ready," Claudia said briskly. "A bath first, I think, then we can discuss the necessary rites."

The woman was delighted, as well she might be. It was a great honour for the Portus Temple to host the Princess and attend to her before her wedding, even if she'd had to agree to subterfuge.

"Does the Goddess favour me?" Julia asked hesitantly. It had been a bit of a cheek to expect everyone to believe that she was somewhere she wasn't.

"The Goddess favours all those who seek her blessing before marriage," Claudia replied confidently. "You will be undergoing the ceremonies of purification ready for your new state, so it isn't a problem."

Julia felt a little relieved at that, even though she'd known that nothing would have happened without the Goddess' agreement. Juno, the Queen of Heaven, was a powerful ally, even if her own marriage to Jupiter didn't always run smoothly.

Claudia rang a bell and two slaves appeared. "Enjoy your bath, Your Highness" she said.

Julia thanked her and followed the attendants, glad that she would get a proper wash for once. The *Tempest* was a wonderful Ship, but didn't have a bath house on board.

Later, washed, massaged and perfumed, she chose a blue silk gown with contrasting shawl and sat staring at her reflection whilst a slave arranged her hair. She wasn't particularly sunburned, she decided, though her cheeks did have a touch of colour. It would all be hidden under make-up anyway. Slowly, the Princess of the Blood appeared in the mirror one piece at a time, pampered and primped to within an inch of her life. It was just as much of an illusion as the one she'd taken off, though not half so enjoyable and more of a mask than Owl had ever worn.

The slave stepped back, eyes downcast and hoping for approval.

"Well done." The woman's face relaxed and she curtseyed low. A knock at the door heralded the High Priestess, her face alight with news. She waved the slave away.

"Your Highness, I've just received a message. His Majesty is coming to see you off!"

Part of Julia was glad that she would see her brother again, even if he would inevitably drag most of the Court along with him, but she was surprised as well. She wondered whether her uncle knew yet, then remembered that Raven would be able to let him know.

"When will the King be arriving?"

"Tomorrow. You'll be leaving the next day, Highness."

Julia nodded.

"Then we must be ready to greet him. Tell me what I have to do first."

*

Artorius entered Portus to an excited and hastily–decorated city. Royal voyages to the rest of the Empire usually began from Dubris, so the local authorities had no intention of wasting the opportunity to impress, whilst thumbing their noses at their sister port.

As Julia had surmised, the long procession was full of expensive carriages and chattering courtiers. She was in position on the temple steps with the Priestesses, waiting to perform the official welcome. The roar as her brother alighted from his carriage startled the pigeons and made the horses shake their heads nervously.

Artorius acknowledged the cheers and strode eagerly up to greet her with a kiss.

"Dear sister! Here we are at last!"

She smiled at him. "Yes. Thank you for coming all this way."

He looked pleased. "It does me good to get out of Londin and I'm going to stop off at Rufus' country place on the way back. He has a hunting lodge in the nearby forest, you know."

Of course. He wouldn't have made the trip solely on her account. She could see her cousin and the Senator waiting patiently behind him and, behind them, Admiral Albanus looking resplendent in full naval uniform. She gave them all a gracious nod.

"Hail, cousin! You're looking lovely, as always," Marcus grinned.

*And you're a useless waste of space, as always.*

"Dear Marcus! How wonderful it is to see you!"

A calculating look flashed in his eyes before vanishing again, so rapidly that she thought she'd imagined it.

"And Senator Rufus! Lady Drusilla! How are you both?"

The great bear of a man beamed at her. Drusilla looked elegant, as always. They were probably the only sincere ones in the party.

"All the better for seeing you, Your Highness!" Rufus boomed. His wife smiled.

"I trust that everything has gone smoothly, Your Highness?"

For a second, Julia didn't know what Drusilla meant, then realised that she was referring to the religious rites.

"Indeed. The Goddess is most gracious."

"Excellent! We'll be offering a sacrifice to her ourselves, on your behalf. Just think, you'll soon be a married lady!" Their proud faces said it all and she did her best to smile back.

The party moved through into the temple to offer their respects. The gilded statue of the Goddess, arm raised in blessing, towered over them as they burned incense.

The King paused and announced, "We are presenting a pair of unblemished she-goats to honour Juno."

There were murmurs of approval from the assembled clergy. The temple had arranged for an official reception, so they were ushered through into a large hall set up as a banqueting room.

Everyone took their positions as slaves scurried here and there with basins and ewers full of scented water for the guests to wash their hands. Not all courtiers had made it this far, but the numbers were made up with local nobility and prominent businessmen, the latter usually richer than the former, though not occupying the closest couches to the King. Julia nodded to those she knew whilst the others waited to be presented, her face showing nothing of her true feelings. It was going to be a very long afternoon.

*

The Royal party's civic duties continued well into the night, and Julia was intensely relieved when she could retreat at last to the relative quiet of her chambers. Now it was late morning and, the requisite prayers and invocations to the Goddess being completed, she was being readied to be taken out to the *Tempest*. It was time to bid farewell to Britannia, at least for the foreseeable future.

Julia felt like a lonely rock in the middle of a turbulent sea. Slaves and servants hurried around her checking chests and boxes full of her belongings, or the ones she was being permitted to take with her. Some had had to be left behind, to be used by any future members of the family; that was, if her brother actually got around to marrying and producing an heir. Priscilla, her aged lady-in-waiting was sitting opposite her, tears making watery channels in her thick, white make-up

"Calm yourself," Julia said, wearily. "This day had to come."

The old bat knew that she'd be pensioned off somewhere now that her useful days at court were over. She'd only been retained because she'd been a friend of Julia's grandmother, the old King's late queen. She had to be pushing seventy by now.

"I wish I could come with you, my poppet," Priscilla sniffed, "if only because you'll have nobody in Gaul!"

"I'll have new ladies," Julia told her, which set the old dame off again.

"You should be allowed to take people you know!" she wailed. "How can strangers attend you? It's not right!" Rheumy eyes peered at her through the paint, looking like a pair of crows embedded in a chalk cliff.

"I can take some things," Julia told her.

"Yes, but things aren't people!"

Julia suddenly pitied the old woman. She'd cared for her in her own way, whilst making mincemeat of any younger attendants who tried to get into her Princess' good graces. Also, her propensity for afternoon naps had certainly helped to conceal many a surreptitious lesson. Julia leaned over and patted her hand.

"Don't be sad, Priscilla. I shall tell my brother how kind you've been to me. He'll look after you."

Priscilla seemed a little mollified. "Our dear King! He will, won't he?"

"Or you could go and live on your son's estate."

Priscilla sniffed. "I could indeed. That household needs a firm hand, if you ask me! My grandchildren need to be brought up properly. Aelia could do with my guidance."

She compressed her wrinkled lips together into a determined red line, the light of battle already in her eye. Julia thought it didn't bode well for her luckless daughter-in-law.

"What a good idea," she said sweetly. "I'm sure they will all benefit from your wisdom and experience."

Priscilla looked happier, before her face crumpled again as the last of the crates was carried out.

A slave hurried up and bowed.

"His Majesty is here, Highness!"

They both stood as Artorius swept in. For once, he wasn't accompanied by Marcus, only two of his guards who took up their station outside the room.

"Dear sister! Lady Priscilla!"

He smiled at them as they dropped into curtsies. Priscilla took his offered hand as he helped her to rise and Julia fancied that she could hear the creak of bones.

"Your Majesty," the old woman quavered.

"I have come to bid a private farewell to my sister. Have no fear, my Lady, you will be rewarded for your long and loyal service to my family."

Priscilla was delighted, murmuring thanks as she left. Artorius immediately flung himself on her vacated couch. "Oh, my head! I thought last night would never end."

Perhaps you shouldn't drink so much," Julia observed, tartly. Her brother pulled a face.

"It was excellent wine. Anyway, you seem ready." He twisted his head to observe the empty room.

"Just about."

"Oh, cheer up. In a few days you'll be Queen of Gaul and have that old fool eating out of your hand, if I know you."

She stuck her tongue out at him and he laughed. It was an old game and, for a few moments, they were children again.

"Don't do that when you're crowned," he teased. His face softened in sympathy. "Look, I know it's rotten to have to leave, but you might not be there long and then you can come back."

"And then you'll marry me to somebody else."

"The Gods might grant you a son, so you could rule Gaul on his behalf," he pointed out.

Julia preferred not to think about how she'd get to that point. The idea of pregnancy and childbirth revolted her.

"And if I don't?"

"Then we'll think of something else. You're young and will still be eligible. Perhaps we can find you a husband more to your taste."

*Like that would ever happen.*

When she didn't answer, he sat up and snapped his fingers.

"Nearly forgot! I've brought you presents."

The doors opened and two slaves brought in a large cage, carrying it carefully between them. Behind the ornate bars, on a branch, sat a small marmoset with a mournful expression wearing a little red velvet hat and jacket. A piece of apple was clutched in its tiny fingers. Julia's heart sank.

"Isn't he cute?" Artorius exclaimed.

"Does he bite?"

"Oh, Gods, I hope not. I asked for a tame one." He clucked at the monkey, who looked back at him warily. "I thought he'd be company. Silvia has one and she loves it. I know you're not keen on dogs," he added.

*Not the yappy little things that I trip over in court.* She had to be thankful for that much. She wouldn't have minded something large that could go for the throat. Naturally, Artorius had asked his mistress for a recommendation. She wouldn't have put it past the woman to propose this out of spite. The King was examining her face hopefully and she couldn't help but think that it bore the same expression as the monkey's.

At last, she relented. "It's very thoughtful of you," she said, with as much sincerity as she could muster and his face cleared.

"I bought you a new personal slave, as well," he said. "You need more than just one girl to attend you."

"Oh? I thought I'd only be allowed to keep Melissa."

Julia had been dreading losing everyone else she knew. Melissa had been with her since childhood and they'd grown up together.

"I insisted the Gauls accept another. This one's been trained and will be waiting for you on board the Ship." Julia sighed inwardly. Melissa would have to keep an eye on the new girl during the voyage over.

*A trained monkey and a trained slave. Which had cost more?*

"Parisius will give you lots of jewels and things as well," he said, as if that was the thought uppermost in her mind. "He'd better treat you right, or he'll have me to deal with."

He meant every word and, impulsively, she went to him and gave him a hug. He might be the King, but she still remembered the noisy little boy charging down the corridors on a toy horse and terrorising the slaves with a wooden Excalibur. Now he had the real one and all the responsibilities that came with it.

"Take care," she said, gazing into his face. "Find the best advisors and listen to them. Don't be rash or hasty and keep the favour of the Gods, both the new ones and the old."

He nodded, suddenly serious. "I will. And yes, I'll get married, sooner rather than later."

Their father's untimely death hung between them for a painful moment.

"Don't be so trusting. Everyone has their own agenda, except possibly Rufus. I'd always listen to him."

"And our cousin," Artorius said, "He's family and he loves me."

"Of course, but he doesn't have the experience," she replied, tactfully. "Will you come with me to the harbour?"

He feigned indignation. "Yes! I'll stand and wave my handkerchief. It's a pity about the *Victoria*, but the *Tempest* is a fine Royal Ship."

"Your fine Royal Ship."

"Oh yes," he grinned.

Julia's gaze returned to the monkey. It was chewing on the apple and watching them, much as if they were performing on stage for his benefit. Artorius followed her eyes and burst out laughing. "Isn't he funny? Glad you like him. Well, I must go. More dignitaries to meet, including that factory owner. What's his name? Freed all his workers."

"Cardo. Be nice. He's rich and influential in these parts."

Her brother snorted. "All right." He stood and adopted a regal pose. "I'm having my portrait painted. I have to stand like this for *ages*."

He was still such a child.

"I know –," she began, but he interrupted her.

"You worry too much, Julia. Everything will be fine, you'll see. Remember, I want to be an uncle!"

She had to smile.

\*

Portus harbour was just about the busiest Maia had ever seen it. As well as a plethora of smaller Ships, the *Regina* lay at anchor not far distant and the two larger vessels dominated the scene. Maia knew that her old schoolmate was furious that she hadn't been chosen to carry the Princess and had retreated into herself to mutter and sulk.

The other Ships seemed more amused than anything.

<She's a one!> *Blossom* laughed. <So predictable. Did you expect anything better from her? I didn't!>

<I thought she might have matured a little,> Maia replied. <It seems not.>

<Her? Hah!> the *Leopard* said scornfully. <I've had enough of her complaining down the link. Let her sulk. She'll soon

change her tune when she realises that nobody's listening anymore.>

<Let's hope so,> the *Intrepid* Sent. <I just feel sorry for *Tempest*, having to deal with the silly little chit.>

Maia felt a little better knowing that she had the support of the other Ships. Didn't the *Regina* realise that she was storing up trouble for herself? Ships had longer memories than most and a bad start didn't help to foster sisterly bonds.

<It's only a short trip and we won't have to say much to each other, with any luck,> she said.

<Nobody'll 'ave much to say to 'er, full stop,> *Persistence* interjected.

Maia was kept busy as boat after boat arrived to disgorge its contents, then returned for more. She worked her cranes continuously and could feel her holds filling as she settled a little lower in the water.

"I feel so heavy!" she complained to Raven, who was returning from some business of his own on shore.

"It won't be for long," he replied, absently. The ancient Mage seemed a little preoccupied as he climbed aboard and she wondered what was on his mind.

"I need to see the Admiral," he told her. So there was something up. Maia knew better than to ask and relayed his request to Pendragon. She'd find out later anyway. It was very difficult to keep things from a Ship aboard her own vessel.

"Send him down," was the reply.

"He'll see you now," she told her Mage, before her curiosity got the better of her. "Is everything all right?"

He pursed his lips. "I'm hoping it's nothing. Certainly nothing you need to worry about, Maia. Concentrate on making sure everything's stowed properly. Who would have thought that one girl required so much stuff?"

"She's representing her country," Maia said. "I know how that feels."

"Yes, you do. So get representing!"

She shot a look of annoyance at his retreating back and went to grumble at her Captain instead. Leo had made his way on to the quarterdeck and was discussing weather with Sabrinus.

"There are no warnings," the lieutenant was saying.

"Good." Leo was bundled up, to stop the cold getting into his wounds, even though the day was mild. "Let's hope a certain Goddess is amusing herself elsewhere. A quick trip there and back and then we'll get new orders."

Sabrinus agreed. "Where do you think we'll be sent, sir?"

His Captain frowned. "There are rumours from the west, but then again, there are always rumours from the west. There's been talk of piracy, too, off the Isles of Canaria. We might have to go there and patrol."

Sabrinus grinned. "I hear they're nice this time of year."

Leo shared his enthusiasm. "Better than freezing our arses off in Britannic waters!"

"Better pray we're not to go north."

Maia formed her Shipbody alongside them and returned their salutes.

"How's it going?" Leo asked her.

"I was just saying that I feel heavy," she said.

"I'm not surprised, with this lot. The Gods alone know what's in all those crates."

"Dowry, probably," Sabrinus said. They watched as another load was swung on board.

"The Princess will be here soon," Leo said. "It's good that you've already met her. Have you?" he asked his second.

"No, sir," Sabrinus replied, "though my father claims to know her well."

He would, Maia said to herself. Surely Sabrinus must be aware of his conniving father's political ambitions?

"Is the state cabin ready?"

"Aye, sir," Maia replied. It had been fitted out with luxurious furnishings, hangings, and sundry other bits and pieces, all for a short voyage. It would only take her a day to get to Coriallum all being well, after which Julia would be formally greeted and taken to Lutetia, the capital of Gaul, where her new husband was waiting for her.

Another voice hailed her.

"Ma'am? There's a new slave here for the Princess. Says she's a gift from the King."

Maia switched her attention to the small boat bobbing alongside. The girl huddled at the stern and swathed in a thick cloak, looked up at her vessel with wide, frightened eyes.

"Bring her aboard," Maia instructed, watching as the sailors steadied the slave and helped her up the ladder.

It wasn't long before the girl was standing forlornly on the deck, already looking a little green.

"What's your name?" Maia asked.

The slave flinched. "Latonia," she whispered.

"Don't worry. It won't be a long voyage," the Ship assured her. "If you need anything, just ask and I'll do what I can to help. Batacarus will show you to the Princess' cabin. Melissa will tell you what to do." She pitied her already. Being an indentured servant had been bad enough, but to be bought as a present didn't bear thinking about.

The girl bobbed a curtsey, eyes lowered and scuttled away after her escort.

Maia magnified her view of the city. Crowds were already gathering on shore to bid their Princess farewell. It wouldn't be long now. Sure enough, a message tone rang in her head.

<Tempest. The Princess is embarking. Stand ready.>

<Acknowledged.>

Faint cheers could be heard, carried on the favourable wind blowing off the land. Was her mother near? Maia sensed that her sister wasn't far away. She hadn't spoken to Pearl in a while and hoped that she would find the time to visit. The boats that had been ferrying goods were pulling away now, eager to be out of the way before the royal arrival. Her crew hurried to get into position ready to greet Julia. Most were excited at the thought of having a princess on board, unaware that they'd been seeing her for weeks. Her Captain was already in his best uniform and she saw that Pendragon was in his cabin being attired for the occasion. Her marines were formed up, still as statues, all the hours of spit and polish making them gleam in the spring sunshine. Osric prowled up and down the lines, checking for anything amiss. The only noises apart from the cheering were her pennants snapping in the wind that danced through her rigging and the cries of wheeling gulls.

There! A hint of shimmer, high in her mastheads. Pearl was around to enjoy the show after all. Maia thought of Sending to her, but decided that she'd better keep all her attention on the job at hand. There would be time afterwards.

She could see the boat now, the Great Dragon of Britannia rippling at the stern, though it was being blown this way and that, which rather spoiled the effect. The Princess was sitting stiffly under a canopy of cloth of gold, surrounded by attendants. Nobody could ever have guessed that she had been the quiet Little Owl a few short days before. Pendragon emerged on to the quarterdeck and returned their salutes.

"All is ready, Admiral," she told him.

"Good. Let's do this."

*Poor girl, to be delivered and dropped off like a parcel left on the doorstep.*

This time, there was no climbing up a ladder. Maia gave her formal permission and the Princess was hoisted on a chair and swung gently aboard, swathed in a beautiful, fur-lined cloak. Maia admired it very much. How many times would she have given her eyeteeth to have owned something so warm and luxurious? Now she could have had one, she had no need of it at all.

The crew stood to attention, trumpets sounded and greetings were made. Pendragon looked genuinely pleased to see his niece, as did Leo. Sabrinus was introduced. Through it all, Julia's face retained the same gracious expression, as impenetrable as any mask.

*That makes two of us.* Maia made her salute and exchanged pleasantries, then the Princess was escorted below, being fussed over by her maids. One by one, the rest of the Royal party was brought aboard, including a small, balding man, dressed in elaborate Mage robes. She glanced at Raven. His face was impassive, though she sensed him bridle.

<I take it you don't like this one?> she asked him. His mouth twitched slightly.

<He's one of Bullfinch's yes men.>

The Mage had come up by chair, gripping the ropes with whitened knuckles. He didn't look particularly thrilled to be at sea. His watery blue eyes fixed on her Shipbody, then slid across to her officers.

"Welcome aboard, Mage Lapwing," Pendragon said.

"Highness." Lapwing bowed unctuously, then remembered his manners. "*Tempest.*"

"Mage Lapwing."

She wondered if he'd ever seen a Ship before from the look he gave her. She thought he seemed a bit jumpy, but maybe he was always like that. It was clear to see why Raven disliked him so much. He nodded to his fellow Mages.

"I'll show you to your quarters," Magpie offered.

"Ah, yes, of course," Lapwing said. His voice was high with a whiny edge. "Will we be setting off shortly?"

His eyes darted about the deck as if expecting to be whisked into the open sea in a trice.

"Soon," Raven said. "Let's hope we don't have a rough crossing, eh?" Lapwing gulped.

"Indeed," he answered, before Magpie indicated that he should follow him. The two of them headed below decks where a cabin had been vacated for his purpose.

<Odious little man,> she Sent to Raven and felt his agreement.

<He should have been called Lapdog,> was her Mage's reply and she had to struggle to keep her face straight. <He'll be reporting back directly to Bullfinch. At least we won't have to bring him back with us. He's representing the Britannic Mages at a conference in Lutetia, so we'll be rid of him when we get to Gaul. It could have been worse. Bullfinch could have decided to come himself.>

<Why didn't he?> she asked him.

<He hates sailing, plus it would mean leaving someone else in charge.>

She overlaid her sight to the state cabin, now the temporary home of the Princess. Julia was sitting in a chair whilst Melissa was unfastening a bejewelled tiara from its nest of elaborate curls. It must weight a ton, she thought in sympathy. A cage stood beside her, containing a small marmoset, the sort that sailors often bought in tropical markets. It looked rather well-fed and didn't seem impressed by its surroundings, staring instead at its mistress.

"Thank the Gods that's off!" Julia exclaimed, stretching her neck and rolling her shoulders.

"Your Highness, I hope your accommodation is to your liking," Maia said. The maid jumped and looked around her wildly.

"Oh don't be such a goose, Melissa! It's the Ship speaking. Go and fetch me some wine," Julia snapped before her tone moderated and she addressed Maia. "It's all lovely, thank you. I know everyone must have gone to a lot of trouble. State cabin?"

"Yes. We kept it just for you. You're its first occupant."

Julia stared wistfully around the cabin.

"I don't suppose I could bribe you to take me somewhere else instead? I've always wanted to see the Carib Islands."

"So have I," Maia admitted, "but I'm afraid I can't help you there."

"No. I didn't think you could. So, off we go to Gaul instead."

She didn't sound too thrilled at the prospect, Maia thought, but she wouldn't have been either if their positions were reversed.

"At least we'll spend some time together," she offered. Julia's new slave was busy chopping up fruit for the marmoset. Now that she had removed her cloak, Maia noticed that she was a pretty, golden-haired girl.

"Yes, there is that," Julia said, before lapsing into silence.

"What's your monkey called?" Maia asked, thinking that a change of subject was in order.

"Well. I was going to call him Marcus, but I thought it wouldn't be fair on the beast," Julia said, her face deadpan. "He doesn't really have a name, more of a use. He likes to eat everything I do, if you see what I mean."

*She thinks she might be poisoned.* Maia felt a trickle of alarm. Julia turned to the maid. "*Tempest*, this is Latonia, my new slave. She was a present from my brother."

The girl bobbed a curtsey, eyes firmly on the floor. "We've already met, haven't we, Latonia?" Maia said.

"Yes, ma'am," the girl whispered.

216

"She's very quiet," Julia said. "It makes a change. Melissa never shuts up."

"If there's anything you need, Your Highness…"

Julia smiled tiredly.

"About a week's worth of sleep. How long do you think the voyage will take?"

"With a fair wind and a calm sea, only about ten hours, Highness."

"Do feel free to take your time, won't you?"

"I wish I could," she replied. "Your uncle is hosting a formal dinner in his quarters this evening –."

Julia groaned.

"I'm not putting all that stuff back on," she declared. "Latonia, please find me something more comfortable, will you?"

The girl scurried off.

"Thank the Gods she's gone. *Tempest*, if I throw myself overboard will it look bad?"

"I'm afraid it would."

"Damn. At least this new girl gives excellent foot rubs. I think I'll keep her. Not sure about the monkey."

Maia looked at the little creature. "Is it trained?"

"Yes. Don't worry, it won't crap everywhere."

"The *Augusta* hated monkeys."

"I know. Did you know that my uncle used to have one? He gave it away because she didn't like it. That's how much he loved her. Perhaps I should give him this one."

"I think he's rather sweet," Maia said. "I always wanted a monkey to ride on my shoulder. You should give him a name."

Julia looked up, her eyes full of mischief. "I know who he looks like."

"Who?"

"Teg!"

They both burst out laughing, startling Latonia who was returning from an adjacent closet with a new gown over her arm.

A subtle alteration in the pull of the sea alerted Maia.

"The tide is with us," she informed Leo.

"Inform the *Regina*, and weigh anchor."

"Forgive me, Highness, but I'm about to make sail," she explained.

"Of course."

Maia withdrew her attention and applied herself, running her Potentia through her capstans to wind up her heavy chains and anchors from the bed of the harbour.

<Tempest to Regina. We're ordered to weigh anchor,> she Sent.

<Acknowledged,> came the curt reply. Maia didn't let it bother her and scanned her decks. The marines had returned to their posts and her crewmen to their duties. Some of her crew were chatting as they worked.

"I ain't never seen a Princess before," Teg remarked.

"Aye, I think there was a woman somewhere under there," Hyacinthus riposted. "Looked like a temple statue, she did."

"It'll take old Parisius all night to get through those layers," Batacarus joked, but Drustan, returning from seeing the unfortunate *Bonaventura* safely to port, had heard him.

"You men, enough! Show some respect!" He glared at all three of them, then relented. "Get back to your duties. Any more and I'll have you flogged."

They dispersed hastily, knuckling foreheads as they went. Her third lieutenant shook his head.

"Sailors will be sailors," Maia reminded him.

"Well, I could hardly say they were right could I?" he said quietly, a twinkle in his eye. Maia rolled her eyes at him.

Once her anchors were secured at the catheads, she made sail and set her bow towards the coast of Gaul, leaving Portus harbour and the little boats that were bobbing about hoping to get a good view of proceedings. Slowly, then with increasing speed, the two Ships left Britannia behind them, slipping away on the tide to skirt Vectis and the dreaded Needles, on their way to Gaul at last.

\*

The Royal Progress made good time as it headed out of Portus, speeding along the arrow-straight road towards its next destination. Senator Rufus had offered to host a three-day

218

hunting party, much to his Sovereign's delight, and everyone was looking forward to eating, drinking and partying at his expense. It was no small thing to accommodate the King and his entourage, but everyone knew that the Senator could afford it.

"I'm glad Julia's going to be settled," Artorius said to his cousin. Marcus stifled a yawn.

"So am I, Sire. It'll be you next."

Artorius grimaced. "Don't remind me. Some plump Gallic maid, I've no doubt."

"You could always put in an offer for a Northern girl –."

The King snorted. "You must be joking, though I hear they're – shall we say – adventurous?"

His cousin smirked. "Who told you that? Leo?" The King grinned. "He'd know," Marcus continued, rattling yet another pair of dice. His face fell at the resulting score.

"Dog, again! Your luck's changed!" Artorius crowed.

"And not for the better," the Prince grumbled. "We must be nearly there."

He stared moodily out of the window. They were passing through dense forest, cut back from the road to deter thieves and robbers. A side road appeared, bordered by lawns and leading to a pair of impressive gateposts, each surmounted by a rampant bear. They had reached Rufus' estate.

"I can't wait to get out of this thing," Artorius muttered. "We should have time to get a ride in before evening, don't you think?"

"Assuredly, Sire."

They clattered for a mile or more down the road, eventually coming into view of the villa. It was small by royal standards, but large by anybody else's and provided a welcome retreat from the grime of Londin. The Senator and his wife were waiting to greet them and Artorius felt himself relax. He'd spent happy times here as a child and the sight called forth many pleasant memories. Official duties could go hang. He was going to enjoy himself.

"Welcome, Sire!" Rufus bowed low as Artorius descended and the King greeted him warmly. Lady Drusilla was next to her husband and received a kiss.

"I would like to have a ride before the light fades," Artorius told the Senator. "I've been too long in the carriage."

"Is that wise, Sire?" Rufus asked. If he'd planned for anything else, his face didn't show it.

"I can get a couple of hours in and I'll take my crossbow just in case."

"Perhaps an hour, Sire, before dusk."

Artorius strode along the familiar path to the great front door, past servants bowing to either side and stood in the atrium whilst Marcus, as was protocol, removed his cloak. The old place hadn't changed much. The same familiar statues of Minerva and Hercules stood in their accustomed places to greet him and he thought how much they'd shrunk. He remembered being so small that he only came up to the top of their plinths. Everything spoke of home, hearth and happiness and he wished he could stay longer than the three days that were planned. He'd just have to make the most of them, starting now.

His personal attendants hurried forward to pour scented water over his hands and dry them on fine cloths, whilst the little fountain splashed into the pool into the centre of the atrium. "Ha, Senator. Do you remember hauling me out of there as a child, when I'd decided to cool my feet on a hot day? I didn't understand why everyone was so cross with me!"

"You ruined an expensive pair of sandals, I remember that much," Rufus laughed, his eyes twinkling.

"I was a young limb of Pan, was I not?"

The courtiers, lining up behind, echoed his laughter.

"Sometimes, Sire," Lady Drusilla said, "I feared you would take a chill, running about with wet feet."

"You took great care of me," Artorius replied.

That had been true enough. No risks could be taken with the heir to the throne. Every cough and sneeze led to a horde of panicking servants calling for the Court Adept to come and pour noxious substances down his throat and wrap him up like an Aegyptian mummy ready for the tomb. The only time he could truly feel like himself was when he was outside, riding through the countryside. Then he could pretend that he was just the son of an ordinary nobleman, without the cares of Britannia and the weight of his heritage digging into his shoulders with iron claws that would only be loosened by death.

He supposed that people envied him.

"A light repast is laid out in the small triclinium," Drusilla offered.

"Excellent. I could eat something, but I'm not that hungry really. Are you cousin?"

Marcus, following two steps behind, shook his head.

"No. I ate some snacks in the carriage whilst you were taking all my money. Why don't we have a drink and a quick bite, then we can change and go out?"

Artorius brightened. "Good idea."

He strode towards the little private dining room where more intimate gatherings were held. The central table was set with dainties and sweets and slaves brought drinks in silver buckets of crushed ice. He lay on a couch and selected some choice titbits. The white wine was cold and clear, with aromas of summer fruits. He nodded to the Senator in appreciation.

"A fine vintage."

"From my own vineyards, Sire. I'll have several cases sent back to Londin with you."

"Most generous." He smiled at his old friend. "Even better on a hot summer's day, eh Marcus? Let's hope we get plenty of those in the coming months."

"Certainly." Marcus was picking at a dish of duck in sauce. He ate a little, then pushed the rest aside, opting to empty his glass instead. "It's been a wet spring, so we need some good weather. I hope that Julia's having a good crossing. She'll be there shortly."

"I miss her already," Artorius said. "I hope she does well, though she'll have to guard her tongue. I hear that Parisius has a temper. He won't put up with some of her fashion choices, either, alas! They're far more conservative in Gaul, or so I hear."

"You are correct, Sire," his host said. "I pray to the Gods that she produces a son soon, then she will have fulfilled her purpose."

"Indeed."

They chatted for a while, enjoying the selection of delicacies. It made a change to be part of a small gathering for once. The rest of his nobles were eating in the larger formal hall. When he felt he'd had enough, the King signalled to one of his attendants. He would go and change into something more suitable for riding, then spend what remained of the day at leisure before the evening drew in. He was looking forward to it. Rufus and Drusilla exchanged significant glances, then the Senator called a slave over and had a quiet word. Artorius looked at him quizzically.

"Just a little surprise I arranged for you, Sire," Rufus explained. "I was going to give it to you tomorrow, but now seems more fitting."

Artorius dressed for riding then went outside, his guards trailing after him. He was surprised to see that his usual mount was absent from the courtyard and turned to his host with a raised eyebrow.

"Forgive me Sire, but I thought you might like this one," Rufus said.

The King followed his gesture to where a magnificent bay gelding was being trotted in. Its saddle was richly decorated with gold and inlay, as was the bridle and stirrups. He fell in love with the animal instantly.

"He's magnificent!"

The horse tossed its head as he approached, but otherwise stood docilely enough. He ran his hand down the smooth neck, examining the beast with a practised eye.

"A generous gift indeed, my friend!"

The pleasure on the old Lord's face was plain to see.

"He hasn't been named as yet. We've just been calling him 'His Majesty's horse'. I bred him specially."

"And kept the secret all this time." Artorius clasped his old friend's arm. "You have always been faithful to my house, my lord. Now we'll have to think what to call him." The King pondered the question for a moment, before the answer came to him.

"That's it! He'll be a fast runner?"

"None faster, Sire."

"Then we shall name him Zephyr, as he will challenge the wind itself!"

The pronouncement was applauded by the company. Marcus strolled over to inspect the princely gift.

"I envy you, cousin! He's beautiful. May he carry you swiftly and safely!"

Artorius beamed at him, before vaulting into the saddle. Zephyr snorted and pricked up his ears, clearly as eager as his new master to be away and running. The other horses were brought, but the King was waiting for no-one.

"Ho, Marcus! Catch me if you can!"

"Majesty, wait!"

His cousin's plea fell on deaf ears as Artorius dug his heels into Zephyr's flanks and the horse sprang forward like a ball from a musket. The King's whoop of joy faded rapidly into the distance as his entourage hastened to mount. His escort of guards were first, their leader swearing under his breath as he tried to catch up, followed by Marcus and the others. The ladies had decided not to ride out that day, preferring to bathe first, so at least they weren't inconvenienced by the King's rash action.

"I wish I still had that much energy," Rufus said to his wife. "He reminds me so much of his father."

"Let him have his sport where he can," she chided him. "Besides, if you hadn't wanted him to ride so swiftly you should have given him a slower horse!" She laughed at the guilty look on his face, "I remember when you would have given him a run for his money."

"Forty years ago I would have."

They smiled at each other, as theirs was a happy marriage, and went back into the villa to prepare for the evening's festivities.

*

Zephyr was everything Artorius had hoped he would be. They soon left the manicured grounds behind and entered the forest proper, green meadows and the odd tree giving way to thicker woodland and narrower paths. The song of birds and the steady beat of the horse's hooves were the only sounds he could hear and he revelled in the blasts of fresh spring air on his face. He had far outpaced his companions but found that he didn't care; he'd stop soon enough to let them catch up with him and then they could all ride together. It was only fitting that he got to try out his new horse's full speed first so he could make his cousin even more jealous.

The blow to his back was savage and unexpected. Icy numbness shot through him, spreading through his torso and down to his toes and fingertips in an instant. His vision fogged, even as he tried to call for help. Artorius slumped over Zephyr's neck and the horse stumbled at the sudden shift in his rider's weight but didn't fall, continuing to gallop on as the King slipped sideways.

He was dead before his body hit the ground.

# X

The first signs of trouble appeared just before nightfall. Maia felt the wind pick up and shift direction, swinging around to blow from the south and forcing her to adjust her sails. At the same time, a line of ominous cloud blotted out the setting sun and she saw that it was bearing down on them with unnatural speed. She notified Leo immediately.

<You say that the front is coming from the west, but the wind is southerly?>

<Aye, Captain.>

Hs brow creased and she could feel his unease. <I don't like the sound of that. Are you making headway?>

She was struggling, even using all the Potentia she could muster to propel herself forwards.

<I'm being pushed back. The wind is strengthening.>

*As if something is trying to stop me.*

The waves were rising higher as well, as the ocean responded to the changing conditions. She alerted Pendragon, who promptly appeared on deck to take a look for himself and consult with Leo. His expression told her all she needed to know.

"We'll have to tack," he told her, after a quick debate with his Flag Captain. "There's no other way, not in this." He turned his gaze westwards. The storm front was bearing down on them rapidly and, at this rate, they would be caught. Messages of alarm began to come in over the Ship link.

"Other Ships are reporting high winds and mountainous seas to the west, Admiral. It's a nasty squall and it's heading straight for us."

Pendragon muttered a curse. "There's no shelter nearby. Bear south-east and see if it blows itself out by the time it gets to us. The *Regina* will follow our lead."

Maia adjusted her course as the sky darkened and the thunderheads piled higher.

"Princess, we're in for some rough weather," she informed Julia. To her credit, her passenger seemed more interested than worried.

"Melissa's already throwing up," she told the Ship, "but Latonia's made of stronger stuff, as am I. Don't worry about us."

"I'll ask Hawthorn to attend her," Maia said. She could hear Melissa retching in the background.

"I'll send Rowan with a remedy," Hawthorn answered, when she told him. "She isn't the only one struck down."

"Tell Raven we'll need a shield," Leo announced, bracing himself as her vessel began to pitch. "And possibly Magpie as well. This isn't getting any better."

The Mages responded and, just as they began their work, the *Regina* flashed purple. She'd been a bit quicker and Maia could see that she had stabilised. A few instants later, she felt her Potentia interlock with that of her Mages and the heaving and bucking lessened considerably, much to everyone's relief.

"I'm still unable to make progress," she informed Leo.

"Keep us as steady as you can," he said. "It has to pass over before too long."

She raised her eyes to the heavens. "It seems to be circling," she said.

"This smacks of the Divine," Pendragon said. "Get Danuco here now. I need his opinion."

The Priest appeared, looking pale.

"Well?" Pendragon demanded.

"We must stay here, my Lord," Danuco informed him. "We mustn't proceed to Gaul." The man was almost in tears. "I just did a reading and the omens are terrible. Some great calamity is about to befall."

"We obey the Gods," Pendragon said, grimacing. "Learn what you can, as quickly as you can." Danuco hurried off. "Damn it! Raven! Any word from the Collegium?"

"I can't reach anyone on land," Raven said calmly, his voice deadened further by the swirling magic. "Magpie?"

"I can't either." The younger Mage's eyes were wide. "Why aren't our speechstones working?" He glanced across at his colleague in bewilderment.

<Maia, I'm asking Milo to contact his Controller.>

She searched for the Agent and found him busy dosing the green-faced Melissa with a potion and helping her to her bunk. A moment later he shook his head, his dark eyes troubled.

Raven turned to Pendragon. "Admiral, it appears we are cut off from the mainland."

Pendragon and Leo conferred quietly.

"A localised effect?" Leo asked.

"I can't reach the *Regina*," Pendragon said abruptly. "*Tempest*? Over to you."

Maia opened the link, noticing that it was fainter than usual. <*Regina*? Can you hear me?>

<Yes, *Tempest*.>

<Stay put! This isn't a natural storm.>

<I know,> the *Regina* replied. Something about her tone was off. She sounded almost gleeful. <You'll be all right. It will pass in a few minutes, then we must return to Portus as quickly as possible.>

<What? We have to get to Gaul!>

<You'll be getting new orders shortly,> the other Ship said calmly. She broke the link, leaving Maia more confused than ever.

"New orders? Has she lost her mind?" Pendragon snapped, as Maia relayed the conversation.

"There's more afoot than we know," Raven said. "She definitely said the storm would pass soon?"

"Yes."

"Then may I respectfully suggest that we're ready to make a run for it when it does?"

Pendragon swung round to question the Mage, when suddenly a streak of silver pierced their shield and halted, swirling several feet above the deck.

"A Tempestas!" Leo shouted, backing off.

"It's all right, I know her!" Maia reassured them. "She won't hurt us."

"*Don't be afraid.*" Pearl's voice was insubstantial, fading in and out as it was carried on the air. "*I am permitted to bring news.*"

"What's happened?" Maia asked her. The swirling slowed.

"*Your King is dead. Murdered.*"

The creak of the rigging and slap of the waves were the only sounds. Her crew's faces were suddenly transformed into tragic masks and Maia half expected the chorus to start up a lament, as if they were all performers on a stage.

"How?" Pendragon's voice was soft but shock and grief boiled from him.

"*A spelled arrow. It was not human-made.*"

"This storm?"

"*Sent to detain you. Do not return to Portus.*"

"We'll never get to Gaul with this wind."

"*Go west,*" Pearl replied. "*Await further messages. The Gods favour you.*"

A brief blast of air and she was gone, shooting upwards almost too fast for the eye to see. As she vanished into the clouds, the wind slackened and the storm began to abate as quickly as it had appeared.

"My son," Pendragon whispered. "Does he live? Surely he would have died before allowing his King to come to harm?"

"No news may be good news," Raven said.

"May the Gods protect him!" Pendragon said. "There's nothing I can do from here, alas! My poor nephew!" He turned to his officers, mastering his emotion. "You heard her. *Tempest*, lay in a course westward. We'll make for the Isles of Sillina until we have more information. Tell Danuco to make sacrifices to Jupiter and Neptune, together with offerings for the dead. We are in mourning as of now."

"My lord," Raven said urgently. "Give no outward sign to the *Regina*. I think she knew already."

The Admiral understood immediately. "A coup?"

"I fear so."

"Then we must leave immediately, under Potentia if we must. If the wind isn't in our favour, at least it isn't totally against us now."

As he spoke, Maia felt the pressure against her rigging and sails shift, as if air was being blown directly into them from an easterly direction.

"We have the wind, sir. Don't ask me how."

They all felt it.

"Drop the shield and go with all speed!" Pendragon ordered. "Officers, to me."

The message came through the link as he was speaking.

*<Tempest*. This is Admiral Albanus. Return to Portus immediately, by order of the King. Acknowledge!>

"King? What King?" Leo spat. "Surely, Admiral, you are –"

"It seems not," Pendragon interrupted. "*Tempest*, you have your orders."

"Aye, sir."

She swung away westwards as he spoke, every shred of sailcloth stretched to its limit, aided by the force of her Potentia to cleave a path through the waves. She felt Raven and Magpie linking their power to hers, like strong arms lifting some of the weight and boosting her abilities. Her vessel picked up speed rapidly, leaving the *Regina* in her wake.

*<Tempest*, acknowledge!>

"Silent running!" Pendragon snapped. "They can think what they like."

"Bloody traitors!" Leo muttered under his breath.

Sabrinus stood to one side, looking from one to the other in obvious distress.

"My lord, Captain, I had no knowledge of this," he said urgently. "I don't know what my father's doing or what's happened. I pray that he's no traitor!"

Pendragon nodded abruptly.

"I believe you, but think! Is there anything you can tell us?"

Sabrinus shook his head miserably. "I've been away at sea, my lord. I know my father has ambitions, like many men, but…" he spread his hands helplessly. "He never took me into his confidence."

Another message came, but this time it was for Maia's ears alone. *<Tempest*. This is *Regina*. Return to Portus immediately. You have authorisation to disobey your officers.>

Silent running included other Ships, so much as she was tempted to demand to know what was happening, Maia refused to answer. This didn't deter the *Regina*.

<Don't be a fool! It's all over for Pendragon. There's a new King now and we're bound to obey him. Don't worry, nobody will be harmed.>

She could hear the lie in the *Regina*'s voice even as she spoke. Had she forgotten that more came over the link than mere words? It was then she knew that her sister Ship had not only known of the plot, but had been a willing participant. There was no coercion here. A dozen little incidents began to click together in her mind, creating a picture out of jumbled and seemingly irrelevant pieces.

Albanus' attention to her. His daughter's change of heart. The little hints about knowing which side to choose. Click, click, click. Maia had no doubt now who the new King, whoever he was, would choose to be his new Flagship, Royal or not. Or maybe Tullia had been promised even more? She'd probably chosen her own name as well; an indication of her father's limitless ambition.

<There's still time to change your mind!> *Regina* insisted, until Maia shut down the link with the equivalent of a door slam. Silent running it was, though that meant that she couldn't get in touch with anybody else. She would have given a lot to talk to *Blossom* or *Patience* and had no idea what the *Victoria* was thinking. Would they be defiant, or follow these new orders? For sure, they'd all be wondering about this new King.

Her vessel skimmed over the ocean like a seabird in flight, putting as much distance between her and her treacherous sister. She couldn't keep this up for too long, but it would suffice to get her to the Isles of Sillina. Once there, all they could do was wait and see what news would arrive.

The friendly wind in her sails pushed her onwards, for her and her alone. Maia sent up a silent prayer to her mother who was surely giving her aid and felt the breeze surround and enfold her, like a loving embrace.

\*

Caniculus trailed along in the King's wake all the way from Portus, and sighted their destination with relief. Rufus' hunting villa was adequate, but didn't have the necessary accommodation for the sheer number of servants and hangers-on that accompanied the Royal Court. Tentage had been erected out of sight of the main house and the lesser orders were being directed there to wash and get something to eat. Large kettles were steaming over fires, containing food or hot water, and the whole place had the air of a military encampment. Various servants dressed in the Senator's livery were marshalling the crowd; Caniculus had to admire the organisation involved.

He tied his horse to a rail and gave the beast a rub down and feed before trotting off to see what he could grab for himself. It took a quick sluice with some warm water and a bowl of stew before he felt ready to resume his duties, which was basically to skulk around and keep an eye on proceedings. He didn't rate an invitation to the villa itself, but checked around the camp for signs of trouble. It only lacked an hour or so to sunset and he was just beginning to prepare for the night shift, or as much of it as he could manage, when a clatter of hooves alerted him. A familiar figure galloped past on a magnificent horse, heading for the woods.

Caniculus swore viciously. Where was the King's escort? Cries of dismay sounded behind him as he pelted to the stables, flashed his badge and grabbed the nearest mount from a startled groom.

The mare was rested and willing, prepared for one of the guests, but this was an emergency. He spurred her on, knowing that Artorius would be well ahead by now. Alone.

Every warning sense he possessed was shrieking at him and he knew better than to ignore it; it had saved his life more than once – not Potentia as such, but a remnant from some far distant ancestor. Ahead of him, the hoofbeats faltered, changing rhythm and Caniculus cursed again. The young fool had probably fallen off and a sprained wrist was the best outcome he could hope for. Behind him, on the edge of hearing, he could make out the escort, late and lagging behind.

There was something lying across the track. Caniculus reined in the mare, just as a shadow slipped away into the undergrowth. He tried to make it out, but it had gone. A deer, maybe? He turned back to the crumpled object on the ground. Damn and blast it, the King had fallen after all and probably knocked himself out. The horse was long gone. He dismounted and ran to the prone body.

Artorius' gaping mouth and staring eyes told their own story. He looked very young and startled by his sudden end.

Dear Gods. The King was dead.

Caniculus thought fast. He had perhaps thirty seconds before it would become a scene of chaos as everyone arrived, and he had to use what little time he had to his advantage. He checked the body quickly for signs of trauma.

The evidence lay underneath. A wooden shaft fletched with black feathers lay snapped under the body, its point buried in the corpse's back. He pulled it out and shuddered as the point dissolved into smoke, leaving a smell of burning as it sealed the wound. Caniculus knew spelled shot when he saw it. Fae arrows were bound with the essence of their victim, such as bits of dried blood or hair, and never missed, killing almost instantly.

Caniculus shoved it back and wiped his hands on his tunic. Then his eye was caught by the King's sword. It had come loose from the hanger and lay to one side on the beaten earth, its richly decorated scabbard dim in the fading light. Without really thinking, he picked it up and shoved it through his belt, before slapping his horse's rump and sending her into the forest. He'd just hidden in the undergrowth when the escort came trotting down the track, led by Prince Marcus and half a dozen armed men. There were no civilians. The Prince reined in his horse with a jingle of harness and gazed down at the sprawled body of his cousin.

The smirk of triumph on his face said it all and Caniculus knew he'd been right to trust his instincts.

"The King has had an accident," the Prince stated, twisting in his saddle to face the soldiers. "The same fate as befell his father, don't you agree, Macro?"

The Captain of the Guard nodded. "Obviously, Highness. He was struck down by the Fates."

"See to it."

The heavily–built man dismounted and went to the corpse. Caniculus didn't think he'd disturbed the body too much and this man clearly had other things on his mind. He picked up the pieces of shaft and hurled them into the bushes, then calmly broke the dead King's neck. The sharp crack made Caniculus wince, even though the poor lad was long past feeling it. He cursed Marcus for the traitor he was and prayed that the Gods would avenge Artorius' death.

*You're the only one who knows,* a little voice whispered in his head.

It wasn't a happy thought. Aware that the Gods helped those who helped themselves, he left Marcus to deal with the body and fled back towards the villa, praying that he wouldn't be too late.

Caniculus got there several minutes later. He leaned against a low wall, forcing himself to calm his racing pulse and wheezing lungs, before thrusting the sword into a clump of bushes and entering the courtyard. Contacting his Controller was out of the question, as who knew how far the rot had penetrated? There was only one man he could trust now.

"I think that the King will approve," the Senator was saying to another man whom Caniculus recognised as a lanista, owner of the local gladiatorial school. "He's always enjoyed the Games, so a few bouts would please him and I'd like to showcase our area's talent."

The other man nodded, happy at the chance for his men to perform in front of such an august company, then his eye fell on Caniculus and he paused. Rufus, alerted, glanced around. He knew the Agent of old.

"We'll speak later to finalise the details, Regillus," he said smoothly. The man bowed and left, not without casting a curious look in Caniculus' direction. The Agent waited until he was gone before approaching.

"Senator. Don't react," he said in a low voice. "The King has been murdered with Fae shot. Marcus has taken the crown and we are all in grave danger. Who do you trust? We have to get word to the Emperor."

He watched as something died in Rufus' eyes, but the old man gave no outward sign in his posture or bearing. The Senator had been brought up in the ancient Roman tradition and would grieve later.

"My Mage, Nuthatch. He can Send directly to Avocet, who's accompanying the Governor. I know he can be trusted. Come."

The two men strolled casually into the villa, Rufus leading as if nothing were amiss. Anyone watching would think there was a problem with the wine, or maybe the flowers for tonight's festivities hadn't arrived yet and they were going to consult with the Steward. Around them the preparations continued as usual; slaves scurrying on errands, workmen erecting wooden structures that would be filled with fireworks or explode with showers of rose petals on command. Much thought, time and money had been poured into entertainments for the King's amusement. Now their bright colours and joyful aspect seemed like mockery and Caniculus fancied he could hear the echo of the Fates' laughter.

The Senator knocked on the door and entered, to find his Mage poring over a dusty scroll and muttering to himself. Nuthatch was immediately attentive.

"You need to Send to Avocet," his patron said without preamble. "The Governor's life may be in danger. The King has been murdered and Marcus has assumed the crown."

He might have been discussing the weather Caniculus thought, filled with admiration. Nuthatch dropped the scroll he was reading and it snapped together with a dry rustle of papyrus.

"What shall I say, my lord?" he asked, shakily, his ruddy face greying.

"Just what I've told you. I'm presuming that Marcus will bring the King's body back here and expect me to bow down before him, the traitorous dog. You have certain proof of his involvement?" he asked Caniculus, who opened his hands helplessly.

"Only what I witnessed with my own eyes, but the Gods know the truth of it. Macro snapped the King's neck to make it look like a riding accident."

Rufus nodded.

"He's acted now that the Admiral is out of the way. Cei's first in line to the throne, not his son, and Julia after him. This vile deed was planned well in advance."

"There have been strange comings and goings, with portals opening up near the palace," Caniculus confirmed.

Rufus closed his eyes briefly. The years seemed to be piling on him minute by minute as he worked out what to do next. Nuthatch began to recite in a steady monotone as information came through his speechstone.

"Avocet acknowledges. 'His Excellency is aware of the situation through Divine warning and awaits instructions from the Emperor. The Princess Julia and Admiral Pendragon are still aboard the *Tempest*. May the Gods protect you, Senator.' End of Sending."

Nuthatch finished speaking and fixed worried eyes on them both. The normal sounds of the villa seemed as if they were coming from far away in another time and place where dreadful things weren't happening and everything was well.

"What shall we do now, sir?" Nuthatch asked anxiously.

His patron took a deep breath. "Get the Lady Drusilla and head for the coast. Take a boat to Gaul – not a Ship, they may be compromised. Her safety is of paramount importance. I shall confront Marcus."

"And when he denies it?" Caniculus asked. The Senator's eyes narrowed.

"I'll make him swear his innocence before Gods and men. But if he doesn't, I'll kill him where he stands."

*

It wasn't until the *Regina* had long disappeared over the horizon that Maia slackened her headlong flight, permitting her Mages to grab some rest. The wind was still aiding her and that, together with her store of Potentia, would keep them going at a steady clip towards the Isles of Sillina. The two larger islands were garrisoned, and would be a good place to replenish her fresh water and maybe get extra supplies, as no-one knew how long she would have to stay at sea and it was best to plan for all eventualities.

Magpie had gone below to snatch a few hours' sleep, leaving Raven on watch beside her on the quarterdeck. It was full dark now, but she hadn't lit her lamps on the Admiral's orders. From time to time she could see other vessels passing in the distance but she sailed on, like one of the fabled ghost Ships that haunted the edges of the ocean.

"We need to know what's going on," Raven remarked. She could see him clearly through the darkness and knew that he could see her – the only two people on the vessel who didn't need

235

light to find their way. To everyone else they would be two black shapes conferring in the night. "Is there a Ship you trust?"

Maia thought for a few moments. "I would have said *Blossom*, but she was in Portus last I heard and may be compromised."

"True," he sighed. "We mustn't put her in danger. Who's at sea?"

One Ship immediately sprang to mind. She couldn't believe that her friend would betray her confidence.

"I could try the *Patience*," she offered.

"Do it."

"The Admiral –"

"I know what he said, but needs must. A private message. Sound her out, but if you suspect anything at all, break the link. Give her no details of our location or where we're heading."

Maia opened the link a crack and visualised her friend, taking care not to alert anyone else who might be listening. It took finesse, but she'd grown in skill over the past weeks.

<*Patience*,> she whispered. She felt her mind touch the other Ship's with the lightness of a feather.

<*Tempest?* The Gods be praised! You're not sunk with all hands?> Her friend's relief flooded the link.

<What? No!>

<I thought it strange. We couldn't understand why there was no distress call, but that's what we've all been told. You sank in the freak squall, along with the Admiral and the Princess.>

<You know that the King is dead?>

She could feel the *Patience*'s misery. <We're getting messages from Albanus. He says that the King fell off his horse and broke his neck, and that Marcus is King.>

<He's not!> Maia hissed back. <Albanus and the *Regina* are traitors! The Admiral should be King, not bloody Marcus!> And to think the Admiral was worried about the fate of his son. Gods of Olympus! She would have to break the news gently. <Don't say anything to put yourself in danger. Can you trust your Captain?>

<I think so, but what can he do?>

Maia thought quickly. < If you trust him, take him into your confidence. Get to the furthest port you can find and make up some excuse to stay there. If anyone asks, we haven't spoken, understood?>

&lt;I understand,> *Patience* replied. &lt;Believe me, I'm glad the Admiral's alive. He should let everyone know.>

&lt;There's been some sort of block on communications here,> Maia explained. A horrible suspicion began to creep up on her. She'd had to use all her skill to talk privately to *Patience*. More little pieces were forming a pattern. &lt;I have to go.>

&lt;Take care, and may the Gods protect you,> *Patience* whispered. She knew better than to ask *Tempest*'s destination.

&lt;And you.>

Maia broke the link gently, scanning for the trouble she now knew that she carried with her.

\*

It was like a scene from some ancient tragedy, Caniculus thought, with all the leading players gathered and positioned on stage ready to speak their lines. Dusk had fallen and the villa's lamps were lit, casting their soft glow on the dismal scene and making it all look even more unreal. He almost expected to see an audience on tiered seats watching from the shadows, eagerly awaiting the action.

Marcus and the Senator stood facing one another, whilst to one side the covered shape that was all that was left of King Artorius the Tenth lay on a hastily–improvised bier. Bewildered nobles hovered around, like an impromptu chorus. Caniculus melted unobtrusively into the gloom, fearful for Rufus. Nothing he said could dissuade the Senator from challenging his enemy directly and the Agent hoped that Drusilla had already escaped with Nuthatch and some trusted servants, as her husband had commanded. The Senator had had no time to bid her farewell and was insistent that he had to buy her time.

"We share your sorrow," Marcus announced, his face a mask of grief. "Alas, my Royal cousin has been slain by the dread hand of Atropos, his thread cut far too soon. Also, I have just received the dreadful news that my father and sister are lost at sea in the storm that destroyed so many vessels today. As the last remaining Pendragon, the kingship falls to me."

The Senator regarded him, stony-faced. "Tragic events indeed, but I fear that I will require you to take an oath before I can give you my allegiance."

Marcus frowned at the interruption. "An oath? On what?"

"I want you to swear by all the Gods that you had no hand in these deaths, by word or deed," Rufus said implacably.

Marcus shot him a look of surprise.

"Surely you can't think that I had anything to do with this? It is the will of the Gods!" He looked about him for sympathy. "My heart is broken and now you accuse me!"

"If you are innocent," the Senator continued, "then you'll have no problem doing what I ask. Place your hand on your cousin's corpse and swear."

Marcus glared at him. "I am above suspicion! I was nowhere near the King and I have a dozen or more witnesses to prove it!"

"By deed, or command," Rufus said evenly. "How convenient that the King should die, just as his sister and uncle are reported lost at sea."

"You have no grounds for this baseless accusation!" Marcus growled. His face reddened and a pulse beat visibly in his temple.

"Well then, you can swear with a clear conscience and I will accept you as Sovereign."

Marcus spread his arms in seeming disbelief.

"All right, if this is what it takes to convince you!" He scowled at the Senator, then strode over to the bier and its grim burden.

The watchers held their breath as the Prince placed his hand on the body.

"I call upon the Gods to witness that I never conspired to cause any harm to my cousin. I am innocent of his death."

There were a few moments of silence, then Marcus removed his hand and stood back with a confident air.

"There. Are you satisfied now, my lord?"

A tiny sound filled the stillness and people's heads turned to locate the source. A woman gasped, then another. A hand pointed and ashen faces turned to the source of the noise, eyes focusing on the body under the cloth. A stain was spreading across the fabric. Blood, black in the lamplight, dripped steadily to patter on the earth.

"The victim accuses his murderer!" A low female voice spoke from the crowd, the words penetrating the horrified stillness.

"No! It's natural! Take the body inside!" Marcus shouted.

The air suddenly became thick and charged as unseen presences made themselves felt. Caniculus shivered as every hair stood on end. It seemed there had been an audience all along.

"I call upon the Gods to witness that you are forsworn, Marcus Pendragon, kinslayer and murderer of your anointed King. You will answer to me here and now!"

The Senator threw off his toga and produced a sword in one easy movement.

"Draw your sword, wretch!"

Marcus looked at him sadly. "Ah, my lord, you are mistaken. Macro?"

A shadow detached itself from the crowd and stepped behind the Senator. Before Rufus could react, the knife was across his throat and a single cut spilled his life.

"Does anyone else think I'm guilty?" Marcus asked, glaring at the horrified onlookers. "No? Excellent. Macro, see to the traitor's body. As you can all see, there has just been another assassination attempt here before your very eyes. Clearly Senator Rufus was the instigator of this terrible business and tried to cover his tracks by accusing me! Didn't he provide the horse for my cousin to ride? He must have summoned the unnatural storm as well."

No-one met his eyes. Marcus had too many friends here and they were all armed. Caniculus had heard of Naevius Sutorius Macro, the head of the Prince's personal bodyguard and an unscrupulous, ambitious man. He would doubtless have planned to have back-up nearby – Marcus wouldn't have left himself defenceless. Sure enough, he could hear the ordered tramp, tramp of a body of soldiers heading towards the villa. It was clear that those whose silence couldn't be bought would meet the same fate as Rufus. It was time to go.

As he retrieved Excalibur and slipped away into the darkness, an owl hooted mournfully above his head. For a second he thought he saw the moonlight glint on a high, plumed helmet and heard the rustle of a woman's dress.

Swallowing hard, he prayed to any Gods who were listening that they would grant the Senator eternal bliss, whilst his cowardly killers would get the justice they deserved.

A low rumble of distant thunder echoed his prayer, as if Jupiter himself had heard his plea.

*

Maia reviewed the facts. The fleet believed her sunk, or rather she corrected, had been told to accept that. Even were her Shipbody at the bottom of the ocean, she would still be able to call for help, so they must have smelt a rat. That left her sisters in a difficult position, as she knew that most Captains would obey the orders they were given without question. She could only hope that Fabillus was different, or at least trusted his Ship. But why would Albanus announce that she was sunk, when all she had to do was broadcast the opposite?

Unless he was counting on her to be already dealt with.

*

Julia stood in her cabin, too restless to sit down or stand still. The news hadn't sunk in yet. It seemed inconceivable that she would never see her brother again in this world and that, even now, his body was being prepared for burial. She'd tried to contact her uncle, but he'd sent Lieutenant Amphicles with orders for her to stay in her cabin no matter what. She'd felt the Ship spring into life, her oaken bones creaking with the speed of her passage, and wondered what in Hades was going on.

"*Tempest!*" she said aloud. "Please tell me what's happening!"

"There's been a coup, Highness." The Ship's voice echoed in the cabin. "I'm taking you out of harm's way. Please accept my deepest sympathies on the loss of your brother."

Julia swallowed the sudden lump in her throat. The *Tempest* had been the only one to remember that he wasn't just the King.

"Now that Artorius is dead, my uncle is King," Julia said.

"It isn't as simple as that, Highness. Please, stay in your cabin. I'll give you more information as soon as I have it."

240

"Is my cousin dead too?" she asked. Marcus might be a waste of space, but he was family. The Ship paused.

"There's no official news as yet."

Julia's stomach lurched. The Gods forfend that Marcus was somehow caught up in this.

"Please keep me informed," she said stiffly. Beside her, Melissa and Latonia were watching her with frightened eyes. Even Teg the monkey had stopped eating, as if aware of the tension in the air. Julia turned away, composing her features with an effort of will before coming to a decision.

"Melissa, fetch wine. Latonia, get me the walnut box with the brass lock out of the domed chest. Quickly!"

The slaves hurried to obey, the former disappearing off to the stores and the latter retrieving the box. Inside, nestled in their velvet–lined compartments, were two pistols. Julia took them out and checked them over before reaching for the powder, ball and wadding.

"Look out!"

Latonia's scream gave her a second's warning as Melissa abruptly re-appeared, a knife glinting in her upraised arm and her face contorted with purpose.

\*

<Raven!> Maia Sent, urgently. <We're in danger!>

She contacted Leo simultaneously. <Trouble's aboard! What's the best way to sink a Ship?>

<Gunpowder,> he replied instantly. <I'm on it!> She heard him barking orders to double the guard on the magazine, deep in her bowels, even as she turned her eyes to the Mage quarters. Both Magpie and Raven were prostrate on the deck, one still and the other writhing weakly.

Horrified, she opened her link to him, but met only a roar of pain and confusion.

<Captain, something's wrong with Raven!>

Before he could react she had already found Milo and repeated her message. The Agent immediately sprinted off to the Mage quarters. Maia sped through her vessel and formed in the cabin.

"Raven!" His eyes opened and she saw that he was in agony. "Poisoned…" he gasped. She clasped his hand and alerted Hawthorn.

The Adept rushed to his pharmacy, frantically grabbing items from shelves as Milo burst in through the cabin door, his eyes wild.

"Raven's alive," she said. "I'm not sure about Magpie."

The younger Mage's face was slack and the light had left his face. Milo didn't waste time. He grabbed Raven's head and forced something that looked like a small discoloured egg between the old man's lips.

"Swallow!"

Raven convulsed, but his throat moved as the charm went down. The echo of running feet heralded Hawthorn, throwing himself to his knees by Magpie, another toadstone at the ready. He felt for a pulse and muttered a charm, but it was clear that he was too late.

"He'd already succumbed," Milo told him. Hawthorn glanced at him bleakly and moved to Raven, who had gone limp in Milo's arms.

"Let's get him to his bed," the Adept said, as Maia relayed what was happening to both her commanders. Leo was coming below, on Pendragon's orders. Suddenly, the Admiral's mental voice cut off as pain lanced through the link. She screamed an alarm as Milo said "Where's Lapwing?"

Several images overlapped in Maia's vision; her felled Mages, Julia wrestling with Melissa, blood dripping from Latonia's shoulder, and Lapwing standing next to a rigid Pendragon, a look of intense triumph on his face. Sabrinus hovered to one side, face white and his sword at his feet, clearly unwilling to risk the Admiral's safety.

"*Tempest!*" Lapwing called to her. "You will do as I say, or he dies."

"I understand," she replied instantly, whilst praying that he wouldn't carry out his threat. She had to get to Julia.

Maia burst up into the state cabin, just as the Princess shouted a word that threw her attacker into the bulkhead. The slave's body smashed into the wood and Maia pinioned her before she could get to her feet. The girl struggled weakly, but a Ship had more than ordinary strength.

"Hold her still," Julia said. Maia's attention was still focused on Lapwing. She needed to get to Pendragon.

"Lapwing has the Admiral hostage," she said. Julia blanched. "You have to help him!"

"Go," Milo said, appearing in the doorway. "I'll question Melissa."

The look of chagrin on his face told her that he regretted leaving his post so quickly. He gestured, and Maia felt Melissa go rigid as the spell took hold.

"As will I," Julia growled. She took one look at the Agent's face. "Milo, you weren't to know. Latonia, you've done well and shall be rewarded. Let me see."

The slave was pale, pressing a bloody cloth to her wounded shoulder. "It's just a scratch, Highness."

"Can you walk?"

Latonia nodded. "Then go to the Adept."

Maia had already left, taking up position just outside the Admiral's cabin. As she went, Milo was just starting on Melissa.

"Tell us what you know, or you'll die here and now."

Julia fixed her slave with a stony glare and the girl flinched.

"Nothing. I know nothing," she muttered, her eyes fixed on the floor.

"We don't have time for this!" Milo looked around, picked up a discarded shawl and wrapped it around his hands. He patted Melissa down, checking her for tell-tale markings, mindful that she might be of the same ilk as Morgan, the deadly Fae spy. He'd expected to find something, but she seemed clean.

"Who do you answer to? I *will* hurt you." He produced a dagger.

Melissa grimaced. "Lapwing."

"What were you promised? Freedom and money?"

A quick jerk of the head.

"And what were your orders?"

The slave glanced at her mistress, but refused to answer. Milo's mouth twisted in disgust.

"You were to finish what he started, I presume? The Princess wasn't to leave this Ship alive and neither was the Admiral. Two more dead Pendragons."

She gulped.

"Why?" Julia asked her. "You've been with me for years."

Melissa raised her head and glared with eyes that brimmed with hate.

"And I'm worth about as much as that monkey, aren't I?" She spat on the floor. "That's what I think of your poxy Empire!" Suddenly she laughed. "It won't last long when the Fae arrive, believe me. You're all slaves now. You just don't know it yet."

She slumped to the floor, giggling hysterically.

\*

Maia emerged slowly into the cabin, her eyes fixed on Lapwing.

"What are you doing?" she demanded, more to buy time than anything else. She had no doubt in her mind that the treacherous Mage was behind the attack on Raven and Magpie and now Melissa had confirmed who the real players were.

"Taking control of this vessel," he replied confidently. "The world has just changed and your allegiance with it. You will obey me now."

Her heart sank.

"I obey my Admiral!" she snapped.

"And he obeys the King."

"He *is* the King, you slimy rat turd!"

Lapwing smirked, not at all discomfited by her insult. "You have a new King. King Marcus. Swear fealty to him and your Shipbody won't be prised from your vessel, weighted and sunk mid-ocean."

A groan escaped Pendragon's lips.

"Oh yes, of course. You didn't know," Lapwing said to his prisoner, full of mock sympathy. "Your son is the King now and he, together with our new Fae allies, will bring in a golden age. You should be so proud!"

Maia checked on Leo. He had joined Milo in the Princess' quarters with as many men as would fit, all armed and with more outside. Julia had grabbed a pistol, her face set. Melissa lay still on the deck, her eyes vacant.

&lt;Leo!&gt; she began.

"That's enough of that," Lapwing sneered, divining her intent. He spoke a word and her Captain collapsed, weapons falling from numb fingers. The rest of her crew followed suit, dropping like puppets with their strings cut. Pendragon stood, unable to move or even Send to her. Beads of sweat rolled down his forehead as he fought in vain against the compulsion laid upon him.

Lapwing laughed.

"Naturally, we'll have to clean house first. Can't have unnecessary royals cluttering up the place, can we?"

Maia wanted nothing more than to rip the smug expression from his face, but knew there was one thing in her favour – the Mage's nature dictated that he prolong their agonies for as long as possible for his own satisfaction. There was a sudden recognition that she was on very familiar ground. His gloating expression reminded her instantly of her former mistress.

She knew she couldn't grab him as she had Melissa, as he could kill the Admiral with a word. She had to knock him out if possible. That wouldn't have been a problem on deck, where she could have choked him with her ropes, but here in the Admiral's cabin her options were limited. Maybe she could play along?

"Please, Mage Lapwing," she begged, adopting her most pathetic voice. "Forgive me. I don't to be sunk! Spare me, I beg you. I'll be a good Ship!"

He didn't seem immediately convinced, but she saw him relax a little as she pleaded. He was her enjoying her submission.

"Very well," he conceded, as magnanimous as any God. "Albanus thought you'd know what was good for you. Turn the vessel around and make for Londin with all speed. Oh and don't expect any help from your sister Ships. They're receiving new orders as I speak."

Sure enough, a message was finally coming through from the Admiralty and she recognised the voice of Albanus. "All Ships. All Ships. Long live King Marcus! Return to port immediately. Remember your duty!"

Maia cast a stricken look at her Admiral, the cords of his neck standing out as he fought the spell and desperately tried to think of something that could save them all.

*

The insistent tone brought Milo round, beating at his ears like a dozen gongs and rousing him from the spell-induced coma. He rolled over, taking in the scene. Julia and the marines had fallen in tumbled heaps on the floor like carelessly–thrown dice, to lie where they would.

He crawled over to her, noting the slow rise and fall of her breast with relief. He'd feared she was dead, but this had to be some sort of sleep spell. The warning that the singing stone was emitting told him of its origin and he cursed quietly.

More Fae magic.

"*Tempest?*" he whispered, praying that the Ship wasn't incapacitated too.

Her voice sounded next to his left ear. "I'm with Lapwing. He's holding Pendragon hostage in his cabin. I've been ordered to return to Londin immediately and I'm pretending to obey for now."

"Good. String him along. Is anyone else awake?"

"Just us three."

"What's the swine doing now?"

Lapwing had seated himself in the Admiral's chair and had helped himself to brandy.

"He's sitting drinking."

"I'm not surprised."

Milo knew Lapwing of old. He was Bullfinch's shadow, always at his shoulder and smarming around powerful men, but he wasn't particularly full of Potentia himself. Still, he was far more proficient in magic than Milo, so a direct assault using that method would be unwise.

"Tell me if he moves," he directed the Ship.

He would have to think of another strategy.

"How are you awake?" she demanded. The singing stone was warm against his breastbone, even through its pouch, as if it was working hard. He shut off the tone before it deafened him but this was an added bonus he hadn't counted on. Still, it was Fae magic and he knew of one thing that would disrupt it. Lapwing would have to be expending enormous amounts of energy to keep his spell going at sea.

"I have a magic amulet," he told *Tempest*, knowing that the simplest explanations were usually the best.

"Oh."

"Tell me, is he looking tired?"

Her reply was instant. "Yes. He seems to be concentrating on something."

"Excellent. Try to get him to leave the cabin."

"All right."

Milo was already feeling better, though the air around him seemed thick, like syrup. He went to the nearest marine and pulled out the man's sword. Standard naval issue, nothing fancy, but it had one massive advantage. As soon as he touched the steel hilt the atmosphere cleared, as if a veil had been lifted and he could breathe more easily. Now he had to trust that *Tempest* could think of something clever to lure Lapwing out.

*

Maia was racking her brains. How could she get Lapwing to move? She reviewed her records, looking for anything that might give her an excuse, then hit on the man himself. She'd seen a list of Mages once, in Raven's cabin; some sort of register that the Master Mage kept, probably to remind himself who was who down the centuries.

For once she blessed her perfect recall. Third shelf down, sixth book across. She flowed through to his quarters and found it. Yes. It was there, the entries going back more years than she cared to think about, all named after birds and most of them long dead. She flicked through the pages, starting from the back where the ink was fresher. One name, that of Kestrel, was already crossed out and she shivered. He must have been the youngster murdered by the *Livia* in Portus. Back she went, searching. It felt more like an ornithologists' guide, except instead of plumage, song and nesting habits, it had appearance, date of ascension and strengths.

She was cursing the fact that it wasn't alphabetical like the register in the Foundling Home, when, at last, her eye fell on his entry, listed between Avocet and Buzzard.

"Small, obnoxious little toady. Out for what he can get from others whilst doing the minimum himself," Raven had written. It seemed that he'd stepped up to the mark on this mission, doubtless so he could claim a rich reward. Was Bullfinch in on it as well, or did Lapwing have even higher ambitions? Further down the page, Raven had penned an addendum. "Good with holding spells, but not much else. Assigned to Londin Collegium, little field experience."

*Little field experience.* That meant that he wouldn't know about Ships and their ways.

Maia smiled mirthlessly as she formulated a plan. She checked on Raven, who appeared to be sleeping peacefully. His colour had already improved, or as much as it ever would and she guessed that his curse had protected him from the worst of the spell. It was time to act.

She slipped into her vessel and followed the familiar path through to the Admiral's quarters. Pendragon was still standing rigidly to attention, his face grey, though she fancied she saw a flicker of recognition in his eyes. She couldn't let herself be distracted now.

Lapwing looked up as she formed against the bulkhead.

"Yes? I take it the course is set?"

"Aye, sir," she said meekly. She'd played about with her rigging and was currently executing a series of manoeuvres that she thought would allay his suspicions.

"Excellent." When she didn't leave he sighed. "Well, what is it?"

"Naval protocol, sir," she said, praying that he wouldn't think to check. "As you're now technically my Captain, you have to swear the Neptune oath.

She adopted a helpful expression. As she'd hoped, he didn't have a clue what she was talking about. Any sailor could have told him that the Neptune oath was sworn on entering naval service and had nothing to do with their current situation.

"Oh, very well," he said crossly. "If it's the rules. What do I do?"

"You just go to the altar, lay your hand upon it and swear to obey the Law of Neptune," she said. "It will appease the Earthshaker."

"All right," he said with bad grace, "but you're coming with me. I can just as easily kill the Admiral from on deck as I can here, so don't get any ideas."

Maia's feigned innocence was the result of long practice. She'd learned from an early age never to admit to anything and she'd counted on him not wishing to offend the God of the Sea.

"Aye, sir."

"After you."

She glided over to the door and opened it, keeping herself in his line of sight as she entered the passageway, the little Mage in her train.

Milo was waiting for him. The Agent swung the blade in a perfect arc, putting all his skill into the cut. Lapwing stood for a moment, mouth agape in a silent scream, before his head left his shoulders in a slow tumble. It hit the planks with a dull thud and rolled, finally coming to rest against the bulkhead. The rest of him crumpled into an ungainly heap. Milo regarded the bloody remains with distaste, before cocking his head as if listening to something beyond ordinary hearing.

"Can you feel it? The spell's broken!"

"Thank the Gods!"

They found Pendragon kneeling, exhausted and supporting himself with his hands. Mingled sweat and tears coursed down his face and he didn't meet their eyes as Maia and Milo gently lifted him and helped him to a chair. They both knew that the shame of his son's actions would remain with him for the rest of his life.

Milo poured him a glass of brandy which he accepted with a shaking hand.

"I take it that Lapwing is dead?"

"Aye, sir," she answered, as cries of alarm sounded from all over her vessel. She was hastily reassuring her crew when Leo strode in, followed by the Princess. He looked almost as drained as the Admiral, but his shoulders sagged with relief on seeing them. Maia noticed that he had blood on his shoes.

"Orders, Your Majesty?"

Pendragon's eyes flew open, as if he hadn't realised. Maia could only admire him as he pulled himself together, relying on decades of naval discipline and duty.

"Proceed on our original course. Captain, I want to know the list of casualties. Julia, thank the Gods you're all right."

The Pendragons exchanged looks that spoke more than words, though outwardly they remained calm. Maia thought that if it had been her uncle, she would have rushed to him, but seemingly the Royals were different.

"I am, though my maid Melissa turned on me. If it weren't for the slave my brother bought me, I could have been killed as he was."

She swept to the floor in an elegant curtsy.

"Your Majesty."

Leo and Milo bowed, but he waved them up, clearly uncomfortable.

"There'll be time for all that later."

*When I've dealt with my son.* The unspoken words filled the room as if they'd been shouted.

"Lapwing was using Fae magic," Milo said quietly. "It was fortunate that I had protection against it and that *Tempest* made full use of her wits to lure the traitor out."

The Admiral's eyes softened as he focused on his Ship. "I never doubted you for a second," he said. "Well done, all of you."

He fixed Milo with a quizzical gaze.

"Agent Milo, Majesty. Raven assigned me here to protect the Princess. I was responding to an emergency in the Mage quarters when she was attacked by her slave."

"All part of the plan to distract and weaken us," Pendragon said, his mouth twisting. "Is the viper dead?"

"Captured, Majesty. She's already confirmed under questioning that there is Major Fae involvement. They are returning."

A fierce light appeared in the Admiral's eyes. "Get as much out of her as you can, Agent, then I'll hang her from the yardarm. Please proceed immediately." Milo bowed and slipped out. "Where are Raven and Magpie?"

Maia checked. Her surviving Mage was sitting up, being tended to by Polydorus.

"He and Magpie were poisoned. He survived, but Magpie didn't." Yet another face that would fade into the past, consigned to the roll of the heroic dead.

"A grievous loss. Any other casualties?"

"Only the traitor, Majesty," Leo replied. He was ashen-faced and Maia remembered that he'd been Marcus' friend as well as the King's.

"Then it could have been worse. You are all dismissed to your duties. It will soon be dawn, thank the Gods. Have Danuco take the morning service to offer thanks for our deliverance."

"Aye, Majesty," Leo said. "Please, you should rest."

Pendragon's eyes were shadowed and he seemed to have lost much of his vigour in the preceding hours, but he nodded, albeit with reluctance.

"I agree. I leave the running of the vessel to you and *Tempest*. You are all dismissed, save you, ma'am."

Maia watched them leave, Leo giving orders as he went. A party of sailors was already cleaning up the mess in the passageway.

"*Tempest*." Pendragon leaned back in his chair and locked gazes with her. "You've only been a Ship for a few short weeks and you've already had to deal with more than most see in fifty years. Do you know that our ladies' usual complaint is that of boredom?"

She couldn't help snorting as his lips turned up in a weary half-smile.

"Now you're going to be faced with even more perils. A spell to subdue a whole Ship isn't normal."

"No, Majesty."

He stared into the dregs of his brandy. "And to think we were worried about the Northern Alliance! Oh, I don't say that they aren't still a threat. They'll take advantage of any opportunity to harry us, treaty or no treaty, and if we're weakened by an attack from the west it will leave our eastern shores defenceless. We have to finish this as soon as possible."

Neither of them mentioned the personal consequences.

He straightened. "I'm Sending to the Fleet. I'm afraid that loyalties will be tested and long-standing friendships broken beyond repair. I hope that you weren't close to the *Regina*?"

Maia pictured the spoilt, selfish girl her sister Ship had been, though there had been good times as well. She understood all the gifts and kind words now as being simply a means to an end. It touched her that, in the midst of his own pain, he spared a thought for her feelings.

"No, Majesty," she replied. "The *Regina* has forfeited any loyalty I might have had to my classmate."

"Then let us hope that others are of the same mind," he replied. "Prepare to Send." She sensed him composing his thoughts, then she joined her power to augment his message, which rang through the link with the full authority of the King and Crown.

"All Ships! This is Admiral Cei Pendragon, aboard the *Tempest*! I am now your King by right of birth and I declare Prince Marcus to be a traitor to Britannia and to the Empire. Ships! He has allied himself with the ancient enemy and will bring our land to ruin, abandoning the Gods and his people. Now is the time to fulfil your sacred duty! Gods save the Empire. Gods save Britannia!"

Familiar voices began to answer. One after another, Ships began to pledge their allegiance, calls echoing through the oaken bond. Maia began to count them in and knew that the Admiral was doing the same.

The battle lines were declared and every Ship knew it. Old Gods against New. Father against son. Ship against Ship.

The worst of all wars, civil war, had begun.

# DRAMATIS PERSONAE

## Mortals

Maia Abella – Royal Britannic Ship.

Tiberius Valerius Severianus Leo – her Captain.

Lucius Albanus Sabrinus – First Lieutenant and Second-in-Command.

Claudius Atticus Amphicles, Marcus Faustus Drustan – Second Lieutenants.

Danuco – Ship's Priest, loyal to Jupiter.

Big Ajax – large, quiet crewman.

Hyacinthus – old crewman.

Teg – old crewman, friend of Hyacinthus.

Corax – Purser.

Pertinax – Ship's cook.

Vinicius (Sprout) – Ship's boy.

Cunomoltus (Monkey) – unlucky crewman.

Osric – Captain of Marines.

Musca – Master Gunner.

Batacarus, Caphisus – crewmen.

Vestinus – Ship's Carpenter.


HMS *Blossom* – A three hundred year old training Ship.

Gaius Plinius Tertius – Captain.

Heron – Mage.

Campion – Adept.

Scribo – crewman.

Cap'n Felix – Scribo's foul-mouthed parrot.


### *Admirals*

Lord High Admiral, HRH Cei Julius Pendragon Mordrawd, uncle of the King.

Lucius Albanus Dio – Senior Admiral and father of the *Regina*.


### *Agents*

Milo – former apprentice Mage, now one of the Government's chief troubleshooters. Nicknamed Ferret.

Caniculus (Little Dog). Friend of Milo.

Foxy, Hart – fellow Agents.

Favonius – Civil servant and spymaster. Has fingers in many pies.


### *Ships*

HMS *Patience* – formerly Briseis Apollonia, Maia's best friend from the Academy.

HMS *Regina* – formerly Tullia Albana, daughter of Admiral Albanus.

HMS *Persistence* – a wise old Ship, friend of the *Blossom.*

HMS *Cameo, HMS Leopard,* – also close to *Blossom.*

HMS *Jasper* – the biggest gossip in the Fleet.

HMS *Augusta* – the oldest Ship and Flagship of the Royal Navy

HMS *Diadem*, HMS *Victoria*, HMS *Imperatrix*, HMS *Justicia*, all Royal Ships.

HMS *Emerald* – terrified of krakens.

HMS *Livia* – executed for murdering her Captain, Maia's father, in a fit of jealous rage. She returned as a Revenant to claim Maia as her own, but was destroyed.


## *Mages*

Raven – an ancient, blind Master Mage.

Robin – Raven's former apprentice, now a qualified Mage-Artificer.

Bullfinch – Prime Mage, head of the Londin Collegium.

Wagtail – Mage to HMS *Persistence*.

Lapwing – an unctuous Londin Mage.

Avocet – Mage to the Imperial Governor.

Nuthatch – Mage to Senator Rufus.


## *Royals*

King Artorius the Tenth – recently ascended to the throne after the death of his grandfather, Artorius the Ninth.

Admiral Pendragon, his uncle (see above).

Prince Marcus – his cousin, Pendragon's son.

Princess Julia – his elder sister.

Prince Julius – his father, killed in a hunting accident some years previously.


## *Miscellaneous*

Pholus – Chief Naval Architect and Centaur.

Naevius Sutorius Macro – Head of Prince Marcus' Personal Guard.

Gnaeus Proculus Aquila – Chief Priest of Jupiter, Londin Temple.

Emrys Brigantius Silvius – Captain, HMS *Regina*.

Fabillus – Captain, HMS *Patience*.

Senator Madoc Britannicus Rufus - Advisor to the King and Raven's friend.

Lady Drusilla – his wife and friend of Princess Julia.

Melissa – Julia's slave since childhood.

Latonia – slave bought for Julia by King Artorius.

King Parisius – elderly King of Gaul.

Ceridwen – High Priestess of the Mother Goddess.

Claudia Modesta – High Priestess of Juno's temple in Portus.

Helena Quintilla – Matrona, in charge of candidates at the Naval Academy in Portus.

Branwen – servant at the Academy and Maia's friend.

Marcia Blandina – Maia's former mistress and murderess (deceased).

The Cyclops – her henchman (executed).

Captain Lucius Valerius Vero (deceased) – Captain of the Livia, husband to Aura, father of Maia.


## *Immortals*

### *The Twelve Olympians*

Greek names in brackets

Jupiter/Jove (Zeus) – The Thunderer, Ruler of the Olympian Gods and God of the Sky.

Juno (Hera) – Queen of the Gods and his sister wife. Patron of marriage and childbirth.

Neptune (Poseidon) – God of the Sea.

Pluto (Hades) – God of the Underworld.

Minerva (Athena) – Goddess of Wisdom.

Mercury (Hermes) - Messenger of the Gods, patron of merchants and travellers.

Mars (Ares) – God of War.

Ceres (Demeter) – Goddess of the Earth.

Vulcan (Hephaestus) – God of Fire and Artificers.

Apollo – God of Music and the Arts, Light and Prophecy. Bringer of plagues. Associated with the sun.

Diana (Artemis) – Goddess of the Hunt, protector of maidens. Twin sister to Apollo. Associated with the moon and Maia's enemy.

Bacchus (Dionysus) – the God of Wine.


### *Other immortals*

Aura, Goddess of the Breeze and Maia's mother. Wife to Lucius Valerius Vero.

Pearl – a Tempestas, spirit of the air and Maia's twin sister.

Cymopoleia, Goddess of Storms. Aura's sister.

Echidna, Mother of Monsters, deceased.

# TIMELINE

*AUC (AB URBE CONDITA) – from the founding of Roma, as Maia's dates are reckoned.*
*Dates from our world in brackets – Before Common Era/Common Era*

**Year 1 AUC**
**(753 BCE)**
Founding of Roma.
**698 AUC**
**(55 BCE)**
Julius Caesar visits Britannia.
**743 AUC**
**(10 BCE)**
Emperor Augustus makes a pact with the Sea God, Neptune.
Sacred oak branches begin to be grafted on to vessels.
**796 AUC**
**(43 CE)**
Emperor Claudius invades Britannia.
**814 AUC**
**(61 CE)**
Boudicca (Boadicea) leads a rebellion against the rule of Roma.
**875 -881 AUC**
**(122 - 128 CE)**
Building of Hadrian's Wall.
**1146 AUC**
**(393 CE)**
Birth of Artorius Magnus.
**1163 AUC**
**(410 CE)**
Roman Empire in crisis. Civil war in Britannia as rivals vie for the throne.
**1165 AUC**
**(412 CE)**
Civil War ends. Artorius acclaimed High King of the Britons and forms Britannic Legions. Merlin gathers Mages and forms Collegium.  Artorius and Merlin lead the Legions on a march to Roma and rescue the Empire. Goths and Vandals bought off and retreat to the East.

**1167 AUC**
**(414 CE)**
Empire stabilises. Major Fae return to Britannia. Artorius
returns with his Legions.

**1170 AUC**
**(417 CE)**
Great Fae Wars. Artorius receives Excalibur.

**1174 AUC**
**(421 CE)**
Major Fae defeated at great cost and driven overseas to
Hibernia. Merlin disappears.

**1210 AUC**
**(457 CE)**
Artorius dies. His son, Mordrawd becomes king.

**1436 AUC**
**(683 CE)**
Northern Alliance formed between Scandinavian, Baltic and
Germanic peoples. Hostilities increase.
First Ship, the *Britannia*, created.

**1548 AUC**
**(795 CE)**
HMS *Augusta* installed.

**1567 AUC**
**(814 CE)**
The Great Blight.

**1579 AUC**
**(826 CE)**
Battle of the Oceanus Germanicus

**1730 AUC**
**(912 CE)**
Jupiter's decree bans the creation of demi-gods.

**2028 AUC**
**(1275 CE)**
HMS *Livia* executed. Maia born.

**2044 AUC**
**(1291 CE)**
Marcia Blandina is killed. Maia enters the Naval Academy.

## *Place names*

Londin/Londinium – London

Portus – Portsmouth

Durobrivis – Chatham

Noviomagus – Chichester

Kernow – Cornwall

The Wall – Hadrian's Wall

Caledonia – Scotland

Hibernia – Ireland

Gaul – France

Hispania – Spain

Italia – Italy

Roma - Rome

Pictland – The North-East Highlands, Scotland

Britannic Ocean – The English Channel

Mare Germanicus –The North Sea

The Isle of the Dead – Isle of Thanet, Kent

Deva – Chester

Dubris – Dover

Vectis – The Isle of Wight

Yr Wyddfa – Mount Snowdon

Lutetia – Paris

Vada Volterrana – the Italian port of Volterra

Coriallum – Cherbourg, Northern France.

# Author's Note

Thank you, dear Reader, for choosing this, the third book about Maia and her world.

I'm currently writing the fourth, which I hope to publish this year (2022), as long as I don't get any more surprises heading my way. Last year was interesting in that I had to move both house and area. Things got a little hectic. Zeus and Hades, my Feline Overlords, were not impressed.

As always, I'd like to thank my friends, who've encouraged me to carry on no matter what. Also, Nick Hodgson, my eagle-eyed proofreader and Thea Magerand, my awesome cover designer. You can find more of her work at ikaruna.eu.

Please check out my website at **emkkoulla.com** for more information. You can also sign up to my mailing list to receive a **FREE novella and short story**, plus monthly (ish) email letters about what I'm up to.

I can also be found on Twitter **@EKkoulla** and the Ships of Britannia page on Facebook. I'd love it if you said hi!

Lastly, if you've enjoyed this book, please could I ask you to **leave a review on Amazon**? It's tough for independent authors, and every single one will help other readers to find these books. Even a few words will really help. Thank you again.

The next book in the series will be THE TRIUMPH OF MARS. Stand by for more action!

Printed in Great Britain
by Amazon

37288470R00158